The Cornish Rebel

NICOLA PRYCE trained as a nurse at St Bartholomew's Hospital in London. She has always loved literature and completed an Open University degree in Humanities. She is a qualified adult literacy support volunteer and lives with her husband in the Blackdown Hills in Somerset. Together they sail the south coast of Cornwall in search of adventure.

The Cornish Rebel

NICOLA PRYCE

CORVUS

Published in paperback in Great Britain in 2023 by Corvus,
an imprint of Atlantic Books Ltd.

1 3 5 7 9 10 8 6 4 2

A CIP catalogue record for this book is available from the British Library.

Paperback ISBN: 978 1 83895 919 7
E-book ISBN: 978 1 83895 920 3

Printed in Great Britain by CPI Group (UK) Ltd, Croydon CR0 4YY

Corvus
An imprint of Atlantic Books Ltd
Ormond House
26–27 Boswell Street
London
WC1N 3JZ

www.atlantic-books.co.uk

MIX
Paper | Supporting
responsible forestry
FSC
www.fsc.org
FSC® C171272

For Ali and Chris Mitchell

Cast of Characters

FALMOUTH

ON BOARD THE BRIGATINE *JANE O'LEARY*

Mary James	*Master's wife*
Pandora Woodville	*Passenger from Philadelphia*
Captain James	*Ship's Master*

THE QUAYSIDE INN

Benedict Aubyn	*Turnpike Trust employee*
John Loudon McAdam	*Road builder*
Marcus Cartwright	*Turnpike Trust clerk*

RESTRONGUET CREEK

ST FEOCA MANOR: SCHOOL FOR YOUNG LADIES.

Founded 1774

Joseph Mitchell   m.   Elizabeth Curnow
b.1720   d.1790   b.1723   d.1800

Harriet   Abigail   m.   James Woodville
b.1760   b.1762   d.1800   b.1750

Pandora   b.1780

Grace Elliot	*Pupil, now teacher*
Annie Rowe	*Retired housekeeper*
Richard Compton	*Prospective inheritor of St Feoca Manor*

FEOCA SCHOOL GATEHOUSE

George Penrose	*Groundsman for St Feoca School*
Susan Penrose	*Housekeeper for St Feoca School*
Kate Penrose	*Daughter*

DEVORAN FARM (*OWNED BY THE SCHOOL*)

Samuel Devoran	*Farmer*
Jane Devoran	*Wife*
Gwen	*Daughter*
Sophie	*Daughter*

FEOCA MILL (*OWNED BY THE SCHOOL*)

Jacob Carter	*Miller*
Martha Carter	*Wife*
Mollie	*Daughter*

ST FEOCA SCHOOL GOVERNORS

Lady Clarissa Carew	*Philanthropist*
Reverend Opus Penhaligan	*Retired clergyman*
Mrs Mary Lilly	*Philanthropist*
Mrs Angelica Trevelyan	*Ship company owner and former pupil*

TREGENNA HALL: NEIGHBOURING ESTATE

Sir Anthony Ferris	*Wealthy landowner*
Cador Ferris	*Eldest son and heir*
Olwyn Ferris	*Daughter*

TRURO

TURNPIKE TRUST MEETING

Lord Entworth	*Turnpike Trust Chairman*
Marcus Cartwright	*Clerk to the Turnpike Trust*
Henry Trevelyan	*Ship company owner*
Jonathan Banks	*Land agent*
Major Trelawney	*Local militia*
Francis Polcarrow	*Trainee attorney*
Meredith Trelawney	*Friend of Benedict Aubyn*

Esse Quam Videri

To be, rather than seem to be

The Hero's Journey

Stage One: The Call to Adventure

Stage Two: The Supreme Ordeal

Stage Three: Unification

Stage Four: The Hero's Return

PROPOSED TURNPIKE ROAD
FROM TRURO TO FALMOUTH

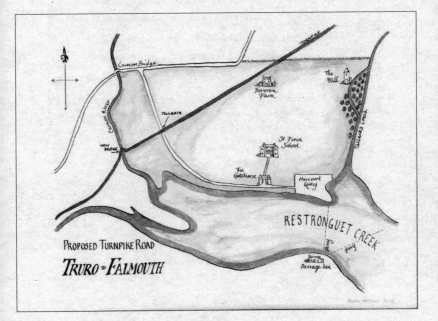

PROPOSED TURNPIKE ROAD
TRURO TO FALMOUTH

*Required with immediate effect: a teacher, or a lady
who has held a position as governess, is invited to apply
for a position in St Feoca School for Young Ladies.*

*The applicant must be educated to a high degree, be in her
thirties, and be steadfast in her support of female education.*

Salary and conditions of service will be discussed at interview.

All applicants to write to Lady Clarissa Carew of Trenwyn House.

Stage One

THE CALL TO ADVENTURE

Chapter One

On board Jane O'Leary, *Falmouth*
Sunday 22nd March 1801, 12 p.m.

The ship was rising and falling, the wind tugging at our cloaks. 'There – on that promontory – that's Pendennis Castle.' Mary James handed me the telescope and an outline of turrets and battlements sharpened into focus.

'The soldiers have got their telescopes trained on us.'

Around us, angry white crests peaked and broke; a fresh burst of spray carried on the wind and Mary clasped her cloak tighter. 'They'll be expecting us. Mr Trevelyan's very particular about letting them know we're coming. They'll recognise our flags. One shows we're from America and one shows we're carrying grain.'

This was Falmouth, *England*, the home of my childhood. Tears welled in my eyes. I was a child again, gripping my mother's hand, staring back at the same squat battlements: an inconsolable child of six, devastated to be leaving St Feoca and the family I loved.

In her early thirties, Mary James was far stronger than she looked. 'I shall miss our talks, Clara. I've loved your company.'

3

Slim and agile, she could haul a rope as well as any man. Her voice drifting on the wind, she slipped her arm through mine. 'I love your tales of gods and goddesses – and all your talk of grand receptions and fancy dinners – the concerts, and fetes in Government House. It's as if I've been there – that I've been using fine bone china and dining with naval officers in their gold brocade.'

I smiled with what I hoped looked like conviction and she smiled back. 'But you know the best part? The best part is you being friends with the Governor's daughters. I've not been to Grenada or Dominica, but it's like I've been wearing fine silk gowns and going to balls and soirees.'

'And I've learned all about the wind and currents, and how to set sails. You and Captain James have been so good to me. I can't thank you enough.'

Shouts echoed across the deck, the men hauling on the ropes. Above us, the sails tightened, the bow heading inland to the safe waters of Carrick Roads. Before long, Pendennis Castle would rise to our left, St Mawes Castle to our right.

Captain James came to my side. 'I said I'd get you here, and here we are. It's been a good passage, Mrs Marshall. You must sail with us again. Not an enemy ship in sight. I've never known the winds so favourable.' A thick-set man with a weather-beaten face, he put his telescope to his eye. 'No doubt it's all down to your gods and goddesses. Had a word with your friend, Poseidon, did you?'

'Maybe the odd word!'

'We'll get extra for arriving early. Mr Trevelyan's good like that.' He scanned the entrance to the harbour. 'They'll make us anchor. We're the first grain ship from America for several years and they'll want to check we're not carrying hessian fly. There's urgent need for this corn. The harvests failed again last year – there's severe shortages. I gather there's been food riots. Let's hope we don't meet any trouble.'

'Trouble, Captain James?'

'As to who gets to distribute the wheat. The navy want it, the army want it, and the people want it.'

A mist hung above the town, the waves calmer now we were in sheltered water. Seagulls circled above us, a smell of manure drifting across the water. Just visible, a church tower rose above a cluster of granite roofs. Nothing but grey: grey houses, grey sky, grey sea. No reflections dancing on an azure bay, no bleached beaches, no fiery hibiscus flowers the size of saucers; no scorching sun, no oppressive heat. No one demanding money from me. Clutching my gold locket, I breathed in the air of my childhood. *We're home, Mama. We're home.*

Captain James scanned the quayside with his telescope. 'We should make one hundred and eighty shillings a quarter.' A green and red flag fluttered from the wharf and he examined it carefully. 'Yes . . . there it is. We've got the signal to anchor.' Swinging round, he shouted, 'Starboard thirty degrees. We'll anchor in Flushing, behind that naval frigate.'

Mary's smile was apologetic. 'I'm so sorry about your luggage, Clara. There are some very unscrupulous people on the quays in Philadelphia – we should never have let it happen.'

'No . . . please don't blame yourself. I should have guarded it better, but trunks and clothes can be replaced. Papa can bring some more clothes when he comes.' I dived beneath my cloak and reached for my letter. 'I've written all about how very kind you've been, and what a comfortable crossing we've had. Will you post this to him when you get back?'

'Of course I will.' She read the address. '*Reverend J. S. Turner, Headmaster's House, Germantown Academy, Philadelphia, Pennsylvania.*'

I hoped my smile looked convincing. 'The Academy couldn't do without him. He's very well thought of. He has a doctorate in Divinity and the boys love him. They converse with him in Greek and Latin. He's an inspiring teacher as well as a brilliant scholar.'

Falmouth looked smaller than I remembered, or did I remember it at all? It was hard to know what my memories were and what I had been told. Mama hardly ever mentioned Falmouth but her tone always lifted when she spoke of her parents. Her smile would broaden, her eyes fill with love, as she recounted stories of Grandfather's treasure hunts, his love of riddles, his knowledge of flowers. Her memories had acted like light in the darkness, a beacon reassuring me of home. But there was always a stumble when she mentioned her beloved elder sister: always a catch to her voice. *What would Aunt Hetty think of you slouching like that? Back straight — never forget you come from English gentry.*

Mary must have read my mind. 'Not quite Philadelphia, is it? But don't judge it from today's weather. Cornwall's very beautiful. In the sun, the houses in Truro shine like gold.' Her eyes softened. 'I hope we've been of some comfort to you, Clara. We so feel for your loss.'

I felt for the gold band on my third finger. 'You've brought me great comfort. Thank you.' Far greater comfort than she would ever know.

'So you're to teach in your aunt's school? How will you get there?'

Mama's voice had been a whisper: *The ferry for the Passage Inn leaves from Falmouth Quay. From there, take another ferry across Restronguet Creek. The gatehouse is on the water's edge. You won't get lost. Tell the ferryman Aunt Hetty will pay.*

I tried to sound strong.'I need to take the coach to Penzance. My aunt's school overlooks the sea. Father tells me it's very straightforward and easy to find.'

Inching forward under two small sails, Captain James rechecked the chart. A row of smart houses lined the quay, a group of men watching us from behind a stack of lobster pots. 'What's our depth?'

One of the crew was bending over the bow with a knotted chain.'Five fathoms . . . four fathoms . . .'

'Drop anchor.' The anchor splashed and Captain James took the wheel. The stern swung round and started pulling against the rope. A crowd was gathering, children watching from the window of a grand house. 'Seems to be holding. Good.' Hardly a timber creaked, a stillness on the ship we had not felt for six weeks.

Across the water the houses of Falmouth were hardly distinguishable in the grey mist. The sound of oars carried across the water: a rowing boat was splashing towards us. 'Here are the Excise men. They'll need to see your papers. They'll check everyone's health records and if there's any sign of fever they'll stop us unloading.'

Mary reached for my gloved hands. 'Fortunately, that's not the case. I shall miss you, Clara.' There was kindness in her eyes. 'You're very lovely, my dear. I'm sure you'll find someone else to love as dearly as you loved Mr Marshall.'

'Thank you, Mary.' With her holding my hands, I could not cross my fingers.

She reached up to prevent a rope from swinging too near my face. 'Why not collect your belongings and we'll ask them to clear you first? Jack can take you ashore once your papers are cleared. It would be a shame if you just missed the coach.'

I clutched my bag, my fear subsiding. My papers were in order – *Clara Marshall, born 1780, Philadelphia, Pennsylvania*. No one had noticed the 1730 had been changed to 1780. The fine drizzle was strengthening to steady rain and I pulled my hood further over my bonnet. Jack's rowing was strong, the water calm, the inner harbour of Falmouth full of ships. Placing the oars in the bottom of the boat he leaned over to catch the chain. The boat tipped and I grabbed the sides. 'Mind these steps, Mrs Marshall, they'll be slippery. Best hold the rope. What a downpour!'

I was home. *Home.* A huge wooden crane towered above us, a group of men unloading the hold of a ship. Harnessed oxen waited in a line, a man shouting instructions. Gripping my skirt, I climbed up the steps to the quayside, the stench of fish guts turning my stomach. An empty cart rumbled past and I only just leapt out of its way. Standing on the cobbles, I felt light-headed, almost dizzy.

'You all right, Mrs Marshall? Everything swaying? First you need to find your sea legs, then you need to find your land legs! It'll pass.' He looked around, my bag in his hand. 'Mrs James says to find the coaching inn. Where's that, d'you think?'

Puddles were forming on the cobbles around us, yet I had good sturdy boots and a thick woollen cloak. I kept my hood pulled low. 'Jack . . . please don't wait on my account. They'll need you back on the ship – I can ask these people where to go. Thank you dearly – but I'll be fine.' A notice caught my attention: the paint was peeling, the board hanging at an angle but it was exactly what I needed to find – *Ferry to Passage House Inn. Every two hours.*

'No, Mrs Marshall, I'll see you to the coaching inn.' Jack readjusted his collar against the driving rain. 'We'll take shelter beneath that overhang – looks like some sort of office. They can tell us where to go.' Hurrying along the wet cobbles, I glanced at the dilapidated sign. The writing was only just visible. *Ten o'clock, then every two hours. Last ferry eight o'clock.* The church bells had just sounded half past two: I had an hour and a half to wait.

Suddenly my shoulder was wrenched and I stumbled forward. A man reached out, trying to steady my fall. 'I'm so sorry. Are you all right? I didn't see you under my umbrella. It was very clumsy of me.' He was quietly spoken, full of remorse.

'No, it was my fault. I had my hood too low and my head down. I didn't see you.'

Drawing me under the overhang, he kept his umbrella above me. 'Are you hurt? Only that was quite a jolt.'

9

The rain from my hood dripped onto my cheeks. 'No, I'm fine.'

Jack squeezed into the shelter next to us. 'First time in England, and here's the rain they tell you about! Are you all right, Mrs Marshall? That was quite a bump.' Flattening himself against the wall, he raised his hat. 'I wonder, sir, if you know where the Penzance coach leaves?'

The man looked to be in his late twenties. He stood tall, if a little slight of build. His cheeks were gaunt, a furrow between his brows. There was mud on the hem of his coat, his boots scuffed, yet his voice was educated. 'Yes, from the Coach and Horses. I'm going there now.' He wore a heavy overcoat, buttoned to the neck, his umbrella clasped between thick leather gloves. Holding the handle towards me, he smiled a half-smile. 'Please, use my umbrella. The inn's just round the corner – I'll be happy to show you.' Pulling up his collar, he bowed. 'Benedict Aubyn, at your service.'

'Thank you, Mr Aubyn, you're very kind.' Turning to Jack, I tried to hide my relief. 'Mr Aubyn will show me the way and if I've missed the coach, I'll come straight back to the ship.'

Mr Aubyn followed my gaze. 'You've come off that grain ship? I must say she's a welcome sight.' He seemed strangely shy, a true English gentleman. *Just like you told me, Mama.*

'We've come from Philadelphia – though Cornwall is my real home.'

The strange half-smile again, a sudden lightening in his eyes. 'Welcome home, Mrs Marshall. I'm sorry about the weather.' Benedict Aubyn stepped into the rain. 'And you haven't missed the coach. It leaves at four, but you'll need to book your seat. I suggest we go now — before that black cloud drenches us further. May I take your bag?'

I knew to keep a tight hold of it. 'Thank you, but it's no weight at all.'

He looked around. 'You have other luggage?'

Jack shook his head. 'Mrs Marshall's a widow. She got taken advantage of. All her luggage was stolen.'

A flash of anger crossed his eyes. 'How despicable. Well, let me assure you, Mrs Marshall is safe with me. I shall escort her straight to the inn where she can get warm and dry.' Jack seemed to hesitate, but as the rain was building he nodded. Mr Aubyn pointed up the street. 'Shall we go now before this cart blocks our way?' Stepping into the road, he bowed to Jack. 'Good day, sir. A safe passage home.'

We turned the bend, and I swung round. Jack was watching and I waved goodbye, or so Benedict Aubyn must think. I had to memorise the way back.

Chapter Two

Everywhere, people were running to get out of the rain. Busier on the ground than it looked from the sea, Falmouth was crowded, the narrow streets twisting and turning, the rooftops almost meeting above us. I was used to straight, broad streets with wide pavements, not the ancient thatches on some houses, the beams on others. People's accents sounded strange, even the church bells sounded different. We joined a long street and headed up the hill. Brick buildings with brass plates and polished front steps lined the pavement: a shop selling bonnets, another selling portmanteaus. A dressmaker, then a milliner's shop, the smell of baking drifting across the street. Boys were wheeling barrows, a knife grinder busy beneath an arch.

Benedict Aubyn stayed by my side, stepping into the road when the pavement narrowed. Alleys led up the hill to our left but our way was forward, towards the main square with a horse trough at its centre. 'There – across the square.' Benedict Aubyn pointed towards a busy inn. Through the arch, stable lads were sweeping up horse dung, chickens squawking, the ostler shouting instructions. The rain dripping from his hat, Benedict pointed once again. 'We need to go round the side to buy tickets.'

The ticket seller was behind a polished counter, the times of coaches chalked onto a blackboard above him. Handing him back his umbrella, I tried to hide my panic. 'Thank you, Mr Aubyn – I'm afraid you've got rather wet on my account.'

The same slight half-smile, this time with a downward glance. 'It's of no consequence.' Taking off his hat, he closed the umbrella, shaking it through the door on to the pavement outside. The woman in front of us was handing over her money and my fear spiralled. Benedict Aubyn was clearly not leaving.

'Please don't let me keep you. I'll be fine, now. Thank you.'

His hat removed, his brown hair looked slightly dishevelled. Slightly too long, and slightly too curly, he drew it from across his forehead. 'I'm early for a meeting – the least I can do is see you get your ticket.' Through an arch, the taproom looked to be bursting, the voices deafening. 'Then I'll show you to a private area where you can wait in peace.'

Without his hat, his eyes looked slightly too narrow, his nose slightly too long. His forehead was furrowed, his cheeks even more gaunt. The woman in front of us was putting her tickets in her purse and Benedict Aubyn stepped forward. 'One ticket for Penzance – *inside*, if you please.' He turned, the same shy kindness in his eyes. 'They'll announce its departure in the inn, but best to be ready at least ten minutes before.'

'That'll be three shillings.' The ticket seller did not look up.

Adjusting his glasses, he started writing in the ledger. 'Name please.'

A knot twisted my stomach. 'Maybe, I won't go today. Maybe, I'll go back to the ship and leave tomorrow when it isn't raining.' I must have been blushing. I know I was stammering. I was usually so good at lying.

Benedict Aubyn was clearly perplexed. 'But it's very likely to rain again tomorrow – once this rain sets in it can rain all week!' He stopped, as if with sudden understanding. Reaching inside his pocket, he drew out his wallet. 'The name's Mrs Marshall.' He kept his eyes on the ticket seller.

My blush deepened. 'No . . . please . . . I can't accept this.'

'All your luggage stolen, and straight from Philadelphia? You've no English money, have you, Mrs Marshall? In which case, it's my pleasure to help.' Handing me the ticket, he smiled his shy half-smile, again with the same downward glance. 'Follow me – I'm afraid it's going to be a bit of a crush.' He led the way through the crowded taproom, his voice rising. 'May we come through? Excuse me, if we can just pass?' Inching ahead, we began making progress through the dripping coats. 'Looks like everyone's come in to get out of this rain.'

Gripping my bag, the crush was considerable. Elbows jolted me, the haze of tobacco smoke stinging my eyes. Heavy beams crossed the low ceiling, a huge fireplace at one side, groups of men sitting on benches beneath the small leaded windows on the other. The innkeeper was serving ale from a barrel, aproned girls weaving their pewter jugs through the crowd. Benedict reached for my arm. 'It's just through here.'

He pushed open a door to a murmur of men's voices, too soft to distinguish what was being said. Elaborate oak screens partitioned the room into separate stalls and with each enclave affording much needed privacy important conversations were clearly taking place. Like the private pews in churches: like Grandfather's church. A memory flashed of me hiding beneath the wooden screen as Grandfather preached from the lectern above.

'This one's free.' Benedict stood back to let me pass. 'The cubicles can be booked for private meetings. Some like to do business in the taproom but you can't hear yourself think in there.' He looked round. 'There's the clock – so you'll know when to leave. You'll be safe here.'

Diffuse light filtered through the rain-splashed windows, a fire burning in the grate. A group of women sat in high-backed chairs by the fireplace, the surrounding murmur of voices sometimes animated, but always muffled. I braced myself. Now he would make his move. Now, in the privacy of the cubicle, just like all the other *gentlemen* in Government House. Yet he turned to go.

'I'll see you get some ale.' No sudden push against the oak panelling, no groping for my breast. No hand sliding beneath my cloak and up my thigh. No leer as if I should expect no less. Just a flash of his sad half-smile and a downward glance. 'Goodbye, Mrs Marshall. I hope you have a comfortable journey. Penzance is a very interesting town. You have family there?'

Thrown by his sincerity, my cheeks burned like fire. 'Yes – my family. I'm going home.'

'I'm sure they will be overjoyed to see you. Good day, Mrs Marshall.'

'Thank you for your kindness.' Guilt ripped through me. He needed nourishment. He should have used the money for a meal.

'Not at all.' There was sadness in his shrug, a look of loss as he turned away.

The serving girl bringing the ale assured me I had nothing to pay and my guilt deepened. The men in a cubicle nearer the door were leaving and, as it would be easier to see the clock, I decided to take their place. Settling myself, the door opened and through a small crack in the screen, I saw Benedict Aubyn re-enter the room with two men. He took down the piece of paper pinned to the cubicle next to mine. 'We're in here – I've booked for an hour. Shall I order you something to drink?'

The taller of his companions shook his head. 'I've had sufficient, thank you.' He had a Scottish accent. Sombrely but smartly dressed, he was in his late forties. Beneath his wide hat he had heavy brows, a clean-shaven chin and a long nose. His coat dripping in one hand, he grasped a leather bag in the other. 'Unless you'd like some, Mr Cartwright?'

The second man shook his head. 'I've plans to dine later.' Short and stout, his face florid, he seemed to be having difficulty squeezing along the bench. His high-pitched voice grew terse. 'We're not here on a fool's errand, I hope, Mr McAdam?'

The Scottish man hung up his coat and slipped along the bench opposite. His case snapped open, and I heard the rustle of papers. 'I believe not, Mr Cartwright.' Silence followed, just the swift movements of Benedict Aubyn as he settled himself on the other side of the screen.

Curiosity is not a crime, Mama — curiosity is how I found out. Following my father was one thing, but eavesdropping on a kind and generous stranger? I sat rigid, knowing it was wrong, yet I could not help myself. Resting my head against the warped panel, I pressed my ear against the black wood. It was not my fault it was riddled with cracks and holes. Not my fault I could overhear their lowered voices.

Chapter Three

B enedict Aubyn cleared his throat. 'I've decided I'll take the
position. With added considerations.'

I heard a slow exhale of breath, then the high-pitched
voice. 'Excellent. You're far the best candidate. We want you,
Mr Aubyn . . . here are our terms. You've proved yourself a
shrewd negotiator – and the Trust admire you for that. They're
offering forty guineas per annum *plus expenses*. Read this at
your leisure . . . it's a two-year contract – though you'll see the
first six weeks are considered probation. Prove you can do
the job, and there'll be *rich rewards*.'

I hardly recognised Benedict Aubyn's voice, yet he was
sitting right behind me. No longer charming, he sounded hard-
nosed, callous. '*Rich rewards* is what I'm after, Mr Cartwright.'

'Indeed, Mr Aubyn. Rich rewards are what we're *all* after.
The Turnpike Trust are men of rank who *expect results* . . . if
you understand what I mean?'

'I do understand you, Mr Cartwright. Which is why the
considerations I have set out here must be met. I want fifty

guineas per annum, and ten per cent of every land deal I negotiate. Plus ten per cent of every mile I save . . . a free pass through all the tollgates . . . and ten per cent of every advantageous contract I pass your way.'

Papers slid across the table, a deep intake of breath, a pause, then the high-pitched voice edged with anger. 'These terms cannot be met. They said you'd be *amenable*, Mr Aubyn. Not arrogant and self-seeking. I can assure you these terms will be found unacceptable. Mr McAdam, you've wasted my time. Your protégé has overreached himself.'

The Scottish voice again, soft, calm. 'My protégé is the best there is. If the Truro to Falmouth Turnpike Trust can't agree to his terms there are other trusts lining up to employ him. No surveyor knows the land like Mr Aubyn, and not to employ him would be a false economy. I've seen his plans. Even allowing for his ten per cent, your sponsors will reap vast rewards.'

'What plans? Let me see them?'

A soft laugh, but the same hard edge to Benedict's reply. 'Only when I'm fully employed by your trust.'

The anger returned, and with it a note of sarcasm. 'You're not the man I was led to believe you to be. I was expecting a *gentleman*, sir.'

On the other side of the screen, Benedict Aubyn's voice remained steady. 'That's as it may be, Mr Cartwright. I may not be as *malleable* as you expect but I have the skills you need. And I come at a price.'

The Scottish voice again, smoothing the waters. 'I'll not be in Falmouth for much longer. Within six months I take up my position as surveyor to the Bristol Turnpike Trust. I've taught Mr Aubyn everything I know about road building. He's the man you want. In fact, I'd go as far as to say he's the man you *need*. Pay him what he asks and you'll not regret it.'

Outside the rain was lessening, though drips still clung to the window. I hardly dared to move but edged forward to see the clock. Another fifteen minutes and I would leave. No sound came from the other cubicle, and I supposed Benedict Aubyn to be reading the contract. A commotion made me look up: the women from the fireplace were leaving.

'That looks in order. I may not seem a gentleman to you, Mr Cartwright, but I give you my word I shall deliver *exactly* what the Turnpike Trust ask of me – an efficient route from Truro to Falmouth to link with the Penzance and Newlyn turnpike. Once my considerations are approved, I'll bring my plans to the next meeting.'

'Just sign the contract, Mr Aubyn. Your considerations will be approved.'

The women were picking up their luggage and preparing to leave. Perhaps I should slip out with them? Yet I pulled back, unable to resist looking through the small crack behind me. Benedict Aubyn was signing several papers, the stout man heaving himself along the bench, a deep scowl on his face. 'Don't let us regret this, Mr Aubyn.'

It was too late to leave. Benedict Aubyn rose to see the stout man to the door and I held my breath, desperate for him not to see me sitting so close. The Scottish man reached for his coat, smiling as Benedict shook his hand. 'Thank you, John. I won't let you down. You know what this means to me.'

20

'I know all about *growing expenses*. Bairns have a habit of growing! Especially wee lasses with their frocks and ribbons!' He paused, his voice softening. 'You've done the right thing, Benedict. It's not an easy decision, but it's the right decision.'

'The truth is, it's the only decision.'

They were getting ready to leave and John McAdam's voice turned serious. 'You're absolutely certain there are no obstacles? She sounds ... well — let's put it this way — I've heard she's a prickly, middle-aged spinster rather set in her ways. She may not view your new route as progress.'

I held my ear against the crack. Benedict Aubyn's voice was a whisper. 'The word is she's bankrupt. The school's all but closed. There are no pupils left and her staff have been dismissed. My offer will be a *godsend* to her. I can't see her putting up any objection at all.'

'Get that land, and you'll get access to the river.'

'Indeed. Get access to the river and a new bridge will take twenty miles off the old road.'

There was a soft laugh. 'Which means an improved access to Harcourt Quay. Your first lucrative land deal, Ben. I congratulate you. Rich rewards indeed.'

Distaste soured my mouth. He was not a gentleman at all. He was just like every man in Government House; just another greedy, manipulating, unscrupulous man who thought nothing of cheating some poor middle-aged woman out of her due.

'How's work progressing on the shore road? You should be finished soon.' John McAdam was just on the other side of the screen, if he took two steps backwards he would know I had overheard everything.

Benedict Aubyn replaced his hat over his curls. 'Going rather slowly but going well. I'm a stickler for your rules and they don't like it. I'm insisting on a depth of six inches and all small stones. Followed by another six inches once that's consolidated.'

'Good man. And not one single stone over the size of a walnut?'

'Not one single stone!'

John McAdam put his hand on Benedict Aubyn's shoulder. 'Remember, the stones must be broken sitting down – that's the important consideration. A woman sitting on a straw mat by the side of the road can break more stones in a day than two men with pickaxes. Remember that.'

'I will.'

Benedict Aubyn closed the door behind them, and I glanced to see if the rain had stopped. A woman was running across the courtyard, her cloak drawn round her. She was calling, obviously anxious to catch someone's attention. Coming immediately to her side, Benedict Aubyn held his umbrella over her. She was clearly agitated, pleading with him, yet he kept shaking his head. I could almost read her lips, *Please, Ben . . . please*. His answer must have upset her as she held a handkerchief to her eyes.

Still he shook his head, his lips tight, both of them frowning, and I pulled back as he glanced round the courtyard. Reaching into his heavy coat he drew out his wallet, immediately pressing what could only be money into her hand. I saw her draw back, trying to refuse. *Please don't, Ben.* Again and again. *Please don't.* Yet he kept insisting she take his money. Reaching for her hands, he held the money firmly between her palms.

Silently, she bent her head and he put his arm around her shoulder, hurrying her out of the courtyard towards the road. The clock struck quarter to and I knew I must hurry.

The rain had lessened to a fine drizzle and I crossed the road, weaving my way between the on-comers, retracing my steps as fast as I could. The crane was still lifting barrels from the ship, the *Jane O'Leary* still swinging at anchor. A crowd had gathered outside the tavern, a fiddler playing. Across the dock, a row of people were waiting for the ferry and I heard the splash of oars. People at the top of the steps were picking up their baskets and I ran the last hundred yards, catching my breath as I stood staring down at the ferry I had imagined more times than I could remember.

'Take care, mind yer step.' The ferryman helped me on to the boat. It was wider than I expected, with rows of seats and a makeshift tarpaulin covering one end. A woman squeezed along as I approached.

'Room fer one more under here.' The tarpaulin barely covered us, but at least I would not be seen by Mary as we passed the *Jane O'Leary*. 'That's a big bag ye have there, my love. Been away?'

A lump caught my throat. 'Yes.'

She smiled. 'Well, yer home now, aren't ye?' Tears pooled in my eyes, a sudden desire to cry. I had been so brave, yet now I was on Mama's ferry the enormity of my journey seemed almost too great. 'Lord, bless ye, love! There's no accountin' fer life, is there?'

I could hardly speak. *Aunt Hetty will adore you, and you will adore her.* The ferryman's coat dripped on to my cloak. 'Tuppence please.' He rattled the coins in the bag around his waist.

'Miss Harriet Mitchell will pay. I believe you run a tally for those going to St Feoca School for Young Ladies?'

His scowl darkened, an immediate sneer of contempt. 'Ye think I run a tally fer a woman with not a penny to her name? Tuppence, please, miss, or ye get off my boat.'

The other passengers were staring at me. A couple nudged each other, one making the sign of the cross. 'Well . . . perhaps I can return with it tomorrow . . . when I have the tuppence from Miss Mitchell?'

'*When I have the tuppence?*' he mocked. 'Like as well ye'll be lost to the devil and *never* come back.'

Reeling from his tone, tears sprang to my eyes. 'Please, sir . . .'

The woman next to me reached for her purse. 'Here. Let the poor girl alone. Here . . . poor love. Take no note of him. Here . . . one good turn, an' all that.' She thrust two pennies into the ferryman's hand. She was middle-aged, her hands raw. In her basket was an onion, two potatoes and something I did not recognise as a vegetable.

'Thank you . . . I'll repay you. Where do you live?' A sudden thought made me reach for the leather bag hanging from my shoulder. 'Or maybe you'd like one of these? Please choose one. I believe you could sell them for more than tuppence.'

Reaching into the purse, I pulled out some shells I had painted on the ship. Cupping them in my hand, I held them towards her. 'Please take whichever one you like best.'

She gasped, her raw hand flying to her mouth. 'But these are so good! Look . . . how can this be? A ship . . . and this one . . . ?' She reached tentatively towards them as if the shells were too exquisite to touch. 'A shoreline . . . an' . . . *flowers* . . . an' bless me, that's a cat. Oh, I'd love that one, but ye must sell these, my love, not give them away.'

We had cast off from the harbour wall and were entering the wide waters of Carrick Roads. The wind was freshening, the waves building, and I pulled back beneath the rough canvas. 'No . . . I insist.' I handed her the oyster shell with the portrait of a black cat. 'She's Miss Mabel – a ship's cat. I insist you keep her.'

'Ye painted these, my love?' She reached for the painting of the *Jane O'Leary* in full sail. 'Look . . . see, everyone?' Touching the arm of the man huddled beside her, she whispered, 'Give the girl some money an' ye can have this beautiful ship.'

Another man leaned forward, another and another. 'Let's take a look.'

Before I knew it she was cajoling the other passengers, smiling, winking, telling them they would regret not giving something so precious to their loved ones, and I smiled back, shrugging my shoulders, amazed by how well my shells were liked. The leather purse lay empty and she reached for my hand. 'There ye are, my love, that's three shillings and nine-pence. Who'd have thought it? There's no accountin' for life.'

The drizzle was penetrating my cloak, the air cold, the

25

water grey; black clouds formed a heavy band above us. I could hardly see Restronguet Creek, let alone recognise it; just the splashing of the oars, the swell of the waves, the water swilling round my feet. Just the smiles of my fellow passengers and the first money I had ever kept gripped tightly in my fist. 'Does another ferry go across the creek?' I asked.

She nodded. 'Ye needs ring the bell – loudly mind, an' vigorously! That usually brings him from his ale. See that thatch just coming into sight? That's the Passage Inn. The Harcourt Ferry leaves from there. Ye can't see much today, but it's just across the water.'

The quay Mr McAdam had mentioned. I swung to face her. 'Harcourt Quay?'

She shrugged, wrapping Miss Mabel in her grey handkerchief, tucking her safely down her bodice. 'Aye, my love. Harcourt Quay. There's a gatehouse through to St Feoca.' Another woman crossed herself, another and another, and her eyes sharpened. 'Come straight back if needs be. Ye've money enough fer a room in the inn now. Come back if needs be.'

Chapter Four

The fresh air did little to sober the ferryman. Scowling that he needed more than one passenger, he tripped and fell at my feet. 'Need three at leashht.'

Only by paying him triple did he agree to take me, and I sat on the wet seat, gripping my bag. The light was fading, dusk falling, the fine drizzle soaking the seat beside me. As we drew closer, a grey tower loomed through the mist and my stomach tightened. 'St Feoca Gatehouse?'

'Was the larsht time I came.' His cape dripped from his shoulders, his hat pulled low. 'Shall I wait? Only, ye're likely to come shtraight back.' He seemed to think that was funny, his laugh turning to a hacking cough. Oil lamps were burning on the quayside, flickering against a warehouse, lighting up the sign *Haye Copperhouse Merchants*. Pulling the boat against the wall of vertical slates, he pointed to an iron ladder. 'Up there.'

I ascended, the depth marked beside me . . . eight foot . . . nine foot . . . ten foot. I had no recollection of buildings, yet several lined the quay. Lamps were burning against their doors, the sign *Carnon Streamworks* and *Chasewater Company* just visible through the drizzle. The place looked deserted, no sign of life in any of the dwellings just the rain and mud, and huge piles of stones heaped on the cobbles. Picking my way around them, I started walking towards the gatehouse of the school.

It seemed immediately familiar. Built of grey stone, the arch towered above me. Solid and austere, it had four pointed windows beneath a row of crenellations and two windows on either side of heavy iron gates. *It's like a castle*, Mama had whispered; *they say it dates back to fourteen eighty*.

The windows were shuttered and I knew I must bang on the door, yet a sudden memory made me catch my breath. I was a child again, clinging to the gates, the pain so vivid it cut me like a knife. Aunt Hetty was turning from me, crying, refusing to say goodbye. I was shouting after her, Father gripping my arm, dragging me away. I was trying to break free, desperate to run back to her and tell her not to cry. That I would return very soon. That I wanted to draw beetles and butterflies with her. That I wanted to study worms with her through her large magnifying glass.

I gripped the gate like I had done as a child of six. It rattled in my hands and I pushed it gently. It opened, and I started walking up the long drive. The ruts in the road looked newly repaired, the surface firm beneath my boots, though it was hard to see with no moon to guide me. It seemed strangely quiet, the trees lining the drive indistinguishable against the night sky. My memory was of oil lamps burning against the front door yet there was no sign of light. A brazier should be casting shadows against the ancient tower; I should be hearing laughter, the sound of singing from the chapel. The courtyard should be filled with running footsteps, the clatter of plates echoing across the cobbles from the kitchen.

Mama's drawings had kept the school alive, kept my hopes alive. The buildings formed three sides of a square: the ancient stone monastery ahead of me, the tower and chapel to my right, the new wing with its large windows to my left. I remember the carriages sweeping round the yew tree to the front door before going through an arch to the court-yard behind. Yet the front door was closed, there was nothing, not even a light. No lamps were burning, just a faint smell of woodsmoke drifting through the drizzle.

Walking through the arch, the courtyard looked just as deserted. I stepped closer, peering across the cobbles. Light was filtering through the window of a downstairs room and I drew back, my black clothes concealing me from sight. The light was coming from the kitchen and I fought my sudden tears. A lamp was burning on the dresser, a fire roaring in the hearth. Two people were in the room, a grey-haired lady sitting in a rocking chair, and a young lady laying out a fine lace tablecloth. The young woman's hair was the colour of ripe corn, her movements graceful, her back straight. She was laughing, smiling at the old lady. She seemed to be singing, picking up plates and placing them on the table. Standing back, she adjusted the crystal glasses and reached for a silver candelabra to place at the centre.

She turned round, and a stab of jealousy twisted my stomach. She was beautiful, like my mother — a delicate, English rose. Poised, elegant, she had all the attributes Mama wanted me to have and a terrible feeling of inadequacy flooded through me: Aunt Hetty would find me *ungainly*. She would think me too tall, too thin, my feet too big, my hands too large. Worse still, I had a snub nose, uncontrollable black curls and more freckles than were seemly. I had no accomplishments: I could not play a single note and had never learned any songs to please an after-dinner audience. Father made it quite clear – I was a woman men might employ as a governess but they would never seek to marry me.

The beautiful young woman looked down at her laid table. Smiling, she lit the candelabra and left the room. The grey-haired lady rose and walked stiffly to the range. Reaching for a cloth, she lifted a heavy iron skillet on to the table and my heart swelled. She was Annie, the housekeeper, though I hardly recognised her. She looked frail and anxious, her eyes darting to the window as if she thought someone might be watching her.

I took a step nearer, my heart jolting. The beautiful young woman was holding open the door, a lady entering – Aunt Hetty, my beloved Aunt Hetty, and I gripped my cloak. Two years older than Mama she looked poised, elegant, far younger than Mama and far taller too. I had forgotten her striking, rather formidable features, and memories came flooding back – the mischief in her smile when I brought her worms for us to study, her conspiratorial wink as we hid behind the gate so no one could see us. Not pretty like Mama, her looks had grown severe, her eyes sharper, more intelligent. Her hair was brown rather than fair, a band of a grey sweeping from her forehead down the right side of her face. She was wearing mourning, like I was, a band of black lace on her cap. A gold locket hung from a chain round her neck and I reached beneath my cloak, clutching my own. *Mama, we're home. We're home.*

Just in time, I remembered to slip the ring from my finger.

My knock was tentative and I watched them swing round in fear. A lump in my throat was choking me, I felt unable to speak, yet I had to shout as they began closing the shutters. 'Please, please let me in... I'm sorry I didn't let you know I was coming. I'm Pandora. Your niece... I'm Pandora Woodville. I've come back.'

The beautiful young woman unlocked the door and I knew to curtsy with my back straight and my chin in the air. Desperate to sound eloquent, I tried not to gabble my words. 'I'm sorry I couldn't let you know I was coming... forgive me for intruding like this.'

Across the room, Aunt Hetty gripped the back of her chair, her face ashen, her mouth tight. 'Take off your cloak, my dear. And those wet shoes. You may not have told me you were coming, but that has not stopped me from expecting you. As soon as I heard about...' Her voice caught and she reached for a candle. 'Get warm... have something to eat. I'm going to retire to my room. I will see you at nine tomorrow morning. Miss Elliot will see to your comfort and show you where you can sleep.'

I held her stare, a thousand knives piercing my heart. No warm embrace. No sign of love. No holding me, no asking me about my mother and how she died. No questions about my journey. Just her stiff upper lip and haughty tone, her chin in the air, her penetrating eyes. I could hardly stop myself from crying. 'Thank you. I'm so sorry...'

At the door, her silk skirt rustled as she swung round. 'Sorry?' Her voice dropped to a whisper. 'Sorry that my prayers have been answered? That I have finally got you home?'

The door shut and Miss Elliot reached for my cloak. 'My goodness, you're very wet . . . Rain pooled on the flagstones around me, my footprints leading from the door. 'Your hem's completely soaked. Maybe you should change into something dry before we eat?' Her voice was as sweet as her smile was gentle. 'Come, sit by the fire while I go and light the one in your room. Get warm, Miss Woodville. You must have had a very long journey.'

Annie Rowe was staring at me. Holding up her eyeglass, she shook her head. 'You haven't your mama's looks, have you, my dear? You always were an ungainly child.'

I forced back my tears. 'No . . . Mama was very beautiful.'

'Come to the candlelight.' Her face was a mass of wrinkles, her skin almost translucent. I remembered her with dark brown hair yet now it was grey and thinning, parted in the middle, and coiled on both sides. She stretched out her arm, a heavy shawl wrapped around her shoulders. Her black brocade gown seemed rather too big for her, her velvet cap edged with black lace. 'Your hair's a terrible mess but that can be addressed.' Her bony finger slipped beneath my chin as she turned my head. 'Dear me. You're the spitting image of your grandmother.'

A bolt of hope shot through me. 'My grandmother was a lady.'

'She was. Indeed she was. A *real* lady.' A faraway look filled her watery eyes. 'I was Mrs Mitchell's personal maid before

I became her housekeeper. We were of an age. Your mother was a wonderful lady. We all adored her.'

Now my cloak was off, I could feel the chill in the room. Despite the fire, the stone walls seemed to retain the damp. More memories came flooding back: the table groaning under the weight of garden produce, a huge basket of lavender waiting to be made into bags. Mama's laughter rang across the kitchen, Annie Rowe smiling down at me, scolding me for climbing trees when I should have been sewing. And always my adored aunt, popping her head round the door, telling me she had found a new butterfly or a fat beetle and I must come quickly. The memories were so real, tears welled in my eyes.

Annie Rowe slipped her arm round my shoulder, a smile lighting her pale face. 'Don't cry, Abigail. You mustn't mind Harriet. She's a very private person . . . she'll be ready to see you in the morning. She'll forgive you in time, but she's right. Your mother doesn't approve of you marrying that man. You mustn't go against your mother's wishes.'

I stared back through my tears. She seemed lost in her own world. 'But I'm Pandora, Miss Rowe — I'm Abigail's *daughter*.'

Miss Elliot was watching us from the door. She seemed to glide across the room. Taking Annie's hand, she led her back to her seat by the fire. 'Miss Woodville must be tired after her journey. I'll take her to her room now. The fire's lit, and the bed sheets are airing. Miss Woodville is *Abigail's daughter*, Annie. You remember now? It's been a bit of a shock for you, hasn't it?'

She lifted my bag, smiling as she walked to the door, and I reached for it, not wanting her to carry it. Who was she?

33

Clearly not a servant as she was dressed so beautifully, but she was too young to be a teacher. She must be all of seventeen. I had no idea how to behave – should I let her take my bag or carry it myself? She was obviously prepared to light a fire and collect my bed linen, but she was not a maid.

She seemed to sense my thoughts. 'I'm lately a pupil here, Miss Woodville. My only wish is to be a teacher. At the moment we've no maids . . . we're just the three of us, and Susan, that is, who lives in the gatehouse. Annie is . . . Well, I think you saw how she slips into the past more often than not. But your room is ready – I'll bring you some hot water.'

She held up the candelabra and I followed her down a stone corridor with an arched doorway on one side. Candlelight flickered against the bare walls, an oak door opening to a vast hall with a vaulted ceiling. A set of worn steps wound from the right and I gripped the banister with its carved figurines. It was as if Mama walked beside me. *You used to peek through the banister like one of the angels.*

The stairs led to a long corridor lined with heavy oak doors, the smell of beeswax mixing with lavender. Miss Elliot walked swiftly, her candlelight flickering on the ornate panelling. Glimpses of unlit brass lanterns flickered in the light, slates with names written in white chalk. Pausing by a second flight of steps, she looked up at them. 'These lead to Miss Mitchell's private rooms. The three bottom steps creak so she knows if anyone's coming up.'

A memory stirred, a sense of childish excitement. 'I remember these steps. I think . . . I might be wrong . . . but did my grandfather have his study up there?'

She smiled, pointing me further down the dark corridor. 'His study's at the top of the tower – through the arch at the end. I came just after Reverend Mitchell died, but I knew your grandmother. Mrs Mitchell was a wonderful lady, we all adored her. She was kind and gentle, and I was so sad when she died.' Grace Elliot looked just like an angel, just how Mama must have looked. 'Miss Woodville, I can't tell you how happy I am you've come. Miss Mitchell needs you. She's only just heard about your dear mother's death and I think you saw how hard she's taken it.'

She opened a door to a room lit with candles, a fire burning in the grate. 'The room will soon warm up.' A bed with a canopy stood in the centre, a dressing table with a large mirror on one side, a desk laid with writing utensils on the other. Two pairs of thick brocade curtains were tightly drawn, a pile of bedlinen folded neatly on a chair. 'Have you other luggage, Miss Woodville?'

I shook my head. 'My trunk and other bags were stolen in Philadelphia. I've only got a nightdress and one change of clothing. Miss Elliot, whose room is this?'

'It's never used – it's always kept in readiness. Miss Mitchell insists on it being aired every day.' A flicker crossed her beautiful face, her eyes welling with tears. 'It's the room your mother used to share with Miss Mitchell when they were children. Miss Mitchell has always kept it ready for your mother's return.' Her voiced faltered and she looked away.

I could hardly speak. 'Would you mind if I stay up here? I'm rather tired. Perhaps, I can come down and bring my supper up on a tray?'

'I'll bring you a tray. I'll make your bed and I'll bring some hot water.'

It was all I could do to hold back my tears. 'I'll make my bed, Miss Elliot. You've been very kind. I don't expect you to run after me like this.'

She held her delicate handkerchief to her eyes. 'Will you call me Grace?'

Sudden emptiness filled me. I could not help it. She knew my grandmother, she had *loved* my grandmother, and my grandmother would certainly have loved her. 'How long have you been at St Feoca, Grace?'

She paused at the door. 'Ten years. I was seven when I arrived. I was an orphan. My aunt scrimped and saved to send me here. When she died, Mrs Mitchell kept me as a charity girl. I owe everything to your family, Miss Woodville. That's why I stayed when everyone else left.'

Her voice sent a chill through me. 'Why has everyone left?'

She clutched the cross hanging round her neck. 'Miss Mitchell will tell you. She doesn't like us to speak of it.'

Taking off my gold locket, Mama's portraits smiled back at me. I had painted them on shell and cut them to the exact shape. Hardly seeing for tears, I put it on the dressing table and shook out my stiff clothes. All were salt-drenched, and not just from the sea. Ten years ago, I had been eleven. Ten years ago, Father had promised us we could return to St Feoca.

Chapter Five

I woke to the swishing of curtains and grey light filtering into the room. "Tis another damp day. Looks to be settling in good and proper.' I did not recognise the voice, nor the woman bustling round my room. Hooking back the heavy curtains she stood, hands on hips, staring at the hem of my dress. 'Seawater? Should have been rinsed through last night. It always leaves a mark.'

The fire was lit, a tray of steaming oatmeal and a bread roll on the table beside me. She seemed amused. 'I've been in and out, and you sleeping like a log! I'm Mrs Penrose — but you can call me Susan. I'm from the gatehouse. I have to say . . .' She swallowed, as if unable to find the right words. 'That, filthy wet hem and muddy footprints apart, it's good to have you here.'

She plumped up my pillow and I sat back, smiling at her. 'It's very good to be here.'

She raised her eyebrows. 'Miss Mitchell won't like your hair. Nor does she like anyone being late. Your boots are still wet; you should have stuffed them with paper.' She was dressed in

37

a grey serge gown with a white apron and mobcap. In her late thirties, her hands were red, her fingernails cut short. She had an air of everything being a problem, but when she smiled, she turned pretty and good-natured. 'Eat this porridge – you've half an hour to get ready.'

'Thank you . . .' I reached for the tray. I was still half asleep. Though the bed was comfortable, I had lain most of the night missing the motion of the ship.

'You won't remember me, but I remember you. I wasn't Susan Penrose then, I was Susan Lee. My husband's the school's groundsman, and I'm the housekeeper.' She paused, shrugging her shoulders. 'Or I used to be.'

'This oatmeal's delicious. Thank you, Susan.' I pulled back the heavy counterpane and the chill hit me. Even with the fire burning the room was cold. She seemed amused, then frowned.

'It's called porridge here. Now, let me brush your hair. I'll slick it down with water.'

'No . . . water makes it curl more.'

The clock on the table chimed the quarter hour. 'Then I'll fetch up some almond oil. Miss Mitchell doesn't like wild, unruly hair. Nor freckles. Nor slouching. Nor speaking before you're spoken to. Nor being kept waiting. And she won't like this woollen dress, either.'

'I'm afraid all my luggage was stolen.'

Shaking her head, she helped me into my black serge dress, smoothing the lace collar. 'So I heard. This needs a good wash – don't stand in the daylight and she may not notice.' Her brush scraped my scalp and I winced as she fastened my hair in a tight clasp. 'Best not fidget. There's nothing Miss Mitchell hates more than girls who fidget – except girls who laugh too loudly – and those who snigger behind their hands. And only knock once and wait for her to call you in. And curtsy deep. Don't sit till she tells you to, and don't start conversing until you're spoken to.'

I reached across the dressing table. 'My headband, I'd like to wear it.' I held up the black ebony headband Mama had given me. It was finely engraved, decorated with mother-of-pearl, and fitted perfectly round my forehead. I held it for her to take, the shells glistening even in the dull light.

She looked thunderstruck. 'No, Miss Woodville! Miss Mitchell will send you from the room if you wear something like this.'

The bottom three steps creaked as I climbed Aunt Hetty's stairs. My knock was firm and I waited to be called in. Her voice was sharp. 'Enter.' Bookcases lined the room, a pile of papers on a table by her chair. Shutting the door quietly, I sank into a curtsy. She was sitting at a desk with letters spread out in front of her. Dim light filtered from the window behind her. 'Come, my dear, sit here.'

She wore the black silk dress and shawl from the night before, the same black lace cap, her silver streak of hair tucked behind a swinging pearl earring. She slipped on her glasses and peered over the top, her skin unblemished, free of wrinkles, though her cheeks looked gaunt, her eyes red-rimmed.

I straightened my back, hoping she would think me lady-like. She did not speak but sat staring down at letters written in Mama's clear handwriting. Slipping one of the miniature portraits from my locket towards her, I broke the first rule. 'Your locket is identical to mine. I've brought you other paintings, but this one of Mama will fit your locket.'

Her elegant hand with its perfect nails reached for the painting. 'Our lockets were a Christmas present. I was twelve, your mother ten.' She held the portrait, gazing at it with tight lips. 'Your father's letter said Abigail died of yellow fever fourteen weeks ago. Is that correct?'

Pain shot through me. 'It happened very fast. We hardly had time to say goodbye. I was with her when she died. I was holding her hand and she told me I should come to you.'

'You were both with her? Your father as well?'

I crossed my fingers under the desk. 'Yes. She closed her eyes and we thought she was asleep. There was a sudden stillness . . . I turned round and she looked so at peace.'

She held the portrait to the daylight. 'You painted this?'

I nodded, opening my own locket. 'It will fit perfectly inside the rim.'

Reaching for the letters, she tied them in a bundle and placed the portrait with them in the top drawer. Taking off her glasses, she rose. 'Is your father in England? Has he come too?'

My stomach churned; all these questions about Father. 'They pleaded for him to stay. He's so highly thought of. His reputation is considerable. There aren't many scholars with honorary degrees of Doctor of Divinity from Cambridge University. Everyone wants him. He's tutor in Germantown

Academy in Philadelphia. That's in *Pennsylvania*.' I was speaking too fast.

'I know where Philadelphia is, Pandora.' She seemed suddenly fierce, not kind at all. 'So, he's no longer schoolmaster in Brooklyn . . . and before that schoolmaster in the grammar school in Columbia, *New York* . . . and before that, private tutor to Lord Howard, Governor General of *Jamaica* . . . and before that, tutor to Mr John Orde, Governor General of *Grenada*? You must be very proud of how his reputation spreads before him. How he was sought so many times for such prestigious positions?'

Somehow, I found my voice. 'Mama loved travelling. She loved Father and was very proud of him. Father worked so hard to give her all she wanted.'

'A far cry from schoolmaster in Truro. So he's coming. He's sent you on ahead?'

She walked to the window, beckoning for me to join her, and we stood staring through the small leaded panes. We were above the central yew tree, the drive stretching through the parkland to the gatehouse beyond. To the left, the old tower and chapel with its pointed stained-glass windows looked dull in the drizzle. To the right, the new wing with its large sash windows and portico looked equally grey. 'Do you remember the school at all, Pandora?'

'Yes – and now I'm back I can remember so much more. But I don't really know if they're my memories or what Mama told me. She talked so much about you and Grandmother . . . about Grandfather's treasure hunts . . . how one pupil nearly drowned trying to get a clue from the well!'

She stood in silence, her face strangely compelling. Her features were striking, as if daring me to look at her. 'You haven't asked me why there are no pupils.'

'That's because Susan told me not to speak first.'

A smile flickered across her lips. 'What else did Mrs Penrose say?'

'That you'd hate my hair, my freckles, my woollen dress, and you'd find my collar shabby. Basically, that I would be a disappointment to you.'

She shrugged her elegant shoulders. 'We'll see what we can do about that. We work miracles here. We boast the finest young ladies, fit for the finest society. Our girls are like the jewels in Cornwall's crown. St Feoca girls are renowned for their wit and good humour, for their elegance and social graces. They are demure, graceful, at ease in any society. They are the cream of the county. *The absolute cream.*'

Her words thrilled me. Maybe, I, too, could become such a lady. 'Do they study botany and mathematics? Do they read Greek and speak Latin?'

Her mouth tightened, her sharpness returning. 'Men do not like intelligence in a woman, Pandora. They look for elegance and a demure smile. They like a biddable wife – not a learned one.' I was a child again, my mother leading me down the stairs from this very room. *Aunt Hetty feels things deeply, Pandora. She can be very sharp and gets extremely angry. We must try not to displease her again.*

She gave a small cough. 'So we can expect your father fairly soon?'

'When he can get away . . .'

'Come.' Her tone was brisk, unfriendly. 'I'll show you round what used to be my school. But first, we shall address your clothes.'

Two doors led from her study and she crossed the room, opening her bedroom door. Her bed was made, the drapes drawn, her dressing table uncluttered: just a silver brush, a comb and mirror, but I hardly saw them. I saw only the portrait of two ladies smiling down at me. One had sparkling blue eyes and golden curls, the other had brown hair, narrow brown eyes and a rather large nose. Both were wearing exquisite gowns — cream silk embroidered with exotic flowers — both with gold lockets round their necks. Beside them was a large vase of lilies: an open book rested on their laps, behind them, a bookcase groaning under the weight of ancient leather tomes.

The painting radiated joy, yet her voice sounded bitter. 'I was eighteen when that was painted, Abigail was sixteen. It was just before she met your father.' She turned, throwing open her wardrobe. 'You and I are of similar heights — I believe any of my dresses will fit.' She started flicking through the row of black dresses, all of them silk or damask. 'Maybe this one?' She held it against me. 'In fact, have these three. This one for the evening, this one for the day, and this one for any visits we may make.'

'Thank you, Aunt Hetty. I'm so grateful.'

'A little less of a *gawp*, my dear. There's nothing more unattractive in a woman. It's very unbecoming. And Aunt Hetty is what a child would call me. You're no longer a child, Pandora, so I'd prefer you to call me Aunt Harriet, and *Miss Mitchell* in front of any pupils.'

43

Her rebuke felt like a physical slap. 'I hope to be useful to you. Like Miss Elliot, I want only to be a teacher in your school. It's what Mama wanted, too.'

'And your father? Does he want you to be a teacher at my school?' She shut the wardrobe, walked swiftly to the door, and I followed with my arms full of her dresses. Once I was wearing one and had oiled my hair and polished my shoes, I might look like a niece she could love. A newspaper lay on her desk. 'You sailed into Falmouth?' she said as she returned to her seat.

'Yes. We were carrying corn.'

'That's good. Wheat ships have been promised for several months, yet none has arrived. The country's facing famine. Demand from the fleet and militia is driving up the price of cattle and sheep. Everything, in fact — corn, potatoes, eggs. Vegetables. It's getting worse. The militia think nothing of dispersing starving crowds with bayonets, and meeting to discuss wages and conditions is prosecuted by fines and imprisonment.'

'I heard the snow lasted until May, and that you had frosts in June.'

'Followed by floods. Uncut hay lay rotting, and unripe wheat blackened. Chickens and geese were battered to death by hailstones and as a result the people of Cornwall are starving.'

'So your pupils left because their fathers couldn't afford the fees?'

Her laughter was hollow. 'Good Lord, no. My pupils come from families untouched by want and hunger. They are shielded from such *inconveniences*.' She indicated I should put the dresses on a chair and join her at her desk. Over the top of her glasses, her eyes pierced mine. 'They may remain untouched by money troubles, Pandora, but, unfortunately, that is not the situation I face. No pupils means no fees, and no fees means no wages for both the teachers and the servants.'

'But surely, Aunt Harriet, if the gentry still have money, your pupils will come back?'

Again the hollow laughter. 'My pupils left because one rather foolish, well, one extremely *stupid* girl took it upon herself to visit St Feoca's Well to divine whether the man her guardian had chosen for her to marry was *honourable*.' Her mouth tightened. 'Whether he *loved her* . . . and *would be faithful to her*.' She breathed deeply. 'This foolish girl was a parlour boarder. I afforded her the privilege of eating at my table. She had her own suite of rooms in the new wing, and her own maid. She was Lord Entworth's protégée.'

'You mean his illegitimate daughter?'

A frown of disapproval creased her forehead. 'No, Pandora, I mean his protégée. She held considerable influence over the other girls – this was last March, twelve months ago. We had our full quota of forty girls . . . I even had a waiting list. I was expecting six new pupils to join us and what happened is beyond comprehension. By May, rumours were circulating, and by June six pupils demanded their parents remove them from my school.'

'Because of rumours of a lapse in supervision?'

'No, Pandora. I dealt with the pupil in question straight away. I was very firm and suggested that as this *foolish girl* was now engaged to be married, she might like to leave the school.

Though, of course, it was all done very delicately with no hint of scandal to prevent her marriage.' She paused. 'No . . . the rumours being spread were that the school was being visited by the *devil*. By September, all but eight had left, and in January not one single pupil returned.'

'But that's ridiculous! How dare they spread rumours like that?'

Her eyes sharpened. 'Of course it's ridiculous. It's ludicrous. But the rumours kept growing. Apparently, there's an ancient myth that the lady of this house once sought the power of the sacred well to divine the nature of her intended. She went at night, in the full moon, and caught the reflection of the devil looking over her shoulder. Of course, she didn't know it was the devil, because he had disguised himself as a handsome young man of good fortune. He told her that he had loved her from afar, and that she must come away with him.'

'But that's just . . . ridiculous nonsense.'

'Of course it is. But Holy Wells are Holy Wells. They are often visited and give great comfort. Many put their faith in them, and if the devil appears, well, then the devil appears.'

'Is the well in the school grounds?' She shook her head. 'In that case, it has nothing to do with the school.'

She looked suddenly tired, her black cap and shawl accentuating the pallor in her cheeks. 'The story goes that the young lady refused his advances and he followed her back to St Feoca Manor and from then on kept trying to lure her away. The story goes that she died of fear and that he cursed the house saying he would *lie in wait* until the next lady of the house visited the well.'

The clock on the mantelpiece struck ten. The last chime rang across the room and I sat fighting my fury. I could feel my cheeks burning. 'How dare they ruin our school like this? How dare they? We can't let this happen!'

Her voice hardened. 'Our school?'

Her tone stung, once again, like a slap. '*Your* school, Aunt Harriet.'

'Almond oil might help tame your hair – your hands are very unkempt . . . and lemon juice may go some way to dampen those freckles. You need to address your posture, Pandora. I may not have a school any more, but the least I can do is get you a husband.'

Disappointment ripped through me. If she only knew how much I had yearned to be here, how every day I had thought of her. How I had put her on a pedestal and ached to come back to her. I stood at the door, my arms full of her dresses, and curtsied deeply. 'I didn't come here to find a husband, Aunt Harriet.' I held my chin uncomfortably high. 'I came here to be a teacher. I don't ever intend to find a husband, but I do intend to get those forty pupils back in to *your* school.'

Her shoulders lifted. 'And what if I don't want them to return?'

I almost reeled at her indifference. Resting her elbows on the desk, her hands were clasped as in prayer, her face serene, no sign of the fury burning mine. 'But you *have* to get them back, Aunt Harriet.'

'*Have* to?' Her eyes were like shards of glass. 'I have work to do . . . I shall stay in my room and we can resume our discussion at three. Tell Miss Rowe we'll take our meals in the dining room. Mrs Penrose can help you with any alterations you may like to make to the gowns.'

No sign of love, no warmth, no asking about my journey; no sign she was pleased to see me. I had been dismissed as if I was one of her foolish girls. I tried to keep the quiver from my voice. 'Aunt Harriet, I'd like to call them Grace, Annie and Susan. If I may?'

She looked down, her mouth tight. 'As you please, Pandora.'

Chapter Six

A mound of curls lay on the flagstones, the fire barely keeping the kitchen warm. Susan put down her scissors. 'Would she mind if you cut it three inches shorter?' I asked.

Annie Rowe pursed her thin lips. 'Yes. She'll not approve at all.'

Susan was equally adamant. 'Not *at all*. This is quite short enough. We'll dress it how Miss Mitchell likes hair to be dressed – the way Grace wears hers. Coconut oil indeed! We don't have coconuts here. Do they really fall from trees?'

Fires in the other rooms were only to be lit for two hours in the morning and on retiring to bed, so the kitchen drew us like a magnet. Grace was at the table, emptying a basket of fruit and vegetables. 'No,' she smiled, 'no coconuts in here! But Sir Anthony does put pineapples in his baskets – Miss Mitchell's very partial to pineapple.'

With only the smallest adjustments, my new silk dress fitted me perfectly. I had washed and oiled my hair and sat with a huge linen cloth around my shoulders. They had been so kind, making up for Aunt Hetty's coldness, and with my hair parted

49

severely down the middle, my high neckline and stiff lace, I hoped she would approve. 'Who's Sir Anthony?'

Their silence cut the air. Annie rose stiffly from her chair. Standing behind me, she rested her hands on my shoulders. 'You're so like your dear grandmother. Did your mother ever tell you that?'

I nodded, but I would not be put off. 'Who's Sir Anthony? Why does he send baskets to Aunt Harriet?'

Again, their downward glances. Annie took the cloth from my shoulder. 'Sir Anthony Ferris owns the neighbouring estate... he's a generous benefactor of St Feoca School. Before her death, Lady Ferris was a governor and, since her death, Sir Anthony has been... very solicitous... of Miss Mitchell and her well-being. His baskets... Well, my dear, you might as well know. His baskets and gifts of game are what feeds us.'

I looked out at the empty courtyard. No hens pecked the cobbles, no eggs hiding where Mama had advised me to look. 'What about the estate's farm? Surely the school has its own farm – I remember visiting it with Grandfather? We used to help milk the cows.'

Annie shook her head. 'There's still the farm but the stables are empty. All but one cow. The rest have long been taken... the pigs, too. They've all gone for the fleet, there's barely a hen left. And what the navy and militia haven't commissioned, the vagrants take. They come at night and everything's taken. Sacks of potatoes... corn... turnips. And even if we had any animals, there's nothing to feed them on.'

Leaning on her stick, she seemed stronger than the night before. 'Unless, of course, you're Sir Anthony Ferris. Tregenna

50

Hall has a walled garden and plenty of armed men to guard it. The fish ponds remain abundant and the glasshouses are filled with oranges and lemons. Sir Anthony has pineapple houses . . . orchid houses, and all the game he can shoot. And not one of us . . . *blames* . . . Miss Mitchell for encouraging his advances.'

'*Advances!*' It was as if a rug had been pulled from beneath me. 'What advances?'

Susan was sweeping my cut hair from the flagstones, Grace arranging orchids in a crystal vase. Annie took my arm, her touch as gentle as a sparrow. 'The truth is . . .' Her voice turned to a whisper. 'Men don't like to remain a widower for long.'

The sound of wheels caught our attention. A mule cart was crossing the cobbles, the driver urging the mule into the barn. Logs were balancing precariously on the top and a couple dropped off as the cart stopped. Susan laid aside her brush and straightened her apron, her eyebrows rising as she looked at Grace. 'He's here. Shall I go, or would you like to see if he needs anything, Grace?'

Grace stopped still, a slight blush spreading up her neck. She was even more beautiful in daylight: pale, enchanting, her blonde hair framed her delicate face. 'No! Of course not! I'm busy with these orchids. You go, Susan.'

Laughter echoed across the kitchen, a sly wink and a nudge as Susan pushed her forward. 'Get along with you. I'll see to the orchids . . . Go tell him where to *put his logs!*'

We watched Grace walk elegantly across the cobbles to the barn. The driver turned and I saw a mass of dark curls. *Don't let it be him. Please, please, don't let it be him.* 'Who is he?' I managed to say. 'Why's he here?'

'He's the road builder — the one resurfacing the road to Harcourt Quay. He's hired my husband's cart for his stones — just till George's foot heals. Miss Mitchell asked for more logs and as George can't bring them at the moment he asked Mr Aubyn to do it.'

Panic filled me. 'Does Mr Aubyn come here often?'

Her smile broadened. 'He comes a lot more since he's seen our Grace! And Miss Mitchell clearly likes him. He mended her ruts and asked for no payment!'

I thought I might be sick. 'Who paid for them, then?'

'The new owner of the quay. He bought the quay a year back and is paying for everything. George says he could have asked Miss Mitchell to pay half, seeing as the shore road runs alongside her land. George says Miss Mitchell's saved a pretty penny!'

The kettle whistled and Susan went to retrieve it. I turned round, my skirt rustled, and I started back at my reflection in the glass: apart from the fear in my eyes, I could have been Aunt Hetty with my tight mouth and severe hair.

I was to meet Aunt Hetty on the steps of the tower and tried to remember how to get there: either I could go up the stairs in the grand hall and use the adjoining arch or I could go outside and cross the drive. A break in the rain drew me to the front door and I stood staring up at the spreading yew tree.

Aunt Hetty came to my side. One glance at my altered appearance and still she frowned. 'You're going to need new shoes.' She looked up at the tower with its stone crenulations. 'Do you remember the tower? We use it for art work — mainly painting and sketching, though *découpage* is proving very popular. There's one room to a floor – three rooms altogether. Up these circular steps.'

'Yes, I do remember it.' The icy chill made me wish I had brought my cloak. Aunt Hetty walked swiftly ahead, almost running up the stone steps. 'That arch leads through to the main house. It was added after the monks left. The tower dates back to fourteen hundred, though it's had considerable repairs.' She stood beneath a carved stone arch. 'We only use the tower rooms in the summer. They dry flowers here – our pupils leave with an extensive knowledge of herbs and their uses.' She opened the door to a central table and rough flagstones. Several lavender bunches were hanging from ancient beams and memories stirred of Mama reading to Grandmother as she sorted through piles of herbs. 'Come.'

She wound up two more flights of heavily worn steps, a rope handrail hanging between iron hooks. Light filtered through narrow slits in the thick walls. 'Here.' Dipping beneath the stone lintel she opened the top door. 'Remember your grandfather's study?' The room was richly panelled, the wooden floor polished and covered in fine rugs. Bookcases lined the walls, a desk in the centre, a fireplace with a stone surround, but whereas the other rooms had barely any light, four large windows overlooked a narrow ledge behind the crenulations. 'Come, I'll show you the view.'

'Grandfather never let me go out there.'

'I should hope not.' Opening one of the windows wide enough, Aunt Hetty squeezed through the small opening and I followed her out on to the narrow terrace, gazing round through the gaps in the crenulations. 'On a good day, you can see Pendennis Castle. Take care . . .'

'Goodness, you can see for miles.' A shimmer of sun broke through the clouds, lighting the vast expanse of Carrick Roads. 'Look – I can see the ships.' Below us, the glass roof of the conservatory glinted in the sun. Edging slowly round, I faced east. The drive to the gatehouse lay before us. 'That must be Mama's creek, and that must be the wood she loved so much. She often told me how you used to row up the creek – just the two of you. How Grandfather sent you on treasure hunts. She said he'd write clues for you and you'd be gone for hours. She said she wrote poems and you drew the birds . . .'

Aunt Hetty turned from me. 'Yes, well, your mother was full of romantic nonsense.'

I forced back my sudden hurt. 'I'm sorry. It's just seeing the creek.'

She pointed to Mama's wood. 'You can just see the roof of the Old Mill. It's all but stopped working. The creek your mother loved is called Tallacks Creek . . . and the wood, Tallacks Wood. But I suggest you stay clear of them. Poachers have set their traps there – that's how George Penrose nearly lost his foot. Sir Anthony insists he should lend me his gamekeepers and I agree George did have a narrow escape, but there's great hardship out there. I believe we can turn a blind eye to the odd lost pheasant and hare.'

The vast park stretched around us. Drawing me to the west side, she pointed out a dirt track winding between brown fields. 'That leads to the farm, though there's no livestock there now. Your grandfather used to like milking the cows.'

'The more I see, the more I remember.'

She pointed me back towards the open window. 'After he died, Mother used this as her sitting room. It was her sanctuary.' She bit her lip. 'The desk is full of their belongings. Books, mainly . . . your grandfather's sermons and old school accounts. I haven't . . . Well, the truth is I need to sort through it all. They're buried in St Feock, if you'd like to visit their graves.'

A pair of iron handles were attached to the side of the tower and I peered down. 'That ladder doesn't look very safe.'

'It's safe enough but it's strictly out of bounds. Mother worried every time Father banked up the fire. He'd overfill the grate and fall asleep. She told Lady Clarissa she was frightened of a fire and Lady Clarissa insisted we install that ladder. Lord Carew had invested in a water-pumping machine and advised us to do the same, but the cost was prohibitive.'

She slipped gracefully back through the small window, seeming only to extend her foot, and I tried to do the same. Holding out her hand, she stopped me from tumbling. 'Who's Lady Clarissa?' I asked, embarrassed by my clumsiness.

'The head of our school governors.' She drew a deep breath. 'The truth is, I'm facing ruin, Pandora. Without fees, I have little if no income. If I'm to attract pupils, I must hire cooks, kitchen maids, laundry maids. The kitchen garden must become productive again. I need gardeners and stable boys – poultry and sheep. I need to spend a considerable amount of money which I don't have to make the school at least *appear* profitable. Even then, there's no guarantee I'll attract any pupils back.'

She reached for a leather account book from the shelf behind her. Opening it at the last entry, she placed her glasses on the end of her nose. 'Mother kept the estate accounts, and I kept the school accounts. The school's income was sufficient for its outgoings. I balanced the books precisely. Mother, on the other hand, tended towards the lenient.' She flipped back the pages. '*In arrears . . . in arrears . . . half-payment . . . payment due next Michaelmas.*' She turned the immaculately written accounts towards me. 'Both Feoca Mill and Devoran Farm have not paid rent for two years . . . and before that they paid only a third. The arrears go back six years. That amounts to no income from the land, despite it being a big estate. No income, only outgoings.' Her mouth tightened. 'Which is why Sir Anthony has made his kind offer.'

'Oh, Aunt Hetty!' Tears stung my eyes. Reaching for my handkerchief, I held my face in my hands. 'I'm sorry. I'm being selfish. Of course you must marry him.'

She drew a deep breath. 'I'm referring to his offer to buy Tallacks Wood.'

I stared at her unsmiling face. 'But you can't!' Pain ripped through me. 'Please don't sell Mama's wood. Mama loved the creek. She always spoke of it. Please, Aunt Harriet, don't sell the creek.'

Her voice was calm, almost flat, her eyes like steel. 'Sir Anthony is very sympathetic to the situation I find myself in. He proposes to plant an arboretum. His woods are on the other side of the creek and he proposes to build a bridle path so my girls can ride their horses through it. He believes my girls need to know about the trees their husbands may want to plant, and he intends to name it Elizabeth's Arboretum in honour of your grandmother. St Feoca girls marry into the grandest families – they have large estates and understanding the management of an arboretum would be of great benefit to them. It is an extremely kind and generous offer.'

I had to bite my lip, force back my tears, not act like a child. I had no right to tell Aunt Hetty to keep Mama's wood. But Mama was in that wood. Her heart. Her spirit. The wood was part of her, her stories about the creek embedded in my soul.

I drew out a notebook from the bag slung over my shoulder. 'These are for you. They're sketches and some watercolours of where we lived. Mainly they're paintings of Mama.' I slipped the notebook across the desk. 'And I painted this shell for you. It's Mama reading by the window. The flowers in the vase remind me of the ones in your painting. She loved flowers.'

Her hand trembled as she took the shell. 'You paint shells?' Turning it over, she examined the unpainted side. 'You think to improve on nature?'

Disappointment ripped through me. Why examine the back, and not look at Mama?

Her voice was hoarse, no more than a whisper. 'Was your mother happy, Pandora? Was your father good to her?'

She started turning the pages of my notebook and I crossed my fingers beneath the desk. 'She was very happy, Aunt Harriet. She loved Father and he adored her. She loved you, too. That's why she insisted I came to you. She talked about you all the time.'

She nodded, breathing deeply. 'Your father loved her, and was good to her? And you love your father?'

I knew I must say the words she needed to hear. 'Father was extremely good to us. He gave Mama everything he could. He

57

wanted to give her the world, and he did. She loved all the places he took us to.'

Once again, her eyes pierced mine. 'Then why have you left him alone in Philadelphia? Why leave your father at a time of such loss ... when the poor man must be grieving and in need of your comfort?'

I felt winded. Her eyes were brittle, challenging, a hint of hostility. *Don't tell her, Pandora. I love her too dearly for that. You must protect her from the truth.* Steadying my nerves, I spoke the words I had rehearsed. 'I was offered a post as a governess but Mama was adamant I come back to your school. Father promised her I could.'

'Can we expect him soon?'

A downward glance accompanied her slight smile and I tried to sound enthusiastic. 'I hope so.'

A soft knock made us look up. Grace peeped round the door, a letter in her hand. 'I'm sorry to disturb you, Miss Mitchell.' Her cheeks were flushed, a slight breathlessness as she crossed the room. 'Only this is from Mr Aubyn.'

Reading the note, Aunt Hetty's smile flickered. 'He asks if he could discuss something and wonders when might be a convenient time to call.' She shrugged, her smile broadening. 'I suppose now is as convenient a time as any. Thank him for his note, Grace, and inform Mr Aubyn I'll see him in the main hall in ten minutes.'

Putting away the ledger, she closed the window and gathered up my notebook and shell. 'Come, Pandora. Let us see what Mr Aubyn wishes to discuss.'

The very words I was dreading to hear.

Chapter Seven

Black beams arched above us, the wooden panelling polished. Silver candelabras were burning on the long refectory table, the fire in the stone fireplace blazing. Rows of logs lay stacked in the fireplace, two baskets brimming with kindling, and I turned quickly from the light. Benedict Aubyn had his back to us. Putting down a third basket, he turned and bowed.

Aunt Hetty's smile was radiant. 'I believe we have you to thank for all this wood, Mr Aubyn. We certainly won't go cold now!'

He smiled his half-smile, respectful, kind, as if he meant it. Without his heavy coat he looked almost too thin. 'It's rather a large room, Miss Mitchell. Once it gets cold, I should imagine it's hard to get warm. I can make more deliveries if you like. I find chopping wood strangely satisfying.'

Aunt Hetty held her hands to the fire. 'May I introduce my niece, Miss Pandora Woodville? She's lately arrived from Philadelphia – on the grain ship.'

I had to turn and face him: I had to curtsy, try to look at ease. He bowed, his black jacket and cuffs dotted with sawdust, his dishevelled hair flopping over his eyes. Running his hand across his forehead, he swept it to one side and his eyes caught mine. There was hesitation, definite hesitation, a coldness in his voice. 'How do you find England, Miss Woodville?'

'I find it rather wet . . . though this sunshine is very welcome.'

Mistrust flickered across his eyes. 'You arrived on the grain ship?'

'Yes. A very good journey . . . thank you.' I had to breathe, stop myself from gripping the chair.

Aunt Hetty remained warming her hands. 'To what do we owe the pleasure of your company, Mr Aubyn?'

He cleared his throat. 'My request stems from an appointment I've just been offered. I'm here, not as the road builder you know me as, but in the capacity of my new employment – as surveyor for the Truro to Falmouth Turnpike Trust.'

Aunt Hetty smiled. 'Congratulations, Mr Aubyn. You've done well. That's a very prestigious appointment.' She turned and held out her hand. 'Come to the fire, Grace. Your arrangement of those orchids is quite charming. Come, do join us . . .'

Walking elegantly across the room, a beautiful blush coloured Grace's cheeks. 'I'm very fond of flowers. Are you, Mr Aubyn?'

Benedict Aubyn nodded. 'Very. Though I'm more interested in the ground they grow on. I would argue rocks and minerals are just as beautiful. In their pure state, crystals are every bit as alluring as flowers.'

He shook the wood dust from his jacket, his eyes locking mine. 'At least you didn't have far to go once you'd arrived in Falmouth, Miss Woodville — no tedious coach journey to suffer?' His tone remained pleasant, though there was no mistaking the accusation in his eyes.

Aunt Hetty smiled again. In a short space of time, Benedict Aubyn had acquired more smiles from Aunt Hetty than I had since I arrived. 'Did you know my father collected minerals, Mr Aubyn? He amassed quite a collection – they're over there, under his portrait.'

Leading him to a large glass-topped cabinet, she smiled up at the portrait of my grandfather in his grey wig with its curls down each side of his round, almost jovial face. Dressed in a black jacket, black breeches and white cravat, he had one hand on the arm of his chair, the other resting on a large book. His spectacles lay on the table beside him. The book was his beloved Bible and my heart jolted. He looked every bit as kindly as I remembered. Every bit as lively.

Aunt Hetty held up her candle and light flickered across Grandfather's face. 'My father was the Reverend Joseph Mitchell. He was Dean of Exeter Cathedral before he returned to Cornwall to start his school.'

Grandmother's portrait was by his side. Also grey-haired, she looked back at me with the gentle eyes I remembered. There was her rather snub nose, her engaging smile. I could almost smell the rosewater she always wore. Behind her were bookshelves, a smaller book in her lap. Dressed in grey, her demure velvet cap was edged with lace.

Aunt Hetty's voice turned wistful. 'My mother, Elizabeth

Curnow, was from Cornwall. Her father was the Bishop while we were in Exeter. We spent our childhood among the cathedral buildings. When my grandparents died Father brought us back to Cornwall. They'd always wanted to have their own school – Mother, even more passionately than Father.'

A fierce glance in my direction and I knew Benedict Aubyn was biding his time. A prickle of sweat ran down my back. I would repay him his money and insist I had got the place names muddled. Yet why should I be the one to fear? *He* was the one chasing *rich rewards*.

His back to me, he was studying the portraits with quiet interest. 'These are very fine paintings, Miss Mitchell. How old were you when you left Exeter?'

'Fourteen and very proud to have our own school. Mother became headmistress – we always assumed Father would take charge, but he insisted it was Mother's school.'

Hands behind his back, Benedict Aubyn leaned over the glass cabinet, his hair falling forward. 'These are fine specimens.' He bent closer. 'Carbonate of copper, such a lovely blue . . . crystals of copper ore from Wheal Providence.' Examining each mineral, he read where they had been found and the date they had been added to the collection. His voice hardened, 'Arsenate crystals of copper ore.'

Aunt Hetty looked at Grace, a slight smile. 'Grace has made a study of them, haven't you, Grace?'

When *I* blushed, I burned bright crimson, but Grace's cheeks looked like delicate rose petals. Demure, eyes down, she was all elegance and shyness, an enchanting example of feminine confusion. 'This is only half the collection, Mr Aubyn

... there are more exhibition boxes in the library. I find minerals absolutely fascinating.'

Resuming his study, he clasped his hands behind his back again, clearly engrossed. 'Do you have a favourite, Miss Elliot?'

'There are so many . . . such vibrant colours. I think, maybe it's this blue carbonate of copper, but this green lead ore is just as beautiful.'

Benedict leaned closer. 'From Wheal Mexico. You know why it's called Wheal Mexico?'

Her eyelashes fluttered, a downward glance. 'I believe it's because of the rich seam of silver ore they found.'

'Indeed.' He seemed lost in his own world, his eyes scanning the beautifully presented minerals. 'See here? These pale green crystals on white quartz from Wheal Pool? They have their own smelting house, and their galena – their lead sulphide – yields as much as forty to fifty ounces of silver to the ton.'

Her eyes widened. 'Is that making them a fortune?'

'Enough to get by!' Turning to the second display, he became engrossed again. 'But for real profit, look no further than this – Herland Mine, in Gwinear. You've heard of it?' Grace shook her head, her hair shining in the candlelight. 'Have you heard about it, Miss Mitchell?'

Aunt Hetty looked amused. 'No. But do tell us. It's not a specimen that's ever drawn my attention.'

'It may look inconsequential but last year the silver cross-course in Herland Mine yielded over 115 tons of silver ore. An extraordinary amount. Partly smelted on site, it realized over £5,600. Just from August to April!'

Rich rewards, indeed.

Grace remained by his side, the two of them discussing the names of the minerals and how to pronounce them. Clearly very knowledgeable, Aunt Hetty looked increasingly proud of her. Benedict Aubyn leaned further over the cabinet. 'That's a lovely specimen of menaccanite. Did you know it was a Cornishman who discovered titanium – in the magnetic black sand just the other side of Falmouth?'

Such politeness. Such manners! *You may be fooling them, but you're not fooling me. You're here to fleece my aunt out of her land.*

'Yes, I did. In Manaccan. Reverend Gregor was a friend of my father's. He gave Father that sample just before he died. I hear from him from time to time.' Aunt Hetty looked back across the room. 'You've brought a leather case with you, Mr Aubyn?'

He seemed unable to tear his eyes away from the cabinet. Or was it the thought that Grace might take him to the library?

'I wonder if we may sit down? I'd like to spread out some papers.' A glance in my direction and I felt my cheeks burn.

You made that woman in the inn deeply unhappy. And you have daughters!

Crossing the room, he picked up his bag and drew out Aunt Hetty's chair. Doing the same for me, he finally seated Grace and sat between us. The brass clasps snapped open and Aunt Hetty drew a deep breath. 'A map, Mr Aubyn? That can only mean you're planning a new road.'

He looked slightly shaken and I tried to hide my smile. 'If I may just show you?' It was not the voice he had used to negotiate his ten per cent commission, more the voice of a pupil who had got his Latin wrong. Unrolling the map, he glanced at

Grace. Smiling, she leaned towards him, offering to hold down the edges. Aunt Hetty remained impassive, though I sensed her breathing quicken. 'I'd like . . . that is . . . I've come to ask if I may survey your land?'

'Do you need my permission, Mr Aubyn?' Not quite the sharp rebuke I knew to my cost, but certainly a tone he could not fail to understand.

He swallowed, reaching for a printed page and holding it to the candlelight. '*Legally*, the Turnpike Act governing the Truro to Falmouth Turnpike Trust grants the Trust power to access any land for the purpose of widening the road . . . and for obtaining stone or gravel to maintain the road. And for the purchase of land. That is . . . to buy land to widen an existing road . . . and . . . or . . . for the express purpose of building a new road.'

'So the answer is no, you don't.'

He swallowed again, a slight heightening of his colour. 'Not *as such*, but I'd prefer it if you gave me your permission.'

I held my breath.

'Then you have it, Mr Aubyn. I appreciate your candour.'

He looked almost believable, not a wolf in sheep's clothing at all. His clever use of solemnity was a winning ploy, his quiet praise of the portraits and minerals highly effective. Neither overly friendly nor condescending, he hardly sounded enthusiastic. Cleverer still, he had not tried to charm or cajole her but had appeared to want to please her. A polished performance, considering how much money was at stake.

Leaning over the map, he pointed to Truro. 'The present turnpike leaves Truro and cuts south-west, taking in Carnon

Hill before crossing at Carnon Bridge, which is extremely narrow and causes considerable delays. Then it cuts south, down St Piran's Hill. The road was the old pack horse route but it's too steep in places. It's become insufficient for our growing commerce. The Post Office and Falmouth Packet Company use it extensively and there's a constant need to supply the fleet in Falmouth. In short, they need a quicker route with less gradient.'

Aunt Hetty's elegant finger trailed across the map. 'So I imagine you intend to cross my land, *here*, no doubt following the cart track I use to go to Truro. I should imagine you'll skirt the top field and follow the contour of the hill. That will give you less gradient and will avoid the low-lying pasture which is prone to flooding.' She drew a deep breath. 'Or *was* prone to flooding. Then, I should imagine, you'll seek to build a new bridge, probably *here*, in Devoran, at the head of the creek, before the river widens.' She smiled up at him. 'Which would directly link to the shore road, which you've just widened to Harcourt Quay.'

Yes, Aunt Hetty. Yes. Yes. Yes. At ten per cent commission on the new bridge, plus his share for negotiating the toll house.

A fierce blush scorched his cheeks. 'That is correct.'

'Which would take several miles off the road as it now stands.' I could hardly conceal my smile. *Twenty miles, Aunt Hetty. At ten per cent a mile saved.* Her immaculate nail traced the map. 'Very useful for the tin-streaming company whose hideous embankments are ruining our creek. And the barges carrying ore from the mines. But what I can't decide, Mr Aubyn, is whether you plan to position your road to the west

66

of my farm or to the east? Positioned to the east, and you effectively cut the farm from my school.'

He loosened his neck tie. 'Any farm cart or harvest cart – any movement of your livestock – would be exempt from toll charges. As would anyone going to church.' He cleared his throat. 'But if the road *were* to cut your farm from the rest of your estate . . . you could sell the farm for quite some profit – even a small portion of the land would make you a profit.'

Rich rewards indeed. His first profitable land deal. Yet he kept his voice diffident, no trace of the riches coming his way. 'It's only a suggestion . . . but perhaps you could relocate your farm nearer the school? I believe some of your pupils keep horses? Perhaps, a purpose-built stable nearer the school may be a happy outcome of the new road?'

Aunty Hetty raised her eyebrows. 'You have permission to survey my land, Mr Aubyn.' I sat in silence, my mind a medley of confliction: if she sold that piece of land it would mean not having to sell Mama's wood. Aunt Hetty watched him roll away the map. 'Dine with us, Mr Aubyn, once you've surveyed my land.'

'Thank you, I'd be delighted.' He looked suddenly shy, neither grasping nor willing to profit. A masterful performance: charming her with his good manners, bringing in the logs, mending the ruts in the drive at no cost to herself. He rose, bowing to us in turn. Glancing at my ringless third finger, his mouth tightened. '*Miss* Woodville.'

Aunt Hetty shut the door behind him. 'What a solemn young man he is! Do you think he ever smiles? Grace, my dear, you were extremely knowledgeable about the minerals. I think you rather impressed him.'

The rose petals returned to her cheeks. 'I'm sorry, Miss Mitchell. I believe I was rather too forward in my enthusiasm. It won't happen again.'

In the candlelight, Aunt Hetty's skin looked flawless, her silver streak framing her right cheek. She had extraordinarily high cheekbones, a tall forehead, her pearl earrings swinging as she turned. Striking, yet formidable, a smile played on her lips. 'Not at all, my dear. I was thinking how very well you looked together.'

I had to turn away. Aunt Hetty was so proud of her. She was more like a niece to her than I was: beautiful, sweet Grace who was everything I wanted to be.

'As it happens, I rather like him. He's clearly a gentleman — despite him wanting to rob me of my land! He has charming manners and I find him rather endearing, even if a little... shall we say... sombre?' Her smile broadened as Grace pretended not to understand. 'I think we need to find out a little more about Mr Benedict Aubyn, don't you?'

Find out more, and she would like him less. Find out more, and she might sell Mama's wood. She turned. 'Pandora, it's time we did something about those heavy boots of yours. I think a pair of daintier shoes is required.'

Chapter Eight

My borrowed shoes were delicate leather, pointed and as soft as velvet, the heels crafted from mahogany. Impractical yet dainty, they made me feel like a lady. I wanted to keep them for best but as Grace showed me round the new wing, it was clear *best* was something Aunt Hetty took for granted. The boarding rooms were sumptuous, even the top bedrooms where four girls slept in two beds showed no sign of scrimping. Each window, of every room, had polished brass fixtures, rich damask curtains and matching brocade ties.

'The bed linen's kept in the laundry — on shelves with warm pipes to keep it aired.' She ran her finger over the iron bedstead and smiled at the lack of dust. 'Every girl has her own bedside table for her mirror and brushes. They're allowed four drawers but share the wardrobe. I was in this room until a year ago. Then I moved into one of the single rooms...' Her voice faltered. 'Because I was to become a pupil teacher.' There was something in her look. A sudden swallow.

69

'What is it, Grace? Weren't you happy? Were the girls unhappy?'

She smiled, brushing off my sudden disquiet. 'Oh no. Very happy. We were all very happy. Some happier than others. It's easy for rich girls to be happy – sometimes at the expense of the poorer girls.'

'They were unkind to you?'

She turned, a catch to her voice. 'No, never. Well, not unduly. I was never seen as a threat. I was just so grateful to be here. They thought me too poor to attract any of their suitors so they were never *that* unkind. Come, we'll go up these stairs.'

The top rooms had polished wooden floors and chairs beside the tables, their huge sash windows overlooking the conservatory below. The rooms were allocated by the fees paid, the lower rooms being the most splendid, gradually decreasing in space on the top floor. There was one rug in the top rooms, two rugs for the rooms with two girls, and any number of Persian rugs in the suite used by parlour boarders. Twenty girls in all, with a room allocated on each floor to a senior boarder who was about to leave and was in charge of the girls on her floor.

The rugs were rolled up, the horsehair mattresses covered with dust sheets. Despite the obvious chill, the rooms smelled fresh, with lavender bags hanging from the iron bedsteads and bunches of thyme above each of the fireplaces. Grace paused. 'I think, maybe, well, do you think Mr Aubyn is the answer to our prayers?'

Maybe the answer to your prayers, sprang to my mind but I

smiled. 'Selling some of the land will enable Aunt Harriet to restart the school. How many maids did she employ?'

'Five general maids . . . three kitchen maids . . . and two laundry maids — along with Susan, who's in charge. Then there's the post boy and George used to help with the grounds . . . and there's the stable boys. And three gardeners.'

Part of me did not want to discuss Aunt Hetty's affairs with Grace, yet I needed to know everything. 'Why did they leave?'

Her hand trembled against one of the bedposts. 'They would have stayed — in times like this, they'd have stayed for food and shelter. They left because they were *terrified*.'

'Of some silly nonsense? Honestly! Superstitious nonsense shouldn't close a school!'

I must have sounded angry as she turned away. She had a beautiful curve to her neck, a perfect complexion, cornflower-blue eyes and rosebud lips. No wonder Benedict Aubyn had spent so long at the mineral table with her. 'It was horrible, Pandora. It wasn't just talk, or silly nonsense. People *saw* him — the girls *saw* him. They said in the full moon the clouds parted and there he was, standing with a huge staff, his face . . . like a skull. Like he was dead.'

'They saw the devil?'

Clenching her fist against her mouth she breathed deeply. 'I told them it was nonsense but they wouldn't listen. They said whenever they went to close the curtains he'd be staring in at the window. Once they found a dead raven on the hearth. Pandora . . . I didn't tell Miss Mitchell half of what they told me. I didn't know what to do.' A tear ran down her cheek. 'I felt so sad for dear Miss Mitchell. This is her whole life.'

'But it was only that foolish, vindictive girl. No one saw anything because there was nothing to see. Just that vengeful girl spreading fear. Young girls can be very impressionable!' My cheeks were burning. 'You stayed, and Susan and Annie stayed. And now I'm here nothing's going to stop us getting the school back to how it was.' I stopped. 'Grace, are you all right?'

She wiped her eyes with her lace handkerchief. 'Maybe it's not Mr Aubyn who's the answer to our prayers. Maybe it's *you*, Pandora. I'm so glad you've come.' She turned quickly away and I felt suddenly chastened.

She only has Aunt Hetty: she stayed because she has nowhere else to go.

Closing the door, we descended the sweeping staircase to the hall with its black and white flagstones. The music room had a piano and several wooden music stands, the other two classrooms had desks and chairs. Opening a glass door to the conservatory, she lifted her chin. 'We have concerts here in the summer. Mostly, our assemblies are held in the chapel but in the summer we hold all sorts of activities. The girls learn to dance and we put on plays. We've done some very grand performances. The girls' parents come with hampers of food and it's really quite wonderful. It's a chance for their families to visit the school.'

A family she did not have. Above us, the glass roof arched like a cathedral. 'We have a pavilion as well and play all sorts of games — like archery, and cricket.' She slipped her arm through mine, leading me on to the terrace. 'We take our meals out here in the summer and watch the swallows. The girls like to watch their horses . . . over there.'

The lawn swept down to a paddock, ringed by a group of trees still bare of leaves. 'Does my aunt ride?'

She shook her head. 'I've never seen her ride. More often than not Miss Mitchell stays in her rooms. She spends whole days up there. Since your grandmother died she hardly comes down at all. It's almost as if she's lost the will to fight the closure.'

I tried to hide my panic. 'I can't let that happen.'

Grace nodded but did not smile. 'I don't think Mr Aubyn will be able to convince Miss Mitchell to sell the farm. Their family's been there longer than Miss Mitchell has. The farm provides the school – we used to get our eggs and milk from them, and the poultry, and meat. Our flour came from the mill.' She sighed, a slight tremble in her lower lip. 'Oh, I so wish we could turn back the clock.'

Aunt Hetty kept to her room. With our light lunch of bread and cheese cleared away, Susan and Annie were polishing silver candlesticks. They had a strict routine for keeping the school aired: each morning Annie would open and shut the windows in the old buildings for an hour, Grace would take care of the new wing and chapel, and Susan would see to the laundry rooms, by stoking the fire to keep the hot air pipes warm behind the stored bedding.

A fortnightly rota was to polish the floors, clean the windows, shine the silver, dust the paintings and turn the beds. Mid-afternoon, Susan would return to the gatehouse, Annie would make a light supper, and Grace would sew, visit the church to attend the gravestones, or play the pianoforte. Aunt Hetty remained in her room or took solitary walks.

With them all back in the kitchen, it was my chance to ask. 'Surely, I can do something to help? No one's been allocated Grandfather's walled garden – why don't I try to get the garden productive again?'

My suggestion was met with a shrug of Annie's thick shawl. 'Your grandfather loved that garden! He'd put on his big leather apron and be out there for hours! He'd come back covered in soil and your dear grandmother . . . how she scolded him! And he'd just smile and say, *But we must cultivate our garden.* And he'd give her a beautiful rose and she'd blush like a timid bride!'

'Did they love each other very much?'

Annie seemed less forgetful today. The same age as my grandmother, her eyes were bright, but compared to Susan's robust polishing, her movements were frail, her touch no more than a feather. 'Such love you've never seen.' Putting down her cloth, her bony fingers rested on the table. 'But he was wicked, your grandfather! For all him being a dean! He used to chase your poor grandmother round the great hall with a *toad* in his hands! How Miss Harriet loved that, but your mother, bless her dear heart, always shrieked and ran away!'

'Then I'm going to restore it.'

Susan shook her head. 'You'll not get the garden back to how it was – the leats have run dry. Even with all this rain they're silted up. They're stagnant, and fetid. We've either too much water and the fields flood or too little and the parkland dries. We've none flowing to the walled garden, nor the Abbot's Pond round the side.'

Grace was washing the dishes, the kitchen warmed by a huge fire burning in the grate. This was the smaller of the two kitchens, the bigger one having a scullery and larder attached, though the unused doors were shut and padded against the cold draughts blowing from the laundry. The clock struck three and Susan put down her cloth. 'I'll be off, then. I'll send Kate up with the new soap. Kate's my daughter. She's eleven now and very bonny.'

Swapping her mobcap for her bonnet, she reached for her cloak and I followed her into the watery sunshine. Across the cobbles, the iron gate to the walled garden was hidden in shadow. Susan handed me the key. 'There, see for yourself. It'll take some doing.'

The lock was stiff, and I stared in despair. More neglected than I expected, a jumble of brown stalks overspilled the small box hedges lining the beds. A broken wheelbarrow lay propped against the wall; Grandfather's shed still in one corner, a stagnant water trough in another.

'I remember running along these paths — I thought they were like the spokes of a wheel.'

Each red-brick path led to a central well. The iron wheel was still there with the large handle just as Mama had drawn it. A wooden bucket dangled beneath the thatched roof and tears stung my eyes. Being there without Mama was so painful, her death suddenly so raw. Not having her with me felt overwhelming, as if the need to get to St Feoca had somehow masked the depth of my sorrow.

Susan slipped her hand through my arm. 'Do you remember your grandfather's sundial? He was that proud of it – he said it was accurate to the minute!' Raised on a plinth, the brass dial caught the sun, casting a shadow between the roman numerals. Carved beneath the rim was an inscription.

'*Pereunt et imputantur*,' I read. 'They perish and are reckoned to our account.'

Her eyes widened. 'You read Latin?'

Tears blurred my eyes. 'It's by the poet Martial. He's warning us to use the hours well – not waste the time we're given.'

For all her organising bustle, Susan went suddenly still, staring at the sundial in silence. A blackbird was singing, a robin perching on the well. Sheltered from the sea breezes, the garden seemed warmer, enveloping me, as if wrapping its arms around me. *But we must cultivate our garden.* I could hear Grandfather's voice, feel Mama by my side. 'But . . . but there's a grille covering the top of the well! There's no water in the leats and you've blocked the well?'

Susan shrugged. 'It's better . . . least it was *thought* better.'

'Because a pupil nearly fell down it and could have drowned?'

She glanced at the potting shed. 'No, it wasn't that.' Shaking her head, she turned to leave.

'Why keep a grille over the garden's only water source? Please tell me.'

Her lips tightened. 'Miss Mitchell ordered it. It was the first *unnatural* occurrence. The gardeners reported a foul smell coming from the well. The water was clearly tainted. George brought a chain and hook . . . and pulled out a carcass of a sheep. The head had been severed.'

'That's horrible. But it was just mischief – just the girl causing mischief. That girl had no idea of the consequences of her prank.'

Susan pointed to the shed. 'Only, she denied it. She was scared witless. I know because I was with her. She didn't have the keys to the potting shed, which is where the head was found. There was smears on the window . . . writing . . . only it was more like signs and ciphers. The devil's signs written in blood.'

I felt suddenly sick. 'How *awful*. How dare they?'

'A year ago it was. It was taken very bad. Several girls left straight away, others wrote to their parents asking to leave.'

'Well, I'm going to get this garden productive again!' Never had I felt so angry. 'Susan, you're going to Falmouth?' She nodded and I opened the bag hanging across my chest. 'I painted these shells on the way over. I've sold some before – for six- or ninepence each. Maybe a shilling for the more elaborate ones? Can you buy what I might need?'

Her eyes widened. 'You painted these?' I nodded, and she wrapped them carefully back in their cotton. 'I'll try to find seeds or potatoes. I might find some hens. They'll help scratch the soil. Your grandfather used to let his hens turn over the beds.'

'Buy what you can.' I had never worked in a garden and had no idea where to start. 'I'll wear my old dress and boots. I'll use gloves and give Aunt Harriet a surprise.' She turned to leave. 'Susan . . . maybe while you're in Falmouth, you could ask – just in conversation – what people at the Coach and Horses have to say about Benedict Aubyn?'

Beneath her bonnet, her fair hair nodded. Her eyes turned serious. 'Indeed I will. Mending her drive – chopping and stacking all those logs? That man wants something. Do you think he's going to make an offer for Grace?'

'I don't know. Either way, it's best to know more about him.'

Her frown deepened. 'While we're talking . . . I don't like to worry Miss Mitchell, but I'll be glad to tell you. This morning's the third time I found the kitchen door unlocked. I'm first in of a morning and I have my own key. Three days I've arrived to find Annie asleep and no one stirring, yet the back door was unlocked. Annie's getting more and more confused; I hope she's not wandering off at night.'

$$\diamond\!\!\!\diamond$$

I pulled my damask curtains rather too sharply. Dinner had been a trial of manners and I had clearly failed. I had tried to hold my cutlery like Grace, delicately wrapping my napkin round my forefinger, copying her dab the corners of her mouth. I had even sipped my wine like her, stiff-backed and upright, the lace ruffle of my high neck not touching my chin.

Eating in the dining room was a ridiculous notion anyway, the food cold before it reached the table. But that was nothing to the humiliation I felt. No, Aunt Hetty, I can't play the piano. Nor the harpsichord. Nor the violin. Nor can I sing. Nor play cards. Nor do I know any of the modern poets your girls like to discuss. I can't recite Shakespeare or Milton, and I have absolutely no idea who John Donne is.

It was not that I wanted Grace's beauty. Nor her talents. It was not her fault she loved my grandmother, nor that my grandmother must have loved her dearly. It was just the unfairness of it all, the terrible sense of loss. I did not want to *be* Grace: I just wanted Grace to be me. If we had come back ten years ago, I would be elegant and refined. Worse still, Mama would still be with me. She would have taught me the piano. We would have played duets, sung in concerts, read all the books in the library.

Chapter Nine

Wednesday 25th March 1801, 8:00 a.m.

With Aunt Hetty staying in her room, the day looked full of promise. Changing back into my old serge dress, my familiar boots were exactly what was needed on the brick paths. Annie looked amused. 'If you must, you must. Mind you don't get dirty.' Wrapping a huge leather apron round me, she chose a big bonnet and handed me a robust pair of gloves.

The gate opened easily, the blackbird greeting me with his song. It was all so unfamiliar: no mimosa, no hibiscus, no drill of the cicadas nor whirr of humming birds, but limp brown stalks and the smell of dank earth. The robin watched me test the wheelbarrow and my spirits lifted; the fruit trees against the wall would soon blossom, the roses already showing new shoots.

Susan had sold my shells, and I was the proud owner of a sack of sprouting potatoes, a pound of dried beans, and five point-of-lay pullets. Stretching their necks, they were watching me from the soil they were turning over. 'You can be *Rose*, you can be *Honeysuckle* . . . you, *Bluebell* . . . and you, *Lily of the Valley* . . . and you can be *Snowdrop*. Mama's favourite flowers.' The potting shed would make a temporary house for them.

Peeping inside, I almost expected to see Grandfather. His utensils hung from wooden hooks and I picked up a hoe, a rush of pleasure stinging my eyes. It was as if I was meant to be here, in his garden, where we had gathered peas and eaten strawberries fresh from the beds. The sound of whispering made me turn. Two girls were staring at me through the gate. Putting down their buckets, they stood in silence. 'Don't be shy . . . come in, the gate isn't locked.'

The tallest girl grabbed the other's hand, her brown eyes almost too large for her thin face. Both looked petrified. 'Ye've got hens?' she asked, squinting into the sun as she bobbed me a curtsy.

'They came yesterday. I'm Pandora Woodville, Miss Mitchell's niece.' They curtsied again, deeper this time, their eyes downcast. They must have been no more than ten and twelve, both wearing ragged clothes, their jackets too small for them, their boots scuffed. Both had dirt on their faces. 'Come closer, don't be shy. Do you like hens?'

They nodded, edging forward, the elder clutching the younger one's hand. 'We're from the farm. We've brought the milk. Miss Elliot's just taken it.' She pointed to the empty buckets.

'Come and see what I'm doing – I'm digging the garden to plant these potatoes. What are your names?'

They edged closer still. 'I'm Gwen . . . and my sister's Sophie.

81

She don't talk. She hears, but she don't talk. Ye keeping the hens in the shed?'

'For the time being. When we've got the seeds planted they may have to move to the barn. Do you like flowers?' They both nodded, the younger sister staring at me with equally big eyes. 'Have you never talked, Sophie? Only you seem to understand?'

She hung her head, biting her bottom lip, and Gwen answered for her. 'She used to talk all the time. Couldn't stop her. But since that day, she hasn't said a word. She don't speak to no one.'

'Since what day?'

Both girls looked down: both crossed themselves. Tears filled Sophie's eyes. She tugged on Gwen's sleeve in an attempt to stop her from talking but Gwen shook her head. 'It's all right, Sophie.' Her dark eyes were defensive, staring up at me in angry defiance. 'The day they brought the devil into the house.'

'Well, that's just silly talk.'

'No . . . it weren't. It happened. They took the track behind our farm. Kept asking fer *St FeoKKa* but they weren't speaking proper. Afterwards we heard it was the devil's language. He was in the box on the cart. A huge box – like a crate – and Sophie showed them the way to the farm. Just like the profagy.'

'Prophecy? Like a story that was foretold?'

'Yes. *The Comin' of the Devil*. Just like in the story . . . the devil's helpers asks a girl the way. An' she never speaks again. Never. Cause the devil took her tongue. Cause he didn't want them to know how he enters houses.'

Tears began rolling down Sophie's cheeks, her thin hands wringing. Gwen put an arm round her shoulders and they turned to leave. 'Wait,' I called. 'Come closer... open your mouth please, Sophie.' Slowly her mouth opened. 'Yes, that's just what I thought – a perfectly good tongue. There was *no* devil, and *no one's* taken your tongue. I've never heard such nonsense. It's a wild, made-up story and I'm really cross. Really, really, cross that anyone could be so unkind as to let you believe that nonsense.'

They turned to leave again. 'Wait... it's only a thought, but I could do with your buckets, and your help. Would your mother mind if you came and worked for me? I'll pay you a penny a morning and I'll feed you.' Sophie smiled and I saw the hope in her eyes. 'It's just we can't use the well with it being covered, but see that water trough full of stagnant water?' They nodded, not needing to look. 'If you empty out the leaves and all the rotting stuff, maybe you could fill it with fresh water from the pump by the barn? Would that be too hard for you?'

Sophie smiled, shaking her head. *Not too hard at all*, she seemed to be saying.

Gwen stepped forward. 'We don't have to ask. Mamm sent us to see if we could get work. She'll be glad ye took us on. Miss Elliot said she's no need of help, but we're that glad to do anythin'.' She picked up the hoe and raised her eyebrows. 'Ye'll need a pickaxe or a proper spade, Miss Woodville. Ye're just ticklin' the top with this. Ye got to get deep down. Not that bed over there... that's herbs. That'll come back nice. And not the one ye're digging... that's an asparagus bed. Won't do no good.'

'Asparagus bed! You know the garden?'

She smiled a shy smile. 'An' we can't use our buckets fer dirty water. Ye know about contagion, Miss Woodville? There's good water and there's bad water. Never mix water with milk in case it's the bad water.'

'I wasn't thinking.'

'It's all right. We can use the fire buckets hangin' in the barn.' If Gwen's hair had been washed it might have had gold streaks in it but it lay in lank curls around her face. Sophie's hair was darker, her features more delicate. Dashing to the potting shed, they dragged back a large fork and a small spade. 'We'll use these. After we've done the water trough.'

Their shy smiles seemed to act like balm, the garden enveloping me, the hens clucking. The robin perched on the spade and warmth flooded through me. My yearning was over, my dream come true. I was home – back in my family's home. It was as if Grandfather and Grandmother were with me, as if Mama was just out of sight.

Scooping out the rotting leaves, the girls emptied out the stagnant water. Gwen stood, looking up through a mass of tangled branches. Squinting into the sun, she pointed to the bricks. 'There should be a drainpipe there . . . see it's broken? There's a gutter along the wall behind the honeysuckle. It should drain into the trough. Then it should drain through this spout into a bucket.'

'Oh yes. You're very clever, Gwen.'

She shrugged her bony shoulders. 'Not really. I don't learn nothing. Not *real* learning.'

Footsteps stopped by the gate, an angry shout. 'What are

you two doing?' Grace had not seen me and her voice rose. 'This is very naughty of you. I sent you home. You mustn't go in the garden. Where did you get the key?'

Stepping forward, I caught her sudden shock. 'It's all right, they're with me. I've taken them on as gardeners. We're going to feed them and give them a penny a morning.'

Her hands flew to her chest. 'But we can't just employ them like this. Have you asked Aunt Harriet? We must ask her first.'

Aunt Harriet? Aunt Harriet! Anger filled me. A wave of fury. She may have lived here these last ten years but Aunt Harriet was my aunt, not hers. *My aunt.* This was *my* family's garden. Not hers. She was assuming too much. I had to breathe, fight the image of a cuckoo in the nest. Of course, this was her home but she was not family.

She seemed oblivious to my burning cheeks. 'How will we feed them? We've little enough already. I know their mother, Pandora . . . she won't accept a *penny* a morning. She'll ask for more. And it's money Aunt Harriet doesn't have.'

Again, Aunt Harriet! This was my grandfather's garden. My grandmother's school. Fire flamed inside me. She may see Aunt Harriet as her guardian, she may even love her, but she was *not family*. Aunt Hetty could be as proud of her as she liked, but she was *not family*.

Again, she seemed oblivious to her mistake. 'I'm sorry, girls; it's just we have so little ourselves. I'm sure you understand.'

Putting down their utensils the girls hung their heads, their smiles replaced by nods of resignation. Seeing their disappointment made something in me snap — she wanted to be a teacher, so let her be one. Let her be the pupil teacher she so craved to be. I fought to keep my voice steady. 'I know it's not enough, which is why we're going to give them an hour's lesson every day.'

'An hour's lesson . . . *a day?*' Disbelief held her in shock.

'We're a school – they need teaching and we need pupils. Don't you see how important this is? We can show *my* aunt how committed we are to restarting her school.'

If I had been Aunt Hetty, I would have told her not to gawp. 'Pandora, are you certain about this? I think you should ask her first. Only I don't think anyone will like this. Not Annie, anyway. If they come in, they'll have to wash and change into their Sunday best. They can't come into the house like this.'

'No . . . maybe not. So, we'll teach them in the barn.' Gwen and Sophie's eyes kept turning from one of us to the other. 'You'd like that, wouldn't you, girls? Somewhere you'll feel comfortable and safe? Miss Elliot likes the barn – she doesn't mind going in there at all!'

The more I thought about it, the more certain I became. 'Do you know Kate Penrose from the gatehouse?' They nodded and I smiled. Grace was clearly still in shock; I hadn't forgiven her, but this was making it a lot better. 'I'm going to ask Kate to join you. There will be three in our school. And I think we should make it two hours, don't you, Miss Elliot? Let's say three thirty-minute classes with a play break between each class.'

Grace could hardly find her voice. 'Play break?'

My gloves were covered in soil, dirt on my apron. The blackbird seemed to be singing louder, the sun shining brighter. It was as if I could hear Grandfather laughing. 'Yes, *play breaks*. Where the girls get to skip and play hopscotch and hoopla.'

The first chance of being alone, Susan drew me to one side. 'Have you a minute?' I nodded and she lowered her voice. 'It's about what you asked me to find out.'

We moved to the window and her smile faded. 'You're right, Benedict Aubyn *is* staying at the Coach and Horses. The rest of the road builders are staying across the creek in the Passage Inn, but he's in Falmouth . . . and you're right, he's not the man we take him for. Least not according to Jenna who's serving there.'

I nodded. 'Go on.'

'She says all that *butter wouldn't melt in his mouth stuff* is a ruse. Women like that sort of thing. They see him as vulnerable and slightly . . . well, *unworldly*. All sombre and lost, like he's in need of a good woman's love. You know, impeccable manners to hide the truth?'

'Yes, I do know. Go on . . .'

'All those curls and thin as a rake? Well, it clearly works as she says he's one for the ladies. More women visit his room than she's had hot dinners! That's what she said. A steady stream. One woman left in tears. Another had two young girls with her – and she said he gave the girls a present and they hugged him.' She took a deep breath. 'So maybe not suitable for our Grace?'

'Did she say where he's from?'

'Bristol. That's all I know, apart from him quibbling over the

87

price of his room. She says he's counting his pennies.' Swapping her mobcap for her bonnet, she hung her apron on the hook and reached for her jacket. 'There's rice pudding, and in case Annie forgets there's that potted crab to finish. Are you going to join them?' I must have looked confused. 'In the music room? Annie loves to hear them play.'

The door was ajar, music filtering across the hall. Aunt Hetty and Grace were sharing the piano stool, their backs straight, their fingers flying across the keys. Annie was listening with her hands clasped, her eyes shut, and I stood fighting my tears. It should be *me* sitting by my aunt, *my* fingers flying across the keys. It should be *my* straight back, *my* head nodding, *my* hand turning the page of the music. Pain twisted my gut. Father had never bought the piano he had promised Mama, and Mama had stopped asking for one. Breathing deeply, I smiled as I entered.

Candlelight accentuated Aunt Hetty's high cheekbones. 'Good night, Pandora.' Her voice softened. 'You've been very quiet tonight. You hardly ate a thing.'

I swallowed, knowing I could put it off no longer. 'Aunt Harriet, I think I'm about to incur your displeasure. I take complete responsibility. Grace advised me to ask you first.'

'But you went ahead anyway? What have you done?'

'I can stop it any time but I thought, well, as we're a school, we should be teaching pupils, so I've suggested to Gwen and Sophie from the farm, and Kate from the gatehouse—'

She pursed her lips. 'I know who Gwen, Sophie and Kate are, Pandora.'

'It's just . . . I thought to restart the school, so I've suggested they should have afternoon lessons in the barn in lieu of payment for helping me in the garden and Grace has agreed to teach them.'

She drew a deep breath. 'A good marriage would be far preferable for you both.'

Her words stung like a wasp. 'I don't want to be married. And I'm sorry I asked Grace. I'll teach them – it'll be *my* school, *The Barn School*. They're bright and clever and have a right to learn every bit as much as your high-society girls who, it seems, are only taught how to please a man – how to alight from a barouche, embroider, simper and smile.'

Her eyebrow shot up. 'Goodness, Pandora. A little less passion, please.'

'I'm sorry, Aunt Hetty, but I do feel passionate. Very passionate. Sophie doesn't speak but she understands everything – she's as bright as her sister, but what chance does she have if people claim she helped the devil?'

'Helped the devil?'

'Some nonsense about her showing the devil the way in to the house. Aunt Hetty, when your pupils return, I'll move my school to their farm. We'll hold our lessons there and you won't even know it's happening.'

She drew a deep breath and I knew to expect her displeasure. 'You've forgotten Mollie from the mill. I believe you'll have four girls in this Barn School of yours.' There was a flicker of a smile. 'And I don't approve of a cold barn. Your pupils are welcome to use the library. They'll need a fire. I suggest Grace gives them three half-hour lessons with a ten

89

minute break between each — so they can *skip around* and play *hopscotch* and *hoopla*.'

I felt suddenly sick. 'Grace has already told you?'

The smile faded. 'No, Gwen did. And you're right, she's an extremely bright child.' Her silk skirt rustled as she made her way along the corridor. Stopping, she turned. 'Before I forget, we've been summoned to a meeting with the school governors tomorrow. Wear your best silk and be ready at two o'clock. Lady Clarissa is kindly sending her boat. The meeting's to be held at her country home — Trenwyn House. Goodnight, my dear.'

Chapter Ten

Thursday 26th March 1801, 11:00 a.m.

Dressed in my silk gown, my hair pinned painfully in two clasps, I stood back so that Annie could admire her work.

'I'll see to the hens,' she said. 'I'll give them the potato peelings. Don't go anywhere to get messy – I suggest you go and read in the library.'

Halfway down the corridor I nearly collided with Grace. A notebook in one hand, she was barely visible beneath a huge bundle of material. 'Oh, there you are!' She looked radiant, smiling in obvious excitement. 'I've been working out my lessons... Have you a moment?'

The heart of the old priory, the library had four arched windows and ancient worn flagstones, a huge stone fireplace at one end and dark oak bookshelves along two walls. Putting her material on the table, Grace held out her notebook. 'I thought the first lesson should be letters and reading... and the second, numbers and simple adding, but maybe the last lessons could be different each day? Maybe atlas work... then herbs and their uses...then drawing and painting...and music. Perhaps the last lesson of the week could be manners and etiquette. Or maybe we should do more sewing?'

It was wonderful to see her so excited. Now she had Aunt Hetty's approval, Grace seemed unstoppable. Her cheeks flushed, her eyes shining, she pointed to the material. 'These dust sheets are hardly worn. They're clean and perfectly good material – I thought to make the girls some smocks. I think they'd like that, don't you? Only that will make them feel ...well...special.'

I left Grace spreading out the dust sheets. Not certain where to go, I crossed the covered bridge to the tower. Aunt Hetty had given me permission to use Grandfather's study and, rushing up the spiral staircase, I was slightly breathless as I opened the door. Light shone through the large windows and though desperately cold, the room seemed instantly welcoming. I could feel my grandparents' presence, a vivid memory of Grandfather sitting by the fire.

Wooden panels lined the walls, the bookcase crammed with ledgers and red leather boxes, and I hesitated, knowing not to get my dress dusty. The desk was highly polished, there was no ink, and sitting in his chair would hardly pose a risk. My skirt rustled like Aunt Hetty's as I sat, filled with a sense of connection. Moving every two years had made me feel rootless, yet here, I felt I belonged.

A row of box files caught my eye and I drew one from the shelf – 1774–1779, the start of the school. Opening it carefully, I sifted through the contents. Interspersed between accounts were letters from prospective parents, several from attorneys and two from governesses seeking positions as teachers. Most accounts were for fencing material or work done to the land – ditch digging, stone clearing, the application of lime – and three from the miller, Jacob Carter, agreeing terms for supplying flour to the school.

No letters were signed by my grandfather, but notes had been jotted on several correspondence – *received with thanks . . . to be asked again . . . an honourable gentleman.* I stifled a laugh. *This man is a rascal!* At the bottom of one, *Daylight robbery!* I could imagine Grandfather reaching for his pen. Only twice was there a hint of anger. *This man is a profligate fraudster. Thankfully, the matter is now closed.*

The last letters were a series of correspondence. Tied in black ribbon they looked more formal than the others, their official red seals making them bulky. Untying the ribbon, most bore the same embossed heading – Henry Asquith & Sons. Attorneys at Law, 15 Pydar Street, Truro. Dated 1778, they spanned May to July, the first catching my immediate attention . . . *Hereby enter into the agreement to purchase ninety acres of land between the adjoining estate of St Feoca School, owned by the Right Reverend Joseph Mitchell, and the estate of Tregenna, owned by Sir William Ferris of Tregenna Hall, both properties being in the parish of Feock in the county of Cornwall.*

Unfolding the thick parchment, a map showed a strip of land between the two estates carefully outlined in red pen. Running west to east, it stopped just north of Tallacks Wood, with St Feoca Mill remaining within the school's estate. So too, Devoran Farm.

The letter continued *Sir William thanks you for your generous*

*response and is delighted for the opportunity to construct a drovers'
lane along the perimeter of his estate.* And written in my grandfather's hand, *Delighted for the opportunity to mend the tower and
construct a conservatory!*

Aunt Hetty would have been eighteen, Mama sixteen, the
date of the painting in her room. Perhaps Grandfather had
used some of the money to pay for their portrait too? I could
picture them sitting round the fire with a celebratory drink,
toasting the plans for the new conservatory.

I had to be careful not to be late, Aunt Hetty had silenced
the chapel clock because the girls had complained it kept
them awake and, scooping up the letters, I prepared to go.
Yet two words suddenly struck me as strange – *generous
response* – and reading them again, they seemed out of place.
What if Sir William had approached Grandfather for the land,
and not the other way around?

Two smaller letters were still to be read and I picked
up the first. It was from Sir William Ferris, Sir Anthony's
father.

*Tregenna Hall
15th July 1778*

To The Right Reverend Joseph Mitchell
Dear Sir,

*Your response to my request for land has been generous
indeed.*

*My wife and I welcome your kind gesture and appreciate
the sentiments behind it. Indeed, we look forward to a closer*

association between not only our neighbouring estates, but our families.

Yours in appreciation,
William Ferris, Bart

Grandfather's reply made me catch my breath. Written underneath, *And how much will you rob me of for her dowry?* I reached for the next letter: it was from Anthony Ferris.

Tregenna Hall
31st July 1778

To The Right Reverend Joseph Mitchell
Dear Sir,

Your generous offer for the drovers' lane gives me such hope.

I believe you are well aware Miss Harriet holds complete possession of my heart. My love for her knows no limit.

As yet, I am constrained by the terms of my inheritance but in five months' time, on my twenty-fifth birthday, expect me to come knocking on your door at dawn, or even at the stroke of midnight, such will be my hurry.

I remain your obedient and expectant servant,
Anthony Ferris Esq.

Written underneath in Grandfather's writing, *Omnia vincit amor.*

Love conquers all. I caught my breath. Grandfather had acted generously to show his consent — Sir Anthony and Aunt Hetty were to marry. They had been in love all those years ago, yet they did not marry?

Hurrying down the steps, a blonde-haired girl was standing in the doorway of the library, her blue eyes sparkling. 'You must be Kate, Susan's daughter?' I said, still reeling from the shock. *They were in love. They were to be married.*

She bobbed me a curtsy. 'Yes, Miss Woodville.' She had the same strong jawline as her mother, the same blonde hair. Taller than Gwen and Sophie, her clothes were clean, her hair neatly brushed. Even in the dull light her mobcap looked starched and spotless.

Through the open door, Grace pointed to her cut pieces. 'Kate's just had an excellent idea. She suggests the girls embroider their names on their smocks. Isn't that clever? I've got plenty of coloured silk threads, but maybe we should sew them on to a piece of fabric first? In fact, I'm beginning to think *making* the smocks should be included in our lessons. Oh dear . . . there's so much to consider.'

Aunt Hetty was waiting by the front door, a stout umbrella in one gloved hand, a basket in the other. Wrapped in a warm cloak, she nodded towards another cloak and basket. 'Wear that, my dear. Put your pumps in the basket. Lady Clarissa's boatman is to meet us at Harcourt Quay. Bring that other umbrella, though it looks like we may be lucky with the weather.'

Sir Anthony Ferris and Aunt Hetty were in love. They were to be married!

Rushing to the kitchen, I collected my stout shoes and returned more than a little flustered. Something had prevented Aunt Hetty and Sir Anthony Ferris's marriage, and now he was a widower, Sir Anthony Ferris was free to press his suit again. I felt winded, reeling from a sudden sense of emptiness.

'I think we'll be lucky,' Aunt Hetty said, setting off down the drive. 'Sometimes Lady Clarissa sends her coach but when the tide's in, it's a delightful drift up to Trenwyn House.' Her complexion looked flawless, the hood of her cloak pulled over a fetching black bonnet. She wore the same pearl earrings, a mother-of-pearl brooch, her look so refined, my stomach twisted. She could have married into any of the great families; she was elegant, dignified, intelligent. She would make a perfect Lady Ferris.

Halfway down the drive, she stopped. 'Lady Clarissa will try to soften things, but the truth is I'm being summoned to tell me the school must close.'

I felt struck as if by a bolt. '*Close?* Aunt Hetty, you *can't* allow that.'

She started walking again. 'Allow me to finish, please, Pandora. It's not my decision, nor is it theirs. It's in the *constitution*. The terms my father laid out are crystal clear. Why else would he appoint four people of impeccable standing to oversee the school? They have the final say. The School Board – or governors, as we call them – have a statuary duty to uphold the constitution of St Feoca School for Young Ladies.'

'Well . . . if it closes we'll just start another!'

Her mouth tightened. We reached the gatehouse and she smiled at the heavy-set man with black hair leaning on crutches by the open gates. Touching his hat, he bowed. 'A good day for the river, Miss Mitchell.'

'Indeed, George. Just the right tide. How are you?'

'Stronger by the day. Thank you.' He pointed to his bandaged foot. 'Back at work in no time.'

Restronguet Creek lay before us, the tide lapping the banks, the thatched roof of the Passage Inn just visible across the water. Dull, overcast, it held the same grey colours as when I arrived, yet this time there was more activity. Yawls were drifting on the river, a fisherman casting his nets. Next to the gatehouse a mule was harnessed to a large cart, a group of men working on the road. Two were pushing heavy wheelbarrows, two wielding pickaxes, two bending over their newly laid stones. Standing by the side of a large heap, I caught the distinct stare of Benedict Aubyn.

An egret flew into the air, a flash of white feathers and yellow feet, and Aunt Hetty's voice turned stern. 'I'm afraid the situation the school is in is legally binding. It's not just a matter of starting over again. According to the constitution, once the school is no longer viable, St Feoca *legally* reverts to the heirs of the estate. And there's nothing I can do to change it.'

'The heirs of the estate?'

Her voice hardened. 'The only surviving male heir is Mr Richard Compton of Birmingham – my father's cousin's son. The constitution states that if the number of pupils falls below ten, and there are fewer than three teachers for a period of six months, the school is considered to have failed and the estate reverts to the heirs of the estate, as laid out in my father's will.'

I was reeling, her words making no sense. 'But Aunt Hetty . . . you *can't* let that happen.'

Two coal barges were moored against the quayside, a man issuing instructions. The quay looked bigger in the daylight, the offices busy, *Walter Reed and John Carne Merchants* written in red paint across the largest building. A rowing boat was squeezed between two barges, the boatman securing it to a ring. Aunt Hetty waved and the boatman doffed his cap.

'The last pupil left in November, Pandora, and I have been the only teacher since. According to the constitution, that leaves me three weeks. The governors are going to tell me that I've run out of options – that they've given me every chance.' She turned at the sound of footsteps. 'Ah, good day, Mr Aubyn. I see you're progressing *somewhat* with your new road.'

His bow was strangely formal. 'Good day, Miss Mitchell. Progress is slower than I'd like but the quality is good and that's what counts.' He held out his arm. 'May I help you over these loose stones? At least the rain's keeping off.' He was wearing his heavy overcoat and large hat, his glance at me severe.

He, who was proposing to fleece Aunt Hetty of her land!

The boatman joined us, also holding out his arm for Aunt Hetty to take. 'Thank you, Seth. That's very kind.' Crossing the wooden plank she settled herself on the bench in the boat.

With her back turned, Benedict Aubyn whispered, 'When are you going to tell her you're a married woman, Mrs Marshall?'

He sounded just like Father. *Just like Father*. 'I'm *not* married. My papers were a mistake. A *necessary* mistake.'

99

Beneath his large hat, his eyes held mine. 'Who are you? What's your motive for coming here?'

I stared back, almost too shocked to speak. 'My motive? You think I'm here to *rob* Miss Mitchell? Really, Mr Aubyn!' Never had my cheeks burned so fiercely. 'And when are *you* going to tell her you're to receive ten per cent of every lucrative land deal you negotiate? Ten per cent of every mile you save? A poor, unfortunate headmistress . . . let me remember. *Rich rewards* were the words I heard used. *My offer will be a godsend to her . . . I can't see her putting up any objection at all.*' I could hardly keep my voice civil. 'You saw my grandmother's portrait and how alike I am to her. I am who I say I am – it's *you* who needs to be honest, Mr Aubyn.'

There was accusation in his eyes, yet a look of embarrassment as if I were telling him something he did not want to hear. 'I am honest, Miss Woodville.'

The boatman returned and held out his arm. Trying to hide my fluster, I slid along the bench next to Aunt Hetty in what was clearly a much-cherished boat. Aunt Hetty trailed her glove along the polished wood. 'This was a wedding present from Lord Carew to Lady Clarissa. She's taught her whole family to row in it – including all her grandchildren.'

Benedict Aubyn placed the ropes in the bow and stood staring across the creek. Aunt Hetty smiled her thanks but I kept my eyes straight ahead. Others may fall for his lost-boy looks, the vulnerability in his eyes, the sense he was struggling with his emotions, but I knew too many men like him: all smiles and politeness in company but revealing their true nature once we were left alone.

Stage Two

THE SUPREME ORDEAL

Chapter Eleven

The boatman, a powerful man in his mid-sixties, began negotiating our way round the hulls of the coal barges, his oars slicing the water in a gentle rhythm. Mama had often described how the water could change in an instant: one moment inky black and ominous, the next grey and mysterious, then sparkling blue to reflect the sky. High tide would bring waves lapping the wooded banks, low tide revealing vast stretches of mud. Wading birds would scuttle along the strewn seaweed, curlews would call, egrets and herons stand like statues. Seagulls would screech and circle above. She loved everything about Restronguet Creek, the dankness, the smell of rotting vegetation, the white branches dipping below the waterline.

'There's more commerce than I thought there'd be. Mama never mentioned the barges.'

'She'd only remember a scattering of cottages. Since she left, the crofts have become businesses and the boathouse is a repair yard. The quay's under new ownership – hence the road repairs.'

Passing the wooded entrance of Tallacks Creek, I caught a glimpse of St Feoca Mill with its thatched roof and large waterwheel. Trees were crowding together, branches over-hanging the water. It was as if Mama was next to me. *You never forget your first kingfisher . . . the sandpipers are my favourite . . . or maybe it's the owls at night.*

Aunt Hetty pointed above the shoreline. 'That's Feock. Look up, and you can see the roof of Tregenna Hall where Sir Anthony lives. Lady Clarissa's house is that large building straight ahead, above the bay.'

Two very grand houses, both with vast estates. Seeing Sir Anthony's house sent a stab straight through me. 'I think Grandfather was a beast, Aunt Hetty. How could he abandon you like that? To agree a lease that throws you to the mercy of the heirs of the estate? Did he think every woman should get married – that you'd be happy to let the school go once you were certain of a good match?'

'Every woman should get married, or at least try their very hardest.' Her voice was hard, matching my own. 'And your grandfather didn't abandon me. There's ample provision for me under the constitution. I can expect a yearly allowance from the heirs of the estate, to live how and where I choose. The lease has merits for a single woman.'

'But you might have married a schoolmaster who loved your school.'

'Like your mother?' Her voice cut like ice. 'No, Pandora, I told Father in no uncertain terms that I was *never* going to marry and this was his way of protecting me. I am fortu-nate in that once the school closes, I will receive a generous allowance. You will not. Nor will most women. A woman's only security is through marriage. Yes, she may be a governess or a teacher, but she has no security should she fall ill, or when she is old. Grace certainly must marry. Her looks and accomplishments must be used to her advantage.'

A shiver ran down my spine, her words spoken so vehemently. Grace was right: Aunt Hetty was not fighting the closure at all. I felt dizzy, the realisation so disappointing I had to grip the seat. She had told her father she would never marry because the man she loved had married someone else. And now he was free, the school felt a burden to her. I had to turn away. Of course I was happy for her. Of course I wanted her to be with the man she had always loved, but for her to abandon the home I had spent so long trying to reach was completely unbearable. Why not let me take her place?

A small jetty projected into the bay below Trenwyn House and, reaching for a hook, Seth tied the boat firmly alongside. 'Looks like the clouds are passing. It might even clear.' He held out his hand, helping us along the wooden planks on to the shore.

Aunt Hetty returned his smile. 'Thank you, Seth. Are the family well?'

'I'm a grandfather again – another bonny lad. That'll be three now.'

Swapping her sturdy boots for her satin pumps, she straightened, looking up at the nearby trees. 'Ash before oak, we're in for a soak.'

Seth shrugged his huge shoulders. 'Let's hope not. Oak before ash, we're in fer a splash. We don't need any more

105

soaking, Miss Mitchell. A splash will do. We need good clear months of sun. There's been enough soakin".

Above the sweeping lawns, four people were watching us from the vast terrace in front of the house. It was like stepping into Mama's drawings, the house exactly as she had painted it; two storeys with eleven large windows facing the river, a stone façade beneath the roof, a balustrade around the terrace. Even the vast stone urns were where she had placed them. Mama had described the walled garden but not the shrubbery, and Aunt Hetty seemed to read my mind. 'This has been newly planted. Your mother and I often came here for tea. She was born the same year as William, Lady Clarissa's eldest son. Everyone thought they might get . . . Well, never mind, it wasn't to be. Your mother was very fond of Lady Clarissa — and so was your grandmother.'

The gravel on the path sparkled even in the dull light. Leaving the shrubbery, we were met by a tall woman wearing a flowing blue silk gown and an elaborate headdress over her soft grey hair. 'A safe passage, I hope?' Her voice rang like cut glass, her eyes full of warmth. 'Miss Woodville, how lovely to see you again. I remember you as a little girl. My goodness, aren't you the image of your dear grandmother?'

Curtsying deeply, I fought my pang of regret. If Mama had married her son, Lady Clarissa would have been my grandmother. Slipping her hands through our arms, she led us towards the terrace. 'I'm so sorry to hear of your dear mother's death, Miss Woodville. You have my sincere condolences. We all hoped she would return. But . . . well, that wasn't to be. We have you now, and that must be such a blessing for your aunt.'

Her words were spoken with such kindness and tears stung my eyes. *No, Lady Clarissa, not a blessing at all, I'm actually rather a hindrance. A nuisance to be married off.*

A sapphire brooch sparkled at her throat, a pair of diamonds clipped to her ears. On her wrist, a collection of shells swung from a gold ribbon. 'I'm afraid this is all very formal, Harriet. You know the reason we've convened this meeting? Though it clearly pains me, what has to be said *has to be said*.'

'Of course, Lady Clarissa. You've been very kind to give me so long.' Aunt Hetty smiled at the man and two ladies waiting on the terrace. 'It's always a pleasure to see everyone. It's just the circumstances that are difficult.'

The elaborate stone urns were planted with clipped lavender, just as in Mama's paintings. Only in her paintings they were bursting with colour, the water behind them a glorious blue. Lady Clarissa led me forward. 'May I introduce Miss Mitchell's niece, Miss Pandora Woodville? This is Mrs Lilly, and this is Reverend Penhaligan. Both members of the Board of Governors.'

Reverend Penhaligan was dressed in a black jacket and breeches; the white bands on his collar dipping as he bowed. 'Delighted to meet you, Miss Woodville.' In his late sixties, he had a kind face and a ready smile but he looked frail, a pair of thick glasses beneath his heavy white brows. Mrs Lilly's returning curtsy was elegant, her smile pleasant. Dressed in a plum-coloured velvet gown and jacket, her white hair was held neatly beneath a matching velvet hat. She looked kind and respectable, her eyes searching my face as I curtsied.

'How like your grandmother you are, Miss Woodville.'

Lady Clarissa turned to the second lady. 'May I present Mrs Angelica Trevelyan, our newest governor, and a former pupil of the school. She's recently taken Lady Ferris's place on the board.'

'I'm . . . delighted . . . to meet you.' Mrs Trevelyan's appearance made me immediately tongue-tied. Tall, graceful, her dark hair bouncing in curls around her face, she was elegant, refined, quite the most beautiful woman I had ever seen.

'Was your journey from America comfortable, Miss Woodville? No untoward mishaps or inclement weather? No enemy ships?'

'No, it was very pleasant. I was scared . . . at first . . . but it was very pleasant. Very comfortable and not uncomfortable . . . at all.' She was mesmerising, young, joyful, smiling as if she was used to people being struck by her beauty. 'I came on a grain ship. All the way from Philadelphia to Falmouth.'

'It's a little chilly . . . let's go inside.' Lady Clarissa pointed to the French window. A footman opened it and as I entered I looked back across the terrace. The sun had broken through the clouds, Falmouth just visible across the vast expanse of blue water. 'That's Pendennis Castle,' she whispered. 'Your mother used to love this view. She used to play cricket on the lawn with my sons. She was a good friend of my son, William. Your mother was much loved by us all.'

The footmen pulled out our chairs. The table was set with delicate cups and saucers to rival the best at Government House. A silver tea urn stood at one end, a large fruit bowl in the centre. Two gold-rimmed plates spilled over with ginger-bread and strangely cut biscuits, and I caught the pride in Lady

Clarissa's eyes. 'My youngest grandchild made the biscuits for us.'

The tea poured, and the biscuits left untasted, Lady Clarissa drew a deep breath. 'I had better start our meeting. First, a very warm welcome to Miss Pandora Woodville, niece of Miss Mitchell.' She glanced at Reverend Penhaligan, who reached for his quill and dipped it in the ink pot. A large minute book lay open on an empty page. 'Those also present are Lady Clarissa Carew, Mrs Mary Lilly, Reverend Opus Penhaligan, Mrs Angelica Trevelyan and Miss Harriet Mitchell. This meeting has been called to discuss the future of St Feoca School for Young Ladies.'

Clasping her hands as if in prayer, she sighed. 'It gives me no pleasure to remind everyone of the strict constitution to which we are all contracted.' She glanced up. 'The fact is we are facing the imminent closure of the school.' Holding up a closely written page she balanced her glasses on the end of her nose. 'Section three requires there to be no fewer than ten pupils and three teachers for the efficient and serviceable running of the school. And it is my painful duty to inform the board that for the last six months there have been *no pupils* and *one teacher*.' She looked up. 'The terms detailing the demise of the school are outlined in section four. If the above criteria is not met for six months, then St Feoca School for Young Ladies will be considered unviable and consequently must close. We are now at that painful point in time.'

Aunt Hetty was sitting opposite the vast French windows, looking not at Lady Clarissa, but across the lawns to the sparkling sea. It was as if she was not listening but was elsewhere:

serving tea on her own grand terrace or showing us round the pineapple house in Tregenna Hall. Perhaps she was preparing for a sumptuous dinner. Maybe she was imagining her wedding night when Anthony Ferris would finally take her in his arms.

Lady Clarissa's voice caught. 'It is my very painful duty to ask each member of the committee if they believe the criteria have been met.'

Murmurs of sadness filled the room, each governor shaking their head. 'Has every avenue been explored?' Mrs Lilly had a soft Irish accent, her frown of concentration deepening. She seemed an amiable lady, genteel and rather pretty.

'I believe it has, Mrs Lilly. We've all tried . . . not least Miss Mitchell . . . but the sad fact remains, according to our constitution, the criteria have been met. After that terrible nonsense, no pupils have returned. There have been fewer than ten pupils in the last six months.'

Still Aunt Hetty stared across the terrace. She was showing no sign of concern, no sadness, no interest. Why say nothing at all? Why not at least *attempt* to save the school? I could feel my cheeks begin to burn.

Still silence, a resigned shrug, and my cheeks burned hotter. 'But . . . but . . . Lady Clarissa, we *do* have pupils.' I was speaking too fast. I needed to slow down. 'And we have *three* teachers – Miss Mitchell, Miss Grace Elliot and me – we have *three pupils* with another about to start. Please . . . *please* give us more time. We only need six more girls and the school will be saved.'

Lady Clarissa swung round. 'You have pupils . . . my dears, this is wonderful news!'

Reverend Penhaligan's quill rested mid-air. 'They've returned? After all that trouble? This is excellent news. Just what we need to hear.'

Aunt Hetty's mouth tightened. 'None of my previous pupils has returned; our new pupils never left. Miss Woodville is referring to the daughters of the families who work on the estate – Gwen and Sophie from the farm, Kate from the gatehouse and Mollie from the mill. Pandora has restarted our school, only our new pupils cannot pay fees. In lieu of payment, they're to work as maids and gardeners, and while I'm supportive of the idea in general, I remain anxious as to the economic feasibility behind her philanthropic gesture.'

I reached for my handkerchief. 'Thank you, Aunt Hetty. Thank you. We can do it, I know we can. We have three weeks to find six more pupils...'

Lady Clarissa lifted her finger in the air. 'Miss Woodville, I'm afraid I must stop you. My dear, were you never told to walk before you could run? The board will never accept this. The school must pay its way. The school governors will never sanction pupils who work as servants. Pupils are pupils. Teach your estate girls as much as you like, but the governors will not accept them working as servants. We need a *clearly* thought-out, *meticulously* balanced account sheet as to how the school will pay for itself. Your enthusiasm must be backed by hard economic figures. Am I right, Mrs Trevelyan?'

Angelica Trevelyan's beautiful face looked strangely disquieted. I had expected a smile but a frown continued to crease her brow. She kept glancing at me, her expression increasingly grave. 'Absolutely, Lady Clarissa. You can't fill the school with servants and teach them instead of payment. Are you a teacher, Miss Woodville? Have you the necessary qualifications?'

A note of hostility had entered her voice, her eyes sharper. I had been nervous of her beauty before, but her new tone sparked sudden resentment. 'My father's a great scholar – a Doctor of Divinity. I've learned everything I know from him. I'm wholly proficient in Latin and Greek and my mathematics and reasoning are second to none. I've always dreamed of returning to St Feoca – to teach under my aunt's guidance. I want nothing more than to follow in her footsteps.'

She wore a cream silk band threaded with pearls around her forehead. My borrowed silk dress was very fine, but it was buttoned to the neck, tight-waisted and sweeping to the ground. Her cream gown was high-waisted, almost below her bosom, her hem showing off her shoes. Tall, elegant, she looked like one of the Greek nymphs on the vases I had studied. Even allowing for my mourning clothes, I felt a drudge by comparison, my dress too voluminous compared to her slim silhouette. She said nothing but her eyes showed she clearly did not like me – as if I had somehow displeased her. Perhaps she thought me too drab to be a teacher, that I would suck the joy of learning from my pupils and bury them in dusty tomes to conjugate verbs in a language they would never use.

Her voice was measured. 'You say you have three weeks – is this correct, Lady Clarissa?'

Lady Clarissa flicked through the papers on the polished mahogany table. 'Yes . . . but if we go by calendar months, we could probably stretch it to four weeks. Why don't we end this meeting and meet again in three weeks? That will leave us just

112

one week to resolve this.' Whisking off her glasses, she stood up. 'Miss Mitchell, there's rather a lovely nest in the wisteria by the side of the house which I think you may like to see?'

We rose and I would have joined them, but Reverend Penhaligan raised his hand, implying he would like a word. The others left, and he cleared his throat. 'Your grandfather was a wonderfully kind man, Miss Woodville. I knew him in my professional capacity. He was always very generous with both his time and his compassion.'

'Thank you, Reverend Penhaligan. I hardly remember him. I wish I had known him better.'

'It must have been very hard for you to be away from your grandparents – but I sense his spirit in you. I believe he would approve of your *servants'* school. He was interested in everything and everyone. I sent many a young curate to him for sage advice, and they always came back with a renewed sense of purpose. He inspired people. Perhaps that was his greatest quality. That and his love for humanity.'

Mama would have sat at this table, looking out of the three large windows. A portrait of Lady Clarissa's children hung above me – five strapping sons and one daughter. The eldest son, William, looked strong and handsome, with thick-set shoulders and a mass of blond hair. *But . . . well, that wasn't to be*. Everything could have been different. Mama could have lived a life of privilege: she could be here still, running down to the jetty to welcome Aunt Hetty.

Reverend Penhaligan rose stiffly. 'As your grandfather is not here, I wonder if I may offer you some advice, Miss Woodville? Pursue this idea . . . you have my support, but you need sound financial backing. Truro Grammar School has successfully negotiated endowment places. Establish endowments, my dear. Organise a committee for fundraising – wealthy philanthropists who share your vision. Raise money, invest it wisely, and use the income to endow your school.'

Like fog lifting, my mind started clearing. 'Thank you. Maybe . . . well, maybe I should ask the ship owners . . . or the mine owners . . . or maybe the smelting companies? Reverend Penhaligan, who is the richest man in Truro?'

He shrugged, his heavy white eyebrows lifting. 'Generally, the belief is Mr Silas Lilly has the greatest wealth. But there are plenty of others with considerable fortunes.'

We were at the French doors, about to join the others on the terrace. The Irish lady was beautifully yet plainly dressed, showing no sign of wealth or privilege. 'Does Mrs Lilly know Mr Lilly? Are they related? Maybe we could ask her to intervene on our behalf?'

He smiled, a slight nod to his head. 'Mrs Lilly knows him very well. She's his wife. And Angelica Trevelyan is his daughter.' His voice dropped. 'They are two of the wealthiest philanthropists in Truro, and both active reformers for women's education. Between them, I believe they can save your school, Miss Woodville.'

⊗

A frown had settled on Aunt Hetty's brow. Though all politeness and manners, our departure seemed strained and she remained silent as Seth fought the current back. Tight-lipped and stern, she avoided all conversation. Only when we reached the end of the drive did she speak. 'We've been invited by Sir Anthony to visit his son and daughter tomorrow at Tregenna Hall. It's very attentive of him and shows great kindness. He's sending his coach at midday.'

Her words sent shards of ice through me. 'Must I go?'

The same tight lips, the same stiffness. Something had changed in her, a sudden hostility. 'Yes, Pandora. It would be unheard of to refuse such a kind invitation. Only, maybe tomorrow you could be a little less *outspoken?*'

I opened the front door and she swept past me. Tears blurred my eyes, not from anger or frustration, but from deep upset. 'I've done something very wrong, haven't I? You're cross with me, aren't you, Aunt Hetty? I thought you wanted us to restart your school. I thought . . . *deep down* . . . you approved . . . that you're pleased I want to save it.'

Drawing off her gloves, she laid them on the side table. 'That's not what concerns me.' Her back turned, and I heard a deep intake of breath.

'What have I done, Aunt Hetty? All I want to do is to please you but it seems I only anger you.'

She kept her back to me. 'Well, my dear. If you don't know, then there's no point in me telling you.'

Chapter Twelve

Fighting my tears I watched Aunt Hetty mount the stairs. My cheeks were burning, my throat tight. Something had changed in her, a definite shift in affection. I had tried to please her in every way. *Every possible way.* Moulding myself in her image, copying the way she walked, the way she talked, aching from holding my chin so high and my shoulders back. Trying to be a niece she could at least approve of, if not love. Even if she wanted to marry Sir Anthony, she could surely allow me to take over the school? She could teach me her ways – at least give me a chance. Why be so curt?

I was a child again, being led down her stairs by my mother, heartbroken that I had done something wrong. Well, I was twenty-one years old now: I was my own person. I was not perfect, not beautiful, not elegant or refined. I spoke with a different accent and lacked society manners, but she would just have to take me how I was. I had had enough of trying to please her.

Sweeping along the corridor, Grace's sewing basket on the

library table caught my eye. It was brimming with lace and ribbons and exactly what I needed. She was in the kitchen reading to Annie. 'Oh, Pandora, you're back. How was your visit?'

Eager questioning followed and I did my best to describe the beautiful house and fine views. Their curiosity at an end, I could finally ask the question foremost in my mind. 'I wonder if I may I borrow your sewing basket, Grace?'

'Of course . . . take anything you need. Can I help you?'

I drew a deep breath. 'No, I'm just going to make a few small adjustments to my gown. It won't take long. I don't need any supper. Would you mind telling Aunt Harriet I'm retiring to my room and won't be down for dinner?'

Her beautiful face clouded, her hand reached for my arm. 'Oh dear. That doesn't sound good. Please tell me it's not bad news, Pandora.'

I smiled back into her troubled eyes. 'Oh no! It's very good news . . . or at least it will be. It just needs a little thought. The school is definitely going to keep open – definitely. There's no question of closure.'

Too tired to continue, I secured my needle and rubbed my eyes. The last candle was guttering and I would finish in the morning. The new seams needed to be encased and the lace on one sleeve still had to be slip-stitched, but from the outside the gown looked finished. Undoing the waist had been easier than I thought and by cutting away half the bodice, I had raised the waistline. Best of all, removing three panels from the skirt had slimmed it right down. The sleeves now ended in lace below my elbow and a panel sewn beneath the now too-high hem gave an impression of an underskirt. Without wanting to be too boastful and, taking into account hers was cream and mine was black, it was an exact copy of Mrs Trevelyan's gown only without the pearls and decorative beads.

It was as if Mama had directed my needle. I was convinced the mothers of Father's pupils tore their dresses just so Mama could adjust them, but Mama would not agree. She was being used but never saw it. Why pay an expensive dressmaker when the tutor insisted his wife was adept at mending? My head was throbbing, my neck aching. The fire was dying, the room growing cold; even so, a breath of fresh air might help me clear my head.

Opening the window, my emptiness returned: Mama would have sat like this, watching the night, listening to the owls hooting across the creek. She would have looked up at the moon, knowing her future could be with William Carew. A title and a grand estate! She could have remained close to her sister, and beautiful Trenwyn House could have been hers. Yet she gave it all up for a penniless schoolmaster?

A shiver made me pull my cloak tighter. The sky was clear, the moon shimmering on the glass conservatory. Across the lawn, the outline of the still bare trees stood stark against the creek beyond. The night was cold, the air smelling of salt, the faintest scent of jasmine drifting on the breeze. About to shut the window, a movement caught my eye and I searched the darkness: not a fox, nor a badger, but something running from the house along the perimeter of the lawn. A deer perhaps? The hedge thinned and I caught my breath. A man, bending double, trying to keep from being seen.

I drew back, gripping the ledge. *There's no curse on the house, no curse.* I scanned the woods again. The prowler was nowhere to be seen. My hands were shaking, an icy chill running down my back. He's a poacher. Just a poacher. A hungry man seeking food for his family.

Friday 27th March 1801, 8:00 a.m.

'You look tired, Pandora. Is it the excitement of going to Tregenna Hall?' Brighter in the mornings, Annie handed me a cup of camomile tea but catching a glimpse of Susan crossing the yard, I knew to hurry.

'Tell the others I'll be down in time to leave.'

Returning with a bowl of warm water, I locked my door, and started twisting each flattened curl back to shape. They started to bounce, swinging as I shook my head, and I began to recognise myself again. Father said men hated unruly curls, that by shaking them so defiantly I showed a rebellious nature; that it made me look coquettish, *unintelligent* – more like a spaniel than a respectable woman. Well, I did not care what men did or did not like, nor did I mind if Aunt Hetty thought likewise.

Reaching into the top drawer, I drew out my ebony head-band. It was black, like my dress, and I slipped it round my forehead. Clipping my mother-of-pearl earrings in place, I licked my finger and outlined my brows. Better still, I added a touch of almond oil and arched them into shape. All I had to do was pull my new gown over my head and, if my measurements were correct, it would slip over my bosom without the need to re-tie the laces. It fitted perfectly and I breathed deeply. I was not being rebellious: I was twenty-one and merely wearing my preferred choice of clothing. I would wait in my room until five minutes to twelve, then I would descend the stairs and face Aunt Hetty's wrath.

She was standing by the open door watching the finest coach I had ever seen draw to a stop. 'They're rather splendid, aren't they? Sir Anthony's extremely proud of his four greys. Make sure your foot is free of your skirt when you step up. The coachman will offer you his gloved hand, and you may rest your gloved hand *lightly* on his. Oh, goodness! We *are* being honoured!'

I caught a flash of blue silk in the window. 'Who's that in the coach?'

'That, my dear, is Mr Cador Ferris, Sir Anthony's only son and heir to the estate. I can assure you, he's utterly charming.' She turned and her smile vanished. Her cheeks flushed, her mouth tightened. 'What on earth . . . ?'

I had to hold firm, yet under her glare my confidence seemed misplaced. My legs began shaking, my courage ebbing. 'Please don't be cross, Aunt Hetty. I knew if I asked, you'd forbid it. It's just Mrs Trevelyan looked so beautiful in her gown and headband. I don't mean to defy you but I don't feel myself dressed how I was . . . Everyone kept likening me to Grandmother and that made me feel very old and rather dowdy.'

'Your grandmother was never *dowdy*!'

Regaining her composure, she smiled across the driveway at the gentleman jumping from the carriage. Tall, assured, an elegant blue silk jacket stretching across a pair of broad shoulders, Cador Ferris smiled from beneath a lock of blond hair. 'I've been commanded to escort you to Father...' His eyes widened, a blush spreading across his handsome face.

Aunt Hetty looked from him to me and I caught a sudden gleam in her eye. She smiled broadly. 'My niece, Miss Pandora Woodville, is lately from Philadelphia, Mr Ferris.'

'Miss Woodville. An honour to meet you...' He seemed confused, as if I had wrong-footed him, his smile rather endearing for all his wealth and standing. He looked away but not before I saw him take a second look and a stab of pleasure shot through me. Not a gluttonous stare like the men in Government House, but a friendly glance showing definite approval. 'Philadelphia? That's rather different! How very exciting... I shall enjoy hearing all about it, Miss Woodville.'

He handed me into the carriage and a tingle of excitement made me almost stumble. It was definitely an appreciative glance. Father had been too long from England and must have forgotten gentlemen in England liked spaniels.

Chapter Thirteen

Returning Cador Ferris's smile, I said very little while he and Aunt Hetty kept up a lively conversation: Sir Anthony was looking forward to showing her the plants in his orchid house, the brown trout in the pond had survived the winter, the fountain in the sunken garden was in full flow. They had manured and clipped the roses and were pleased with the new fig trees. The orange and lemon trees in the orangery were showing signs of blossom and the peach trees looked to be thriving. The aviary had been re-netted, and the peacocks were as noisy as ever.

I sat studying our route. For such a near neighbour, our journey was ludicrously circuitous. Taking the newly resurfaced shore road, we followed the creek past a series of ugly embankments. A dredging barge was obscuring the river mouth, the words *Carnon Streamworks* painted on the hull. Only after half an hour did we join the turnpike and, straight away, we were caught in a backlog. Oxen carts slowed us at every narrowing, the coach drivers growing increasingly impatient, and just one glance at the gentle slope on Aunt Hetty's land showed Benedict Aubyn to have a point.

Cador Ferris must have thought I was smiling at him. 'We're very nearly there...'

A pair of grand gates led to a long drive and I caught a glimpse of the wide waters of Carrick Roads. The tip of Tallacks Creek was just ahead and sudden distaste soured my enjoyment. Surely this was the strip of land Grandfather had sold to Sir William? Aunt Hetty was even more animated, smiling and nodding, pointing out the pheasants, asking if Cador had seen any March hares, but fury filled me. This was not a drovers' lane at all, but a grand drive with young oaks lining both sides.

We turned a bend and I caught my breath. Built of gold stone, Tregenna Hall stood reflected in the bluest lake. Shimmering in the spring sunshine the symmetry was perfect, an exact mirror image of the elegant house with its crenulated façade and shallow roof. Every bit as grand as Lady Clarissa's, the two floors had ten large windows. A circular drive swept round an elaborate sundial to a porticoed front door.

'Do you like the house, Miss Woodville?' Cador Ferris asked with a shy smile.

'It's... beautiful... the reflection... it's perfect.'

'We've nearly two acres of lakes – it's a haven for herons, kingfishers, wild mallard, visiting geese and all sorts of other wildfowl.' Two footmen stood like statues by the front door, their red uniforms embroidered in gold thread. They rushed forward, pulling down the steps, and Cador Ferris seemed strangely hesitant. 'Welcome to Tregenna Hall. Ah...here's Father. He must have been watching for the carriage.'

I stared across at the welcoming smile of Sir Anthony Ferris – the man who was soon to take Aunt Hetty from me. I had no reason to dislike him – he had prior claim over her, and I should be welcoming their happiness – yet one look at his square chin and short grey hair, his immaculate cravat and impeccably tailored jacket, and my loneliness spiralled. Tall, impeccably dressed, broad-shouldered, he looked an exact older version of his son. 'A comfortable journey, I hope? Welcome, welcome...this is such a pleasure.' He was charming, attentive, obviously intent on pleasing us; casting sideways looks at Aunt Hetty when he thought no one was watching.

Tall and graceful, her blonde curls falling to her shoulders, Olwyn Ferris appeared as hesitant as her brother. Curtsying, she smiled. 'It's such a lovely day...we thought maybe you'd like to see the gardens – if it's not too cold?'

Indicating across the drive to an iron gate, Sir Anthony held out his arm for Aunt Hetty and we followed close behind. The blue trimmings on Olwyn's velvet bonnet matched her eyes, her gloved hands slipping into her velvet muff as we began our tour of the sunken lawns and granite terraces. Every now and then her hand would slip from her muff to point out a plant in the herbaceous border and I tried to stifle my growing disquiet. Aunt Hetty looked so comfortable at Sir Anthony's side.

Worse still, these sounded like the exact flower beds Mama described, her descriptions always ending with a wistful sigh, an echo of regret at how much she missed an English country garden. Friendly and attentive, smiling with encouragement, yet with downward glances and hesitancy of speech, Olwyn Ferris seemed approachable and kind. Both brother and sister were giving me such a warm welcome and their respect for Aunt Hetty was obvious. As if reading my mind, Cador Ferris cleared his throat. 'Father thinks very highly of Miss Mitchell. In fact . . . we all do.'

'I believe they've known each other a long time.' The ache grew fiercer. Olwyn Ferris could only be seventeen, Cador about my age. Both were well-nourished, strong-boned and elegant, with fine features and aristocratic bearing. 'I'm so sorry your mother has passed away. My . . . mother—' I had to stop.

'We're equally sorry for your loss.' Cador's voice was hardly more than a whisper. 'Father told us . . . Please accept our sincere condolences. Mother died two years ago . . . it does get a little less painful, but no easier. We miss her every single day.' He held out his arm and I slipped my hand on his, walking behind Sir Anthony and Aunt Hetty through a wisteria tunnel in the Long Walk.

Stopping outside a glass house with tall, arching windows, Olwyn addressed Aunt Hetty. 'We thought we might take luncheon in the warmth of the orchid house. Papa thought you might enjoy watching the butterflies. Several have already hatched. Papa thinks we should build a separate butterfly house.' Reaching up, she pulled the rope of a brass bell.

A table had been laid with fine china, sparkling crystal glasses and gleaming silver. Aunt Hetty seemed delighted. 'What a lovely idea.'

Sir Anthony took her cloak and I caught her radiant smile. Her hair was dressed in a softer style, her black gown clearly her best. Made from iridescent silk it caught the light, shimmering as Sir Anthony pulled out her chair. Momentarily, his hand rested on her back and my stomach churned. I must not be selfish. I must not feel this dislike of him. Aunt Hetty looked beautiful. At forty-one she could be ten years younger. Elegant, witty, intelligent, it was no wonder Sir Anthony could not take his eyes off her.

Plates of cold meats arrived, a basket of freshly baked bread, jars of pickle and apple sauce, a tray of potatoes. There was asparagus from the hot house, braised fennel, a bowl of roasted artichokes, a plate of hard-boiled eggs, their yolks whipped with cream. I could hardly eat, hardly breathe, hardly talk.

Jealousy gripped me, not the gut-wrenching envy I was expecting but sharp pangs of longing: I did not resent their beautiful home, nor their two-acre walled garden, their rills, their fountains, their herbaceous borders and hot houses; not their innate good manners, their charm, their shyness despite everything they had. It was not their possessions making me feel so empty but the fact they could have been my cousins. My family. Aunt Hetty could have lived here, and Mama and Father could have taken over the school.

Olwyn was clearly thrilled by how well the meal was going. Clasping her hands, she threw a shy look in my direction. 'What a lovely day this is turning out to be.'

A flood of warmth burned my cheeks and I had to keep my eyes from watering. I was sitting in a butterfly house with people who thought well of me. I was no longer dreaming;

this was actually happening. 'Your names are quite lovely,' I managed to say. 'They conjure up a world of chivalry. Wasn't Sir Cador one of King Arthur's knights?'

Cador Ferris glanced at his father. 'I'm afraid so... and there's absolutely nothing I can do about it!'

Sir Anthony's returning smile was rueful. 'I believe you lived in Dominica before moving to Philadelphia, Miss Woodville?'

'I was just thinking how very like Government House this is. Only we needed to be fanned with huge palm leaves to get the air circulating. We had a butterfly house, or rather the Governor did. His daughters and I used to draw the butterflies. We often sat like this and took refreshments – in the cool of the evening.'

Cador Ferris leaned forward. 'How very exotic... in fact, how thrilling.'

'My father is a renowned scholar, a Doctor of Divinity. It sounds rather boastful, but he's highly sought. Our apartments overlooked the lawns of Government House. You can imagine all the balls and receptions. I was educated with the Governor's daughters... we grew up like sisters and...' I reached for my handkerchief. These were not false tears, these were very real tears. 'I'm sorry...'

A flood of compassion filled Cador's eyes. He seemed strangely affected. 'How very difficult for you. It must have been hard to leave them.'

Putting away my handkerchief, I shook my head. 'Father's pupils have a habit of growing into young men. No appointment lasts for ever. After a while, I grew to anticipate our moves. We travelled all over the West Indies, but when I was

127

fifteen the situation started to get dangerous and Mama worried terribly. Father was about to take up a post in Jamaica but with Britain at war... and the slaves' uprising... Father decided to take a senior position in the grammar school in New York. Then we moved to Philadelphia. The yellow fever epidemic had left several vacancies.'

Aunt Hetty remained staring at her empty plate, but Sir Anthony leaned forward. 'What's Philadelphia like? I believe it's very prosperous – an immensely busy port?'

He had piercing blue eyes, an unwavering stare. 'Yes... it's busier than both New York and Brooklyn. We lived off Market Street behind the President's house.' His interest was suddenly unnerving. Had he known Father? He would certainly have known Mama. 'We often saw President Washington before the government left Philadelphia. Father used to take me to some of his speeches. He taught many of the sons of the government officials... he was invited to attend functions... to give lectures.'

Cador Ferris had the same blue eyes, but not the same assurance. He offered Aunt Hetty another glass of elderflower cordial. 'I hope you don't find Cornwall too quiet after all the places you've lived, Miss Woodville? Can we hope you might stay, or will you return to your father?'

Aunt Hetty remained straight-backed and still. 'I'm going to stay. I want to help Aunt Harriet in her school. Now that I've returned, nothing will prise me away. I've been longing to come back.'

Sir Anthony put down his cup. 'But you must miss your father, Miss Woodville? Can we hope he's to join you? What an asset he'd be to Truro. He'd be just as highly sought here. We have lectures in the assembly rooms and I imagine he'd draw quite a crowd.'

I could hardly trust myself to speak. 'I hope so.'

Our sorbet finished, Sir Anthony rose. 'Would you like to take a look at the pond, Harriet? The moorhens are nesting just the other side of the bulrushes.'

Harriet. He had called her Harriet. There was no mistaking the affection in his voice, nor the tenderness in his eyes. No mistaking the brush of his hand against her back as he leaned to draw out her chair. Inside, a knife twisted. There was nothing I could do. Like him or not, I was going to lose Aunt Hetty to him.

Grace piled several more logs on to the fire but, even so, Annie pulled her shawl closer. Her shock at seeing my alterations subsiding, Susan conceded. 'Well, I think you've done a grand job. I saw the way Mr Ferris looked at you. You've made a conquest there, and who can blame you? Aim high, my girl. There's beauty in those bold looks of yours.'

Grace nodded in agreement. 'You do look beautiful – like an Italian noblewoman or a Spanish princess.' She looked down. 'I saw how Mr Ferris looked at you as well. What's the house like? They say it's *very* grand.'

'It's very beautiful. The reflection in the lake takes your breath away. But we didn't go into the house, we had luncheon in the orchid house. Sir Anthony was very keen to show the butterflies to Aunt Harriet.'

129

Singing drifted across the yard outside – *Fe Fie Foe Fum . . . I smell the blood of an Englishman.* Gwen and Sophie from the farm were swinging a long rope, Kate from the gatehouse singing as she jumped. Susan pulled up a chair. 'I'm not sure I'll be able to drag Kate home.' Her voice dropped. 'According to the rumours, Sir Anthony wants to endow our school an orchid house. Your grandmother loved orchids . . . and he thinks Miss Mitchell should build an orchid house in her memory. But there's more to it than that . . .'

'Hush, Susan.' For such a frail lady Annie could sound very sharp.

Susan merely shrugged. 'It's best Pandora knows. 'Tis well known there was never any love lost between Sir Anthony and his wife. Rumour has it—'

'That's enough, Susan!' Annie's eyes were pinprick sharp. 'What she's saying is that Sir Anthony wants to gift Miss Mitchell the funds for an orchid house but Miss Mitchell won't hear of it. She'll accept his generous food baskets, but she won't take a penny. Time you took Kate home, Susan.'

Picking up her cloak, Susan smiled from the door. 'You did a grand job today, Grace. Three happy children who don't want to go home! I'd say you're a born teacher.'

Dusk had fallen, the warmth of the fire filling the kitchen. I left Grace and Annie playing cards but halfway to my room, a creak on Aunt Hetty's stairs made me jump. 'Aunt Hetty, I didn't see you in the shadow!'

There was no returning smile. Holding out a letter, her voice was brittle. 'Why would Mrs Lilly invite you to visit her in Truro?' She was clearly angry.

'I think Reverend Penhaligan may have suggested it to her.'

'And why would he have done that?' Aunt Hetty had been charming all day, yet the coldness in her voice was chilling.

'I asked him who we could approach for endowments and he suggested—'

Her gasp sent shivers through me. 'That we turn to our governors ... and *beg*?'

'No, not at all. It was a conversation we had when you were on the terrace. He said Grandfather would like the idea of endowments ... but Aunt Hetty, if you sell some of your land we won't need to ask for endowments. The new road might have come at just the right time.'

'Perhaps I should make myself perfectly clear. I am not going begging to Mrs Lilly, nor to anyone else. Goodnight, Pandora.'

'But it would save the school! Aunt Hetty – if you sold a strip of land north of the proposed road, you wouldn't notice the loss and you'd have more than enough money. There'd be good work for a blacksmith and a saddler. Even a cooper and a wheelwright. Sell *six* leases, Aunt Hetty. Why not encourage a printing press ... or a soup kitchen for the poor? The land is bound to be worth more now there's talk of the new road.'

Her voice cut from the darkness. 'Have you considered what I might think? Have you even thought that I might be tired of the struggle ... tired of the whole business of education and the expectations of foolish girls with little more sense than donkeys? Charged with constant discipline and unremitting responsibility? Perhaps I should explain the *reality* of running a school? I have worked *tirelessly*, Pandora. *Tirelessly*. For a pittance of a wage . . . not a moment of free time . . . and next to no thanks.'

Her emotion was raw, her voice breaking. I had clearly spoken too harshly. 'I'm sorry. I've been selfish and not considered you at all. I can understand, honestly I can, but why not let me help? Please, Aunt Hetty. Please give me a chance to start the school again. We won't have the same expenditure if we educate poorer girls. With no horses and no carriage rides, no frippery and social climbing . . . with no coming here to meet the *right sort of people* our expenses will be so much less. Please, Aunt Hetty. Please let me try.'

Her voice dropped. 'I can't sell any land, even if I wanted to. The land's held in trust, and the terms of the constitution are extremely favourable to me. When the school closes, I can expect an annual income of *three hundred* pounds – that's exclusive of rent, which will be paid separately. That will see me very comfortably settled. Why should I put that at risk? Will your father grant me such favourable terms when he joins you in my school?'

I could hardly speak for my rush of fear. 'Please don't give up the school. Can we come to some sort of arrangement? You won't need to teach.' It was all I could do to keep my voice steady. If we could not sell any land, then Mrs Lilly's endowments were the only things that could save us. 'When has Mrs Lilly invited me to visit?'

'She hasn't set a day.'

'Would I have your permission to visit her in Truro?'

'By yourself?' From the shadows I heard her deep intake of breath. 'I believe you'd go even if I forbade it.'

She must not hear the catch in my throat. 'I'd much prefer to have your permission.'

A rustle of silk, a voice from halfway up the stairs. 'Do what you please, my dear. No doubt you have your instructions.'

Chapter Fourteen

The brightness of the morning did little to expel my sadness. Aunt Hetty and I should be setting off together like a loving aunt and niece. Instead, my sleepless night had made me tetchy. All night I had agonised over her words: Aunt Hetty had clearly had enough. Worse still, she was probably secretly engaged to Sir Anthony. Of course, she had every right to find happiness, but so did I.

I was not hot-headed, nor was I disobedient. Nor was I showing my rebellious nature as Father would have said, it was just time was running short and waiting for Aunt Hetty's approval would take too long. I had travelled by myself from Philadelphia, so I could certainly make it to Truro and back! Besides, the mule was already harnessed and waiting by the gate.

George Penrose scowled down at his bandaged foot. 'I'd take ye if I could, Miss Woodville... I've plenty needs doing. The work's piling up; but the truth is I've hired the cart out and it's not mine fer two weeks.'

'Please, Mr Penrose. I have to get to Truro.'

He shook his black curls. 'Ye'll have to wait and catch the up-going tide.'

Footsteps sounded behind me, a familiar voice with its hint of derision. 'I can take you, Miss Woodville. As it happens, I have business in Truro.' Benedict Aubyn was doing up the top button of his large overcoat, his hat pulled low over his brow. He looked stern, barely smiling as he pointed to the cart. 'It would be my pleasure.'

'I'll return by ferry, Mr Aubyn, so it'll be one way only. You can add my fare to the money I owe you.' Without waiting for his help, I slipped quickly on to the driver's bench.

He sat the other side and took hold of the reins. Flicking them, he cast me a sideways look. 'I'm afraid it won't be as comfortable as Sir Anthony's coach.' The mule plodded forward, taking us down the rough track and through the park. Behind us, the windows of St Feoca glinted in the early sun. I could almost feel Aunt Hetty's eyes burning my back.

'We'll go past the farm, then cut north to the turnpike by the gates of Tregenna Hall.' He sounded defensive, even angry. 'And you don't owe me anything. Your fare to Penzance was freely given and I don't expect repayment. I thought you a grieving widow in need of help, that's all.'

'Grieving, yes, but not a widow. I took a married name for my safety. A man can't appreciate what it's like to be an unmarried woman who journeys by herself.'

He seemed affronted. 'I do appreciate exactly what it's like. That's why I offered to buy your fare.' There was an edge to his voice I could well do without.

'I don't mean to argue with you, Mr Aubyn. If we're going all the way to Truro, we might be better off talking about the weather, or the state of the fields.'

'Do you like to travel alone?' He stared ahead, a frown creasing his brow.

'Yes. The freedom is liberating. I know it's considered dangerous and foolhardy, so you don't need to tell me the risks.'

'Alone, from Philadelphia?'

'It gave me space to think for myself. Men do not allow women to think for themselves. No . . . don't answer that. I think maybe we should enjoy some silence.'

He glanced round. 'You see men as controlling, Miss Woodville? I'm interested in your views. Your aunt has led a very independent life. Do you wish to be like her?'

'It's not my view, Mr Aubyn, it's more of a fact. Men consider women their property — that's how they view us. Either they shield us like delicate orchids and allow us to go nowhere or, if we do dare go somewhere, they brand us as forward and inviting trouble. We must either marry and give up our freedom or become drab governesses and spend the rest of our lives avoiding unwanted advances from those who see us as fair game.'

'That's rather cynical, isn't it?'

'Not at all. Until men experience what women experience, they'll never understand. Society does not accept a woman having a life of her own. So yes, Mr Aubyn, I very much envy my aunt. I want to walk in her shoes. To be just like her.'

He urged the mule forward. 'Marriage gives security. It

gives a woman a home . . . and children. The love and protection of her husband.'

I tried to hide my irritation. 'Does it, Mr Aubyn? Or does it just tie her to him? Once married, a woman loses all rights, all independence, and all her own money – which is why I shall never marry. I shall teach instead. Only through education can women hope to thrive independently from men.'

He breathed deeply. 'Many women thrive through security. I think you're being very unfair on men. Maybe you haven't met the right man? A loving relationship—'

'I don't believe in love, Mr Aubyn. Not reciprocated love. One might love, but the other holds all the cards.'

He flicked the reins, urging the mule along the muddy lane. 'Your grandparents clearly loved each other, and my parents . . .' His voice faltered. Wiping his hand across his mouth, he seemed to struggle to finish his sentence. Clearing his throat, his scowl deepened. 'Here's Devoran Farm. This sweep of land is where the new road will rejoin the turnpike.'

'But that's right next to the farm!'

'It's the only option. The gradient's perfect for good drainage.'

The farm looked scruffier than I remembered, the thatch in need of repair. Stones were crumbling in places, paint peeling on the windows. No chickens pecked the courtyard, no cows waiting to be milked. No sign of planted crops, just vast fields of heavy, unploughed soil. We passed the empty stables and Benedict's voice dropped. 'They're struggling. They've no income. They've told me they're not averse to change; it's only

137

their loyalty to Miss Mitchell that keeps them going. Put yourself in their shoes...'

Fury filled me. The arrogance of the man! 'They're tenants of St Feoca School and it's not their decision to sell the farm. You've no right to discuss it with them.'

His mouth tightened. 'Maybe not. But they asked. They're highly intelligent people. They deserve my respect and I gave it to them.' He coaxed the mule forward.

'In future you should consult my aunt, not her tenants.' Silence ensued, both of us scowling, both staring ahead with tight lips. The oaks lining the drive to Tregenna Hall drew closer and he must have seen me glance towards Tallacks Wood. His eyebrows rose. 'Perhaps you might be persuaded to change your mind about marriage? Mr Ferris seems a pleasant man. His father's estate is profitable, the family have vast mining interests, and I believe they have a house in London.'

I bit my tongue, but not for long. 'He also has a very beautiful sister who I imagine commands a hefty dowry. Maybe you should set your sights on her? You might do better to find an heiress to marry.'

His frown deepened. 'You don't like me very much, do you, Miss Woodville?'

'I overheard you in the inn, Mr Aubyn. What I heard, and subsequently found out, makes me wary of you. You all but accused me of being a fraudster. You thought me capable of robbing a vulnerable woman and it seems just a little ironic that it is actually *you* who intends to profit from selling my aunt's land.'

A small gate led through a bramble hedge and jumping from the cart, he grabbed the mule's bridle. 'Forgive me if

I've offended you. You clearly got muddled between Penzance and St Feoca.'

I nodded. 'An easy mistake.'

'An easy mistake. Though some say Penzance is worth visiting.' Pulling the mule through a patch of mud, he began negotiating a series of ruts. Rain pooled in the puddles, his boots in danger of getting stuck. Alongside us, carriages flew along the turnpike road. 'Truro's behind that copse over there. You can just see St Mary's spire – those masts are alongside the wharf.'

The sky was a cloudless blue, a band of woodland stretching along the Truro River. He kept his back to me, his shoulders broader than I first thought, his grip on the mule strong. 'This track's used by drovers for their cattle. I've got a toll pass but we won't use the road – we'll join it at the gate.' His grip tightened as the mule hesitated. Another carriage flew past, the rumble of an oxen carriage. It was even busier than before, the carts heavily loaded – coal, ore, quarried stone, cut timbers – a steady stream going both ways. In the distance, black smoke rose from tall chimneys.

He kept walking, not looking round.

'The mud's drier now. The ruts are free of rain . . . why don't you come back and sit on the cart?'

He shook his head. 'Because, Miss Woodville, everyone knows everyone in Truro and gossip spreads like wildfire. You may like to travel alone, but your reputation will be torn to shreds if you're seen on the cart with me. It's only another three miles.' He glanced round, a hint of his half-smile and I found myself smiling back.

'No one's ever considered my reputation before.'

He looked down, as if suddenly shy. 'Perhaps it's time someone did. Especially dressed like that. You look very . . .'

'Unsuitable?'

A faint blush spread across his cheeks. 'Not at all. It's just . . . I just think you might be noticed, that's all . . .' He walked on, stooping to examine some flowers. 'Do you remember our English flowers? These are primroses, those in the hedge are hazel catkins. The white blossom you can see is black-thorn.' He seemed to be at pains to make amends.

'I remember them from my mother's paintings. She loved the spring. She said new growth always brought new hope. We didn't have seasons in Dominica – just times when it was less humid. My mother missed the seasons. She missed Cornwall. In Philadelphia, sometimes you can't breathe for the heat, yet in the winter the river freezes and the ice can be two inches thick on the windows.'

He kept his back to me. 'I've heard ships get stuck in the ice and have to wait weeks for it to thaw. My work's taken me to London and more recently Bristol, but now I've returned I realise how much I've missed Cornwall.'

We edged round an orchard still bare of blossom. Ahead of us, chimneys rose high into the sky. 'Mr Aubyn, what do you know about Mr Lilly? I'm going to ask Mrs Lilly to endow places at our school.'

He stopped, staring across the vale to the chimneys. 'He's made money from carpet factories and woollen mills. From his mining interests and smelting houses. From the desolate heaps he leaves on once productive pastures. From felling vast

140

woodlands. From poisoning brooks with the washings of his mine.' He took a deep breath. 'From his fumes of arsenic and sulphur.'

'You sound envious of his wealth. Families are starving, Mr Aubyn. Cornwall needs his wealth. The men need work.'

He smiled his half-smile, the sadness returning to his eyes. 'We need industry and we need men like Mr Lilly. But what we don't need is the toll it takes — working men struggling to get through the day with ugly knots on their skin, with constant deadly sores. With racking coughs and sore throats. Men too ill to work, gasping their last breaths through blue lips. We don't need the vomiting, the abdominal cramps, the tingling in their fingers and toes. Everyone watching their skin darken, knowing there's only one end.' He drew his hand across his mouth. 'Forgive me. It's the high price paid by those labouring in the heat and breathing the noxious fumes that concerns me.'

He sounded so passionate, his anguish leaving me unsettled. Pulling the mule forward, he walked on in silence, his strides longer, his head lowered. We were on the outskirts of Truro, the track merging alongside the turnpike. A steady stream of carts were waiting to go through the tollgate and raising his hand, Benedict showed his pass to the toll keeper. 'Busy today, isn't it?'

The toll keeper touched his cap. 'Mornin', Mr Aubyn. Care to come in? Can I offer you some refreshment, sir?'

Benedict stared down at his boots. 'Not this time, John. I'll get you into trouble.'

Stamping his toll book, the toll keeper shook his head. 'Best be warned. The tinners are back, an' there's trouble brewin'. The militia's been summoned – best take care. Best leave sooner than later.'

Turning towards the centre, we followed the thin channel of brown water snaking between the riverbanks. The stench of rotting debris mixed with horse dung, plumes of acrid smoke wafting from cauldrons on the wharf. Ships with their hulls deep in mud were leaning against the harbour wall, shouts echoing across the river. Whistles were blowing, carts waiting along the quayside, the mules stamping their feet. It was so vibrant, so energising: the men on horseback, the beautiful row of houses along the quay. The church bells ringing. One chimed half past ten, the perfect time to make a morning call.

Gripping the bridle, Benedict wove us skilfully across the cobbles through the mass of laden carts. 'That's where the ferry leaves – the one to take you back to Harcourt Quay,' he shouted over his shoulder. A group of ragged men were walking six abreast, three carrying pickaxes, and Benedict swung round. 'I don't suppose you have money for your ticket, do you, Miss Woodville?' He reached into his jacket pocket.

'I don't need your money. I've something I intend to sell. I've sold them before. I need...' I looked round, 'to find a shop... someone who might buy these from me.' Reaching for my bag, I drew out the four shells I had painted the night before. 'I found these oyster shells on the shore and painted them. One's an oyster catcher, one's a heron, this one's the fishing boat in Restronguet Creek. This one's the garden gate. I'll try to sell one.'

Reaching forward, his finger brushed my palm. 'You painted these? But they're beautiful.'

'I've sold some before. They can fetch up to a shilling each.'

His frown was back, a shake of his head. 'Wait here. There are shops just round the corner. Give me a minute, only I think it best if I sell them — you'll soon be linked to Miss Mitchell and once you are, tongues will wag. I've not been around Truro for four years so no one will recognise me.' Tying the reins to some railings, he darted across the road.

Beside us, a large red-brick house boasted four wide sash windows and a painted front door. It was beautifully pro-portioned, but one look at the brass plaque and I turned quickly away. *The Trevelyan Shipping Company.* Wrapping my cloak tighter, I pulled down my hood. What if Captain and Mary James were in Truro? I nearly jumped when Benedict returned.

'Six shillings, and a bargain at that price. You have a rare talent, Miss Woodville. Make sure Mrs Lilly sends a servant with you to the ferry. These riots can turn nasty.'

A further six men were walking down the quayside, loaves of bread clenched tightly in their fists. They were holding them in the air, shouting in unison. Two held up huge plac-ards saying, *Underweight Loaves* and *Adulterated Bread.* Benedict steadied the mule. Helping me dismount, his voice sharpened. 'Mrs Lilly is expecting you, isn't she? She does know you're coming?'

I crossed my fingers under my cloak. It was so intuitive, I hardly knew I was doing it. 'Yes. Eleven o'clock. Thank you, Mr Aubyn, you've been very kind. I've got good instructions how to get there.' Once out of sight, I would ask the first person I saw.

I looked round. Benedict Aubyn was no longer watching me. Lost from sight, he was surrounded by a group of protesting men. Shouts rang across the cobbles, *Wheat at ten shillings a bushel. Nine pence fer a quatern loaf.* I saw my chance and hurried down a side street.

Chapter Fifteen

Perren Place, Pydar Street, Truro

Truro was far more beautiful than Mama had described or how I remembered. I was used to the straight grid of Philadelphia, not the winding streets with their timber-framed houses. Many of the houses looked newly built, their gold stones glowing in the sunshine, their sash windows and railings gleaming with fresh paint. The square was lined with banks and shops, the streets teeming with women gathering in doorways. Men were shouting their wares, horses drinking from a trough. A soldier in red uniform sat mounted on a black mare.

The woman I asked stood staring at the men entering the square. Her voice sounded clipped. 'Mr Lilly? Along King Street, then left at High Cross. Perren Place is the building with five chimneys.'

Hurrying from the crowds, I reached Pydar Street and saw the sign, *Perren Place*. The footman was grey-haired and slightly stooped. Glancing down the street, he frowned. 'Neither Mr nor Mrs Lilly are at home. May I take your calling card?'

Behind me, someone shouted, *Cornish grain for Cornish people. Keep Cornish wheat in Cornwall.* A group of boys ran past. 'I don't have a calling card. I'm Miss Pandora Woodville. Mrs Lilly knows me . . . she's invited me to call. I thought . . .'

'Ye're not from here, are ye? I can tell by yer accent. Mrs Lilly's not here. And when I say she's not here, I mean she's away at her country house. Mr Lilly's in the foundry. I don't mean she *won't* see ye. I mean she *isn't here*. And ye need a calling card.' He made to close the door.

'When will she be back?' I should have remembered what Mama told me about the protocol of social visits.

Through the small gap, his voice sounded urgent. 'Go home, Miss Woodville. There's trouble brewing. Go home. Or get to the church.'

The door shut and a woman grasping a child's hand rushed past. Soldiers with muskets were marching towards me, an officer in a scarlet uniform at their head. Swinging round, he stopped abruptly. 'Halt!' He had thick side whiskers, a bushy moustache. 'They're meeting in the town hall to put their demands to the mayor in a *constrained and civilised manner!*' His face was flushed, his brows knitted. 'Fewer than fifty and we can't arrest them. But the first sign of danger – the first sight of implements being thrown or windows smashed – and I'll read the Riot Act. At the sound of my whistle arrest the troublemakers. We'll not tolerate rioting and sedition. Not on our streets. Not on my watch.'

The ferry back to Harcourt Quay would not be until the tide turned. Crossing the street, I hurried towards St Mary's church, yet as I approached more men in ragged clothes started gathering by the railings. They were clearly starving, their boots held together by rags. A man with a placard began shouting. 'Selling us short is theft. We demand accurate measures. Come, 'tis time to march.'

He started leading the men away, a small crowd of onlookers walking tentatively behind them. Others joined from the sides, the crowd growing, walking quicker, surging forward, straight towards me. To avoid being caught, I squeezed against the railings, searching for a side alley. Glancing up, I saw *St Mary's Street*.

Father had often spoken of how he helped the Master of Truro Grammar School. He had turned down the offer of Master when we left for Dominica, but he used to tell me how his lectures had doubled the numbers. The school was in St Mary's Street and, looking around, I recognised the lane in Mama's drawing. The wall alongside was topped with iron railings, an arched gate leading to an inner courtyard, and a squat building had a bell tower and a wind vane exactly like her paintings. I read the brass plaque – *Master: Reverend Cornelius Cardew: Appointed 1777* – and could not believe my luck.

It was as if everything had pointed me there. Not luck, but The Fates intervening. Reverend Cardew was Master when Father was here and would remember him. I could ask him about endowments, he might even recommend my school to the parents of his pupils. Pulling the rope, a bell rang on the other side of the gate. Above me, the bells of St Mary's church sounded the half-hour.

No one answered and I knew I must wait until lessons ended. A patch of sun lit the wall and I leaned against it. We had left Bristol where I was born, and I was four when Mama had brought us home to St Feoca. Father had worked with Reverend Cardew for two years – two happy years when I became Aunt Hetty's shadow. Mama's two miscarriages kept her in poor health and Aunt Hetty had shielded me from their worries. Where she went, I went. What she studied, I studied. We were inseparable.

One day, it all ended: I overheard shouting, pleading, Grandfather's voice raised in anger. Grandmother was crying, the swish of Aunt Hetty's skirts as she strode across the room. The memory was so vivid, I could feel the tears burning my cheeks. Loud clanging made me open my eyes. The bell in the bell tower was ringing, the boys pouring into the courtyard. A tall youth in a smart jacket opened the gate and bowed. 'Who shall I say is asking for him?'

'Miss Woodville. From Miss Mitchell's school – St Feoca School for Young Ladies.'

The panelled corridor was devoid of windows, the flagstones scuffed and worn. Following the youth, he made me wait outside a heavy oak door and in the dim light I read the first five of the Ten Commandments. Two bewigged men scowled down at me from their elaborate gold frames, and more gold lettering framed the door – *Esse Quam Videri*. To be, rather than seem to be.

The youth returned, gripping his hand. 'Reverend Cardew says it's highly irregular, but he'll see you for *five* minutes.' Holding the door open, he ran swiftly down the corridor.

A voice sounded from within. 'Take a seat. I'm a busy man with work to do.' Sitting at his desk, Reverend Cardew's bald head was bent over a pile of books. Light shone through a small window, the room dark and musty, smelling of tobacco and leather. Bookcases lined the walls, papers spilling over, a mound of periodicals on the flagstones by a chair. 'I don't see people during the day, Miss . . . What was your name again?' A cane lay within easy reach of his right hand.

'Miss Pandora Woodville. I believe you knew my father.'

His hands clenched, his knuckles white. Jolting upright, his eyes above his half-rimmed glasses hardened. 'Woodville?' The steel in his voice matched his eyes. '*Pandora* . . . I remember that ridiculous name. That pretentious, ludicrous name. You think you can march in here . . .' His hand reached for the cane. 'How dare you come here! Has he sent you?'

'Sir . . . I beg you . . .'

'How dare you ask for my time! Leave this moment. I have *nothing* to say to you. Nothing. I made it quite clear to that impostor . . . to that liar . . . that fraudster James Woodville, that if he so much as enters my premises I'd have him arrested. And that goes for any spawn of his.'

I gripped the back of the seat. In the face of such vitriol, I felt the room sway. The anger in his eyes, the hatred in his voice. In his mid-fifties, his bald head gleamed with sweat. 'I'm sorry . . . You don't understand. My father spoke so highly of you.'

'I find that hard to believe!'

'Sir, your anger must be misplaced. My father, James Woodville, is a Cambridge scholar . . . he has a doctorate in Divinity. Might you be thinking of someone else?'

Standing up, his whip flicked against his open palm. 'Mr

James Woodville, assistant tutor to this school? My recollection of him is very clear. The man was a fraudster. Your father is a fraudster.'

'No . . . no.' I had to sit down. 'To slander my father's name like that—'

'Not slander. It's God's truth. And well he knew it.'

All air seemed sucked from the room. 'You are mistaken, sir. He's written several books. His thesis is highly acclaimed . . . it's stocked in academic libraries all over the world. His doctorate—'

'His doctorate was written and awarded to another man. Your father's *cousin*, I believe. A man five years his senior and also residing in Cambridge. A renowned and highly acclaimed scholar who your father knew *very well*. He grew up in his shadow and had the audacity to claim his work as his. Your father is a liar and a fraudster.'

'No . . . no . . .' I gripped the arms of the chair.

'Miss Woodville, I believe this has come as quite a shock.' A lessening of his anger, although the bitterness remained. 'Your father worked here under false pretences. He almost cost me my position.'

'No, sir. You are mistaken.'

'No. Listen to me! You need to know the truth. I was less qualified than he purported to be and was on the point of losing everything. Then, I found out – merely by chance – that he couldn't explain a reference in the work he said he'd written. So I did my research. I wrote to the *real* author of the work, and I received a long and erudite explanation. *From his cousin.*' The cane wrapped his palm. 'I was ready to have your father arrested. Horsewhipped. Gaoled for the fraudster he was. Only my regard for your grandfather held me in check.'

Words stuck in my throat. 'No one . . . knows . . . no one has ever known.'

'Your grandfather knew because I told him. Believe me, I told him. I knew your grandfather from my time in Exeter. He was a kind and generous patron to me. My wife was from Exeter and we knew him from the cathedral. He helped me obtain my curacy. But for your grandfather, your father would have been exposed as a lying fraudster.'

'My grandfather intervened?'

There was spittle on his chin, beads of sweat on his forehead. 'He pleaded for me to say nothing – he promised your father would leave Truro, immediately, and never return. And only because I owed your grandfather so much did I give way and promise to keep my silence.'

'Father left for Dominica – he's never come back.'

Reaching for a handkerchief, he wiped his forehead. 'So it should be. Yet he clearly continues to be a despicable liar. Good day, Miss Woodville. I believe you can understand why I want nothing more to do with you.'

I hardly knew how I left the room. Dizziness made me feel faint. Yet the more I stumbled, the more I believed him. Father was a fraud. A lying fraudster. Mama had always marked the pupils' work, not Father. First Mama, then me, the two of us preparing every lesson he gave; transcribing long passages of the *Iliad* and the *Odyssey*, wading through Herodotus and the teachings of Plato and Socrates. *We* corrected his pupils' translations. *We* did everything. Every piece of work he needed to complete handed straight to us because the day's teaching had *fatigued* him. Always an excuse why we should do it for him — always going out at night, always insisting he had evening lectures to give, evening classes to attend.

All those passages he could not explain. I tried to clear my thoughts. Yet it was blindingly obvious — Mama had taught me everything, not Father. Mama was the scholar. Mama, not Father. And there was more.

I told her I thought Father was untrustworthy, that he was with other women, yet Mama had dismissed my claims, telling me I was too judgemental. But I was right. There were never any evening lectures, no boys needed extra classes. He was not looking after the interests of his pupils but looking after his own interests. His own, licentious, interests.

The bright sunshine dazzled me. Mother must have known Father's lies would keep her from returning to St Feoca. All along, she knew she could never come home. A surge of nausea made me bend double. I must breathe, stop myself from retching. Father had lied every single day of my life and Mother had aided him, stringing me along with her praise and adoration of a man with absolutely no moral principles whatsoever.

Shouts echoed behind me, a group of women waving banners. They were bearing down on me, almost upon me, and I staggered forward trying to get out of their way. My arms were gripped by powerful hands, my body propelled to the beat of steady marching. A shout rang in my ear. 'We'll not be sold short. What do we want?'

Behind me, voices rose in unison. 'We want fair measures.'

I was marching with them, my steps keeping time; great angry strides sweeping us past the church and towards the market. The woman gripping my arm had gaunt cheeks and tattered clothes. Her eyes blazing, she shouted, 'What do we do to farmers who adulterate our corn?'

The returning cry was instant. 'We burn their barns.'

I tried to break free, but the iron grip tightened. 'What do we do to bakers who adulterate our bread?'

'We burn their shops.' This time their reply was louder, gaining in strength. Their shouts were growing fiercer, the heavy tread of boots gathering momentum. I hardly knew where I was going. Everything was a lie. *Everything*. Mama's whole life, her beauty, her intelligence, wasted on a lying philanderer.

A lying, philandering fraudster.

Chapter Sixteen

With little room to move, I was jostled from side to side. Jolted forward, it was all I could do to stay upright. Crammed behind tall hats and broad shoulders, the shouts dimmed to angry jeers. Through a small gap, I saw a man standing on a raised plinth outside the town hall. Holding up his hands, he attempted to get his voice heard. 'I hear your grievances. I hear them. Believe me, I am listening. I'll weigh these loaves and if I find—'

Shouts and whistles erupted from the sea of raised fists. A chant grew. 'Not *if*. Not *if*.'

Across the square, a man shouted down from a window. 'Listen, for once. Listen to what he's saying! Give the magistrate a chance.' He looked prosperous, smartly dressed, shouting at the crowd from a window above the bank.

'Who's he foolin'?' a voice sounded behind me. 'He should be down here . . . on that platform. Not skulkin' like a frightened rabbit. Mayor or no mayor, he's a coward.'

The chanting quietened to a murmur and the magistrate on

the platform tried again, this time with a megaphone. Holding up a piece of paper, his voice was educated, refined, edged with fear. 'I've received your complaints. I have names . . . and the incidences of forestalling you claim to have occurred.'

A voice rang across the crowd. 'Selling corn before it reaches the market is *against the law*. Storing corn to profit at a later date is *against the law*. We don't *claim* anything, sir. We're *telling* you the facts. Money's being made . . . people profiting while our children gather nettles an' fight dogs for potato peelings. Loaves at one shilling and tuppence – who can pay that? We're starving while the farmers prosper.'

Crushed on both sides, I tried to push my way through the shouts. A man's elbow caught my cheek and I winced in pain. A sudden surge forced me forward and a woman grabbed my arm. 'Take care, my love. Keep on yer feet. Stand steady, ye looked washed out.'

Once again, the voice boomed through the megaphone. 'Shortages are to blame. I don't need to tell you that. No corn is being stored. There's just *no corn*. I can find no adulteration of the flour. No chalk or grit's been added. The bakers aren't poisoning you. They're honest men with livings to make.' The rumble was growing again, the murmurs getting louder and a note of steel entered his voice. 'Go home. *Go home*. I have your list of grievances. *I will* see to it. *I will* investigate your claims. I will—'

The sound of crashing glass stopped him. To my right, a deafening shout. The crowd surged forward, and I felt myself almost lifted from my feet. A loud whistle, shouts, a woman was screaming, and I looked up. Red uniforms were forcing

155

their way towards us. 'There . . . that one. Those over there. That woman with the placard. Get that man . . . that one. Round them up.'

Like a wave, the crowd swept forward. I could hear punching, scuffling, angry grunts; a fight broke out, a man with blood dripping from his nose. I tried to break free but the woman beside me gripped my arm. 'Stay upright, my love. Don't stumble or ye'll be trampled.' In her other hand she raised her banner, waving it defiantly.

Another whistle blew, louder, closer, just behind me. I saw a flash of red and pulled myself free. Using my elbows I forced my way through the screaming crowd but a circle of red coats lined the buildings, each soldier with his musket raised. The officer in charge was standing on the platform. Pointing into the crowd I heard him shout. 'Get that woman – the one with the banner.'

My hand was gripped and I fought to free it. 'Pandora, it's me. Quick . . . this way.'

A man jolted me from behind and Benedict Aubyn's hand tightened. 'There are more soldiers behind the town hall. We need to take a side alley or we'll run straight into them. Keep your hood up – cover your face.'

Keeping my hand firmly in his, he forced his way through the heaving mass of people. Fighting to stay upright, I stumbled and nearly fell: a child on a man's shoulder knocked Benedict's hat off and, taller than everyone, he immediately ducked. 'They mustn't recognise us.' The crowd surged round us, almost pushing us over, and his arm tightened round my shoulders. 'Are you all right?'

I felt disorientated, my feet aching from the crush of heavy boots. 'Yes, I'm fine.'

'You look very pale. Your lip's bleeding. We have to get out of here.' I felt myself lifted in strong arms, heard his urgent shout. 'Follow me. This way. All of you, follow me. No... not that way. *Not that way*. You... come with me. All of you... *Come this way*.'

Free of the crush, he started walking, then running, leading the group of women down a narrow alley. At the entrance to the quayside, he stopped. 'Walk now. *Walk*. Throw away your banners and walk. They can't arrest you if you're walking peacefully.' His chest was heaving, his hair falling across his face. Pointing to his cart there was anger in his eyes. 'Arresting starving people!' I felt numb, unable to reply. All I could hear was Father's weasel excuses; see his false smiles, the contempt in his eyes as he looked at Mama.

Lowering me to the seat, Benedict gave a coin to the boy holding the reins. 'Stay on the quayside, Josh. Don't go anywhere near the market.'

The boy seemed pleased with his money. 'No, sir. Thank you, sir.'

All my life, witnessing Father's control over Mother, his manipulation of her thoughts, his clever use of rhetoric. Every day, convincing us we were lucky to live in the shadow of his shining intellect, yet it was Mama who was the clever one. Mama who wrote his lectures and planned his lessons. He was a sham, a fraudster, spewing nothing but deceit and falsehood every day of my life.

Reaching for his handkerchief, Benedict held it against my

lips. 'It's not a cut . . . it's a nose bleed. You've got quite a graze on your cheek. Does it hurt anywhere else?' I shook my head and his mouth tightened. 'It's all right, you don't have to say anything. I know you didn't have an appointment with Mrs Lilly because the moment the trouble started I went there to bring you back.' Flicking the reins, the mule started weaving through the people hurrying from the marketplace.

'It was an oversight on my part.'

Staring straight ahead, his mouth tightened. 'Or was it because you knew I wouldn't bring you to Truro to participate in a riot?'

A flame of anger burned my cheeks. 'I did *not* come here to participate in a riot. I was caught up in it—'

'Arm in arm with the woman leading the march? Miss Woodville, everyone saw you. How you weren't arrested, I'll never know! I've never seen anything so reckless.'

Fury filled me. 'Thank you, but I can do without your lectures. It was an oversight – circumstances outside my control. I'm grateful for your help but I can do *without any lectures*.'

Without his hat, his hair fell in unruly curls across his forehead. Sweeping them to one side, his cheeks were as flushed as mine, his hands tight on the reins. We were almost at the tollgate, the river fuller now the tide was rising. 'An oversight? Like needing to get to Penzance? Like using a false name?'

The crowd was thinning, though shouts still echoed from the marketplace. A woman walking alongside us looked up in obvious surprise. Smartly dressed in a fetching bonnet, she called out. 'Benedict . . . ? My goodness . . . it is you, isn't it?'

Swinging round, Benedict's frown turned to a broad smile. 'Meredith! How lovely to see you. I thought you were in Bath.' Behind us, a musket shot made the mule bolt and Benedict pulled on the reins. 'Stop . . . stop. Oh, I'm sorry . . . he won't stop.'

She was bright-eyed, smiling, jumping quickly back. 'How long have you been in Cornwall?' she shouted as we shot past.

Thrusting the reins in my hands, Benedict knelt backwards on the bench. 'A few months. Can I take you somewhere?'

'No . . . thank you . . .' I heard her shout back.

She must have been too far behind as he swung round again. No longer smiling, his hands clenched on his lap. The mule was behaving perfectly now, the road surface comfortable, and I bit back the words I was itching to say. *Another conquest, Mr Aubyn?*

Holding up his pass, the toll keeper ushered us from behind the steady stream of carts, allowing us to go first. Glancing round, Benedict was clearly still searching for Meredith and my anger returned: another poor woman who had fallen for his perfect manners and sad eyes. I flicked the reins. 'Might as well stay on the turnpike seeing as my reputation can't get any worse.'

'Why get involved?' His voice was harsh. 'Whatever justification for their claims – and we both know there's ample justification – the way they set about that protest is unlawful. There was well over a hundred people there. Presenting a list of grievances to the magistrate is one thing, but marching with placards is quite another. As for breaking windows and starting a riot . . .' Placing his head in his hands, he shook his head. 'You could have been arrested.'

'Well, I wasn't . . . and thank you for intervening, but most likely, I'd have found my way back to the quayside and caught the ferry home.'

He shook his head, a look of incredulity. 'I can't get the measure of you, Pandora. You were in great distress back there. It's as if you're not who you seem to be.'

Like a spark to tinder. Like oil on flames. I gripped the reins, fighting my fury. He sounded so like Father. *So like Father*. I could hardly see for the burning in my eyes. I tried to keep my voice steady but I felt like screaming. 'Don't lecture me on *being what I seem to be* – or not – as you so clearly think the case! I've had a life time of *Esse Quam Videri*. All I can take on how I should or should not behave, how I should be grateful for my education, how I've been given such opportunities.'

Adding fuel to the fire, he pointed to a boulder and seemed to brace himself.

Passing it with no mishap I drew a deep breath. 'I don't need to be told how to drive a mule – just as I don't need to be told how lucky I am to have the protection and influence of a learned man.'

'No . . . of course not. Consider that said. Nothing was further from my—'

'Every night translating that eternal bore Herodotus or Pompous Pericles with his dislike of women. But we're not to question that. Oh no, we're just to do as we're told. Well, shall I tell you something? I don't ever want to read another word of Latin or Greek. Never. Not *one word*. Ever. And as for the *Odyssey* – the great hero Odysseus! That liar and fraudster – perhaps that's where men get their behaviour from?'

I whipped the reins to go faster. 'We're to praise him, admire his prowess, honour him as a great hero, yet all the time he's a lying, cheating philanderer blaming the gods for his misfortune . . . the nymphs for being temptresses. There are just too many goddesses to keep him from returning to his poor wife slaving at home. Oh no, let's keep this journey going, this great Odyssey we're having. Let's promise we'll return but in the meantime I'll be worshipped and bedded by beautiful women who, despite my best attempts, lay spells on me. Not a whoring philanderer, but a victim of magical potions! After all, when a beautiful goddess lies naked at your feet, what can you do but succumb to her charms?'

He grabbed the reins. 'I think we'll come off here . . . we'll take this side lane. I'll stop by that tree.' Hot tears burned my cheeks. Bending forward, I held my head in my hands. Never had I shouted so angrily. Never cried so pitifully. The cart came to a stop, his voice soft. 'We're not talking about Odysseus, are we, Pandora? Did your husband treat you badly? Is that what you're really saying?'

I shook my head. 'I'm not married. I've never been married. Men don't marry women like me.'

'Who said that?' I shook my head and his voice grew stern. 'Who are we talking about, Pandora? Forgive me . . . I shouldn't have lectured you like that. It was overbearing and insensitive. But who are we talking about? Who are you so angry with?'

I kept my face covered, my shoulders heaving fiercely. I felt him dismount, his hand on my elbow helping me from the seat. 'I never cry. I never, ever cry.'

'Well, perhaps it's time you did. What's this all about,

Pandora? Was it because I sounded cross? I wasn't cross at all, just very anxious. Rioters and looters are dealt with extremely harshly.'

Ahead of us, the lane looked dry. Picking up my skirt I started striding away. To show him such weakness was embarrassing. I never cried. I was too strong to cry, too used to holding my head in the air, too used to letting their arrows bounce off my protective aegis, the god-protected shield I always carried.

He followed, leading the mule behind me. I could not stop but kept up my angry pace. The sun was still warm, the hedgerows full of catkins. A gate lay at the entrance to a field and I leaned against it, waiting for him to join me. 'You don't have to tell me anything, Pandora . . . but if you do, I can assure you I won't say anything. I promise I'm a willing and safe ear.'

A blackbird was singing on the hedge beside us. 'I'm not distressed any more. I'm perfectly composed now.' A tear rolled down my cheek, another, and another.

Reaching for his bloodstained handkerchief, he dabbed my eyes. 'I think we all need to talk more. Too many of us hide behind protective shells.'

Closing the gate, we walked side by side along the edge of the field. 'When Mrs Lilly wasn't at home, I thought to wait in the church . . . but then I saw I was near the grammar school and the Master was the same as when Father worked there. I thought to ask him about endowments. My father—' I stopped. 'I'm sorry, I can't tell you.'

'Of course. I understand. You don't have to say another word.' Looking down, the sun caught the shadows under his eyes. He looked tired, his cheeks every bit as gaunt as the protestors in the market. 'I believe Reverend Cardew sees no one during the day.'

There was such kindness in Benedict's eyes, a look of understanding, and my lips trembled. I was in great danger of bursting into tears again. 'Reverend Cardew agreed to see me, but he nearly threw me out. He as good as told me I was the spawn of the devil. He was very abrupt. He said Father was a liar and a fraud, that his qualifications were awarded to his cousin who bore the same name. And the worst of it is, I believe it's the truth. My whole life has been lived as a consequence of Father's deception.'

Benedict remained watching the lane, avoiding the water pooling in the ruts. 'I'm very sorry to hear this.'

'And what I feel is nothing but anger. Father was clearly too arrogant, too contemptuous, too stupid to think he'd be found out. Yet Grandfather found out and he made him leave. Within days of Grandfather knowing, we left for Dominica and I never understood why we couldn't come back. Until now.'

Reaching another gate, he seemed reluctant to open it. Leaning on it, he pointed to a small stream. 'A kingfisher. Did you see him?' I saw a flash of blue and smiled. 'This stream will have to be kept east of the new road. There's very little chance of it flooding but it would be a wise precaution.' His eyes caught mine, blue eyes full of understanding. No man had ever shown me such kindness. His voice was soft, not judgemental at all. 'A lot of stolen identity occurs – certainly, stolen papers and false claims to education. But that's not the reason you ran away, is it? You did run away, didn't you?' I bit my lip. Saying the words somehow made them true. Leaving them unsaid was far easier.

'It's all right,' he whispered. 'Don't answer. I didn't mean to pry.'

Yet I needed to say the words, to rid myself of the bile catching my throat. Because they were true, my life nothing but resentment and crossed fingers. 'Father treated Mother very badly. At first, I thought they were happy. I'd no inkling that Mother was unhappy. But two years ago, her health deteriorated – she developed a racking cough which never improved. She never grew strong again, and Father just stopped pretending. He was ruthless in his treatment of her and expected the same blind obedience from me. When I was eleven, he promised me we would return to St Feoca. Our bags were packed, I'd even written to my aunt to say we were coming, only the ship he took us on was bound for New York. Not Falmouth. And my letter was never posted.'

'How despicable. I'm so sorry to hear this.'

'He's lied all my life. The promotions he boasted of must have all been fabricated but I believed him. I believed everyone was clamouring for his skills. I should have seen through him. It took less and less time for his employers to give him notice – his periods of employment grew shorter, but worse still...' For the first time in my life, I was speaking the truth, not hiding my feelings: it was like lancing a boil. Like allowing out the poison.

'You don't have to tell me if you don't want to.'

'There was always a woman we had to leave behind. We

were always packing our bags, leaving island after island, city after city. Our very own *Odyssey*, he laughingly called it! And all the time my poor mother was growing weaker and less able to cope.'

'I understand your anger and your hurt.' Making his way to the stream, he washed his handkerchief, and returned to dab it on my cheek. 'You have a bruise developing.' He paused. 'Pandora . . . it's none of my business, but does your aunt know any of this?'

His fingers brushed my cheek. 'No, I can't tell her. And I can't tell her about the riot. I'll just say I caught my cheek.'

'I think you should tell her the truth about both.'

I shook my head. 'I can't. Mama made me promise. She never blamed Father. What I saw as weakness, she saw as strength. Her duty. Her stupid, ridiculous pride. Which meant keeping the truth from my aunt because the truth would upset her too much. Aunt Harriet needs to think my mother was happy. I promised Mama.'

'Then you'll just perpetuate your father's lies and never be free from him. I think you should unburden yourself of all this and tell Miss Mitchell the truth.'

'*Esse Quam Videri*. Not live a lie. I suppose you were a Truro school boy?'

He smiled his half-smile, sudden pain in his eyes. 'No, I was tutored at home. First by my mother, then by my father. I learned everything from them.'

We walked on in silence, the school tower ahead of us bathed in sunshine: a glorious spring afternoon with the scent of new growth, warm earth, a hint of salt on the breeze. We were almost touching, our strides in step. Behind us, the mule started to pick up speed. 'He's ready for home.' At the last gate, he stopped. 'See that path? It cuts across to the school. It'll save you having to walk up from the gatehouse.' His eyes held mine. Blue eyes, speckled with grey. 'You will tell your aunt the truth, won't you? Otherwise your father will continue to have control over you.'

I hardly knew what to say. For some reason, I wanted to stay exactly where I was, leaning on the gate with him, watching the shadows cross the parkland. Never had anyone been so understanding, so solicitous of my well-being. Yet I knew to reach for my aegis, hold my trusted shield against my heart. 'Thank you for your kindness, Mr Aubyn. But we mustn't speak of this again.' I began walking, my feet aching, my toes crushed from being trodden on in the crowd. Behind me, his voice sounded urgent.

'Pandora, there's something you need to know. Mrs Angelica Trevelyan is the owner of the Trevelyan Shipping Line. I believe you met her at Trenwyn House. I don't know for certain, but I believe she would have seen your name on the log book – or rather, your borrowed name.'

My heart jolted, but for a very different reason. 'Who told you I met Angelica Trevelyan at Trenwyn House?'

My sharp tone made his cheeks colour. He looked at his hands. 'I think maybe Grace might have mentioned it.'

'During one of your deliveries to the barn?'

I could not help it, the wasp in me was back. I had the measure of men. Sting or be stung. The evening sun was glinting on the windows of St Feoca and I strode forward, my back to him. I had made a foolish mistake. Convincing me of his sincerity like that, making me enjoy his company. Walking side by side, leaning on the gate like that. His gentle touch as he bathed my cheek.

I had been stung too many times to know him any different.

Chapter Seventeen

I could tell by their downward glances that Aunt Hetty must be furious. Susan continued bustling from cupboard to cupboard, her lips pursed. Taking the last of the potatoes from a large basket she held it up. 'Mr Cador Ferris brought these himself. Honest to God, he looked that disappointed when you weren't here.'

Annie held up two rabbits. On the table, a brace of pheasants lay staring through glazed eyes. 'He came in his curricle. He must have been hoping to take you for a ride around the park. He's a very thoughtful young man – extremely kind to come all this way with so much produce.'

Again their downward looks. Grace held up a small sack. 'He brought these beans for you to plant in your garden and the biggest bunch of orchids. I've taken them upstairs. He was very insistent you should enjoy them in your room.'

Finally, Annie spoke their thoughts. 'And us having to say you were indisposed with a headache and couldn't see him!'

'Mr Cador Ferris needs to know I'm free to leave the school

– especially as I didn't know he was coming. Going to Truro is hardly a sin!'

Silence greeted my fierce tone. Susan reached for her hat and cloak. 'You'd better go to Miss Mitchell. She's been pacing her floor all day.' She stared at my cheek. 'That looks sore – it's red and swollen. How did that happen?'

Instinctively, I crossed my fingers behind my back. 'There was a riot in the market – a sudden skirmish and I received a blow.'

Sucking in her breath, she shook her head. 'Miss Mitchell won't like that. Best keep yer face from the light.'

I hardly dared go up her stairs but stood on the bottom step, Benedict's words turning in my mind. *Then you'll just perpetuate your father's lies and never be free from him.* He was right. There should be no more crossed fingers, no more lies. It was time to tell Aunt Hetty the truth.

'Continue . . .' Aunt Hetty remained at her window, staring at the gathering dusk. She turned her gold locket in her fingers. 'So you decided to run away?'

'When Mama became ill, I took over her work. Her expertise in mending was our biggest income. Father was always out and I preferred it that way.'

'She never danced and dined in Government House?'

'No, Aunt Hetty. Never. And I never painted butterflies with the Governor's daughters. They didn't know I existed. Or if they did, they despised me.'

A pulse throbbed in her neck. She swallowed. 'Continue . . .'

'I never told Mama I followed Father that day. I still have no idea if she knew. After she died, he moved in with this other family. I believe the child is his, though I never asked. One night, we had a terrible row. He expected me to continue marking his pupils' work and preparing his lectures. He knew enough to teach but he was lazy. He had me, so why not use me? I hated his hold on Mama. He controlled her every move. All my life I was scared of him but I would never leave Mama because I had to protect her. And she would never leave Father. But that day . . . when I saw him greeted at the door by that other woman . . . when the child ran to him and he picked him up in his arms . . . I was furious. So angry. I could have rushed at him and scratched out his eyes. And the worst was . . .'

'Continue . . . Don't spare me.'

'He just smiled and laughed at me. Then one night, he told me he'd obtained a position for me as a governess in a family who would be *useful* to him. I was to sail to Jamaica and he and his new family would follow. I buried Mama and agreed to his plan, thanking him, telling him I would pack my bags and be ready to leave.'

'Who's Mrs Marshall? You used her papers.'

Sudden weakness almost made my legs buckle. 'You knew?'

'Mrs Trevelyan told me on the terrace when you were speaking to Reverend Penhaligan. She owns the ship you sailed on. She was there when it arrived and went through the ship's log. She told me your name wasn't on the log – only a *Mrs Marshall* was on board. How did you obtain false papers?'

'Mama obtained them. The day she died, she could barely speak but held her locket and pointed to her bottom drawer.

Hanging on the chain next to her locket was a brass key and in the drawer I found a box. The papers were in there. She'd changed the date to the year of my birth. There was a ring, and money.' Tears rolled down my cheek. 'Inside was a note, *Go to Aunt Hetty. Tell her I'm sorry. Tell her I love her.*'

Reaching for her handkerchief, she wiped her eyes. 'Continue, please, Pandora . . .'

'It was as if The Fates had decreed I should escape. Father kept our identity papers. It was how he controlled us. He put us to work and he took and spent our earnings. He bought my ticket to Jamaica and kept hold of my papers. He insisted on taking me to the quayside to oversee my luggage on to the ship. He handed my ticket and papers to the captain for *safekeeping* and waited with me on the deck. I told him I had a headache and needed to lie down . . . that I wouldn't wave him goodbye but I'd get settled in my bunk. He was so sure of his control over me, he just left me and I watched him walk away and buy a bouquet of flowers on the quayside. After a short while, I picked up my bag and walked off the ship and hid for a night behind a pile of barrels. The *Jane O'Leary* was nearly ready to sail. I had booked my ticket the week previously and they were expecting me. I had to lie about my luggage being stolen.'

She blew her nose. 'So everything about loving your father and him coming here was a lie. You ran from him and have made it very hard for him to know where you are. You were to *vanish* from the ship mid-passage?'

'Yes. The captain had my papers. For all intents and purposes I was onboard his ship.'

171

'And here I was, convinced it was your father who'd sent you! You must forgive me, Pandora. I thought he was waiting out of sight, lurking as he always did with that irritating, sly smile which made my blood run cold. Waiting for me to be ruined so he could take over my school. I believe that's what your father always intended.'

I shuddered. 'Why do you say that?'

'Because I know your father's powers of manipulation. I'm not a fool, Pandora. Your mother shielded me from the truth because she loved me. She was in the grip of that man – *enthralled* in the truest sense of the word – and I thought you were as well. Well, anyway, here we have it. You shall write to him directly.'

'I can't! He mustn't know where I am.'

She shrugged, reaching across the desk for her quill. 'Then I shall write to him. My letter will be clear. I shall tell him that, *after* Reverend Cardew has had him horsewhipped and exposed as a fraudster, he shall have me to face. I shall tell him that he's *never* to contact you again, other than to leave you money in his will – in lieu of the payment he owes you for your years of hard work.'

Her eyes brimmed with love. 'But I'll have to explain why my niece came here under false papers. We shall tell Mrs Trevelyan the truth, of course.' She smiled. 'Even so, it's best we have proof of who you say you are. I'll write to the parish where you were baptised and ask for a record of your birth. Why were you limping when you came in?'

'My foot was stamped on . . . these shoes are very flimsy.'

Her pen scratched the paper. 'Perhaps it's better if you stay away from church tomorrow with that graze on your cheek, though the thought you're still unwell will have Cador Ferris rushing here with a physician. You've made quite a conquest, my dear. Three vases of orchids?'

I opened the door and her voice turned serious. 'I meant what I said, Pandora. Running a school like this requires sacrifice – heaven knows, I can vouch for that. You must take your time and consider things very carefully. The choice is either marriage or to be headmistress of St Feoca School. You can't have both.'

Despite my blurred vision, my voice was firm. 'Headmistress of St Feoca School.'

The candles in my room were lit, the fire roaring. On each table a crystal vase was filled with orchids. Next to one was a note with an embossed crest at the top.

Dear Miss Woodville,

   Olwyn and I hope these orchids remind you of your childhood in Government House.

            Yours in friendship,
                Cador Ferris

A tentative knock made me swing round. 'Grace?'

'May I come in?' Her long blonde hair caught the candlelight, her face pale, her eyes glistening. She remained clutching her candlestick, staring at the orchids. Even more beautiful in the glow of the candle, her hair hung loose around her shoulders, her eyelashes dark against her pale skin. 'I don't know what to do about church. I don't want to get it wrong.'

A log crackled, a flame leaped. 'Get what wrong?'

'I've been teaching the girls how to walk in line – you know, how to keep their shoulders and backs straight. Mollie's joined us from the mill so now there are *four* in the school. And that makes for a very neat procession . . . only, we used to wear velvet caps and black leather gloves in the winter, and straw hats and white cotton gloves in the summer. And capes. We keep the capes very carefully . . . they're beautiful red capes which we keep hanging among the hot pipes . . . and I thought.' She stared at the orchids, biting her beautiful rosebud lip.

She took a deep breath. 'Only Annie and Susan warned me not to be too precipitous.' She glanced at Cador's note resting against the vase. 'I've sorted the capes and hats and found gloves to fit the girls but when I asked Miss Mitchell if the girls could wear them to church she told me it was not her decision to make.'

I remained staring into the fire. Blowing her nose, her chin rose. 'I don't mean to sound so wretched. Only I thought Miss Mitchell meant it was *my* decision but just now, I realise she meant it was *your* decision if the school is to go ahead. And it's very insensitive of me to want something so badly when I've already been given so much.'

She looked vulnerable, no more than a child. Mama had been her age when she fell in love with Father but unlike Mama, Grace was desperate to stay in the only home she knew.

'Of course they must wear gloves and capes. And velvet hats. And walk in a procession. Our school is *not* going to close, Grace. Soon, we'll have a long list of girls wanting to join us.' I crossed my fingers behind my back. 'We've got no end of patrons interested in offering us endowments.'

She clasped her mouth. 'Oh, Pandora! I'm so happy.'

Smiling, I shrugged my shoulders. 'Take one of the vases . . . in fact, take them all. Orchids like this should be enjoyed by everyone. It's selfish of me to keep them in my room.'

The embers were glowing, the log basket empty. The last of my candles guttered, yet still I could not go to bed. My grief was always more painful in the dark; not lessening, it seemed to be growing worse. The clock had just chimed two; I needed to sleep, not pace the room.

Drawing back the shutter, I stared at the silent lawn. Mama would have stood looking out of the window just like this. She would have stood exactly where I was standing, her life ahead of her, the prospect of two very different paths with two very different men. My sense of emptiness seemed overwhelming, a huge vacuum where once I had felt such love. Mother must have known about Father's deception.

The night was dark, the faintest glimmer of moonlight, the leafless branches swaying in the breeze. Peering into the darkness, a movement caught my eye. The poacher was back. Scanning the hedgerow, I tried to follow his path. A patch of light illuminated his back and I saw the same man running along the perimeter: the same man with the same furtive intent.

This was no poacher. This was a thief. What if Annie had been wandering? What if she had left the back door unlocked?

Chapter Eighteen

The hall was in darkness. So, too, the corridor to the kitchen. Faint moonlight filtered across the pine table and I reached for the tinder box, striking it with trembling fingers. As I feared, the back door was unlocked and, reaching for the key, I turned it swiftly. The embers in the range were still glowing, Annie's clothes hanging over the airer in readiness for the morning. The kitchen looked undisturbed and I breathed deeply. I was being fanciful, that was all. It was just Annie's forgetfulness, just a poacher running from the woods.

Yet the room felt cold, as if a blast of wind had recently blown through it. Lifting my candle, I caught my breath. Damp footprints led to the larder door and I braced myself, knowing we had been burgled. The shelves were bare, the vegetables gone. The basket of eggs lay empty, the two pheasants no longer hanging by their necks.

Nothing else seemed disturbed. Annie's door was shut and I opened it gently, relief flooding through me at the sound of her gentle snoring. A glass with a thick ruby stain lay on her bedside table, the contents of sweet-smelling spirit still lingering. A sound behind me made me jump and I almost screamed. Someone was in the kitchen. Yet all the doors were closed.

He could be hiding under the table, or in the scullery. He could be in the main kitchen or the laundry room. Confront him, and I would be in danger. I must open the door and let him run free. Rushing to the back door, my fingers fumbled with the key. Flinging it wide, I knew to sound firm. 'Leave now. Leave. I know you're in here. Leave now and *never* steal from us again.'

The noise came again, louder, more frantic. It was coming from the pickle cupboard where Annie kept her jars. No one could hide in there, the shelves were too narrow. So not a man, maybe a mouse? The noise grew louder, a frantic scratching – more like a rat, by the sound of the scuffle. Slipping the catch, I jumped back in fright. An enormous black bird was staring at me, his wings fanning my face, and I dodged away, his talons just missing me, scraping my nightcap. Cawing and croaking, he began circling the room, knocking against the shelves, sending cups flying off the dresser.

His powerful wings rustled above my head, his cries raucous, angry, filled with malice. Settling on the dresser, his beady eyes were staring at me as if he wished me harm. Stifling my scream, I backed against the wall and grabbed a towel drying by the fire. Flapping the towel I shouted, 'Get out . . . get out.' He took flight again, circling the room, his claws stretched out as if to grab me. Knocking into the window, he thumped against the glass and I flapped the towel again, forcing him through the door.

I could not stop shaking. With trembling hands, I locked the door and began collecting up the debris, replacing the pewter cups on the shelves, brushing up the broken glass. There must be no trace for Annie and Susan to find in the morning. Grace must never know, or her terror would return. Repositioning the chairs, I hung up the towel and searched the room. About to leave, I saw a huge black feather lying by the grate and I reached for it, hardly wanting to touch it. Burning it in the embers would create too much of a smell, but neither could I risk hiding it. Deciding to bring it with me, I jumped as the clock struck three.

This was not the work of the devil. This was the work of the man running along the edge of the lawn. My candle flickered and I reached for the silver candelabra, lighting all four candles with trembling hands. I would tell Aunt Hetty, only Aunt Hetty: the others must think it was just a theft.

Grateful for the extra light, I crossed the hall and started ascending the stairs. The twisted spindles were casting shadows against the wall and as I drew nearer, I tried to make sense of what I saw. The shadows seemed to be playing tricks: strange shapes looked to be hanging between the banisters. The shapes grew sharper, now unmistakable. Flickering against the wall lay the shadows of three women hanging by their necks.

Steadying myself, I held up my candles and began edging closer. They were dolls. Hideous dolls with pale wax faces and bulging eyes, their mouths twisted in grotesque grimaces.

Two were dressed in black, one had brown hair and a thin silver streak, the other, a band around her forehead. The third doll, dressed in grey, had long blonde hair, cupid red lips and staring blue eyes. All three had nails hammered through their chests. There was red paint on the nails, the nooses round their necks tied in a hangman's knot.

Sinking to the stairs, I fought to breathe. Sickness made my stomach heave. *This is not the work of the devil: this is the work of an evil man.* Moments ago he had been in the house, and on these stairs. I had to put my head on my lap to fight my dizziness. A drop of water glistened on the stair beside me, more drops on the step above: it must be the rain dripping from his coat. The garish faces were staring at me and I knew I must summon up the courage to return to the kitchen for a knife to cut them down.

Yet I stayed rooted in fear. Further raindrops glistened on the steps above. His coat had been dripping on the stairs, yet in the kitchen there were only signs of damp footprints. The drips were coming *down* the stairs, not up them. He had walked past our rooms, past Aunt Hetty, or had he gone up her stairs? Keeping my candles low, I followed the glistening drops. I could hardly see in the shadows. Candlelight glinted on the polished wood yet her steps seemed dry. Running up them, I knocked on her bedroom door, opening it just wide enough for her to hear. 'Aunt Hetty . . . Aunt Hetty . . . we've had a theft. Only it's not a theft, it's the terror starting again.'

She woke, puzzled, her eyes widening as I told her what I had found. Reaching for her dressing gown, she slipped on her slippers. 'Where do the drips lead?'

'Further along the corridor. He must have come through a window.'

Her hair hung loose around her shoulders, her eyes steely in the candles' glow. Tying her dressing gown she lit more candles. 'Come.'

'Has this happened before?'

'There's never been anyone *inside* the school before. A doll was found hanging in the chapel. . . and the sheep down the well. Several dead rooks and ravens were found in fireplaces. A chough was found hanging in the woods. Mainly just sightings at the window. Girls can be very fanciful and it was hard to know what was real and what imagined.'

Following her downstairs, she paused outside Grace's door. 'The drips don't linger – he went straight past her. They're coming along here, which means he crossed the arch so must have come from the tower. It's lucky you saw him running away – any later and these drips would have dried.' Stopping at the circular stairs, she held up her candle. 'Yes. He's come down here.' Her voice hardened. 'He's come from the top of the tower.'

'I've seen him run away before. It's not the first time the kitchen door's been found unlocked. Susan told me it's happened several times – with Annie still in bed.'

The door to the study was shut. Examining the windows, she tried each in turn. 'The latches are all secure. He must have locked it behind him. How did he get in?'

I studied the windows. 'There are signs of scraping on this one – a thin blade can often lift a latch. Once up the fire escape he'd have had plenty of time to work on the windows.'

Taking a deep breath, she studied the room. 'There's no sign of rain pooling. The trail leads straight from this window down the stairs. He hasn't stopped, which means he knows exactly where to go. Which makes me think he's been here before.' Returning to the desk, she opened the top drawer. 'He's probably sat here and read all our personal accounts.'

'But why start terrorising us again?'

Aunt Hetty drew her arms around her chest, as if shielding herself from sudden cold. Despite her frown, she looked younger with her hair loose, her satin dressing gown shimmering in the candlelight. 'Because he's heard we've restarted the school and he's determined that won't happen.'

'But who can be so vindictive?' It was not just the coldness of the room making us shiver.

She swung round. 'St Feoca estate is worth a fortune – I'm not as naive as people think. They want my mineral rights. They want a fast and efficient route to export their tin and copper and they need access to the creek – and out to sea. The new owner of Harcourt Quay hasn't bought it to sit fishing on it all day!'

'Who exactly are we up against, Aunt Hetty?'

Her frown deepened. 'All of them. All think to come trampling over my land for rich pickings.' Turning, she held out her hand. 'I'll take that feather ... I'll take down the dolls and keep them hidden. You said Annie slept through it all?'

'She was sound asleep ... helped by some brandy. I think Annie likes a nightcap.'

'Just as well.' Her mouth was tight, her eyes searching the

room. Outside the wind was whistling, a fresh burst of rain lashing against the windowpanes.

'Shall we get new locks fitted to the windows?'

She nodded. 'And bolts across the door on the other side. We need to feel safe. I'll check the windows and doors every night.'

Chapter Nineteen

Church bells were ringing, the sky grey and overcast. Wrapping my apron round me, I sought sanctuary in the garden. Aunt Hetty had reassured everyone the poacher had run away, that with better vigilance and with her taking responsibility for locking the doors at night, there could be no more thefts of food. The matter was now closed and Susan would go to Falmouth to buy more provisions.

With everyone at church I was on my own in the garden, yet not alone. It was as if Grandfather and Grandmother were in the rustle of the wind, the scent of the jasmine, the clump of primroses beneath the sundial. The blackbird was singing, the robin never less than three feet away, and I breathed in the smell of damp earth. Cador Ferris had been more than generous: Gwen and Sophie had planted his sprouting potatoes and I would plant the beans and peas.

'No...no... out you go.' Rehoused to a coop by the barn, the chickens were now confined to the yard and I shooed them out, shutting the gate behind them. Staring at the well, my stomach tightened. Fury filled me. No one must ever violate Grandfather's garden again. No one.

They would have started the service by now. Slipping off my apron, I locked the gate, my boots leaving clumps of mud as I crossed the courtyard. He would have run this way, cutting behind the washhouse, slipping past the mangle and washing lines to the lawn behind. Too much rain had fallen to be sure of his footprints but even so, I caught his trail. The grass was indented, churned at the gate, a definite set of steps running alongside the wood. Glimpses of the creek showed through the trees; the tide was still out, the banks muddy.

The trail ended at a stile, a track leading through the woods. Heavier boots than mine had recently passed this way and I stopped to look. Not one set, but two running side by side towards the shore road. Overhanging branches made the ground dry and I stopped, unsure which way they had gone. A broken twig to my left meant they must have gone that way. The footprints appeared again, growing deeper, the hedge now a fence, the way blocked by a field gate. By the depth of their prints, I could see they had vaulted it. Two fit and healthy men.

The shore road was deserted, so too the quay. Two fishing boats lay against the wharf, several others beached along the shore. No one was on the quayside, the shutters of the businesses closed and barred. Rain had washed the cobbles and following any further trail looked doubtful.

A pile of stones blocked one exit, the other road led straight to St Feock, but would they risk running through the village? Turning to go, I looked back at the pile of stones. There looked to be an indentation on the top, in fact several indentations, as if someone had recently climbed them. Checking no one was watching, I picked up my skirt and scrambled over the top, sliding down the other side to a clear set of footprints. They must have run along the shore towards the small jetty and I stared at the muddy bank, fighting my disappointment. Of course they would not have led to a house.

A bird called across the water, another answered back. Then stillness, just the lapping of the water against a fallen tree trunk. It was so beautiful even in the dull light, and I started walking along the shore – the entrance to Mama's creek. Birds were singing in the wood, waders scuttling across the glistening banks, and I kept walking as if in my dreams. The thatched roof of the watermill was just visible through the trees, a boat bobbing on the end of a rope.

The sound of braying made me stop. Scampering up the bank, I heard it again. On the edge of the woods, George's mule stood harnessed to a cart, the reins dragging on the ground. Walking towards him, the mule backed away, shaking his head. 'Steady, now. Steady.' I could see the wheels of the cart had left a mark on a track through the wood. The wood set with traps where George Penrose had nearly severed his foot. 'Is anyone hurt?' As if in answer the mule threw back his head, whinnying in distress.

Tying the reins to a tree, I broke off a stout branch to use as a pole and began walking down the track. I shouted louder. 'Is anyone hurt?' Thickets of brambles lined my way, the canopy thick above me. Ivy hung from the trees, the track

185

getting thinner, yet the wheel marks went deeper and I called again. 'Is anyone there?'

A shout answered. 'Yes . . . down here.' The voice seemed to come from below me.

Stamping my pole before I trod, I followed the voice through the thicket. 'Over here . . . but be careful.' There was nothing to see and I edged closer. Hidden behind a dense bush, I saw the ridge of a gully and I peered down a steep shaft. Hands and feet splayed like a spider, Benedict was halfway up it. He looked up, smiling from under his dishevelled hair. 'Careful, the edge might crumble.'

Stepping back, I peered over again. His shirtsleeves were rolled to his elbows, a coil of rope slung across his shoulders. A small pickaxe and a bag bulging with stones hung from his leather belt. Inching his way up the almost vertical gulley, he reached first for a hand grip then for a foothold. Straightening at the top, he wiped the mud from his hands. 'What brings you to these woods when everyone's in church?' His smile was rueful, a slight rise to his eyebrow.

'Aunt Harriet thought my bruise would draw too much attention so advised me against going.'

My cheeks burned under his scrutiny. 'It does look very sore.' Our eyes caught. Gentle, kind, eyes filled with approbation, and I fought a rush of pleasure. His cheeks were pale, his hair swept back; tall, thin, too gaunt, his hair too long, his eyes just a little bit too narrow.

I removed some leaves from my gown. 'Surveying on a Sunday?'

He shrugged, his shirt open at the neck, his prominent

Adam's apple moving as he swallowed. Reaching forward, he put his hand on my arm. 'Come back from the edge. There's a danger of slippage.'

Pulling on his jacket, we walked side by side, the path growing wider as the trees began to thin. Wood garlic and early bluebells lined our way, the wide waters of Carrick Roads stretching before us. The tide was in, only the thinnest strip of shore glistening at the water's edge. Flinging his bag of stones into the cart, he patted the mule. 'Now then, you. No more running away...' Straightening his necktie, he stared across the water. 'I don't know which I prefer, the tide in or out. Both are beautiful.'

I bent to pick up some shells. 'My mother loved this wood... and this creek. Grandfather told her the wood was full of treasure but I think he meant we each have our own idea of treasure – mine is finding these empty shells. Oyster shells are best.'

'You paint very well, Pandora. Have you ever thought of developing your talent?' I said nothing and he looked away. An old brick wall was half-obscured by brambles. 'This must be part of the old quay. Yes... look, Tudor bricks. That wasn't a gulley I was down, it's part of the old workings – part of a disused shaft.' The clouds had lessened, a brightness to the sky. Ships were sailing up the river, the outline of Pendennis Castle just visible. 'Did you come to watch the birds? Tallacks Creek is particularly peaceful, don't you think?'

We stood staring across the silent water. 'Benedict – I'm glad we have this chance to talk. Only, yesterday, I told you things I should never have told you. Not to a stranger . . . not to anyone.'

The warmth in his eyes was disconcerting. 'You were shocked. What you had just learned was very distressing. It's natural you needed to speak of it. I only hope I was able to help.'

A blush made my eyes water. 'What I said was very *intimate*. I'd like you never to speak of it to anyone.'

'You've no reason to ask that. You already have my word.' His voice was sharp, accompanied by a frown.

'And I must thank you for your advice. You were right. My aunt needed to know. So much better to tell the truth.' My throat felt tight, I was in grave danger of crying. The horrific dolls had kept me awake, the thought of such evil making me shiver.

He pointed across the water. 'An egret . . . and a heron. That's a curlew.'

Biting my lip, I stared across to Falmouth. A fisherman was throwing out his net, the surface rippling, gulls dipping and disappearing beneath the water. The air smelled of distant woodsmoke and I fought my emptiness. 'Is that yawl dredging for oysters?'

He nodded. 'Pandora, you've made your dress very dirty on my account – your boots are caked in mud. May I help you clean them?'

'No, thank you – I was muddy before. This is my old gown and my working boots. I was gardening when I decided to go for a walk.'

He looked away. 'You're a keen gardener?'

'I know nothing about gardens but I'm going to restore Grandfather's garden. Apparently he kept saying, *But we must cultivate our garden*; and so I will – for him. I remember him wearing a leather apron and digging the beds.' I was talking too fast. Trying to sound buoyant.

He turned and I avoided his eyes. 'That's from *Candide* – it's how the book ends. Have you read Voltaire's *Candide*?' I shook my head. 'You might enjoy it. It's a satire. A group of characters set off to find Eldorado because they hear the streets are lined with gold. They pit their wits against every extreme and in the end decide all the riches they could possibly want can be found in a garden. No one needs to circumnavigate the world to find gold.' He coughed. 'I'm sorry. That was very insensitive of me.'

His words echoed the emptiness I was already feeling. How could Mama leave somewhere so perfect for a fraudster, a cheat and a liar? 'My childhood wasn't unhappy,' I managed to say. 'But I often felt excluded. My parents would laugh and smile in a secret world of their own. Mama never implied she was unhappy. Not at first.'

'Maybe they were happy. When you love someone so deeply...'

I could not look at him. 'I think Mother was scared of Father. I think the prospect of him leaving her made her...' My throat was too tight to continue. 'I'm sorry, I have to go.'

Rushing from him, he called after me. 'May I see you safely home? Let me take you in the cart.'

I could not stop; my tears were flowing too freely. I had never spoken such words, I had hardly dared think them, yet the truth was staring me in the face. All these years, Mother had been hiding her pain from me, just as she had been hiding the truth from Aunt Hetty.

Aunt Hetty shook her head at my soiled hem, though she relented and smiled. 'You were missed in church this morning; Cador and Olwyn were most concerned. I told them it was only a minor indisposition and you'd soon be well again, which pleased them no end.'

I smiled back. 'How kind of them to be so attentive.'

'Not only that. Olwyn's asked you to join her on a visit to Falmouth for her birthday. She's eighteen on Tuesday and Cador is to take her shopping. They plan to have lunch at the Ship Inn and I said you'd be delighted to join them.' A tingle of trepidation, and I bit my lip: to be singled out for such a special occasion was almost overwhelming. I must have looked scared as Aunt Hetty added, 'They've asked you because they clearly enjoy your company. It's important to make friends of your own age – they're our closest neighbours and I think Olwyn would love your company. A visit to the shops will do you both good.'

Chapter Twenty

Tuesday 31st March 1801, 10:00 a.m.

Aunt Hetty accompanied me to the quayside where we waited for Cador and Olwyn. Wrapped in my warm cloak, I felt almost too hot in the spring sunshine. Shielding my eyes against the dazzle, I breathed in the beauty of the day. The tide was high, the sun glinting like tiny mirrors on the surface of the water. A slight breeze was blowing. 'The wind's from the north-west. Perfect for Falmouth.'

Beneath my cloak my bag held a purse containing ten shillings, my handkerchief and a carefully wrapped shell for Olwyn. Aunt Hetty had insisted I was to buy something to remember the day, some ribbons or buttons, or laces for my stout shoes, and my excitement was mounting. They came into view and I waved. Olwyn was sitting, Cador standing up, holding the tiller of a sleek, well-polished boat. Above them a single sail arched then swung loose as Cador let out the rope. Drifting to our side, both smiled in greeting.

'Happy birthday, Miss Ferris.'

'Thank you, Miss Woodville. Good morning, Miss Mitchell,

isn't it a glorious morning? We've just the right wind for our sail.' She was warmly dressed, a beautiful blue bonnet shielding her face from the sun. Cador secured a rope round the hook and held out his hand to help me aboard.

'We'll drift with the current and the wind. Are you used to sailing?'

I slipped in next to Olwyn, trying not to tip the boat. 'No. This is to be a real adventure.'

Both seemed pleased with my answer, both smiling, fussing over me, making sure I was comfortable. Cador pulled on a rope: the sail went taut and curved to one side. The pull of the wind made the bow turn and we slipped from the quay. 'Falmouth, here we come.' As if free from all constraint, his hair ruffled, his jacket undone, he smiled at Aunt Hetty. 'I promise I'll bring Miss Woodville back in one piece, Miss Mitchell.'

A seagull circled above us, a cormorant diving deep beneath the water. Woodsmoke from the charcoal burners drifted on the air, the sail filling, the boat leaning. Olwyn was clearly trying not to look at the bruise on my cheek. 'We missed you at church. We were worried you might not be well enough to come.'

'I wasn't unwell . . . only a book fell from the top shelf and caught my cheek. I was rather too embarrassed to be seen.'

She smiled in understanding, and we gripped the side as we picked up speed. I felt like pinching myself. For the first time I was not dreaming, not watching from the shore. Not fabricating a story, not imagining what I would love to be doing. I was on the water, feeling the sun on my cheeks, relishing the splash of water against the bow.

Cador remained standing, his words blown by the wind. 'That's Mylor church. It's too shallow here for large ships, but we're fine. We'll skirt round those anchored naval frigates. Whoops!' Foam sprayed across the bow and we screamed in delight. Never had I felt such freedom. Never laughed with such pleasure.

'Cador! You're drenching us.' Olwyn gripped the side, laughing as the sail tugged and the boat tipped. She raised her eyes heavenward, but I could tell she was loving it every bit as much as I was. Rounding the Flushing promontory, the harbour of Falmouth lay glistening in the sun.

'I'll tie up at the Ship Inn. It's where the Flushing ferry leaves but there's usually space. They should operate a ferry direct to Harcourt Quay – I can't think why there isn't one already.'

Falmouth harbour teemed with ships and I scanned the flags. Some were naval frigates or brigs, most were yawls or luggers loading timber. Others looked to be fishing vessels. Relieved the *Jane O'Leary* was no longer in port, I began to relax and enjoy the bustle. The quays were swarming with carts, dogs were barking, seagulls screeching. Pendennis Castle stood grey and austere, yet the sun glinted on the windows of the houses around us, the sky a brilliant blue. Letting the sail flap in the wind, Cador leaned over the side and brought us effortlessly to a stop against the quay. 'This will do nicely.' Strong, tall, undeniably handsome, he beamed at me. 'Not too blown about?'

Laughing, I accepted his hand and he helped me to the side. 'I loved being blown about. It was only the finest spray. Is this your boat?'

'Yes, she is.' He looked down at a dead crab on the cobble by his feet, a slight shrug of his broad shoulders. 'It's a skiff, built to my father's design. He gave it to me for my last birthday. It used to be his – but Mother never took to sailing.' Helping Olwyn from the boat, he looped the rope through an iron hook. 'I'll reserve a private room for one o'clock. That will give you two hours. Is that long enough to buy everything?'

Olwyn looked as excited as I felt. Slipping her hand through my arm, her eyes sparkled. 'Will that be long enough, Pandora?'

I bit my lip. I had never been shopping before and had no idea how long it might take. I was used to things being *passed my way* or handed down from the good ladies of the church. Instead, I nodded. 'Maybe for our first visit! Where shall we start?'

'The milliner! There's one in Fore Street. Father says I must buy a new bonnet and a silk shawl. And Cador wants to buy me a parasol, only he wants me to choose it. What about you? What's on your list?'

The thought seemed extraordinary. But I did have ten shillings in my purse, and Aunt Hetty did say to buy something. 'Maybe some paints?' I whispered. She did not hear me and my courage grew. 'Maybe some paints if we can find any.'

Halfway along the main street Olwyn looked strangely lost. She drew aside to let a party of ladies pass. 'I can't thank you enough for coming. I rarely come to Falmouth. Father says now I'm eighteen he'll have to face the prospect of losing me. He's to host a ball in my honour. What he really means is that he shall invite all the eligible men in the county and see who offers for me. It's rather daunting, yet at the same time exciting. We've lived a very quiet life since Mother died.' She looked around as if not knowing where to go.

The ladies passing us were carrying boxes. One of them looked to be my age and I quickly curtsied. 'Good morning, miss. Forgive me, I'm Pandora Woodville from St Feoca School. Could you tell me where we can find a milliner?'

The older ladies in the party looked thunderstruck to be addressed but the young lady dipped a surprised curtsy. Though shaken, she pointed up the hill. 'Mrs Gould's establishment is on the right. Opposite the bank.'

Thanking her, I could see Olwyn was clearly embarrassed. I had forgotten Mama's strict instructions about social niceties and had revealed my sad lack of social etiquette. Yet we had been heading in the wrong direction and wasting precious time. 'I'm sorry, Olwyn,' I whispered. 'I forgot I wasn't in Philadelphia.'

She linked arms again. 'I would love to have your . . . strength.' She looked down as we walked. 'I can feel it in you. And I admire you for it.'

'Father used to call it my *rebellious* nature.' I took a deep breath, fighting my fear. No one knew about Father. *No one knew*.

Mrs Gould's establishment was far grander than standing outside it led us to believe. A display of hats and bonnets hung along the polished wooden panels, a row of parasols and umbrellas down one wall. A glass-fronted cabinet held rolls of material, each drawer labelled with ribbon, lace or feathers. One was labelled *fruit*, one *birds*, another *butterflies*. Through an open door two women were busy sewing. Silence greeted our entry, a tall, elegant lady swinging round in surprise. 'Good morning, ladies.' She dipped a half curtsy, her chin rising. 'Do you have an appointment?'

Olwyn curtsied deeply, a blush spreading up her neck. 'No, we don't. It's just I'd like to buy a bonnet.'

One glance at me and the proprietor's look turned haughty. Perhaps it was my windblown hair or my flushed appearance. Perhaps it was the bruise on my cheek. Glancing away, she addressed Olwyn. 'Perhaps you should return with your mother, my dear. We are very busy. Another day, miss?'

I was used to being treated with disdain but this was too unkind. Olwyn looked on the point of tears. 'Miss Olwyn Ferris is the daughter of Sir Anthony Ferris of Tregenna Hall,' I said, ushering Olwyn forward. 'We've come to buy a bonnet. It's to be Sir Anthony's gift and he'll be very angry if his daughter is turned away.'

Not dreaming, not fabricating, but telling the truth.

Immediately, Mrs Gould ushered her women from the back, all of them fussing over Olwyn, implying nothing was too much trouble. And nothing, it seemed, would be too expensive. Olwyn reached in her tapestry bag and drew out a note from her father saying as much, and I stood beside her, determined to examine every bonnet. Every one of them, suitable or not. Taking down a beautiful yellow bonnet, Mrs Gould held it up to the light. 'This is one of my finest. We can change the trimmings or adapt the lace. We can make it exactly as you like. Though I think these silk flowers are beautiful. It epitomises spring, Miss Ferris. I believe it will look particularly fetching on you.'

Snapping her fingers, she brought one of her women to her side. 'Some refreshments for our young ladies. A glass of Madeira, perhaps?'

I caught Olwyn's look of surprise and nodded. 'Thank you, Mrs Gould. A glass of Madeira would be very welcome. May we look at your parasols? And where can we buy Indian silk scarves in Falmouth?'

Never had I seen drawers open so fast. Olwyn swung round in delight. At least ten shawls to choose from, each glinting in the sunshine as we took them to the window to examine in detail. 'Which shall I choose?' she whispered, then blushed and smiled. 'And Madeira, too. Pandora, this is such a wonderful birthday. Thank you so much for sharing it with me.'

Carrying Olwyn's boxes, we were bade goodbye with deep curtsies and warm wishes to return another day. Giddy with pleasure, we managed to link arms, smiling, almost skipping back along the main street. 'We've only half an hour. Pandora, where shall we find a paint shop?' She stopped, buoyed up with courage. 'Why don't you ask someone again?'

This time I chose a respectable-looking woman in a warm cloak who looked like a tradesperson. Nodding happily, she returned my greetings and pointed me down a narrow alley. 'There's a good trade in paints. You'd be surprised how many sailors take paints with them. And the militia. They say there's more painting done on ships than polishing! Try the naval store. Mind, the cobbles are rough. Take care.'

Pushing open the store, the smell of oiled leather mixed with polish and tobacco. More a pile of jumble than a shop, we worked our way round large trunks and cases, swinging rope hammocks, piles of pewter dishes and mugs. Wooden buckets hung from hooks, ropes, chains, a whole array of brass instruments secured to boards. The counter was overflowing with warm gloves and hats, pens and paper, notebooks and logbooks. A glass cabinet held sailor's knives, compasses, a huge brass barometer, and we looked around for assistance. A man called from behind a half-folded tarpaulin. 'Can I help you, sir?'

'Do you have any paints?'

'Oh, ladies! Forgive me.' A burly man with a full beard appeared. 'I do have paints. A few oils in bladders, and plenty of square cakes and blocks. Down this end of the cabinet I've got a few watercolour sets in fancy boxes – yew, mahogany or satin wood – or I sell them separate.' He picked a large black cat off the counter and held him in his arms.

'Do you have the paints with honey and gum Arabic mixed in them? The semi-moist ones that last longer?'

'Aye, take a look. I've got a few Ackermann, though I've sent to Bristol fer more. They get them direct from Holborn – from Reeves and Woodyer.' He kissed the cat's head. 'Is it fer yerself, or a loved one?'

One glance at the prices and I had to make a decision. I could only afford three of the small cakes – red, yellow and blue. I would blend them to make the other colours. 'These three cakes are perfect, thank you.' I bit my lip. 'I wonder ... do you have any broken ones you can't sell? Only, it's a shame to waste them.'

He watched me count out my shillings and must have seen the contents of my purse dwindle. 'I'll tell you what, I'll give ye that white one fer two shillings. Make that ten shillings, an' ye can have the white as well.'

He escorted us to the door, still holding the fat cat, and clutching our parcels we hurried to the Ship Inn. The proprietor showed us up to a first-floor room and Cador rose to greet us, rushing to take our parcels and hang up our cloaks. The large room had windows overlooking the harbour and across to Flushing. A table was laid with a fine white tablecloth, silver cutlery and a vase of flowers. Crystal glasses glinted in the sun, Cador's smile as wide as the river mouth. 'Looks like you've been successful! That's excellent. I've ordered us roast bass and potatoes, and the new season's asparagus. Then rhubarb tart.'

Never had I imagined being treated with such kindness. It was like every dream coming true – a bustling harbour, wonderful food, the respect in everyone's eyes as they served us. Olwyn and Cador took it for granted, but I wanted to capture the day for ever. So enchanted by their talk and laughter, I almost forgot to give Olwyn my present. Opening it, she had tears in her eyes. 'It's our house – Tregenna Hall. You've captured the refection in the lake perfectly. Surely you didn't paint this?'

Cador seemed speechless. 'You've a rare talent, Pandora. It's beautiful . . . Is this an oyster shell?'

I nodded. 'My last one. I'll have to look for some more now.'

Our meal at an end, we retrieved our cloaks and boxes. As we left, Cador called the proprietor over. I hardly thought what they were saying but as we settled ourselves back in the boat a man carrying a large sack came running over. He bowed, handing the heavy sack to Cador. 'There, sir. One bag of cleaned oyster shells.'

'Oh, Cador . . . how kind. Thank you so much.' I could have been given the King's crown.

He smiled, shrugging his broad shoulders. Looking up at the sail, he seemed almost shy. 'It's my pleasure. Ready to sail back? We're at low tide – it's about to turn our way. The wind's dropped so I anticipate a gentle sail.'

Strong, agile, he hauled up the sail and we skirted round the moored ships, Olwyn and I clutching our treasure. Only mine was a sack smelling of the sea: I would clean them again, dry them, bleach them, then paint them with a wash. An undercoat first, then the painting. Then a thin coat of varnish.

Once round the Flushing promontory, Cador began to sing.

Long we've tossed on the rolling main,
Now we're safe ashore, Jack.
Don't forget your old shipmate,
Faldee raldee raldee raldee rye-eye-doe.

That's the chorus – join in.'

All three of us began singing as if without a care in the world. Never had I felt so free, and never so sad. We could see Trenwyn House where Mother could have been mistress, Tregenna Hall where Aunt Hetty could be living. Or Mother could have married an honourable man and I could have stayed at St Feoca. Cador and Olwyn could have been my cousins. My family around me. Sudden emptiness made my singing hollow.

Pulling up against Harcourt Quay, Cador leapt to help me out. Lithe, nimble, he reached for my hand. 'Thank you for the loveliest day. I've so enjoyed it.'

Reaching inside the boat he handed me the huge sack of shells. 'It's you who's made it so pleasurable, Miss Woodville. We wouldn't have had half as much enjoyment without you.' He looked quickly away, but I had seen the approbation in his eyes. 'Can you manage all these? I can carry them up to St Feoca for you?'

'No, I can manage.' The bow drifted out in the current and he pointed the skiff towards Tallacks Creek. Olwyn was waving, both of them smiling, and I waved back, watching the ease with which Cador handled the boat.

Lost to sight, I turned round: I was not alone on the quayside. Benedict Aubyn had his back to me and was walking quickly away.

Chapter Twenty-one

Wednesday 1st April 1801, 2:30 p.m.

With the climbing roses pruned and the honeysuckle pinned behind a new gutter, I left the girls deciding whose turn it was to hold the skipping rope. Gwen, it seemed, was to skip first, and I left her jumping happily. '*Fi Fie Foe Fum, I smell the blood of an Englishman . . .*'

My thank-you letter to Olwyn and Cador lay ready to catch the post, Aunt Hetty would be in her rooms for at least another hour, and with Grace preparing her lessons and Annie unpacking Susan's new provisions, I slipped off my apron and changed into my satin pumps. I wanted to return to Grandfather's study.

Closing the door, I went straight to the window. In the daylight it was obvious the casement latch was loose and a thin blade inserted through the gap could easily lift it. The bookcases looked undisturbed, nothing seemed to have been touched. Running my hand over the backs of the books I started searching for *Candide*. Sudden nerves tightened my stomach: I had spoken far too freely to Benedict Aubyn.

The thought of Father's lies filled me with fury. He was never kind to me, frequently taunting me, dampening my spirit. *It's in your name, Pandora — Kalon Kakon, Beautiful Evil sent as calamity to man.* Sent as a present from Zeus to Epimetheus for revenge on mankind, sent to lure men from the straight and narrow: *my* fault, not theirs. My evil powers their undoing. I fought my anger.

Father had insisted I painted miniature portraits of the men who might be *useful* to him. I was to paint them *alone* and if they found me charming and accommodating then a little light flirtation on my part would make them even more useful. *It's in your name, your nature, your power to help me.* Did Mama know about that? Well, I was not a plaything to be groped and fondled, not a naughty temptress, a wicked girl with a jar of vices.

Candide was not on the shelves and I gave up my search. Sitting at the desk, I noticed the bottom drawer to be deeper than the others and I pulled it open. A leather-bound Bible took up most of the space and I edged it out, lifting it with both hands on to the desk. It was Grandfather's Bible, the spine creased, a mass of inserted pages written in the same writing as on the accounts. Too full to shut properly, it bulged in front of me and I opened it carefully. *To my dear son, Joseph Sebastian Henry Mitchell, on the occasion of your twenty-first birthday. May God give you the strength and courage to be truthful to yourself in the pursuit of His Glory. Your loving Father, Joseph Peter Everard Mitchell. 4th October 1741.* Tears welled in my eyes. At the bottom of the page was another inscription. *My beloved husband, Died March 15th 1790. May you Rest in Peace.*

The next two pages had lists of names and dates: Grandfather's ordination, his first curacy; his move to Exeter, his promotions; his new jobs rising to Dean. His marriage to *Elizabeth Ann Curnow, August 1st 1757, Exeter Cathedral.* The births of their daughters, *Harriet Elizabeth, 24th January 1760, Abigail Clare, 1st February 1762.* Their baptisms, their move to St Feoca School.

With space running short, the writing at the bottom of the second page became smaller. *The marriage of Abigail Clare Mitchell to James Edward Woodville, St Feock Church in the county of Cornwall, July 1st 1779.* And underneath, *Pandora Harriet Woodville, born Bristol, 1780.* Squeezed at the very bottom, *Abigail and Pandora Woodville left St Feoca School for Dominica: 24th July 1786. Contritum est cor meum.* My heart is broken.

The poor man, having to watch his daughter and grand-daughter leave on such a perilous journey. Footsteps sounded, someone running up the stairs, the door opened and Aunt Hetty smiled. I rose and curtsied. 'I thought I'd find you here.' She was slightly breathless, her cheeks flushed. It may have just been a shadow, but the edge of her sleeve looked wet. There was mud on her boots, a trace of damp around her hem. 'I've been outside looking for you, then I thought—' She stopped. 'You've found Father's Bible?'

'Was Grandfather ill before he died? Mama cried for days when she received your letter. It took ten months to reach us. All that time and she hadn't known. She thought she should have had some intuition, some sense of knowing he was no longer with us. She was bereft.'

Her mouth tightened. 'Yes, well, if your father hadn't moved every two years – if he'd held down a position long enough for my letters to reach you – we might have had better communication. As it is, I think he kept my letters from Abigail.'

Pain shot through me: no doubt she was right. 'How did Grandfather die?'

'Suddenly and very unexpectedly. He was going to give the sermon at church . . . he was late coming down and I went to find him. He was lying on the floor, barely breathing. I couldn't rouse him. We brought him downstairs and called the physician who told us to expect the worst. That evening Father breathed his last. It was horrible. Mother was never the same again. I took over the running of the school. Your grandmother died ten years later, almost to the day.'

I turned the Bible round so she could read it. 'Grandfather hasn't written the date of my birthday. Shall I add it?' She shrugged, making to close it, and I pointed to the entry. 'Why didn't he write the date? Every other entry has the full day and month.'

'An oversight, that's all.' There was something in her voice. A stiffening of her shoulders.

'But he knew it very well. He used to send me birthday greetings in his letters.'

She hesitated. 'He must have forgotten to fill it in.'

'Grandfather was meticulous in recording everything. Look . . . the exact date of when we left, but he couldn't bring himself to write the date of my birth? That's quite horrible of him. Didn't he love me?'

She could not hold my glance. Again, the same hesitancy. 'Of course he loved you. More than you will ever know.

But he obviously . . . forgot . . . that he hadn't written it in full.'

'But that doesn't make sense . . .' Sudden dizziness made me catch my breath. An icy chill down my back. *Never lie on the Bible, Pandora. Grandfather would be horrified*. I gripped the desk. 'Aunt Hetty, I'm not a child. Grandfather didn't want to write my date of birth in it – did he? He didn't want to write it because he couldn't bring himself to . . . Aunt Hetty, what don't I know?'

Her hand gripped my shoulder. 'I wish you hadn't seen that.'

'He couldn't bring himself to write an untruth in the Bible. That's it, isn't it? Did Mama tell you another date?'

'No. Your birthday is January the twenty-third, one day before mine. She told us that date and we've always celebrated that date.'

Yet she had looked away. 'But you know it to be a different date?'

'We know nothing of the sort. That's the date she gave us.'

Sudden realisation made me catch my breath. 'Oh no! No! Was I . . . *forced* . . . on Mother? Was I . . . the result . . . of violation?'

Her voice dropped. '*Violation* certainly. But neither unwilling nor unsought.' Her words were soft, tender, yet brooking no argument. She drew up her chair and took my hand. 'Your mother was in love with your father. She worshipped him with almost dog-like devotion. I used to watch her eyes light up and follow him across the room. She was captivated by him. Your father was an extremely good-looking man with a power about him – a compelling presence. His eyes were mesmerising, hypnotic – pale grey, fringed with dark lashes.

He'd stare at people, as if forcing them to seek his approval, and they'd be caught like a moth in a flame.'

The tightness in my chest was almost unbearable. 'It's so shocking. It's unimaginable that Mama—'

'I know. Unimaginable. And I would have kept this from you if I could.'

'Everyone knew?'

She squeezed my hand. 'Yes, we knew. How else would Father allow his beloved daughter to marry such a scoundrel? Mother was taken in just as badly. If she had only shown the restraint I advised – if she had only listened to my plea that he was not to be trusted – Abigail might have married William Carew. But Mother was taken in by your father as surely as Abigail was.'

'But for them to . . . to . . .'

'I know, it's beyond comprehension. But you must understand your father's attentions were not *unsought* by your mother. Your father was a persistent, calculating man. He had a strong physical presence, a terrible power over her . . . she was like clay in his hands. The truth is he was a ruthless man who wanted our school. And he knew just how to get it.'

'How did they meet?'

'Your father arrived unannounced one night. He said he'd come from Bristol to seek a position at St Feoca. He said he thought it was a boys' school and apologised profusely, saying he would leave straight away. A storm was raging, his clothes were sodden, and but for Mother's kindness that would have been the end.

'He chose his night well. As it was, he stayed for four

months. Not in the house, but in the coach house. He told my parents he would seek a position elsewhere. Father helped him find a post as private tutor in Falmouth but he kept coming back, walking with Abigail . . . rowing with her on the river. Watching birds in the creek.'

'And Grandmother encouraged them?'

'He charmed her as well. He was very pleasing, even Annie adored him. Your mother always had a chaperone, but they obviously found a way to be alone. Abby was only seventeen. After eight months, I told her what I thought of James Woodville. She was furious. Utterly furious. She said it was too late to stop their love. That they'd been *indiscreet* on several occasions. That she had been *intimate* with James so Father would have to let her marry him — and it *had to happen as a matter of great urgency*. That's how she put it.'

A wave of nausea churned my stomach. 'How could she be so reckless?'

'We'd lost her to him. He'd been feeding her lies, drawing her from us. He told her we thought him inferior, that we'd never accept him. His father was a clerk who worked every hour to send him to Cambridge and he told her his background would be considered beneath us. That we despised his pretentions to rise above his station, that Father was jealous of his intellect, and that his birth and upbringing would stop any chance of their marriage.'

'Father always directed Mama's thoughts. I told her she should contradict him when he was so obviously wrong, but she said love was forgiving — that he was misunderstood by everyone.'

'There was no misunderstanding him! The agreement was they would go to Bristol after the wedding and return after eighteen months. Father was prepared to accept him as a son-in-law, but tongues were already wagging – a dean's daughter, married in such haste, sent immediately to Bristol?' She breathed deeply. 'I waved them goodbye, knowing my chances of a good match would never be realised.'

'Sir Anthony . . . ?' I whispered.

She squeezed my hand. 'We were never formally engaged. Within two months of Abby's marriage, Anthony's father announced Anthony's marriage to the daughter of a well-connected family. So I threw all my energy into the school.'

Because of me, she had lost her chance of love. Father's mocking jeer would not leave me . . . *Kalon Kakon* . . . *Beautiful Evil sent as calamity to man*. She handed me her lace handkerchief. 'But we didn't come back in eighteen months. I was four when we returned.'

'The day after they left several silver candlesticks were found to be missing. So, too, a silver plate and bowl, and fifty guineas from the school drawer. Father wrote immediately to Abigail and her reply was stinging. That we'd think James involved in any theft proved us unworthy and cruel. She was furious – how dare we insinuate such a thing? Her fury was uncontained and his victory complete. James Woodville had succeeded in driving a wedge of iron between us.'

A burst of sun lit the room and I breathed deeply. 'But we came back.'

Shutting the Bible, she replaced it in the bottom drawer.

'Yes, and I loved every minute of you being here. I was prepared to put up with your father's weasel ways. He made my flesh creep, but so long as we kept apart, I could tolerate him living here. To be accurate, he took lodgings in Truro while he worked at the Grammar School. You and Abby stayed here.'

'But now I know why we had to leave.'

'Yes, now you know. I was bereft at losing Abby. It was Annie's birthday and we had planned a small celebration. Your father was halfway down the drive and the fury in his eyes will never leave me. He wanted the school and his plans were thwarted. I knew from that moment I would never see Abby again.'

'So Grandfather drew up the constitution and left provision for you, but not Mama. Because he was worried Father would come back and claim her inheritance? Yet you kept Mama's room aired . . . you kept hoping for her to return.'

She wiped her eye. 'I never gave up hope. But it's you I've been waiting for. You.' She smiled. 'I've almost forgotten what I came to tell you. I've just received not one letter, but *three* letters!' Standing up, she shook the creases from her gown. 'Angelica Trevelyan says she has a whole list of names willing to raise funds for your Barn School – though she emphasises that's not the name she used! And Mrs Lilly writes that she's in *negotiation* with her husband to sponsor four girls to bear their costs *entirely*. Which actually means it's a *fait accompli*. And Lady Carew has called for a meeting of the school governors on Saturday afternoon to discuss it all.'

Shame burned my cheeks, Mama with Father, hidden from sight. Mama so foolish I almost despised her. 'How could you let me go with Cador and Olwyn yesterday? And go to Lady Clarissa? I never want to go to Tregenna Hall or Trenwyn House again – nor ever show my face in Falmouth. How can I hold my head up?'

Her back straightened. 'Because that's what we do. We take a deep breath and we hold up our chins. That's what I've always done and it's what you must do.'

I hardly heard her as she closed the door and followed me down the spiral steps. I would rather feel the emptiness than feel such censure. 'Lady Clarissa has also sent some interesting information. There's to be a meeting of the Turnpike Trust and Benedict Aubyn is to present his findings. Apparently, there's so much interest that they've had to hold it in the assembly rooms.'

Because of me, Mama had been sent to Bristol; because of me, they had to marry. The pain was so sharp it cut me to breathe. Aunt Hetty's voice drifted from behind. 'Is that agreed, then? Shall we ask him? Only forewarned is forearmed. I think I'll ask him to dinner tomorrow and he can show us his map.'

'Why not?' I hardly knew what I was saying but curtsied and ran under the arch to the courtyard. The children were still skipping, singing in unison, *Be he alive or be he dead, I'll grind his bones to make my bread.* Fumbling, I opened the garden gate and, leaning against the sundial, I let my sobs escape.

See what you've wrought? Father's voice would not leave me. *Oh yes! I named you well.*

Chapter Twenty-two

Unable to rid myself of the sense of shame, my earrings and ebony band had been on and off too many times to count. My cheeks were the colour of plums. The thought of Mother sitting at my dressing table knowing what she had done filled my every thought. Knowing her disgrace could ruin the family.

The rich aroma of stew drifted from the kitchen. Annie had spent all day cooking, the sound of her pans clattering across the cobbles. Susan had been to Falmouth to replenish our provisions and Annie had smiled broadly as she cut and chopped. 'Of course he'll be hungry. Unless he's so smitten with our Grace he can't eat!' Her laughter had brought blushes, shakes of the head, a wink from Susan as Grace looked away.

Annie would serve the potatoes, but Grace was to collect the stock pot as it was too heavy for Annie. Susan had polished and cleaned the hall, Grace had laid the table. The silver candelabras were glinting in the firelight, the logs blazing, the room full of expectation. Aunt Hetty smiled as I stood in the doorway. 'How charming you look.'

Yet I paled into insignificance compared to Grace. She was arranging the glasses, her beauty taking my breath away. Wearing a pale blue gown with lace at her throat and elbows, her blonde hair was coiled to one side with a matching blue silk flower on the other. Elegant, demure, her neck poised, her back straight, her sweet smile curving the corners of her rosebud lips, she seemed nervous, rearranging the bottles behind the crystal glasses. 'Is this right? The wine is uncorked . . . and the brandy is in the decanter. Will he pour them, or do you think he'll expect us to pour them? Only there's a smudge here I think I'd better wipe off.' Getting out her handkerchief, I could see her hands tremble.

Aunt Hetty turned to the side table. By the vase of orchids Cador Ferris had sent me was a small leather box engraved with gold flowers. Aunt Hetty smiled as she handed it to me. 'These were your grandmother's pearl drops – the ones in her portrait. I'd like you to have them.' I could hardly speak. The pearl drops shone in the firelight and I fought my tears. Hanging beneath a small gold bow, they glistened as I held them up. 'They were given to her by your great-grandfather when she was twenty-one, so it's only right you have them. Here, let me help you.'

Outside, dusk was falling, the lamps on either side of the front door burning. Holding one of her letters to the firelight, Aunt Hetty cleared her throat. 'I've had some very interesting communication about Mr Benedict Aubyn. It seems he's known in Truro – both Angelica Trevelyan and Lady Clarissa know him from old. Both tell me the same thing. Until his recent death, his father was the highly respected Rector of St Kew. His mother is from the Kearne family from St Endellion and is considered a kind and intelligent person – a devoted mother and wife – and much admired by the parishioners.'

She glanced at Grace, the slight rise to her eyebrows bringing an immediate blush. Twisting her handkerchief, Grace looked down. 'The poor man. That must account for his sadness. To recently lose his father . . .'

Aunt Hetty turned the page. 'According to Lady Clarissa, Benedict Aubyn followed his elder brother to Oxford with the intention of joining the Church – like his brother and their father. Lady Clarissa says that never happened. All she knows is that he went to London. Angelica Trevelyan says her husband remembers him at Oxford as being involved with a very *lively* set. Apparently, he was always called upon to play his fiddle at dances and was *indispensable* at social gatherings. If there was food, drink and dancing, then Benedict Aubyn was at the centre.'

Again, the faint flush on Grace's cheeks. 'Goodness. An Oxford man . . . and a bit disreputable?' Her colour deepened.

A smile played on Aunt Hetty's lips. 'Disreputable is the word. According to Angelica's husband, Benedict Aubyn was in the running for several prestigious livings yet one day his room was empty, and he was gone. He never completed his degree. The last thing Henry Trevelyan heard was that Benedict was in London.' She raised her eyebrows. 'I wonder if he was sent down for some sort of misdemeanour?'

A loud knock sounded on the door, and Grace went to open

it. Curtsying as Benedict entered, she looked down in obvious confusion. Taking off his hat, he smiled. 'Thank you, Grace, you're very kind. Fortunately, the rain's kept off.'

I must have looked equally surprised. Certainly, Aunt Hetty's eyes widened. His hair had been cut short, his chin finely shaven. He wore a silk cravat pinned with a silver pin, his cut-away jacket clearly new, his trousers well-fitting. His boots were shining, no sign of mud. He looked commanding, standing with his overcoat on his arm, his hat in one hand, a large bunch of flowers in the other. Reluctant to give Grace his coat and hat, he looked around. 'Let me put them some-where ... over there? No, please. I can leave them here.' Stepping forward, he bowed. 'A small token of my appreci-ation, Miss Mitchell. Flowers from along the shore road.'

Aunt Hetty took the delicately entwined bunch of flowers. 'How lovely ... pussy willow and catkins. Daffodils and helle-bores. And forsythia. A beautiful spring bouquet, Mr Aubyn. How very kind.'

He seemed suddenly shy, turning to the roaring fire. 'The logs are lasting, I see.'

Firelight caught his features: without his mass of hair, he looked more assured, his cheeks sculptured, his chin firm. Aunt Hetty smiled, a slight rise to her eyebrows. 'Could your new haircut be in honour of our dinner tonight, or is it to impress the Turnpike Trust in Truro?

His smile was instant. Shaking his head, he laughed shyly. 'I believe nothing gets past you, Miss Mitchell.'

'I should hope not. Though many are foolish enough to make that assumption.'

215

'Only until they meet you!' He looked shy again, a brief glance at me. Across the room, Grace looked full of admiration. 'I assume you've researched my credentials... made enquiries of my...'

Aunt Hetty nodded. 'Yes, I have. And may I offer you my sincere condolences on the loss of your father. A recent bereavement, I believe? And therefore all the more painful.' She looked round. 'We all offer you our condolences.'

'Thank you.' His hands clenched by his sides, a flicker of pain as he closed his eyes. The mother-of-pearl buttons on his waistcoat caught the firelight, his chest rising and falling. Grace stepped forward. 'May we offer you some wine, Mr Aubyn? Only we have some uncorked.'

'Let me help you.' Following her to the table, he reached for the bottle and read the label; Grace handed him the glasses in turn. Standing side by side like we had stood at the field gate, Grace looked beautiful in the soft yellow glow. Her eyes were downcast, her behaviour demure. He had only bowed to me, stiffly, abruptly, yet she was making him smile, giving him a commission to lessen his discomfort. Intuitive, beautiful Grace. Aunt Hetty was watching, a slight smile as she breathed in the scent of her flowers.

Handing us each a glass, Benedict reached inside his discarded coat and drew out his folded map. 'I'm to present my plans to the turnpike trustees on Saturday. It's the first time I've met them... it's a public meeting. I believe there's quite a lot of interest.'

Aunt Hetty had dressed with great care. Her best black silk rustled as she walked, her pearl brooch glinting at her throat.

Two diamond earrings swung as she talked. Round her shoulders she wore a cream silk fichu with a matching set of cream feathers pinned in her hair. She pursed her lips. 'Indeed, and we shall be there, Mr Aubyn. Wild horses could not keep me from going. Just tell me, are you planning to cut my farm from my school?'

He laid his map on the table. 'No, Miss Mitchell. The road will cut west of Devoran Farm.' He looked pale in the firelight. Now I knew he was in mourning, I could recognise the pain in his half-smile. 'The land east of the farm has streams and natural wells. The land to the west has less potential to flood.'

Aunt Hetty smiled, shrugging her shoulders, indicating she had seen enough. 'You can join us in our carriage to Truro. Lady Clarissa is sending us her coach. There'll be room for you, and your new clothes will not be dusty when you meet the trustees. Enough of business. I believe our meal is ready. Grace, would you mind helping Annie bring it in?'

'Please . . . let me carry anything heavy.' Insisting he must help, Benedict opened the door for Grace and followed her out. She was smiling, sweet and alluring, and my stomach twisted. I felt tainted by association, ashamed of my mother, furious with my father.

Aunt Hetty must have seen me frown. 'Don't be too hard on him, Pandora. I believe him to be honest. He's not proposing to rob me, he's just doing what they've asked of him . . . and if he's the gentleman I believe him to be, then Grace has done very well for herself. He's a fine catch.'

Seated and served, Aunt Hetty gave thanks for our meal

and we started eating. I hardly tasted the rabbit stew, nor the creamed potatoes and turnips. My cheeks burned with shame, everything tasting of sawdust. Benedict was clearly enjoying the meal despite Aunt Hetty's continued probing. Like a game of cat and mouse, every question Aunt Hetty asked was answered with a shy smile or a slight rise of his shoulders.

'So Oxford was not to your taste, Mr Aubyn?'

He reached over to pour her some more wine. 'Oxford was very much to my taste. It was the thought of going into the Church which wasn't.' His voice caught, a slight tremble in his hand. He reached for his napkin and wiped his mouth. 'I had several good offers — livings in wealthy parishes. I'd made influential friends and my future could have been very settled.' He looked down at his plate. 'But, *foolishly*, according to those who advised me, I chose to go to London. I won a scholarship to the Royal Society to study the gravitational attraction on the density of substances — mainly gaseous exchanges.'

Aunt Hetty's knife and fork remained poised above her plate. 'Like the euphoric effects of inhaling nitrous air? Is this *laughing gas* really capable of destroying physical pain?'

If he was surprised at Aunt Hetty's knowledge, he hid it well. 'Yes . . . exactly so. I believe there's every chance nitrous air could be curative. Used to alleviate pain, in fact. Even the pain of childbirth.'

'And you studied these curative gases in London?'

'My interest has always been in minerals . . . in their extraordinary diversity — their vast array of properties. More exactly, how to use these properties . . . how to isolate them into compounds . . . break them down into further, smaller

218

elements . . . and combine these newly found elements with other newly formed elements. To discover, or initiate, chemical affinity between them. Mineral gases can be both curative and *corrosive* – some compounds heal, some poison. There's so much to discover.' His forehead creased into a sudden frown.

'And your father disapproved of your desire to isolate these corrosive gases?'

'No.' He coughed to clear his throat. 'Not at all. My family have always supported my interest in minerals.' There was sorrow in his eyes, the same tenderness as when he dipped his handkerchief into the stream and dabbed my cheek. Drawing a deep breath, he turned to Grace. 'You share this interest, Miss Elliot. Minerals can be very addictive, can't they?'

Annie stood at the door, her clean white apron especially laundered for the occasion. Limping slightly, she lifted the lid from the stew pot. 'Good . . . not a morsel left. And now, we've gooseberry tart with *cream*.' Smiling, she reached for the handle. 'No, no. The pot's empty . . . it's not heavy. Stay where you are, Mr Aubyn. We'll just move the plates to the side and I'll clear up when you're in the music room.'

Hands on his chest, he beamed back at her. 'That was the best rabbit stew, Mrs Rowe. You had rosemary in it . . . and cooked in wine, I believe?'

He seemed suddenly vulnerable, a kind and lonely man in need of company and a good dinner. Annie must have thought so too. She beamed back at him. 'One of Lady Clarissa's favourite recipes.' Her voice turned conspiratorial. 'One of her French cooks from long ago. No garlic, mind. I don't like garlic; onions work just as well.'

He rose and started helping her take the plates. 'And you added wine? And parsley, carrots and celery? A lovely, rich, well-cooked stew. I haven't tasted one so good in a long time.'

Shaking her head with pleasure, Annie sucked in her cheeks. 'Wait till you taste the gooseberry tart. It's cooked with lemons but I've added honey and a touch of brandy!'

With Aunt Hetty's next question his frown returned. 'No, not nearly finished, unfortunately, Miss Mitchell. The men have been delayed not only by the weather but by the ferry. By the time we get from Falmouth we miss an early start. Not to mention the amount of stones being stolen each night! Mr McAdam has strict instructions – he has to prove his new method works. Roads are still being built with heavy stones but suspensions are better, the loads are heavier and it doesn't take much to dislodge the large stones. Once rain gets in, ruts are inevitable. The stones lift, the rain pools, then streams, erosion occurs, and the road becomes impassable.'

'But your small stones are spread evenly and won't rut?'

'Better than that, our stones become impressed and harden – they don't scatter or get pushed to one side.' His voice was kind, his smile gentle. 'They bed down and take the pressure. Coupled with a curve to each edge, a good ditch on either side and a firm base, he believes he can guarantee no ruts – no matter the amount of traffic or weight of the loads.'

'How very clever,' whispered Grace, a flutter of her eyelashes.

A sudden chill made me shiver. I kept trying to bring my mind back to the conversation but I could not help my thoughts from wandering. I could think of nothing but my recent discoveries. Mama had lied every bit as much as Father had. She had lied about us coming home when she knew we could never come back. That day on the quayside we had waited for a ship to Falmouth. Waited and waited, but no ship had come. How could you do that to an eleven-year-old child? How could you tell her she was going to Cornwall, only to take her to Brooklyn? I felt clamped in ice. Frozen. Like the ships in Philadelphia.

Aunt Hetty rose and Benedict stood to pull out her chair. Turning to me, he seemed to sense my distress. 'May I help you? Are you unwell?' I held his glance and shame flooded my cheeks.

'I'm just a little flushed with the fire.' A dean's daughter, a respectably brought-up young woman. There must have been talk. Of course there was talk. Enough talk to make Sir William Ferris refuse his permission for Anthony to marry Aunt Hetty.

Leading us to the music room, Aunt Hetty resumed her questioning. 'Do you enjoy music, Mr Aubyn? Only, I was told by Mrs Trevelyan you play the fiddle?'

'Oh dear! I see Henry Trevelyan has blotted my copybook. My only defence is that he was at the same soirees. He was not always the sober man of business he is today.'

Her laughter rang like a bell. 'Perhaps we can discuss that another time!'

A fire was burning in the music room. Still smiling, she pointed to the piano. 'Grace would be delighted to take her place at the piano, or would you like to play us something?' Opening a cupboard, she reached for a black ebony case. 'A number of my pupils learn the violin. Mr Joseph Emidy comes – or rather *came* – to teach my girls. I don't think this will be too out of tune.'

Opening the case, Benedict drew out a gleaming violin. Plucking the strings, he walked to the piano and placed the violin against his ear. Taking hold of the bow, he swung it several times, adjusting the strings until he nodded. 'Do you have any music?' Aunt Hetty pointed to the cupboard where the violin had been laying and going through the pile, he paused. 'This one.'

He looked so at ease, elegant, poised, his clothes immaculate. His jaw looked stronger, his forehead broad and intelligent. Placing the music on the stand he positioned his violin and began to play. Not a jig but a piece filled with deep melancholy, each sweep of his bow speaking of longing. The pain of loss was mirrored in his frown, each note haunting, plaintive, the music trembling, swelling, filling the room with sadness. Shutting his eyes, he seemed lost to his surroundings.

Such visceral pain, such raw grief: the sorrow of loss mounting, making my mouth quiver. Aunt Hetty gripped my hand, her eyes lost to the distance. His final notes fading, she reached for her handkerchief. "Melodie", by Gluck. From his opera, *Orpheus and Euridice*. What a sad piece to choose, Mr Aubyn. I was expecting a country dance. A jig . . .'

He shrugged, replacing the violin in its case. 'The heartbreak of separation – of believing all is lost. But Gluck saves us from sorrow, Miss Mitchell. He's telling us we have the power to change how things end. In his opera he makes the gods repent and Euridice lives. That's why I played this piece.

We can have dominion over Greek myths. When loss seems so cruel . . . when grief seems overwhelming . . . hope steps in.'

Aunt Hetty wiped her eyes. 'When grief is met by hope.'

Across the room, Grace's eyes were deep pools of sorrow. Aunt Hetty saw her look of adoration and cleared her throat. 'I have a proposition, Mr Aubyn – a two-way, mutually beneficial *business* proposition. We were burgled the other day – just a hungry poacher with a family to feed – but it's left me feeling rather vulnerable. Would you consider staying in the rooms above the coach house? They're very comfortable rooms – and your men could sleep in the rooms behind the gatehouse. Mrs Penrose often puts up the coach drivers and footmen there. It's simple accommodation but it's clean and she'll undercut the price you're paying for food and lodging. That way, you can make an early start on your road, and we'll have the benefit of knowing we are not *unprotected*, so to speak.'

He nodded, thanking her, but my stomach tightened. Aunt Hetty knew exactly what happened to innocent young girls when single men took rooms above the coach house, yet there she was, smiling and showing Benedict out of the front door, and there was Grace, smiling and helping him on with his coat. Smiling in that alluring way, avoiding his eyes with her downward glance. Giving his shoulder a little brush, as if there was some dust to remove!

Annie must have moved his hat and gloves and he turned to look for them. They were by the orchids. 'Ah, there they are.' Reaching for them, his shoulders suddenly stiffened. The open jewellery case was by their side and his voice faltered. 'What beautiful flowers, I didn't see them before.'

Grace smiled, looking at the orchids, repositioning the jewellery case alongside them. 'They are from Mr Ferris at Tregenna Hall. Miss Woodville is very generous to share them.'

Chapter Twenty-three

Friday 3rd April 1801, 10:00 p.m.

The shutters still open, moonlight danced across the roof of the conservatory. I had spent the day altering the second of my gowns and it hung against my wardrobe for the morning. Sewing in the library had seemed a good idea, though watching Grace and Susan running backwards and forwards to prepare Benedict's room proved rather too distracting.

I stared at his un-shuttered window. Mother would have stood just like this. Right here, where I was standing, watching, waiting, anticipating Father's signal. Waiting for the house to grow quiet so she could slip out of the back and go to his room. The shock would not lessen, it would never go away. The more I thought about it, the more disturbing my imagination became.

A light tap on the door and I knew it would be Grace. Her blonde hair was pinned beneath a nightcap, her candle guttering in her hand. 'I'm so sorry to disturb you but I can't settle...'

'Grace, you look distressed. What is it?'

Clutching her shawl, she took a deep breath. 'I couldn't ask you earlier – but I don't know what to do. Sophie from the farm won't take a single step into the house. *Not one*. Gwen says it's on account of the devil's box, which I told them is all nonsense . . . but . . . today . . . Mollie from the mill won't go into the barn. And she's got Kate from the gatehouse saying the same thing.'

'Why won't they go into the barn?'

Twisting her shawl, I thought she might cry. 'Because, today, they found a black feather in the barn. It was two foot long – if not a bit more – and they said it was the *devil's* feather.' She covered her mouth with her hand. 'They say the devil's back.' Her voice was failing. 'That . . . it's his *sign*. Because he said he'd come back. Like the rumours . . .'

'Well, it's complete nonsense. Birds go into barns, and rooks and choughs often lose wing feathers. I hope you told them that?'

'Yes, I did. Of course I did. And I said Mr Aubyn was here now and would protect us . . . but it doesn't stop my problem. I need the girls *together* – in one place – in order to teach them, and they mustn't be frightened or they'll not come to my lessons.'

She looked drawn, her fingers fidgeting as if she wanted to make the sign of the cross. 'Then we'll find somewhere else to hold your lessons.' The vacant stare of the wax dolls flooded my mind and I forced myself to sound steady. 'Use the coach house. There's plenty of space in there and with Mr Aubyn sleeping upstairs the girls will feel safe.'

She nodded, then smiled. 'I'll sweep it clean tomorrow and have it ready for Monday. Goodnight . . . and thank you.'

Across the moonlit courtyard a lamp was burning in Benedict's room. My candle flickered and died, the glow from the fire sending shadows across the ceiling. The moon was glinting on the conservatory, the lawns almost as bright as day and I pulled my shawl tighter. The dolls had been viciously accurate, and now they had left another feather. Across the lawns, the trees were in shadow. Not a movement, no one running away. Just the black silhouette of the woods.

'Who are you?' I whispered. 'Who are you?'

Chapter Twenty-four

Saturday 4th April 1801, 10:00 a.m.

The suspension on Lady Clarissa's carriage was better than Sir Anthony's, yet even so we jolted uncomfortably. Aunt Hetty was dressed in her finest, her hat elegantly on one side. She looked pale, as if she had not slept well. Benedict Aubyn sat opposite me, a series of closely written pages on his lap. Flicking through them, he kept referring to his map. The creek narrowed and I caught a glimpse of the mouths of two small rivers. A large waterwheel was turning, two barges anchored midstream.

Aunt Hetty leaned forward. 'What are those men doing up to their waists in water? Surely the water's too cold! How long have they been streaming this stretch of the creek?'

Benedict leaned forward to see more clearly. 'The Carnon Streamworks? I'd say six months. They're digging new pits — using the overburden to build the dykes to hold back the tide. I believe they've got a hundred and fifty men on their books — each on the lookout for the glint of gold.'

'Gold?' I did not mean to sound so shocked.

'It's tin they're after, but sometimes they find minute quantities of gold – *prills* – they call them. The men carry quills with a wooden plug at one end to store their finds. Sometimes the gold's no bigger than a pinhead but it mounts up. Some find silver.' Dressed in his new clothes, Benedict Aubyn looked professional, his short hair and closely shaven chin giving him an air of gravitas. Yet he also looked tired, shadows beneath his eyes.

Aunt Hetty smoothed her cloak. 'They stream the river for tin and copper. They don't mine it but wash the alluvial sediment from the valley above. It's a race against the tide – hence the need to build dams.'

'There is tin and copper – and gold and silver, in the creek?'

Benedict stared out of the window. 'There is. Further up the valley they use engines to pump the water from the mines. The water is rich in tin and copper and flows through the adits – the huge drains – and makes its way downriver. The sediment gets deposited in Restronguet Creek, where they extract it.'

'Enough to make money?'

His laugh was rueful. 'Oh, yes. Enough to make money. There are forty-five miles of streams, and I know that because I've walked most of them! Twenty-five of them flow through the richest seams and pick up the tin as it flows past. It's lucrative ground. The water mill scoops the water out of the dykes but it's no longer meeting the demand. They need a steam engine to pump the water out.'

Aunt Hetty leaned forward. 'What's happening at the

entrance to Perren Creek? There seems to be more workings than usual.'

Benedict followed her gaze. 'The Perren Foundry is dredging channels for the barges to reach Perranarworthal. Mr Fox supplies machinery for the Gwennap copper mines and he's expanded his foundry. Barges deliver his coal and ship his machinery but the tin streaming works are obstructing navigation. There's a big rumpus going on. Hence the need to dredge the channels.'

'I don't remember Mama mentioning such industry.'

His eyes held mine before looking quickly away. 'They've streamed this river since the Romans. There's always been rich sediment, but now they need to dig deeper.' His voice hardened. 'The next step is to sink shafts.'

It was as if he was warning us, telling us something we should know. His change in tone was not lost on Aunt Hetty. Her frown deepened. 'Your new bridge would span the mouth of the river and benefit all these works.'

He took a deep breath. 'Everyone would benefit, Miss Mitchell.'

'Enough interest to fill the assembly rooms?'

'It seems excessive. But in times like these there'll be great interest. Contracts are to be awarded to build the tollhouses, the tollgates, and to appoint labourers. Other contracts will be for the provision of stones, or to break the stones. There'll be a contract to repair and maintain the road, and the mile-posts, and labourers clamouring to build the road and dig the ditches. Most importantly, they'll give information about the auction of tolls.'

'Auction of tolls?'

'Prospective gatekeepers will be invited to bid for the amount of money they believe the tolls will bring in. The highest bidder usually gets the contract for an agreed number of years. The amount is set, he gets a free house, a weekly wage, and any money *over* the amount he pledges is his to keep. Of course, he may make a loss some years but he still pays the agreed amount each year. Most do very well out of this system.'

Aunt Hetty stared out of the window. 'They'll ask for subscriptions to build your new road?'

'Most certainly. They'll compile a list of subscribers. Many will see this as an opportunity to invest. Any profits – and there are usually substantial profits – will be split between the shareholders and the trust's outgoings.'

We joined the turnpike, our journey continuing in silence. Benedict put his papers into his leather case and stared out of the window. I kept my eyes firmly on the hedgerows, the fields, the carts we passed, or down at my gloved hands, trying not to smooth my skirt, determined I must not play with the beads on my bag. Anything but catch his eyes in the reflection of the window. Perhaps my hat was at the wrong angle, or a curl was out of place. Maybe he thought my pearl earrings too fancy for a trip to Truro, but every time I looked up he was using the glass to look at me, his expression increasingly sombre.

His words kept running through my mind. *We can have dominion over Greek myths.* He had said it with such kindness, his eyes filled with tenderness, yet today he was avoiding looking at me. He seemed distant, formal, staring at my reflection with his mouth drawn tight.

The line of oaks along the drive to Tregenna Hall stretched to our right and his frown deepened. He cleared his throat, pointing to the gate where we had stood side by side, next to the stream where he had dipped his handkerchief into the water. 'Miss Mitchell, may I suggest you reposition your main drive along the lines of the drive to Tregenna Hall? Your cart track could take firmer foundations... you could widen it. The journey to Truro would then be halved.' His voice hardened. 'It would also be very *convenient* for any visits between your two estates.'

'Build similar gates and line the avenue with oaks?' Her gloved hands rested on her lap. 'How long have you been surveying this area, Mr Aubyn?'

He looked up. 'Just under four months.'

'And before that you were in Bristol?'

'Assisting Dr Thomas Beddoes in his laboratory at the Pneumatic Institute.'

'Doing what, precisely?'

He breathed deeply. 'Analytical chemistry – the study of how chemicals interact. We break them down by precipitation, extraction or distillation and we study their melting points, boiling points, solubility, and their reactivity. In my case, it was as gases. I worked with another Cornish man – Mr Humphry Davy.'

She pierced him with her eagle look. 'You left your position at the prestigious Pneumatic Institute to *survey* land?'

Heat seared his cheeks. He gripped the handle of his

leather case. 'Researching gases does not keep a family, Miss Mitchell. There's no money to be earned. It's solely for those with private means.'

I looked away, but Aunt Hetty had not finished. Her tone sharpened. 'Susan told me this morning you've been seen giving money to a woman who frequently visited your rooms in Falmouth. I believe we need to be honest with each other, Mr Aubyn. Are you referring to this lady – maybe she's your wife?'

I thought they would hear the beating of my heart. He smiled his half-smile. 'She's my *sister*, Miss Mitchell.'

'Yet when she leaves her name, she calls herself *Mrs* Aubyn.'

He looked stung. 'That would be Mrs Martha Aubyn, my sister-in-law. And the two girls who accompany her are my nieces. I have no wife, Miss Mitchell. Nor any engagement. I have no money so the prospect of any marriage seems highly improbable.'

Never had such softly spoken words brought such a rush of pleasure. He looked wounded. Wounded, and in pain, yet Aunt Hetty's smile lit her face. Her eyes seemed to sparkle. 'Perhaps you've not heard, Mr Aubyn, that I have a reputation for securing good matches?'

He laughed, but it was with sadness and I felt a sudden, protective desire to see him no longer hurt. His grip on his case strengthened. 'You don't consider me a ruthless land-grabber intent on robbing you?'

Her smile broadened. 'A ruthless land-grabber, no; although you do intend to rob me, Benedict. But I'm prepared for any *proposal* you may throw at me. Forewarned is forearmed, don't you think?'

He glanced at me and I fought not to let my cheeks give me away. Not show any signs of my sudden confusion. Like a veil lifting, like clouds dispersing, like a fog clearing, I could no longer hide my liking for Benedict Aubyn. He was not a fraudster, not a wolf in sheep's clothing, but a gentle man who should not be tramping along moors and rivers but bending over his microscope in his laboratory, combining his elements, mixing and separating his curative and corrosive gases.

Aunt Hetty was still smiling as our carriage passed through the tollgate and headed towards the centre of Truro. Without the rioters, the streets looked empty, the houses glowing in the sun, and I leaned closer to the window, looking everywhere except at Benedict Aubyn. 'Look...a leather shop. A haberdasher...a milliner. What lovely bonnets she has in her window.'

A pie seller was calling across the market square, women carrying baskets. The inns looked busy, a group of warmly dressed passengers waiting outside the Red Hart. We turned right and the spire of St Mary's church was lit by sunshine. The coach driver called the horses to a stop. 'We have an hour before the meeting,' Aunt Hetty said as she gathered up her bag.

Chapter Twenty-five

An air of expectation greeted us, loud voices echoing round the entrance of the assembly rooms. Built as a theatre, the balcony above was already full, a sea of faces peering down at us. The room was crowded and stuffy. Aunt Hetty had wanted no one to see us arrive and we had almost left it too late. Edging our way along the back of the room we found the last free seats. 'Goodness . . . I didn't think there would be this many here! There's far more interest than I expected. Surely they can't all want to bid for the tollgates?'

Six seats were arranged in a row on the raised stage. A group of men were talking with their backs to us, all referring to their fob watches. The clerk's table was on one side, a large map pinned to a wooden board on the other. The man in a brown corduroy jacket looked familiar and I recognised him as Mr Cartwright who had given Benedict the papers to sign. Standing to the front of the stage, he rang a hand bell and as the shouts turned to whispers the men took their seats.

'If we could start…' Mr Cartwright looked round for confirmation. Sitting in the middle of the row of seats, a tall, slim man in his late forties scowled his consent.

'That's Lord Entworth,' whispered Aunt Hetty. 'It was his protégée who caused all the problems. His land is south of mine – just the other side of the creek. He's the Turnpike Trust's chairman.'

'So it's in his interest to build this road.'

She drew a deep breath. 'Next to him is Mr Alfred Horner who holds a high position in the Falmouth Packet Company. His niece was one of my pupils before she asked to be removed.'

I looked at the rotund man in a brown wig. 'So it's in his interest to build the road.'

Her mouth tightened. 'The man next to him, I wasn't expecting to see. He's Mr Henry Trevelyan who owns the *Jane O'Leary*. He's Angelica's husband. He has extensive business interests and owns a vast number of wharfs.'

A handsome, well-dressed man, Henry Trevelyan looked to be in his early thirties. He glanced up through steel-rimmed spectacles – an honest face, serious, but kind. 'I don't know the man in the green jacket,' Aunt Hetty continued. 'I've never seen him before. But the one with the grey hair at the very end is Sir Charles Montague – and his interest lies in the Post Office.'

'I'm beginning to see a pattern, Aunt Hetty.'

Her frown deepened. 'I think we must assume this is not just a consultation meeting to show the route. They've already made up their minds. Mr Aubyn was right. This meeting is to seek tenders.'

Lord Entworth rose and the room went silent. Dressed in silk, he flicked the lace at his sleeve. Looking down at the crowd as if wishing to be elsewhere, he almost snarled, 'This new road we're proposing is well overdue. *Well* overdue. And as Chairman of the Trustees, I shall make it my priority to take this map, in person, to Parliament, and I shall ask, no, I shall *insist*, they proceed to draw up a new Act of Parliament to grant us the right to commence building this new road as soon as is reasonably possible.'

A murmur of assent almost brought a smile to his powerful features. Too cruel-looking to be considered handsome, he was clearly used to getting his way. 'We have the right, gentlemen, to build this road we so desperately need. I believe the money can be raised swiftly. Our industry is suffering . . . progress is being slowed. We need this road *now*. Our surveyor has chosen a safe and sensible route which avoids Carnon Hill and anyone who believes this road to be anything other than progress is indeed a fool.'

The rumble of approval grew louder, everyone nodding, even a few cheers. Allowing himself a congratulatory grimace, he banged his cane on the wooden floor. 'There cannot be *one person* among you who objects to this new route. Not one who does not see the benefit of the miles saved . . . the better gradient . . . the opportunity to widen and add speed to your journeys. Our industry is being stifled. We need our tin and copper to get to the ports . . . our foundries need to get their coal and equipment to the mines. Our Post Office needs quicker communications – a safe road, with a well-regulated system of tolls. And let us not forget, gentlemen, this road will bring our labourers much needed employment.'

The nods were instant, a rumble of agreement. A man shouted, 'You get this through Parliament, Lord Entworth, an' we'll work night and day.'

Another picked up the baton. 'Aye . . . I'll be putting in my tender.'

'So will I. Let us know where we sign. We'll raise the money. We have to.'

The rumble turned to shouts, men raising their hats to show their approval. Lord Entworth turned to the Post Office man with a poor attempt to conceal his self-congratulatory smile. At the desk, a young man in black was writing furiously in a large minute book. Banging his cane again, the room went silent. 'Mr Cartwright can furnish you with more details.' Lord Entworth flicked his coat-tails and sat down.

Mr Cartwright adjusted his glasses. 'As you know, I've recently been appointed clerk to the Trustees.' His face was flushed, sweat breaking on his brow. 'I've long thought this road overdue . . . and yet, we needed the brilliance of our new surveyor to give us a road we can trust to be sound . . . in the best position . . . where we know the land won't subside or be washed away. Where the rock we excavate won't be too hard or too crumbling. Where the gradient won't cause erosion.' He wiped his forehead with his handkerchief.

I, too, was feeling uncomfortably hot. Sitting at the back, we could hardly see through the haze of tobacco smoke. A movement caught my eye. Benedict was being ushered on to the stage among a burst of applause. 'And here he is, gentleman.

I give you Mr Benedict Aubyn, the man with the expertise behind our new road!'

The applause grew louder, cheers sounded, more waving of hats, and Benedict stood out from the side. Bowing in acknowledgement, he looked reluctant to go any further until Mr Cartwright ushered him nearer. Standing by the large map, Mr Cartwright reached for a stick, leaning across his bulging waistcoat to point to the map. His high-pitched voice rose higher. 'Gentlemen, you cannot see this well enough but suffice to say . . . here at the Carnon river mouth we propose to build a new bridge . . . and here, and here, we propose to put the tollhouses. Here, will be a holding pen, and running all down this western side, we shall construct a substantial side-lane for livestock.'

A voice rang from near us. 'Which side of the bridge will the toll be?'

A quick glance at Lord Entworth, and Mr Cartwright cleared his throat. 'South side.'

The rumble of voices sounded displeased and Mr Cartwright's already flushed face deepened to puce. Raising the stick in his hand, he forced a smile. 'There will be jobs aplenty . . . please, gentlemen, you can't see the map sufficiently from where you are. First, I propose a vote. Then I propose you come forward and see the map for yourselves. I shall bring it down. Please address any business directly to myself, and I shall have your interests recorded by my secretary.' He wiped his forehead again. 'First the vote. All those in favour, raise your hands and say aye.'

The shouts of 'aye' were deafening, the raised hands like a

forest in front of us. Aunt Hetty tapped her fingers against her mouth. 'Who is that man in the green jacket? Why don't I know him? I dislike his face intensely.'

I looked up. Across the stage, Benedict was staring at me. Our eyes held and I felt a rush of sympathy. He looked lonely, out of place. He must have known the decision would go his way but there was hurt in his eyes, no sign of rejoicing.

Chairs scraped as people got up to leave. Some went straight for the door, others formed groups and the noise started rising. The committee left the stage and Benedict lifted the map down the small steps at the side. Blotting his book, the secretary shut it swiftly, gathering up his things as two men lifted his table and carried it down the steps.

A flash of red caught my eye. A military man was making his way through the group of otherwise darkly coated men and sudden panic made me look closer. He was not the officer who had led his men into the crowd of starving tinners, but he had the same air of authority. Walking with a stick, his hair flecked with silver, he looked distinguished and handsome. He headed straight for Benedict, who swung round and greeted him warmly. They became hidden from sight. A circle of men were clustered around Mr Cartwright but further commotion was causing disruption. The man in the green jacket was setting up his own table and men were clamouring round him.

Making my way through the crowd, I reached his table. Men were pushing forward, jostling for position, and he raised his voice. 'One at a time, please, gentlemen. Let's go one at a time, shall we? I'll get your details and your interest. No one will leave without me knowing what it is you want and what you can offer me.' He laughed, but without mirth, and if Aunt Hetty did not like his face, I certainly did not like his tone.

On the stage above me, Benedict was shaking hands with Angelica's husband. By their smiles, I could see their mutual pleasure. Talking amiably, they were shrugging their shoulders, placing a hand on each other's backs. A sudden nudge forced me forward and a man pushed past me. 'Mr Yoxall of Yoxall's Wagons. *Oxen* wagons. My business is thriving. I transport goods for the navy . . . provisions . . . booty . . . prizes and such like.'

'Captured gold and silver?'

'Aye, plenty of prize money, Mr Banks. I need somewhere for my oxen, and somewhere for my men. Devoran Farm will suit me perfectly.'

Sudden giddiness made me catch my breath. Another man pushed forward, another and another. A voice spoke sharply. 'I'm interested in that farm, too, sir. I'll turn it into a coaching inn. The farm has a good array of stables, an' its position's perfect. I've three coachin' inns – Penzance, Bodmin and Camborne. Here's my card.'

A tall, well-dressed man elbowed his way forward. 'I'd like a quiet word, Mr Banks. A *quiet* word, if you don't mind.' Scowling at a man intent on interrupting him, his voice hardened. 'I've serious intent, but I'd like my business to remain my own.'

Two or three others nodded in agreement. 'Aye, too many eyes and ears.' Reaching forward, they presented Mr Banks with a series of printed cards and I had to steady myself. With the crush and heavy smoke, I began to feel faint. Mr Banks leaned back in his chair and reached for his pipe, lighting it as the men watched in greedy expectation. The bowl glowing, he sucked in the smoke and exhaled as he read their cards. 'I'm here for a week. I'm staying at the Red Lion. Let's see what I can do for you, gentlemen. Or rather, what you can do for me.'

He had a thick accent, very different to the men he was addressing. Through a gap, I watched him put the business cards in his jacket pocket. The red coat caught my eye again. The major was pressing forward, clearly wanting a chance to speak.

'I wonder if I could . . . ?' He tried again, louder, more forcefully. 'I wonder if I could have a word, Mr Banks?' He bowed stiffly. 'Major Henry Trelawney at your service.' He sounded like a gentleman, his manner courteous, yet Mr Banks neither rose to greet him nor stopped sucking his pipe.

Smoke billowed around him. 'Your business, Major Trelawney?'

'I'm commissioned by the militia. Part of my extensive brief is to find sufficient housing for the troops. Our garrison needs a new billet — we need provision for our regiment as well as visiting regiments when they dock in Falmouth. We have a growing number of volunteers. I need premises with considerable sleeping arrangements and areas of hard standing where drills can be conducted. Where training can take place . . .'

Mr Banks' eyes widened. 'So, ye're after a large property, Major Trelawney? I believe you've found the right place. St Feoca School has all those requirements.' I felt the room spin, my shock making me gasp. Sitting like a giant toad, fat, pockmarked, his smile greedy, Mr Banks raised his eyebrows. 'Right on the creek – the ships carrying your troops could anchor in the deep and the men row straight ashore. I think we can do business, Major Trelawney. Don't see any reason why not.'

There was no air, just heavy tobacco smoke and the smell of sweat. Someone pushed me from behind, another jostled me sideways, everyone pushing forward to lay claim to Aunt Hetty's land. I felt my arm taken, Benedict Aubyn propelling me back to Aunt Hetty. 'I think Pandora could do with some air.'

She rose immediately, following us out, and I breathed deeply. She turned to Benedict. 'Who is that man?'

'His name is Jonathan Banks. That's all I know. He's not a member of the Turnpike Trust. I don't know his connection, nor his reason to be here. Henry Trevelyan hasn't heard of him either.'

The fresh air was cooling my cheeks but not my anger. 'He's talking about your land, Aunt Hetty. He's taking business cards for the farm . . . even the house!'

Her voice was a whisper. 'Will you find out who Mr Banks represents, Mr Aubyn?'

Benedict looked as shaken as we did. 'I'll see what I can do.'

Men spilling from the door began hanging around in groups. 'So, the rumours are right. The estate *is* to be sold.' Other rushed past, hurrying to spread the word.

Aunt Hetty's cheeks burned as furiously as mine. '*Sold?* Who's doing this?' She stared at each of them in turn. 'Whoever he is, he's here. He was at the meeting – in that room.'

We watched Benedict weave his way through the crowd, his frown hardly encouraging. Reaching us, he shook his head. 'I'm little the wiser. He's an agent but he's not saying who he represents. All he'll say is that he's working for your estate.'

Aunt Hetty's cheeks turned ashen. 'My estate? Carrion crows, the lot of them.' She slipped her arm through mine. 'Come, my dear, we have an important meeting to attend.'

Chapter Twenty-six

Town House, Truro

With Town House only four houses away, we had no distance to walk. Lady Clarissa's house was the last in the row and hurrying along the pavement, the church clock chimed twelve. Trees behind the house were rustling in the wind, a sudden crispness in the air. Across the square, the church railings were being painted, a man sweeping the path.

Standing under the ornate porch, Aunt Hetty smoothed her hair. 'Don't knock, Pandora. The footman will open it. He'll take our cloaks and gloves . . . keep your bonnet on. Lord Carew and Lady Clarissa have very liberal views, but in town, they keep to protocol. They leave town in the spring and return for the winter months – they're only here because their daughter's expecting her second child. Ah, here we are . . .'

The door opened to a beautiful bright hall with a sweeping staircase and polished mahogany doors. Dressed in livery, two footmen took our cloaks and gloves and I glanced in the ornate gold mirror, tucking a curl back in place. Both of us looked flushed, the colour in Aunt Hetty's cheeks making her high cheekbones even more pronounced.

Announcing us at the door, the footman stepped back and, curtsying deeply, I felt suddenly overwhelmed. In great danger of gawping, I tried not to stare at the most beautiful drawing room I had ever seen. Light and airy, it had two large sash windows at each end, a view to the church at the front, a leafy garden at the back. The marble in the fireplace seemed to glimmer. An intricate gold clock ticked on the mantel-piece, a series of silhouette portraits hanging in oval frames. The furniture had elegant claw feet, the backs of the chairs inlaid with delicate marquetry: a pianoforte with an embroi-dered piano stool was at one end, a painted screen taking up the corner space. It was enchanting, exactly like Mama had described grand houses to look like – even down to the pale green and gold striped wallpaper, and the chairs upholstered in gold silk.

Dressed in flowing green silk, her matching green turban pinned with an emerald brooch, Lady Clarissa stepped forward. 'Welcome, my dears. Come and sit down... we're just waiting for Mrs Trevelyan and we shall be complete.'

Reverend Penhaligan had risen at our entrance and bowing, pointed to his seat by the fire. 'Miss Mitchell... please, take my seat.' He bowed to me. 'Miss Woodville, your servant.'

Mrs Lilly remained seated and smiled from beneath her velvet bonnet. 'How lovely to see you both again.' I had forgotten her soft Irish accent but remembered the kindness in her face. A beautiful woman, her eyes seemed to sparkle beneath her white hair. 'I have some *very* good news for you.'

Lady Clarissa was studying us carefully. 'Harriet, if I may say, you look a little *unwell*. Dear me, this sudden north wind does not bode well. Come to the fire, my dear.'

Aunt Hetty shook her head. 'I'm very well. It's just we've come from the Turnpike meeting. The plans have been approved for the new road and I have to admit to being rather put out.'

Mrs Lilly glanced at Lady Clarissa and I caught their immediate concern. There was resignation in their looks, resolution, as if they needed to speak out. Mary Lilly clasped her hands in her lap. 'My dear, this is very difficult for you. And very difficult for us.'

Aunt Harriet shrugged, though not from indifference. 'It's not that. I knew about the road plans. I understand the need to slice across my land without a second thought . . . to run roughshod through my hedges . . . to trample my fields. I know all of you – except maybe you, Reverend Penhaligan – have a vested interest in getting this road built. But what I didn't know is that my land is rumoured to be for sale.'

'For sale?' All three gasped. Lady Clarissa sat down, leaning immediately forward. 'Harriet, you must be mistaken. They'll be putting in tenders to be toll keepers, that sort of thing. No one can be selling your land. The land is held in trust. They may apply for permission to work on it, but that's all.'

Voices sounded in the hall. The door opened and Angelica Trevelyan handed her cloak to the footman. 'I've just heard something very shocking. Henry was at the meeting just now. He says St Feoca School and estate is to be *sold*! He says it's all over Truro. People had certainly got wind of it as the meeting was crowded.'

Flushed, and clearly angry, she took a deep breath. 'Miss Mitchell, I have four girls who through no fault of their own find themselves on the edge of untold poverty. Four girls, more excited than you can imagine, whose dream of an education was about to be realised. Four bright, intelligent girls whose only fault is to be born of respectable families who have slipped into poverty and illness. Yet now, I hear the school is to *close* and their dreams of an education is to be whisked away. My fundraising committee have worked *tirelessly* and yet now it must be dissolved, and I must tell these poor unfortunate girls that they must return to their impoverished aunts and grandparents. *Until I find someone else willing to educate them*. It's very disappointing and not what I expected from you.'

Never had I heard such a dressing-down. She was magnificent. Quite magnificent. If we had been by ourselves I would have clapped. Her tirade at an end, Mary Lilly stared at her hands while Reverend Penhaligan examined his shoes. Lady Clarissa sucked in her cheeks and clasped her hands against her chest. Above the mantelpiece the clock chimed and Aunt Harriet drew a deep breath.

'I remember you once gave me a very similar dressing-down, Mrs Trevelyan. I believe it was after the fifth time you ran away from my school. Miss Angelica Lilly, you were then, fifteen were you? But just as fiery and furious. Telling me in no uncertain terms that I should be educating the girls in my charge, not teaching them how to flower arrange and alight from a barouche. And that, my dear, was the reason why I kept my school going. You didn't know it at the time, but your fury gave me such hope. And I can assure you that as long as I live, I shall fight for my school.'

Angelica Trevelyan's eyes filled with tears. 'So the rumours are wrong? We still have a school?'

Aunt Hetty nodded. 'Yes, we still have a school and we have work to do. But someone wants to close our school, of that there's no doubt. We've been the target of malice again – a raven was found in the kitchen, and Pandora found three waxen effigies hanging from the stairs. They want to frighten us again.'

Mary Lilly reached for her fan. 'Who would do such a thing?'

Angelica Trevelyan indicated for me to sit next to her on the chaise longue. I had risen when she entered and had remained standing. My awe of her was complete. She was elegantly dressed in the latest fashion, but she carried a leather case and looked every bit as efficient as the men in the meeting. 'Someone has gone as far as spreading rumours that the school is to close. Well, he won't succeed! We need a list of everyone at that meeting. One of them there will be behind this. May we sit round a table, Lady Clarissa, only I have several papers I'd like Miss Mitchell to sign?'

Resettled at the long dining table in the equally gracious dining room, Lady Clarissa nodded to Reverend Penhaligan. Opening his book, he picked up his quill and with the preliminaries recorded, Lady Clarissa smiled at Angelica Trevelyan. 'Item number one.' She cleared her throat. 'It is with delight I can inform the governors that funding for four *charity girls* has been arranged by one of our trustees. Mrs Trevelyan will now furnish us with the details.'

Angelica Trevelyan opened her leather case. 'I have the names of the four chosen girls. I've formed a committee of like-minded, wealthy patrons who have pledged an annual fee towards their upkeep. The amount available per child is *thirty-five pounds per annum*.'

Aunt Hetty's hand flew to her mouth. 'Oh...oh, my goodness! Oh, how *very* generous! How very...kind.' She reached for her handkerchief and I reached for mine. 'Thirty-five pounds is more than generous. Will you thank your committee... from the depths of my heart? Thank them for their belief in my school.'

Lady Clarissa reached for the papers Angelica held out. 'Can you guarantee these funds for *ten* years?' She sounded doubtful. 'How do we know your sponsors will keep to their word? How do we know they'll not withdraw too soon?'

'Because the money raised will be held securely in a bank. My committee view the education of women as vital. Mrs Fox is particularly keen, as is Lady Polcarrow. Some wish to remain anonymous, others have told me they can't afford as much as they would like to give but they intend to show their support by attending your concerts and plays — and participating at your prize-giving events.'

A faint blush coloured Mary Lilly's cheeks and I knew she must be one of the main benefactors. She caught my eye and smiled her sweet smile and a rush of gratitude flooded through me. Her stepdaughter gathered up the papers. 'So if we could have your signature to say you approve, please,

Miss Mitchell? I can have the girls with you in two weeks' time.'

Sliding the papers across the polished table, Aunt Hetty studied them carefully. Round Lady Clarissa's wrist was a bracelet of broad beans. They had been dried and painted, pierced, and strung on a ribbon. On her other hand, her ring looked to be fashioned from plaited straw. The room was charming with paintings of roses hanging in groups, a family portrait of her five sons and daughter.

Though with such grand proportions, the room was saved from formality by a number of shells and stones displayed on the shelves. A wooden rocking horse sat between the two windows, an abacus on the floor. On the table behind her, a beautiful wooden ark stood with carved white animals spilling from the gangplank. Lady Clarissa tidied away the signed papers and cleared her throat. 'And now, Mrs Lilly, I believe you have made progress with the endowments?'

Mary Lilly nodded at her stepdaughter, who once again reached into her leather case. Sliding yet more documents across the table, her cheeks dimpled. 'I have, Lady Clarissa. I'm happy to say Reverend Penhaligan and I have been very busy and have met with an inordinate degree of success. I believe we will soon raise enough money to cover the cost of the girls from your estate. All four of them.' She glanced down ... Miss Sophie and Miss Gwen from the farm, Miss Mollie from the mill and Miss Kate from the gatehouse.'

Sifting through the papers, she reached for her embroidered glasses case. With her glasses securely in place, she read the agreed criteria. 'They must no longer be considered servants... they must wear the same dresses as the other girls... there must be no difference between endowment girls or fully paying girls. Or the charity girls. We shall not call them by any other name... all must be treated equally. They must sleep with the other girls in the school, though they can go home every Sunday – as can all the other girls.'

Aunt Hetty nodded. 'That's very comprehensive.'

'We are aiming for *thirty* guineas a year for the next six to seven years to see the girls through the school and into gainful employment. This is not an inconsiderable amount and we know it's ambitious, but it equates to what I understand you charge the fee-paying pupils, and we must have equality. Should this be successful, I believe further fundraising and charity events could point the way to further endowments. Maybe, in a year or two?'

For a while, Aunt Hetty had been strangely quiet. Putting down the pen, she sat staring at the papers, as yet unsigned. 'May I speak plainly, Lady Clarissa?' Silence filled the room. Her chest heaved. 'I have nothing but admiration and deep, deep gratitude. You have all been my rock... the school is your school as much as mine... so what I'm about to say has been a difficult decision. I don't say this lightly. I know this vastly important new approach to our school will be the making of it – the future of girls' education is vital – but I, myself, feel unable to remain as headmistress.'

Aunt Hetty remained looking down but I caught their sideways glances. Strangely, none of them seemed shocked or angry. Lady Clarissa cleared her throat. 'My dear Harriet, I think we all understand why.'

Aunt Hetty reached for my hand. 'I intend to hand over the school to Miss Woodville. I will be right behind her and support her in every way possible. I'll gladly teach in her school, if she'd like me to, but I no longer wish to be head-mistress of St Feoca. Pandora has all the passion and drive the school needs now.'

Lady Clarissa's hands rested on the table. 'We have wondered. Only, word gets around. Since you were seen with Sir Anthony at the theatre, on several occasions, rumours have circulated. I believe this is known to you. My dearest Harriet, none of us would want it otherwise. We are well aware of the sacrifice you have made for your school and well, my dear . . . may we congratulate you?'

Aunt Hetty shook her head. 'No . . . My friendship with Sir Anthony is widely talked about, I know, but there's nothing to congratulate me about. I tell you this only because I believe it vital to advertise for another teacher. The constitution says three teachers and we have three, but I don't believe it will be for very long. Miss Grace Elliot is charming and accomplished, and as her guardian I owe it to her to find a good match. Marriage will give her the security she deserves.'

Reverend Penhaligan put down his pen. 'I believe a new teacher is both timely and an excellent idea. We're in the nineteenth century . . . society is changing and our school will reflect this change. We must educate our young women to take their position in society – to give them a chance to be governesses and teachers. To learn bookkeeping . . . accounts. Most will find husbands and use their education in their homes, but the few who don't must leave our school with a chance of good employment. An experienced teacher will add immeasurable value to the school.'

Nods of agreement greeted his words. He drew out a handkerchief and wiped his glasses. 'It will show our school is thriving and signal to anyone who thinks they can intimidate us that we're not to be frightened off. But, I must say I'm filled with misgiving. Grave misgiving. Are you safe in your beds at night, Miss Mitchell? How did the dolls and raven get into the school?'

Aunt Hetty's poise never left her. She looked almost regal. 'An unfortunate oversight. The kitchen door was left unlocked, and it won't happen again. But just to make sure, I've arranged for six strong men to sleep in the gatehouse and Mr Aubyn is to sleep above the coach house. I believe their presence will deter any further attempt at entry.'

Angelica Trevelyan reached for another sheet of paper. 'Henry jotted down everyone he can remember being at the meeting, though obviously there are others he's yet to name. Someone on this list is responsible, and my guess is the name at the very top – Lord Entworth.'

Mary Lilly leaned closer to read the names. 'My husband believes the men from the Streamworks are behind it, but it could be the new owner of Harcourt Quay.' She looked up. A man was hurrying across the square. 'Here's Henry now.'

The footman opened the door and Henry Trevelyan caught his breath. Bowing, his handsome face broke into a shy smile. 'Just carrying out instructions, Lady Clarissa! Forgive me for barging into your meeting like this but Angelica insisted I find out who the agent at the meeting represents.' He turned to

Aunt Hetty. 'He says he's working on behalf of your estate — that he has your interests at heart.'

All colour drained from Aunt Hetty's cheeks. 'My interests!' Her sudden pallor made her look vulnerable. 'He is not working for me, so I can only deduce he must be representing my father's *heir*. After all, he will inherit the land. Yet, if it is him, who could have told him the school was closing? Only the school governors know about the constitution. *Only the governors*.'

She looked at each of them in turn. 'None of you has mentioned the constitution in conversation?' Heads shook, everyone looking as shocked as she was. 'None of you?' Again they shook their heads. 'Not even by accident?'

Finally they found their voices. 'No, never.' 'Not at all.' 'Never mentioned it.'

Their protests grew stronger and Aunt Hetty reached for her bag. 'I'm sorry, I had to ask. That leaves only one other person — the attorney who drew up the constitution.'

Reverend Penhaligan turned back the pages of the minute book. 'The constitution was drawn up by Sir George Reith, residing in Number 1, Pydar Street. His son's taken over the business.' Shutting the book, he took a deep breath. 'We need to ask him if anyone has asked to see your father's will.'

Chapter Twenty-seven

A short walk brought us to a brightly painted front door with the brass plaque *Matthew Reith, Attorney at Law* gleaming in the sunlight. Ushered into an elegant room, the young clerk was apologetic, walking backwards as he bowed. He shook his head, trying to prevent us from entering, but Aunt Hetty swept past him. Left in no doubt she was not to be sent away, he looked increasingly uncomfortable. 'He's out of town...for three weeks at the very least. An important hearing has taken him to Bodmin...then up to London...'

'So who will see me?'

The young man hesitated. 'If it's important, I can send him a letter. Please, allow me...' Tall and dark, his hair cut short, his blue eyes looked intelligent, if a little troubled. Dressed smartly, he had a slim build, broad shoulders and must have been about my age. 'May I offer you a seat, Miss Mitchell? I'm Francis Polcarrow, Mr Reith's stepson. I'm here to keep things *ticking over* until he returns. Only, I'm not qualified to take on any new briefs...'

Aunt Hetty regarded him more closely. 'Mr Francis Polcarrow? Your brother is Sir James Polcarrow? I must say the family resemblance is striking.' Sitting at the proffered chair, she smiled. 'This is Miss Pandora Woodville, my niece, and soon to be headmistress of St Feoca School.'

Bowing, he walked backwards again, seating himself at the huge desk before leaning forward. Cheeks flushed, a slight tremble in his hands, he reached for a pen and a fresh piece of paper. 'If you tell me your business, I can write to my father and receive his instructions.'

'Are you an attorney, Mr Polcarrow?' The young man shook his head. 'Studying law?' A smile and a nod, and Aunt Hetty shrugged. 'And you work for your stepfather? Then, I'm sure you'll be able to help us.'

A drop of ink from his pen splashed on the paper. 'I only started yesterday. That is, I was employed last week. I'm still at Oxford but Father thought it important to get acquainted with the office clerks and find out how they go about things.' Noticing the ink blot, he reached for another piece of paper.

Aunt Hetty smiled her most charming smile. 'The information we require will give you the perfect opportunity to get acquainted with your father's office. A letter will delay us too long. An agent is, as we speak, parcelling up my land, *which is not for sale*. I need to know how my father's will has become public – who has been here to enquire about the school's constitution . . . and who has asked to read my father's will? I believe you keep it here in your safe room?'

Francis Polcarrow's brow creased. Leaning forward, his elegant fingers chose another pen. 'We hold your father's papers and your school's constitution, do we? Could you tell me your father's full name and the date of his death?'

He may have looked flustered, but there was no mistaking his grasp on the situation. Writing quickly, he began a series of searching questions. The room was sparsely decorated, paintings on the wall, a fire burning in the fireplace. Bookcases lined each side with rows of box files, ledgers spilling over the lower shelves, leather volumes crammed along the top. A working room with few embellishments, and I liked it better for its simplicity. Francis Polcarrow was a handsome man, square-jawed and broad-browed, his eyes sharp with concern. Aunt Hetty spoke quietly and clearly, and his jaw clenched.

'This malice first occurred when precisely?' His pen scratched the paper. 'And you believe this latest malice is the work of the same man?' Reaching for another piece of paper, he cleared his throat. 'We have very little time if your father's heir, Mr Richard Compton, believes the land to be his in two weeks' time.'

A concerned look in my direction brought a flush to his cheeks. 'We can presume this enquiry came *before* the rumours started? Which takes us to March last year.' Another piece of paper joined the pile. 'I need the date of your mother's death, as well as your father's death. Let me be quite clear – it was shortly after your mother's death that the devilment began?'

'Yes. My mother died last March. My father died in March 1790.'

Gathering his papers, his frown cleared. 'I think that should be fairly straightforward. I'll locate your school's box and I'll search the attendance diary. My stepfather, like his father before him, recorded everything.' He smiled shyly. 'May I offer you some refreshments?'

We declined and he backed through the door. Tapping the tips of her fingers against her mouth, Aunt Hetty looked drawn. Outside, carts were passing, a few men on horseback. The wind was clearly picking up; men were holding their hats, women gripping their shawls. The clock struck four and Aunt Hetty tapped the table. 'What's taking him so long?'

She began pacing the room, her silk gown swishing across the polished floor. 'This does not bode well. He's just a youth. He'll have no idea—' The door opened and she swung round. Francis Polcarrow was carrying two large ledgers, behind him, a clerk was holding a large box file.

Laying them on the desk, Francis Polcarrow's face remained serious. 'Forgive me for taking so long. I think I have everything we need.' Nodding at the clerk, he reached for the box file. 'Thank you. You've been most helpful.' Waiting until the clerk left, he invited us to come closer. The ledger had markers inserted throughout. Opening the first marker he pointed to a closely written page. 'There's no record of anyone applying to see your school's constitution for the year before the devilment began. No one has enquired. And we can be quite sure of that because here, to make it absolutely clear, is your school file. If anyone had enquired, there would have been a double entry. And there isn't.'

Clearing his throat, he reached for another of the ledgers. 'Nor, I'm afraid, do we hold either of your parents' wills. This is our attendance diary. My stepfather's father – who I'm afraid is no longer with us – visited your school on your father's death to read his will... and we know Mrs Mitchell was at the reading. It was considered clear and straightforward and no further action was taken. Were you there, Miss Mitchell? Did you hear your father's will read out?'

'No. I wasn't present. I was at an important governors' meeting. I had no idea an attorney was coming for that purpose. Mother was there. They should have waited but we were both very upset and I think Mother just wanted it over with. I was told Father left all his personal belongings to my mother – his paintings, his books and his mineral collection – and the estate was left in trust. It was to revert to his heir on the closure of the school. I was told my sister was excluded from the will.'

Nodding, Francis Polcarrow flipped the pages to the next mark. 'My stepfather attended your school to read your mother's will in March. You were there then?'

Aunt Hetty nodded. 'Yes...'

'All your mother's personal goods were to be divided between Miss Harriet Mitchell and Miss Pandora Woodville, with certain provision for Miss Annie Rowe. At least that's clear. But we don't have your father's will here.' Searching through the box file, he drew out an official document. 'This, we do have. It's the constitution where your father leaves very clear instructions that the school is to revert to the heirs of his estate – as outlined in his will – but, as I said, we don't have his will. I've searched everywhere and can only conclude it must be in your possession.'

Pulling out Aunt Hetty's chair, he beckoned for us to sit. Returning to his side of the desk, he reached for yet another piece of paper. Choosing the right quill, he dipped it in the ink. 'I believe I must be blunt. If I'm to help you, I must understand the reason for the constitution.' In the silence, he put down his pen. 'I understand your reluctance. You think me young and inexperienced, but please believe in my integrity. Nothing you tell me will leave this room. Unless you'd prefer to wait for my stepfather's return?'

Aunt Hetty nodded and I spoke clearly, detailing everything I wanted to keep hidden, even the scandal of my birth. He left his pen idle, his eyes kind, shrugging, even smiling, as he drew the story from me. As I finished his brow furrowed.

'Which leads me to suspect the will has been read. This could be officially, or it could have been in your school – either by a person who has come across it by accident or by someone who has gone expressly to search for it. Most likely, the man entering the tower window. Miss Mitchell, to be completely clear, how does your father's heir, Mr Richard Compton, fit into the family?'

Aunt Hetty shook her head. 'We've never met him, just his father – my father's cousin. He came on a rare visit to Cornwall and stayed with us. He was amicable, but neither party instigated further visits.'

'Did his visit coincide with Mr Woodville staying at the coach house? Their visits, were they roughly the same time?'

'No, Mr Compton visited after my sister left. Soon after his visit Father drew up the constitution and asked me to read and approve it. Which I readily agreed to. I had decided not to get married and the thought of a pension after years of teaching was an attractive offer.'

'And Mrs Abigail Woodville and her husband were informed of this change in the will?'

Aunt Hetty nodded. 'Yes. Father asked them to acknowledge receipt of his letter.'

'So Mr James Woodville can be ruled out. He would gain nothing by the closure of the school – which was clearly the intent of the constitution, as I understand it.' Embers glowed in the fire, a sudden chill to the room, and Francis Polcarrow rushed to add more logs. Returning to the desk, he took a deep breath.

'The question we need to ask is who stands to gain the most from the closure of your school? And I believe the answer to be Richard Compton. However, what we need to discover is who *instigated* the closure – was it Mr Compton himself who instigated the terror or did someone with the appropriate knowledge instigate the terror in order to benefit? A chicken-and-egg situation, as I see it.'

'There are more names than you have ink for, Mr Polcarrow. Every member of the Turnpike Trust would benefit for a start.'

'And your estate workers? Would they benefit from a new landlord?' Aunt Hetty remained silent and he glanced at me. 'Forgive me, Miss Mitchell, but I need to know if I can rule them out.'

'There's Mr and Mrs Samuel Devoran in Devoran Farm, Mr and Mrs Jacob Carter in St Feoca Mill, and Mr and Mrs George Penrose in the St Feoca Gatehouse. But none of them knows about the constitution.'

His eyebrows rose. 'Unless they scaled the iron fire steps and searched your study? I don't think we can rule anyone out. But just to be clear – your school needs ten pupils and you have only eight?'

'Yes. Four of our estate girls and four promised endowment girls. We're to advertise for a new teacher and I intend to advertise for more pupils.'

His look was sharp, every bit as eagle-eyed as Aunt Hetty. 'Miss Mitchell, let me advise against advertising for more pupils. Let people think the school has the correct number. If the school is thought to be thriving, Mr Compton has no legal right to invite bidders for land he does not yet own. But another teacher? I thought you already had three?'

Aunt Hetty gathered up her bag and smoothed her skirt. 'We do. But one is to leave us soon. She will soon be married.'

Showing us to the door, Francis Polcarrow's voice dropped. 'I'll arrange a meeting with this agent – this Mr Banks. Good day, Miss Mitchell, Miss Woodville. I'll visit you as soon as I have some answers.'

Above us, the sail finally started to fill and began arching in the wind. Feeling its pull, the men leaned forward, resting on their oars, taking swigs from the gourds hanging round their waists. With the frequent bends and curves, the river was difficult to navigate, yet now we were picking up speed. Wrapping our cloaks against the sudden chill, we watched the wooded banks. Woodsmoke blew from the charcoal burners, the sound of water lapping the bow. There were quite a number of passengers and I kept my eyes on the left bank, desperate not to glance at Benedict Aubyn.

Joining us, he had hurried along the quayside to catch the ferry home. Sitting a little distance away, his hat was pulled low, his fists clenching and unclenching against his leather case. Aunt Hetty continued talking. 'An experienced teacher will bring new ideas. She'll know what they teach in other schools. She must have authority, yet she must be approachable. More particularly...' Dear God, she was about to say it all over again. 'I'm very fond of Grace. Very fond. But I'd be failing in my duty if I don't see Grace marry well. Grace has no security like you have. You have me, but Grace has no one.'

She clasped her hands in their leather gloves. 'Even if we teach our girls to the highest standard required to be a governess, our priority must always be to find them husbands. Grace's beauty and charm are clearly intended for marriage. Everyone looks twice at her...' She glanced where I was avoiding looking. 'I'll be failing in my duty if I don't see her well married,' she repeated.

Whenever I looked at him, my stomach twisted. Her meaning was obvious. Every time she spoke of Grace, her eyes would turn to him, and every time she mentioned her name, a knot would twist my gut. Her voice dropped. 'Mother excluded Abigail entirely from her will. She left everything to you and me – her jewellery, her clothes, her books, her paintings. And that includes all Father's personal books and mineral collection. Everything was to be divided equally between us, but you, my dear, will have it all. My will has already been drawn up. Everything I have goes to you. Like those earrings, which look quite splendid on you.'

We came alongside Harcourt Quay and were helped off the boat. I thought she might start walking but she was clearly waiting for Benedict. 'Mr Aubyn, may I introduce our new headmistress? It's been decided and approved. I present to you Miss Woodville, headmistress of St Feoca School.'

He bowed, his back stiff, a new formality in his address. 'Congratulations, Miss Woodville. I'm delighted. How very ... pleased I am for you. Though I must admit I'm a little surprised. Rumours are rife – does this mean your estate and school are to remain just as they are? Mr Banks seemed adamant everything's to be sold.'

Aunt Hetty's smile was more like a grimace. 'Everything will remain just as it is. Mr Banks is wasting everyone's time. Simply an unfortunate misunderstanding which will soon be resolved.'

I could hardly speak as we walked through the gatehouse and up the long drive. Side by side, his strides keeping pace with mine, none of us was talking, just the sound of our foot-steps on his newly mended drive. He was clearly not going to probe: thank goodness his innate good manners prevented him from questioning us any further.

I hardly ate supper, hardly knew what I said, but kept my eyes down, my hands folded, as Grace played yet more pieces from her extensive repertoire. From now on, this was how it would be. I would listen to the girls playing their music, watch their theatricals, see them grow into beautiful, refined ladies with the skills and education to match. They would be my pride, my joy, my reason for waking every morning. Their welfare my only concern.

Aunt Hetty sat straight-backed and smiling and I tried to do the same. Yet I could feel my back burning. It was the strangest sensation, as if eyes were piercing the back of my neck. I looked round. A man was looking through the window, not the poacher but Benedict. Catching my eye, he looked quickly away. Of course, he would be drawn to the music. Of course, he would want to listen. Standing alone in the dark, watching Grace when he thought no one could see him. Watching with longing in his eyes. His pride, his joy, his reason for waking every morning. Her welfare his only concern.

Stage Three

UNIFICATION

Chapter Twenty-eight

G wen nodded, then shook her head, her freshly washed curls bouncing off her shoulders. 'I know and I'm that grateful. It's more than I want in the whole world, but I can't. Not if Sophie can't. She don't speak . . .'

I smiled. '*Doesn't* speak.'

'*Doesn't* speak. She won't take *one* step in to the house. So it just won't work. And I can't stay in the school if Sophie don't stay.'

'Doesn't stay.'

Her bottom lip trembled. 'Wouldn't be kind. So I have to say no.'

The beans and peas planted, we were watching the robin hopping over the raked earth. Sunshine filled the garden, the smell of warm soil, the scent of jasmine. The blossom on the cherry tree was in bud, the blackbird singing, a pair of blue tits collecting moss for their nest behind the honeysuckle. Sophie watched us from the asparagus bed. Scooping soil around the tender new tips, she was following our every word. Dropping her trowel, she ran from the garden.

Gwen's eyes plummeted and I could see her struggling not to cry. 'We've got the funding, Gwen. We've arranged *endowments*, which means a number of prosperous people believe in your abilities. It's so important to have schooling. It won't be all uppity and fancy. There won't be lords and ladies, just girls of good moral standing, whether they be gentlemen's daughters or farmers' daughters. You're very clever, Gwen. You ask questions I don't think to ask, and you have answers to all my questions. Just think what you could do if you were educated.'

A tear trickled down her cheek. 'I'd be like Miss Mitchell – I'd study things through a maggiflyer.'

'A magnifier? And what would Sophie do?' She remained silent, shaking the earth from her hands. 'Sophie doesn't need to talk to come to our school. She can learn without talking. But she will need to come *inside*. You'll both have your own comfy bed and four drawers each. And lots of good food. The bursary will include your school dresses and a day dress for wearing in the evening. You can see your parents in the yard every day and you'll go home after church on Sunday. Kate and Mollie will be just the same.'

'She likes flowers. Before the devil got her tongue, she said she loved flowers.'

I tried not to snap, but fury filled me. 'The devil *did not* get her tongue. How can anyone let a child think that?'

She was backing away, dipping a curtsy, her eyes downcast. 'I can't join yer school, Miss Woodville. Wouldn't be kind. Sophie needs me.'

My panic was rising. 'Please, Gwen . . . please. I need you, too. I need girls in my school or Miss Mitchell will have to

270

close it. Gwen, I *need* you. Miss Mitchell needs you. Please persuade Sophie to come into the house.'

The sound of chanting echoed across the cobbles . . . *be he alive or be he dead, I'll grind his bones to make my bread.* She turned to go but swung round. For an eleven-year-old, her eyes turned piercingly sharp. 'Mollie Carter says her father drinks. She says he lays about all day. And Kate's father says Mr Carter's a lazy lay-about. But my father says he never used to be like that. He says he used to be hardworking and jolly.'

It was like the gates had burst. I had never heard her talk so freely. 'That doesn't stop you from coming to school, nor does it stop Mollie. It's because the harvests have failed. There's no wheat for Mr Carter to grind. It's enough to stop anyone being jolly.'

'Well, he's not thinking, is he? He's being stupid an' Mollie's that fed up. If he were thinking – if he wasn't lying around drunk all day – he'd use his mill to grind bones.'

'Grind bones?'

She shrugged, scowling back at me. 'Father can't afford fertiliser to put on his fields and Jacob Carter at the mill has no wheat to grind. But he has the mill. So why doesn't he grind bones to give Father? Doesn't have to be fish bones – the fertiliser Father likes has ox bones in it, an' all sorts. Father's cattle's been taken by the navy to Falmouth. There's plenty bones in Falmouth.' She bit her lip, forcing herself not to cry. 'Doesn't take going to school to work that out!'

The chanting stopped, the sound of scampering feet: Sophie and Mollie came running through the gate. Mollie could have been Gwen's twin: the same height, both eleven, both with the same flecks of gold curling onto their shoulders, but whereas Gwen still scowled, Mollie was all smiles. She bobbed a wobbly curtsy. 'Ye'll never guess what?'

Sophie reached for my hand, her huge eyes alive with excitement. 'What is it, Sophie?' She started pulling me across the courtyard, Gwen and Mollie running behind. Stopping under the arch of the coach house, she pointed across the newly brushed cobbles to four chairs arranged in a half circle in front of a large slate. The alphabet was on the slate, copied by a wavering hand. 'Your beautiful lettering? Is that what you want me to see?'

Shaking her head she pulled me slowly forward, leading me on tiptoe to a bale of hay. Smiling, she indicated I should look behind it. Benedict was crouching forward on the ground. 'Twelve eggs. Definitely twelve eggs.' He turned and his smile froze. 'Oh, Miss Woodville. Good morning.'

Gwen rushed next to me. 'Our hens are laying. We thought they hadn't started! Well done finding them, Mr Aubyn. They must be from two hens, maybe three? Look, these ones are speckled. These look darker.'

I knelt on the dry hay, all of us crowding round the nest. Benedict seemed delighted with his find. 'I noticed one of the hens kept coming here. My sisters keep hens and they often follow the new hens . . .' In the small space, his white sleeves brushed against mine and he jolted away. 'I'm sorry . . . here, let me . . .' Picking up several of the eggs, he handed them to Mollie and Sophie.

Our eyes caught, and I could feel my cheeks flame. He must not see the pleasure his smile had brought. Turning to the girls, he seemed strangely flustered. 'If there are, let's see . . . twelve eggs, and we keep two back — because my sisters always say not to empty a new nest — then how many eggs do we have?'

Mollie held up her fingers. 'Ten.'

Straw was clinging to his shirt, his jacket nowhere to be seen; just his white shirt with its sleeves rolled to his elbows, his black silk cravat tied at his neck. 'And how many eggs does it take to make an omelette?'

The three girls giggled, Sophie smiling broadly. Gwen jumped up to take a strand of straw from his newly cut hair. 'That's a silly question. Depends on how many are going to eat it and how many you can afford to use!' Laughing, they seemed so at ease with him.

Mollie screwed up her face. 'I don't like omelettes.'

Gwen raised her eyebrows. 'Have you ever had one?' Mollie shook her head and a chorus of laughter made the girls double up. 'So how do ye know if you like them or not?'

Benedict's half-smile widened. A beautiful smile, lighting his face, making his eyes crease. 'I think Miss Woodville ought to decide how they should be eaten.'

I could hardly look at him. Informally attired, straw in his hair, I caught a glimpse of the man buried beneath his grief. Heat seared my chest, a burning pain. 'Divide them between the four of you — we must count Kate, even though she isn't here.'

Gwen shook her head. Raising her chin, her eyes flashed. 'No. There's *ten* of us in our school. Mr Aubyn found them so it's only fair he joins us. That's us four, Mr Aubyn, Miss

273

Woodville, Miss Mitchell, Miss Elliot, Mrs Penrose and Miss Annie.' She held up all ten fingers and the hairs on my arms rose. She was smiling with her heart and soul, telling me in no uncertain terms that she would do anything to make our school work.

Benedict bowed formally. 'Thank you, Miss Devoran. I'm honoured to join your school.' He turned and started climbing the wooden steps to his rooms and I stood watching but not watching, wanting him to stay. Wanting him to smile like that again.

Mollie clutched her egg and I asked if I could walk home with her. The sun was shining and a walk would do me good. Besides, I wanted to see the mill and meet Mr Carter. The facts were simple: he owed us rent. Grandmother may have been happy to waive his rent, but that was then, and now was now.

Cradling her egg in her palm, Mollie led me round the back of the barn. Skipping sideways, she pointed to a circle of bulrushes round a boggy patch of mud. 'That's the old Abbot's Pond. Father says there used to be trout in there. He used to fish it as a boy.' The more she skipped, the happier she seemed. 'I'm that pleased to be with Gwen and Sophie. I'm that pleased to go to school.'

'I'm pleased too. I'm glad you like them. Do you know them well?'

Like Gwen and Sophie, she was pale and under-nourished, but also like Gwen, she had freshly washed hair and clean hands and face. She even wore the same yellow ribbons. Her smile broadened. 'My mamm's her mamm's sister. But we don't see much of each other since our fathers quarrelled. They don't speak to each other. It's stupid.'

Ahead of us, the mill was half-hidden by the trees. A huge wheel towered above the sloping thatched roof, but whereas the waterwheel attached to the Carnon River Mill had been turning furiously, this one lay still. 'Why isn't the wheel turning?'

She shrugged. 'Works all right when the tide comes in, but the pool behind is silted up. Father's tried to keep it flushed but it just silts up again. Mamm says he's worked himself to drink. The more he tries to clear the silt, the more it builds up.'

'May we look?'

'Course... through here. Mind, 'tis slippery.' Following her round a dirt path, we drew closer to the wheel. The tide was out, the wheel not turning. Pointing to a series of deep brick channels down the side of the mill, she squinted in the sun. 'The tide comes in here and floods this chamber... which leads to the wheel. The wheel turns and the water goes into the holding chamber. Come...'

She put down her egg and balancing along the edge of the brick channel we reached the wheel. The wooden paddles were covered in slime, several strands of seaweed hanging mid-air. 'The millpond's meant to hold the water and when the tide goes out, it's meant to flow back to feed the wheel... going backwards this time. But the thing is... whoops... do be careful, Miss Woodville, this is very slippery.' She was balancing precariously near the edge. 'Back in Grandfather's day it worked. My father worked it as a boy.'

Edging back to safer ground, I stood staring at the mill house. 'I'd like to speak to your mother and father. Will you take me to them?'

Mollie opened the kitchen door. A stained apron tied over her worn skirt, Mrs Carter looked petrified. Her greasy hair was parted beneath a mobcap, her fingers twisting her skirt. 'He's not here . . . he's . . . he's . . .'

Through the open door, I heard the sound of snoring. A man's legs were stretched out in sleep. His arms were hanging by his sides, his head back, his mouth wide open. 'Mr Carter?'

Jolting awake, he swore a volley of oaths. About forty, he was unshaven, his black hair falling across his face. His jacket was stained, his boots scuffed. 'Mr Carter?' I tried to control my anger – the same snores, the same extended legs, Mama in the kitchen doing all the work. Both of us tiptoeing around with the same look in our eyes. 'I shall wait for you next door.' I tried to keep my voice steady, my outward appearance calm.

Mrs Carter offered me a chair by the unlit fire but I knew to remain standing. Mr Carter shuffled in, wiping his mouth, looking every bit as angry as I was. 'And you are?' Glaring at me from beneath black brows, he had the same smirk as Father, the same note of derision. The same dismissive tone. I had always stepped back before, biting my tongue, looking down like Mrs Carter. Mama, always clutching at her apron, the same look of disappointment in her eyes.

'My name is Pandora Woodville, I'm Miss Mitchell's niece. I've taken over the running of the estate and I'd like you to attend a meeting, with Mr Devoran, on Monday. I expect a proposal of how you intend to make the farm and mill profitable again.'

'You what?' There was a lessening in his sneer, a flash of panic in his eyes.

'I want your proposal on how you're going to keep the millpond clear of silt.'

His brows creased. 'I've tried. God knows I've tried. There's no water, no millpond, and no wheat to grind. 'Tis enough having the road builder on my back.'

Mrs Carter's hands flew to her mouth. 'He's a good man, honest he is. He don't mean that, Miss Woodville.'

I gripped the back of the chair. 'The road builder?'

She shrugged. 'Mr Aubyn – the kind man doing the shore road. He said his men could dig here next. He said they were a strong workforce and they could give a week's work before starting the next road. But Jacob gave him short shrift. He sent him on his way.'

A stab caught my ribs. 'Why did you send him away?'

She reached for the edge of her apron, pressing it to her eyes. 'Miss Woodville, 'tis not from want of help. 'Tis from want of money.'

I drew a deep breath. 'Your brother-in-law needs fertiliser for his sodden fields and I believe fish bones – even ox bones – can be ground in mills. What if that's possible? Have you spoken with him? What if you can produce his much needed fertiliser?'

'Let him go elsewhere. We don't speak.'

Each time, backing down, biting my tongue, never holding my ground. Well, not any more. 'Next week, I want you to tell me how you're going to get your mill prosperous again. My grandmother may have tolerated rent arrears but I shall not. Tenants who do not pay their rent will be evicted.'

Mrs Carter gripped the back of her chair, her face so white, I thought she might faint. 'Mrs Carter, you and Mollie can always expect a home in my school, but I'll not tolerate drunks.' Jacob Carter passed a trembling hand across his eyes. 'Will I see you both in church on Sunday?'

Courage filled Mrs Carter's eyes, a drawing back of her shoulders. Lifting her chin, she held herself taller. 'We'll be there, Miss Woodville. Jacob and me, we'll be there.' Rushing to the dresser, she opened the top drawer. 'This is what Mr Aubyn suggests.' She held up a piece of rock. 'He said we should think of grinding gypsum. It's a sort of stone but the millstone will grind it, no problem. Mr Aubyn says they're putting it on the fields in Norfolk an' it's making the pastures grow better. Maybe we should grind that alongside the bones?'

The pain beneath my ribs was back, sharper, more intense. Her eyes were alive with hope. 'He says he could get it fer us. If we find the money, he can get some sent.'

Chapter Twenty-nine

Unwilling to leave the garden, I had to force myself indoors. The sun was stronger, the buds beginning to burst. The birdsong was louder, the smell of warm earth, the scent of new growth. Persephone, in all her glory, breaking free from Hades to be reunited with her mother Demeter. It seemed strangely fitting. Released by her father from his barren underworld to restore the flowers to the meadows, the fruit to the trees, the harvests to the fields.

Aunt Hetty looked pale, she had hardly eaten. 'Aunt Hetty, it's such a beautiful day, shall we go for a walk?' Her smile was followed by a swift shake of her head. 'But it would do you good. Now that the weather's so lovely, might you spend less time in your room? Maybe I could keep you company?' I knew I was speaking boldly, but it was lonely with her always in her rooms. She hardly ever ventured out, and if she did, it was always by herself.

It was not just that. If she left her rooms more often, she would have more understanding of the state of the grounds.

Grace had taken the plates to the kitchen and I seized my chance. 'Aunt Hetty, did you know there's been a terrible falling-out between Jacob Carter at the mill and Sam Devoran at the farm?'

She shrugged. 'They're brothers-in-law. It's probably just a family disagreement.'

'I saw Jacob Carter yesterday and I've asked him to come with Sam Devoran to discuss how they might help each other.'

She seemed preoccupied, hardly listening to me at all. 'Splendid. Then the rift is clearly not as great as you've heard. Gossiping is never advisable, my dear. The most important thing to grasp, being a headmistress, is that it cuts you slightly adrift. It's not easy to hold a position of authority and stay friends with those you employ.' I found it too hard to reply. She gathered up her skirts and was halfway to the door. 'We have a well-stocked library, why don't you read some of the new poetry our girls like to read? Or we have Shakespeare's plays. Your grandfather was a great reader.'

'Like *Candide*?'

She swung round in surprise. 'I should have thought sooner! Father loved that book. Third shelf, on the right. Halfway along. Next to *Gulliver's Travels*.'

Fighting my disappointment, I made my way to the library. The girls were playing hopscotch outside, the sound of jumping echoing through the open window. Aunt Hetty was clearly telling me I must expect the life of a headmistress to be a lonely one, and I must not get too used to her company. Yet St Feoca without Aunt Hetty would be a very lonely place and I fought my sudden sadness.

I found *Candide* straight away; it was clearly a much loved book, the binding scuffed, the pages well thumbed. A slim volume, the print was small but perfectly readable. A piece of paper was inserted in the last page and I recognised Grandfather's writing.

> *You have found the silver and found the gold,*
> *But the greatest treasure you've yet to behold.*
> *What good is wealth (if wealth you've found)*
> *When harvests fail and wither on the ground?*
> *Your grapes may decay and render sour wine,*
> *And minerals can trick you and falsely shine.*
>
> *What good is silver when famine strikes?*
> *What good your gold with empty dykes?*
> *The answer is here, and clear as a bell,*
> *The treasure you seek can be found in a –*
> *So here it is, my curious daughter,*
> *The treasure you seek can only be –*

It was clearly a riddle, no doubt part of one of Grandfather's treasure hunts. I held it to my lips, then my heart. The first clue must have been silver, and this was the clue for gold – the gold of Eldorado. The answer to the next clue must have been water. Grandfather had inserted the riddle between the last two pages and I turned to the last line of the book – *But we must cultivate our garden.* It was as if he was standing behind me.

I turned to leave, but the spine of a book caught my

attention: not the shape, nor the binding, but a small gold symbol lit by a shaft of sun. It glinted, drawing my eye: the symbol of a snake sending a shiver down my spine. It was as if I knew what I was going to find.

The Coming of the Devil.

There was no author, no date; neither was it printed but hastily written in brown ink. Nor were the pages attached to the binding but slipping out as I opened it. Almost dropping them, I hurried to the table. The manuscript smelled musty, a faint odour of smoke. The pages were hand-cut and sewn together with gut. Opening it, a sketch of a raven's feather took up most of the first page; the writing beneath it was cramped and blotched.

When I die, for die I shall, I will know my best is done. Read well, and mark my words, for this is the truth, and those who gainsay this truth will regret their foolishness. I pray you take heed of my warning. For though you hear him not and see him not, he is watching your every move. He is in the turn of the stair, the flicker of the light. In every recess, in the very shadows of every room. Take heed, I implore you, lest you be the next to catch his eye. Written in The Year Of Our Lord Sixteen Hundred and Ninety. This is the true and binding testimony of Alicia Emmery, aged seventeen.

It looked hurriedly written, several ink spots obscuring many of the words. Singed by smoke, some of the pages were too discoloured to read. The first page must have been lost, as it started mid-sentence.

and with trepidation I determined not to answer. Straight away, I felt a nervous expectation, an agitation which I knew I must forbid myself to feel. For it was wrong of me, unseemly, and wicked to thrill at his touch. That he wooed me with such fervour sent a shivering through my body, a yearning I comprehended I must deny. That I was being sinful was too great a burden to withstand, yet as I held his letter to my heart my body burned. From nowhere, I sensed him in the room. 'Leave me, leave me, for you have wrought enough. You have wronged me and I will be ruined.'

He was behind me, yet I saw him not. I felt his hands caress my body, the warmth of his breath upon my neck. The touch of him, the very heat of him: his hands burning, sending such arrows of desire. Yet as I stared in the reflection of the looking glass, I saw only myself, a smile of such ecstasy on my lips. For he was kissing my neck, biting my ear. 'Oh, but you are mine. You are mine. And I shall have thee. It is the price which you must pay for beholding my face. See how you burn at my touch.'

'No . . . no. Leave me. You will ruin me. I shall lock my doors. I shall bar the windows. I shall never be yours.' Yet I knew I was undone. For my neck burned at the touch of his breath. His hands were on my bodice. In the looking glass I could see my laces slowly loosening and I gasped with anticipation. For I knew I was in mortal danger, on the very brink of giving myself freely to the devil. His hands were setting my breasts afire. Unable to resist, I knew to reach forward and pull the bell pull, yet I could feel myself melting, burning, the heat from his body coursing through me. In that moment, I knew I was undone.

I felt only the terrible need to be his. For I had tasted of his lips and my body yearned for him with such sweet fervour.

And yet I was saved. My maid entered, and I shivered in the cold draught that blew into my chamber. 'My lady . . . you are not well. Come, you are burning up, such a shaking in your limbs. You have a fever, a terrible rash on your neck.' Her timely arrival had saved me, and I fell sobbing to the floor.

'You must bar the windows, lock the doors,' I cried with what little strength I could muster. 'My fireplace must be boarded. I must never be left alone.' Yet as I spoke, I heard a rustle and a shadow crossed the beams above me. 'I need a priest,' I cried. 'Bring me my Bible, and my prayerbook.'

A page was missing, another one torn in half. A draught blew in from the window, the sun dipping behind the garden walls. Shadows were lengthening, a coolness in the room. I knew I should take this straight to Aunt Hetty, yet I turned the page.

Behind me, a gust of air blew upon my hair. My limbs turned icy cold, chilled as if by the hardest frost. Yet I fought my desire to turn round. I knew not to look but keep my eyes downcast. If I gave way to temptation I would see a man in the looking glass; the most handsome man there ever was. For I had drawn water from the Holy Well and seen his countenance behind me. Such magnificence you could not envisage, his eyes so blue, his hair softly curling. His lips full blooded, his chin square. He had wooed me so completely and I had thought him a gentleman. Misguided and mistaken, I had believed in the sincerity of his love. Such was his disguise.

And so it was I kept the devil at bay. Or so I thought. I fervently wanted to believe he was banished from the house and yet the more he stayed away from me, the more I craved his touch. I was no longer myself, but a servant waiting for him to do with me what he willed. For I had tasted of his lips and was his for the taking. I could not eat, I could hardly drink, but lay every night in fervent want of him. I could only stare at the shadows, my eyes searching the dark recesses, knowing he was there. Longing for the thrill of his touch.

My physician remained perplexed, my parents distraught. They cried out with anguish, their sobs echoing down the dim corridor. If I did not nourish my body, how could I nourish my soul? And yet I knew my soul had long been lost. I was failing, my bloom fading. I was dying for the very want of him.

Yet, he was there all the time: he had not relinquished his quest for me. 'I shall have thee,' I heard him whisper from the rafters. For I had underestimated his power. He had been playing with us, biding his time. Only now did I understand he had taken full possession of the house.

For he had entered the house in a stealthful manner, bidden welcome, and ushered through the door with great expedience. Disguised was he as a book and sat upon the pile of other books in a box purchased and sent from a land I knew not where. Admired he was and looked upon with great excitement. 'Fools that they are,' he whispered in my ear. 'For I must be invited across the threshold and bade welcome.' Yet my parents knew that not. They knew not that the box on the cart was how he entered this very house. And not one person could ever speak of it, for he laughed with such depravity and said in a manner *most cold and callous, 'Those who direct me henceforth become my henchmen. For I smite them dumb in order that they serve me better. Forthwith, they speak only with the devil's tongue.'*

Gathering up the manuscript, I stuffed it in its leather binder. Hiding it beneath my shawl I ran across the hall.

Chapter Thirty

Halfway up the stairs, I shouted, 'Aunt Hetty... Aunt Hetty?'

The door opened. 'Goodness, Pandora. What is it?'

'Look what I've just found in the library! It was half-hidden on the top shelf, pushed back, yet the light caught this serpent. It's... Well, what do you make of this?'

She was wearing a large apron, her hair slightly dishevelled. Behind her, the door to her sitting room was open. '*The Coming of the Devil,*' she read with contempt. 'This was in the library?' Reading it, her frown deepened. 'There was mention of a diary. I searched everywhere but never found it. It's very simplistic, a rather crude imitation of *The Castle of Otranto.*'

'Surely no one would believe this is written over a hundred years ago? Surely no one would fall for such an obvious forgery?'

'Young girls are very impressionable – especially if they read it at night with shadows flickering across the ceiling.

But what I don't understand is where has it been? Someone's returned this to the library. Why? To scare Grace?'

'Are you sure it hasn't been there all the time and you just haven't seen it?'

Sitting at her desk, she turned the pages as if they would burn her. 'That might be possible. I've been very preoccupied. I did search the girls' rooms but I thought it most unlikely to exist. Just another of the rumours.'

She was remarkably calm, yet my fury was mounting. 'Did the rumours start before or after Lord Entworth's protégée visited the Holy Well?'

'Afterwards. Definitely afterwards.' She paused, looking up. 'Lord Entworth came to see me about her. He was ushered into the library and I saw him there.'

I caught her meaning. She may have sounded calm, but there was anger in her eyes. 'Was he alone?'

'Yes. He had every opportunity to place this in the library. In fact, now I remember, he was standing by the books.'

Behind me, the clock chimed five. 'What does Lord Entworth gain if he gets his hands on your land?'

Her laugh was brittle. 'The bridge will give him access to the tin streaming works. Lord Entworth has considerable shares in the company and you heard Benedict say they needed to sink shafts to gain deeper ground. Lord Entworth would use my land to build a pumping station.'

'So he got his protégée to visit the well in order to set this in motion.'

'It is possible. But you forget,' she looked down in disgust, 'this might have been returned the night those hideous dolls were left. I'm certain it wasn't in the library. Lord Entworth isn't the only one who wants my land. We must think who else would gain by having access to the shore.'

'Everyone involved in the streaming works will gain.'

She grasped her wrist. 'The owner of Harcourt Quay definitely stands to gain. A busy quayside with everyone clambering to export their tin will see his profits soar.' She slid the manuscript across the desk. 'How does this poor unfortunate end? By giving herself to the devil, I presume? It's too ridiculous to waste any more time on.'

I turned the pages, reading quickly. Finally, I reached the end. 'There's a fire. He claims her as flames leap around them. She relinquishes her honour and is consumed by flames. *For I knew not the earthly pain of burning but felt such exquisite ecstasy coursing through me. Yet as I looked into his handsome face, he was smiling. For he is the devil and though I reached out my hand to beseech my parents to save me, my cries were drowned by his laughter—*'

'Enough!' She shook her head. 'No one must read this, least of all the girls.' Placing the singed pages back inside their cover, she locked it in her top drawer.

'Sophie is convinced she directed the devil into the house. Can you remember a box arriving on a cart? She said the men spoke the devil's language. Soon afterwards, she stopped speaking because she was told the devil had got her tongue.'

A flicker crossed her brow. 'A box did arrive. From Augsburg in Germany. It was . . .' She gripped her wrist again. 'Just after Mother died, we had a delivery of a large crate. It was a rather large box for such a small piece of equipment – some instrument – we had ordered. The men spoke no English; so yes, I believe we can place the manuscript from after that.'

'Who saw this box arrive?'

'All the girls. All the staff. It caused quite a commotion.' Standing up, she smoothed her skirt. 'It arrived in view of everyone. Before the rumours started.'

'So the person who wrote that book knew about the box.'

Her cheeks were pale, a pulse throbbing at her neck. 'It links them to the school, doesn't it? Lord Entworth's ward was definitely present, and so was Mr Alfred Horner's niece. Maybe I should go through the list of all the girls here at the time?'

Chapter Thirty-one

St Feoca Manor: School for Young Ladies
Sunday 12th April 1801, 11:00 a.m.

A fine mist was drifting above the creek, a stillness in the air as the girls lined up to be inspected. Their scarlet capes looked as grand as any militia, their boots polished, their bonnets adjusted to just the right angle. Not yet summer, they wore black gloves and velour hats, woollen stockings, and their best Sunday dresses. Scrubbed and gleaming, their cheeks on fire, they looked shy and embarrassed.

Passing muster, Grace began their proud procession, our twenty-minute walk accompanied by nervous giggles. 'Won't they just laugh?' Kate whispered.

Gwen shook her head. 'Not if we don't let them. We're not to be put off. Ye heard Miss Annie. She's that proud of us an' we're not to be put off.'

The church bells of St Feock were ringing, the day warming, the sun burning the mist. Aunt Hetty and I walked behind and Benedict joined us. Looking beautiful in a blue bonnet and gown, Grace seemed more nervous than the girls, constantly turning round to ensure her charges were keeping time. Her obvious excitement made her eyes sparkle, her cheeks flush with her perfect rose-petal blush.

Perhaps I was scowling. Perhaps my anxiety at being seen in church was showing. 'The start of things to come. Gwen's quite right, you're not to be put off.' Benedict Aubyn kept his eyes ahead. Not wearing his overcoat, his grey cravat was pinned with an enamel pin, his double-breasted jacket cut squarely across his shoulders. His hair was freshly washed, his boots gleaming. In one hand he held a Bible, in the other, a wodge of papers.

Leaving us at the church door, he bowed and handed them to Jacob Carter. Smartly dressed, the miller was almost unrecognisable from the drunk who had slouched and scowled only days before. Mrs Carter caught my eye and curtsied but turned straight to Mollie, wiping away her tears of pride. I could not stop to talk: Aunt Hetty was introducing me to the rector. 'Reverend Carew, this is my niece, Miss Woodville, who has lately arrived from Philadelphia.'

Tall, pleasant-looking, with a warm smile, I recognised him from the family portrait hanging in Lady Clarissa's dining room. Her second son, Charles Carew. His wife was by his side, welcoming me back to Cornwall after what they could only imagine had been a very *interesting* life. He could have been my mother's brother-in-law and sudden shame flamed my cheeks. Everyone knew. Everyone. All of them would remember my parents' hurried marriage, their quick departure to Bristol.

Looking away, I caught Benedict's eye. Making his way through the line of people, he stood by my side. 'Have you got your aegis ready?'

My god-protected shield. I had almost left it behind.

The church already looked full. Grace led the girls to the seats reserved for the school, and Aunt Hetty reached for my arm. Smiling, she returned the many nods and curtsies, the smiles of people craning their necks to see me. I thought it unlikely we would find a seat but still she drew me forward. The front box beneath the pulpit was free, Sir Anthony Ferris in the opposite box bowing, smiling, wishing us good day. Next to him was Cador Ferris, and next to him Olwyn was wearing her new lemon bonnet. Both showed great pleasure in seeing me.

Recognising the family pew, I sat where I had last fidgeted through Grandfather's sermons. I could remember his hands gripping the lectern, his playful wink when he finally finished. Today, I sat straight-backed with Benedict beside me. 'No one knows about your father's deception,' he whispered. 'And even if they do, the sins of the father should never be visited on the child.'

I gripped my gloved hands. 'They'll say bad blood runs in my veins. Their looks were not kind. I saw more scowls than smiles.'

'Give them time. They think the school was closed. Yet here you are, like Venus rising from the waves.'

I hardly heard the sermon but sat staring at the altar where Mama had knelt. Mama, whose indiscretions with Father had brought such consequences. A sense of emptiness gripped me. It was as if she was growing distant, as if I never really knew her. The service ending, I gathered up my bag. Sir Anthony held out his arm, and Aunt Hetty accepted it with a smile. Cador Ferris stepped forward, also holding out his arm. Smiling, he indicated we should follow his father and Aunt Hetty down the aisle. 'A lovely service, don't you think?' He hesitated, looking round, and whereas Benedict was free to walk Olwyn down the aisle, he held out his other arm to his sister. 'We were so hoping to see you, Miss Woodville. And such a glorious day.'

Smiling, he greeted the nods and bows as everyone watched us leave the church. Tall, undeniably handsome, his silver tiepin glinted in his silk cravat. Both were dressed elegantly. Olwyn was wearing her new bonnet and a matching yellow silk gown which shimmered in the sun. She held up her hand to shade her eyes. 'Shall we follow Papa and Miss Mitchell? It's such a lovely day to take a walk.'

Aunt Hetty turned, clearly expecting us to follow. People were dispersing from the church and Cador smiled his shy smile, a slight stammer as he pointed out a cherry tree in full blossom. 'Mother loved that tree. It's always the first to bloom.'

Benedict had joined Grace and was smiling at the children. Her excitement plain to see.

'Shall we visit your grandparents' grave, Miss Woodville?' I heard Olwyn say.

'I'd like that. I haven't visited it yet . . . it's just I've been so busy . . .'

Glancing back at Benedict and Grace, I fought my rush of envy. Benedict had stood beside me like a rock. A true friend. Someone who understood me and knew what I was going through. Someone with whom I felt safe: a man of under-standing and gravitas, yet with a sense of humour and a gentle way of mocking me. *Like Venus rising from the waves.* Visions of Venus protecting her modesty with her wet hair flooded my mind; Venus, naked, rising from the waves. Venus, the goddess of love and beauty.

He was offering his arm to Grace, now walking with her in the sunshine. No doubt all the way back to St Feoca where no one would see them slip into the barn. Maybe he would suggest they visit the hens' nest in the coach house to look for eggs? A perfect excuse to take off his jacket and roll up his shirtsleeves. He would reach to see if there were any eggs and she would stretch up to pluck the straw from his hair. Slowly, he would tilt her chin and draw her closer. Was that what Mama had done? Slip into the barn to meet Father behind the straw stack?

Cador stopped mid-sentence. 'Are you all right, Miss Woodville?'

'Yes, very well.'

'Shall we continue walking? There's a bench here we could sit on.'

Olwyn stopped him. 'Why don't we wait here? Miss Woodville, might you want to visit your grandparents' tomb by yourself?' Her voice was full of tenderness. 'Only if this is the first time, I can understand you might like to be alone. We'll wait for you here. It's just a little further on – beneath that apple tree.'

I nodded, biting my lip. Never had I imagined it would be like this. I had always envisaged Mama taking my hand, the two of us walking side by side to lay flowers on her parents' tomb. My emptiness deepened; of course Aunt Hetty should marry Sir Anthony. A blackbird was singing, a tethered goat eating brambles by the fence. A sea breeze was picking up, the faintest wisp of wind against my cheek. Below me, the sea was glinting, around me, the leaves about to burst into leaf, and I forced myself to appreciate the beauty of the place. Anything but think of the haystack; anything but imagine what I was picturing in my mind.

A tombstone caught my eye. Covered by lichen, I could only make out half of the inscription but the name was clear enough.

MISS ALICIA MARY EMMERY †

TAKEN FROM US IN THE YEAR OF OUR LORD
SIXTEEN HUNDRED AND NINETY †

AGED SEVENTEEN †

MAY SHE REST IN PEACE †

Turning, I caught the murmur of voices: Sir Anthony was speaking. 'Please allow me to help, Harriet. Cador was in Truro yesterday and he heard it on several accounts. Why didn't you tell me? You've no need to sell your school. Miss Woodville appears more than capable of achieving this strange vision of hers. Surely, it frees you from all your obligations, yet at the same time keeps your dreams alive?'

Aunt Hetty must have replied but her voice was too indistinct. Whatever she said brought a rush of defence. 'It would be a *loan*, Harriet. Merely a loan. You won't be in my debt. And I don't care how long it takes you to repay me – if indeed you ever repay me. Miss Woodville has no other home.'

'She will always have a home with me.'

'Yes, always – Harriet, that goes without saying – but if that stubborn pride of yours won't allow me to offer you a loan, then please reconsider my offer to buy the wood. You love that wood. I love the wood. It's where we met – where I first saw you.'

'That seems a very long time ago, Anthony.'

'Not for me, Harriet. I see it as clear as the day – you and Abby, sitting in your boat, Abby writing her poetry, you drawing your shells. I often watched you from my side of the creek, the two of you paddling in the water, searching the shore for treasure. Sometimes I'd wait all day, desperate for you to come. Always watching the weather, the tide, listening for the sound of your laughter. I'd watch your antics and admire your sense of freedom. It was *your* creek, *your* wood, and no one could stop you flinging off your bonnets and shaking out your hair. That day . . . when I was sailing and pretended I hadn't seen you . . . was the day I finally plucked up the courage to join you. That day seems like yesterday; I remember it as clear as bell.'

'You fell in the water. Was that on purpose?'

His laughter drifted across the churchyard. 'Of course it was. And you fell in too – was that on purpose?'

'How very young and foolish we were.'

I could see them through the hedge. They were leaning on a gate, looking out across the field. Standing side by side, comfortable in each other's company. He would have been standing in the skiff just like Cador had stood: tall, virile, undeniably handsome. I knew I should walk away and leave

297

them to their intimacy, yet the urgency in his voice drew me back. 'You love that wood, Harriet. I think of it not just as *your* wood but as *our* wood. And if I can gift it to you in any way . . . keep it for you . . . give it to you so it will be yours, for ever, no matter the sale of your estate, then I gladly will. Dearest Harriet, I appreciate you're in mourning. I will not, and cannot, presume. But if you have the same—'

Voices drowned her answer. A man and women were coming towards me, bowing and curtsying, wishing me a good day. Turning away, I stumbled along the grassy path to the large tomb under the apple tree. Seeing my grandparents' names made it impossible not to cry. My emptiness felt overwhelming, Sir Anthony was offering Aunt Hetty the wood as a wedding present. Not Mama's wood. *Their wood.* Tears welled in my eyes. How empty St Feoca would seem without Aunt Hetty. How lonely.

A gentle cough, the rustle of a silk skirt, and Aunt Hetty stood by my side. Slipping her hand through my arm, she stood in silence. 'How beautiful their gravestone looks,' I managed to say. 'How well positioned.' She nodded and I fought my tears. 'How well tended and well loved.' The gentle breeze caressed my cheek, a hint of salt, the scent of flowers. The blossom would soon be out, the bluebells soon carpet the whole churchyard. Everything just as in my dreams yet my loneliness seemed unbearable.

Aunt Hetty squeezed my arm. 'Come,' she whispered. 'Let's go home.'

Chapter Thirty-two

The capes and bonnets returned to their pegs, the girls were clearly reluctant to go home. The afternoon sun was streaming through the kitchen and Annie reached for her handkerchief. 'Breathe into a cloth if your eyes run when you're cutting onions, girls. That's something I learned very young. Not that it's doing any good today!' Grace was singing as she busied about the kitchen, Annie seizing the opportunity to show Gwen and Sophie how to make a rabbit stew. Sitting at the kitchen table, they began watching but not watching, far more interested in what was going on in the yard.

'Honest, he won't go away.' Rushing to the window they stood on tiptoes, their petticoats showing beneath their skirts. 'Mr Aubyn says he followed him home. He said he was over at Hammet's Hill. He just looked round and the dog was there. And ever since, he won't leave his side.'

Putting down my book, I joined them at the window. As did Grace, both of us peering over the girls' heads to watch

Benedict attempt to make a scruffy dog sit to command. 'There, see. He's done it,' cried Gwen.

'No he hasn't. You mind my words. That dog will get your chickens.' Annie had long been shaking her head. The dog was filthy and needed a good bath: he was never to come in her kitchen as he would steal the food.

'Mr Aubyn says the dog was starving. He says now he's washed and fed, he thinks the dog must have belonged to someone. He's not wild, or vicious. Mr Aubyn says the dog seems to want company more than anything.'

Benedict must have seen us all watching. Shrugging, he tried to make the dog sit again. Miraculously it did, and Benedict turned and bowed with a smile. Clapping her hands, Gwen smiled back. 'There. He's a sweet dog.'

'No he isn't. He's filthy and smelly and I'll not have him in my kitchen.' Returning to the table, Annie scraped the chopped onions into the pot and reached for some more. 'And he's not getting any of this. If you must feed him . . . if he has to stay . . . then potato and swede will have to suffice. And maybe the odd bone. *Maybe*.'

Grace was clearly on Gwen's side. 'I think he's lovely, and Miss Mitchell thinks having a dog will be a good thing. He can guard us. I think we'll all sleep better for having a dog in the yard. Oh, look. Oh, that's so adorable. He can't take his eyes off Benedict. Look. He clearly adores him.' Shirtsleeves rolled to his elbows, the sun catching his white shirt; the dog was clearly not the only one who could not take his eyes off Benedict Aubyn.

Resuming her lesson, Annie summoned the girls back to

the table. 'The onions give the flavour. Never skimp on onions, girls. And we shall add a little wine. And parsley. But first, pass me some more vegetables. Those parsnips and that swede.' Wiping her eyes, she breathed into her muslin cloth. 'Turn away, girls, if your eyes begin to water.'

Resuming her tasks, Grace bustled round the kitchen, putting away the last of the vegetables. While we had been at church three baskets had been delivered, two with fruit and vegetables, one brimming with game. 'Sir Anthony never usually sends *three* baskets. Though this basket looks a little different. Maybe it's from another well-wisher?'

The butchering of the rabbit complete, Annie was assembling the rest of the ingredients. 'Pass me that parsnip. Now you must learn to scrape gently. Hold the knife steady and always away from you. You know that, don't you?'

Holding the parsnip, she started scraping off the skin. Reaching for another, she wiped her eyes again. Half the vegetables looked new to me. I was used to very different produce, like yams and plantain, mangos and pawpaw that grew in the gardens of Government House. Mama taught me to make aromatic stews with spices and ginger that burned your tongue and left the sensation of heat in your mouth. Until now, I had not realised how much I missed them.

'Wait! Stop!' Gwen jumped from her stool. 'What is it, Sophie?' Sophie was shaking her head, pulling sharply on Annie's sleeve. 'What's wrong, Sophie?'

Eyes wide with fright, Sophie shook her head, pulling even more forcibly on Annie's arm. Annie swung round. 'What is it, child? You nearly made me cut myself.'

Gwen leaned over. 'No, stop. She's right. It don't look like a parsnip.' Reaching forward, she held it up. 'It's a root. Looks like a parsnip but it's not. It's a root. Look!'

Annie wiped her eyes. 'Why bless my soul. Dear Lord, I didn't see it properly. What with my eyes not being as they were and the onions making me cry. Dear Lord.' The colour drained from her already white cheeks. She looked grey, her hands beginning to tremble. 'Oh my dear Lord. Oh . . . oh.'

'Annie . . . you aren't well. Do you have a pain?' Grace ran to her side, helping her to her chair. Hand on her shoulder, she looked distraught.

'No. 'Tis not me. It's . . . dear Lord. Take a look at that root.'

Grace went quickly back to the table. She, too, turned ashen. Taking the root from Gwen, she held it in the air. 'Go and get Miss Mitchell. Hurry. No. Wait . . . wash your hands. Everyone wash your hands.' Dropping it, she hurried them to the sink and pumped some water. 'Use the soap. Wash your hands well.'

'What is it?' I stared at the seemingly inoffensive root. 'What do you think it is?'

Gwen rushed for Aunt Hetty, and Grace helped Annie wash her hands. 'I can't be sure. I've only ever seen it once but it's something we were taught. If I'm right, it's *mandrake* and very poisonous. People who eat it by accident can die.'

'Come here, Sophie.' I sat, holding her on my lap. She was shivering, her thin frame shaking. I had coaxed her gently into the house, telling her about the crate of instruments and how the men who delivered it had been speaking German. That she was not to be afraid of coming into the house, yet now her terror had returned. 'There now. A simple, easy mistake,' I said, soothing her hair.

Grace gripped the back of the chair. 'Yes, a simple mistake.' As if she might faint, she slipped on to the chair, staring at the mandrake. 'Pandora, it's known as the *devil's claw*.' She put her head on her lap. 'And we nearly ate it. All of us. We nearly all ate it.'

Wrestling free, Sophie ran for the door and darted across the courtyard, the dog at her heels. 'Gwen . . . follow her . . . make sure she's all right.'

Aunt Hetty entered and stood staring at the mandrake. 'Which basket was it in?'

Fighting her dizziness, Grace pointed to the baskets. 'I kept the contents of the baskets separate. There were three. One looked different. It was not like Sir Anthony's usual baskets, it didn't have his bows or the silk lining. I did say, didn't I, that it looked different? But I never thought to . . . that is, I just emptied the contents on to the table for Annie to use.'

Reaching down, Aunt Hetty held up a stoutly woven basket very similar to one the woman had been carrying on my first day in the ferry. 'This basket? It was left with the others? Sometime while we were in church?'

Grace nodded. 'I found it when I came back – next to Sir Anthony's baskets. I didn't think anything untoward. Only that it looked different. But if that's mandrake, it's been very carefully chosen to look like a parsnip.'

Annie gripped the arms of her chair, her knuckles white. 'I didn't recognise it. I was that sure I was peeling a parsnip.'

A chill entered the room, and not just from the open

303

door. Aunt Hetty wrapped a cloth around the root and drew a deep breath. 'An easy mistake. People are scavenging the beaches, picking up every last edible thing they can find. This was an accident – someone simply mistook it for a parsnip.' Shrugging, she walked to the door. 'Someone will tell us who left the basket and this will all be cleared up.' Stepping out into the sunshine, her voice dropped. 'Who recognised it as mandrake?'

'Sophie did,' I whispered. 'The devil's claw. Aunt Hetty, this was no accident.'

'I know. Either they want to scare us or they want us all dead. Go and see if Sophie's all right.'

Crossing the yard, I knew not to search the barn. Sophie had not entered the barn since she had found the raven's feather. She was not in the garden, nor the shed; even the coach house looked empty and I would have turned away but a whisper drew me back. Benedict's voice drifted from behind the straw bales. 'You're safe here, Sophie. The hens know it's safe and the dog knows it's safe. I find it a very safe place.' I edged closer. Through a tiny gap, I saw the three of them kneeling by the nest, the huge black dog with his head on Sophie's lap.

'See? He's not afraid. I think he's saying, *Don't be frightened*, don't you?' The dog's large black eyes stared up at Sophie, and I saw the back of her head nod. 'He's telling us he'll keep us safe, but Gwen says it was *you* who kept everyone safe. It's you we must thank. You recognised the mandrake and that kept us all safe. So all this talk about being in league with the devil is just silly nonsense.'

Silence followed, the three of them stroking the dog's newly washed coat. Benedict cleared his throat. 'What shall we call him? He's going to need a name if Miss Mitchell is allowing us to keep him.' Sophie shrugged her shoulders, Gwen kept silent, and Benedict continued. 'We could call him Dog, but I think he'd like a proper name. See how safe he feels here? What shall we call him? Let's think of a name.'

A hen was pecking the straw beside them yet the huge dog did not move. He remained staring up at Sophie, and Benedict frowned. 'I can't think of a name. Maybe we should just call him Dog.' A tiny whisper and he bent his head nearer. 'What was that? I didn't quite hear.' The tiny whisper grew louder. 'Shadow?' repeated Benedict. 'What a lovely name. Why do you want to call him Shadow?'

Her voice was tiny, as delicate as she was. 'Cos he follows ye like a shadow. An' he's black, an' at yer feet. Like a shadow.'

'That's such a clever name.'

Her voice was gathering strength. 'An' he never leaves ye. A shadow never leaves ye.'

Benedict remained kneeling, Gwen reaching round the nest to tidy the straw. Sophie leaned forward to kiss the dog. 'He still smells. Miss Annie won't want him in her kitchen. He'll need another bath.'

Benedict nodded. 'Yes, and a good chop of this shaggy coat.'

Sophie mirrored Benedict's half-smile. With her hair washed and brushed, she looked like an angel. 'Like ye needed a haircut, Mr Aubyn. When ye first came, ye looked just as lost and lonely.'

A smile, a shrug. 'I think I was rather lost and lonely – just like Shadow.'

'Ye still look really sad sometimes. Like ye want to cry.'

The two girls edged closer, both stroking the dog, both waiting while Benedict seemed to hesitate. 'When you lose someone you love it's hard to be happy – or believe you'll ever be happy again.' His voice was gentle, treating them as equals. 'It throws you completely. The world keeps turning, and you get through the days, but there's such emptiness inside . . . a black void. A lonely dark void you can't climb out of. You live a half-life, somehow getting through the day, but believing you're never going to be happy again.'

Tiptoeing nearer, my heart burned so fiercely I thought it would burst. Seeing him like that, hearing his words, I could deny it no longer. I *loved* Benedict Aubyn. I loved him. The pain grew worse: I loved everything about him. Loved his gentleness, his manners, the way he spoke to me as an equal. The way he listened and took what I said seriously, the way he stood by me in church. Everything, *everything*. I felt sick, a pain ripping the pit of my stomach.

Fighting for composure, I stared through the small gap. I had been drawn to him from his very first half-smile, his immediate concern for my safety; the way he had frowned and stepped forward to pay my coach fare. Yet it was more than that. It was a physical draw, a longing for him to hold me. That first accidental bump as we collided in the rain, the strength in his arms as he carried me from the crowd. His gentle touch as he bathed my bruised cheek. It was everything, *everything*. The evening stubble on his cheeks, his prominent Adam's apple. The ache in my chest burned fiercer. Standing by my side at the gate, side by side with me in church.

I had always longed to stand side by side with the man I loved.

His voice was soft. 'I believe St Feoca has woven its spell on me. Here, I feel a lifting of my darkness. Maybe it's because spring is bringing new life – maybe it's because I've met you two – and Mollie and Kate. Maybe it's because of Miss Mitchell . . . and—' He stopped.

Gwen looked up, waiting for him to continue. He looked down and she whispered, 'Maybe it's because ye've fallen in love, Mr Aubyn? That's really what's making ye happier. Ye've lost yer heart . . . no, honest ye have! And anyone in their right mind can see she loves ye back.' His puzzled frown brought a vigorous nod. 'Yes, honest! Miss Mitchell knows it, and she's *never* wrong.'

His frown deepened; a shake of his head. 'She's talked about it? Surely not?'

'No, course not. She's said nothing. But Mr Aubyn, some-things don't need *speaking*, or *telling*. Course, Miss Mitchell knows. She knows everything. If *we* know, then she knows. And we don't need to go to school to learn that!'

His cheeks looked flushed, a quiver in his voice. 'Please don't speak of this again. You know the way things are. I've very little to offer. Nothing, in fact . . . until . . . until . . .' He ran his hand through his hair. 'Miss Mitchell . . . isn't . . . cannot . . . accept any . . .'

Both girls shook their heads. 'Miss Mitchell's *never* wrong. She said you've got good employment an' good prospects. An' she likes you. Why else would she let you stay in her coach house?'

They were referring to Grace. Dear God, they were

307

expecting him to propose to her. The pain was so fierce I thought I might cry out. I must not stumble, nor catch my foot; I must walk tall, shoulders back, calm, indifferent, like I had always walked, clutching my aegis for protection. Only, it was useless. The gods were laughing down at me from their thrones on Mount Olympus, cheering, jeering, slapping their thighs, bending double with mirth. They knew my protective shield was theirs to withdraw. Riddled with holes, it had proved no defence against Cupid's arrows.

The rabbit stew tasted of nothing, the lemon tart like sawdust, yet I must have sounded joyful because I drew smiles and laughter from both Aunt Hetty and Benedict Aubyn. He had been invited to dine and would be dining with us until he left. Grace looked more beautiful than ever, the four of us sitting in a semicircle watching her fingers fly across the keys. 'Do join me, please, Miss Mitchell.'

Aunt Hetty conceded, agreeing to play a duet. Benedict rose to turn the pages, a frown creasing his brow, and I sat watching with what I hope looked like happy contemplation. The fire was too hot, the room too stuffy, the scent of Sir Anthony's lilies too overpowering. Annie was clearly enjoying the music but I wanted to run from the room. Mama would have sat like this, felt like this: wanting to be with Father, thinking only of him. Wanting to know what he thought, interested in his opinion, yearning to know him better.

More memories. More painful memories. Mama and Father standing by each other's side on the deck of every ship.

The two of them walking side by side, Father's arm through Mama's. Everywhere, the two of them walking into the sunset, along beaches fringed with palm trees, meandering through beautiful gardens. Sometimes jostled by crowds on busy boulevards, but always arm in arm, the two of them engrossed in their own conversation. Laughing, pointing to the setting sun, a new flower, a new tree. Marvelling at the birds with their colourful plumage, buying exotic new fruit from a street vendor, and I would walk behind them knowing they did not need me for their happiness, knowing they were in a cocoon of their own making. A bubble. An all-enclosing, protective bubble of their own making.

Until the bubble burst.

The clock struck nine and my ordeal was over. On her steps, Aunt Hetty reached to kiss my cheek. 'Be very careful that your meeting tomorrow ends in agreement.' I nodded and she turned to go. 'Their quarrel took place a year ago. Samuel Devoran said Jacob Carter had returned inferior flour to him. He accused him of substituting sacks of poor quality corn so he could profit. Which he did.'

'The quarrel's well known and talked about?'

'No, it was never talked about. Gwen told me and Gwen's *never* wrong. She says her father's grain was good quality but the flour in the returned sacks was clearly inferior. Her father accused his brother-in-law of cheating him, but Jacob Carter denied it. That was enough to bring about the family feud. They've not spoken for over a year. You think I live in an ivory tower, my dear, but I know everything that goes on. Tread carefully tomorrow. It won't be easy.'

'Did Gwen tell you about the bones for fertiliser and the gypsum?'

'No, Mollie did. And very happily, I received a letter yesterday from the naval slaughterhouse in Falmouth offering us a consignment of bones. Lord Carew is negotiating a good price, or rather his son Captain Frederick Carew is. He's overseeing a contract for you.'

'Mr Carter's going to be thrilled. Aunt Hetty, it's vital we get the millpond clear of silt.'

Candlelight flickered against the wall behind her, lighting the steps to her rooms. 'I'm sorry we kept you from your book tonight, Pandora. Sleep well, my dear.' She turned. 'Grace has great beauty and considerable talents but she doesn't have your . . . grit.'

I fought back my tears. 'Grit, Aunt Hetty?'

Her cheeks dimpled. 'Your grandfather was particularly fond of grit. He used to add it to his soil. Enjoy finishing *Candide*, my dear. I really must reread it one day.'

Chapter Thirty-three

It was useless to try to sleep, and peering across the courtyard every ten minutes was only making it worse. If Sophie had not recognised the mandrake we would be writhing in agony in our beds. Across the lawns an owl was hooting, the night still, only the faintest moonlight shimmering on the glass roof of the conservatory. Was our prowler only trying to frighten us? If that was his intention, he had certainly succeeded.

Trying to get inside his mind was making my heart race. What if he tried to get through the tower again? Each time, I had seen the prowler at two o'clock. Pulling my cloak round me, I glanced at the clock: it was just before one. Had Aunt Hetty fully bolted the doors? Surely he would return to see if his devilment had born fruit?

Slipping from my room, I trailed my hand along the wall. No candle, no lantern, he must not see any sign of light in the house. Slipping past Grace's door, I hurried along the corridor, across the archway, and up the spiral staircase in the tower. Groping with my hands, I felt the hard bolts on the study door. They were drawn across and secure. So too, the main door leading out to the drive. Everything bolted and secure. No need for my terrible panic.

Returning across the archway, I trailed my hand against the wall again, gripping the banister as I went silently down the stairs. The front door was bolted and barred. Moonlight glinted on the un-shuttered top windows, streaking across the beams, giving just enough light to see my way across the hall to the door of the conservatory. Everything bolted and barred. The downstairs corridor was pitch black, the library windows firmly shuttered. A red glow drew me to the kitchen: the embers were burning, faint shadows flickering across the ceiling. Tiptoeing across the flagstones, I opened Annie's door. She was fast asleep, the tell-tale empty glass on the table beside her.

Annie's rug was over her chair, more logs in the basket. I would settle down and wait. If anyone came, I could ring the huge gong that summoned the girls to their meals. The clock struck the quarter hour and I bolted upright. I was not thinking straight. Our tormenter did not know we had discovered how he entered the house, he would think the tower window still loose.

The back door key was kept under the table napkins in the third drawer; it felt cold in my hand and I gripped it tightly. Taking Annie's rug, I drew back the bolts and turned the lock. There was no sign of life, not even the hooting of the owls. Locking it behind me, I slipped silently across the cobbles.

Clouds obscured the moon, the courtyard in darkness. The barn was too far away, so too, the coach house. I needed to find somewhere to watch the tower in complete conceal-ment. Taking care not to stumble, I worked my way round the old brewhouse where the girls stored their trunks. I knew it would be locked, but the old smokehouse would be open. Half-derelict, the ancient stone building with its huge brick dome was used as a shelter for the gardeners. Pushing open the door, I jumped in fright. A rat scuttled towards me and I stifled my scream. Nothing else moved and I tried to calm the thumping of my heart.

In the darkness I could just make out the shape of a barrel and implements hanging against the wall. My eyes were growing accustomed to the half-light: above me, coils of rope were hanging from huge iron hooks; on the dirt floor, a pile of empty sacks. There was no window, but if I left the door ajar and hid beneath the sacks, I would have a clear view of the fire escape.

A break in the clouds and the tower shone in the moon-light. The barrel was empty and easy to move, the dirt floor dry and, wrapping Annie's blanket around me, I pulled the sacks over me. If the rat came back, I would swipe at it with a pitchfork. The light from the moon would give me a good chance of seeing our tormentor. Unable to get through the window, he would have to return down the iron ladder and pass right by me. If I could not catch his features, I would follow to see where he went, and who was waiting for him.

Despite my cloak and blanket, the smokehouse felt as icy as a tomb. The sacks smelled musty, the blackened bricks retaining the odour of smoke. A sound made me jump and I peered through the darkness. Two eyes were staring at me from the open door. Not a rat, but bigger, and as black as the night. A whimper, then another, and Shadow came silently to my side. Settling himself on the sacks, he looked up at me with glistening eyes. 'Oh, Shadow . . . thank you. Thank you. Not a sound, you understand? No one must know I'm here.'

Stretching out his neck, he laid his head across my lap, the heat from his shaggy coat as comforting as his presence. He lay watching the door and I settled back, feeling safe for the very first time. 'Grandfather sent you to protect us, didn't he?'

Without the chimes from the chapel clock, I had little way to gauge the time. Maybe it was an hour, maybe less. Suddenly, Shadow rose and ran through the door, his barking vicious and furious. Echoing across the cobbles, I could hear him growling. I had seen no one, heard no one, but Shadow was not letting up. Darting past the door, I watched him running back and forward across the courtyard, his barking more and more vicious.

'Hush, Shadow. Stop that! Come here. You'll wake everyone.' It was Benedict's voice. 'Come *here*. What are you barking at? A fox? A badger?'

If that had been our prowler, he would not return. Silence followed. In the moonlight, I saw Benedict pulling on his coat. He was walking past the laundry, Shadow at his heels. 'You mustn't wake everyone like that. You'll have to sleep in the barn. Shadow . . . Shadow, come back!'

Slipping through the door, Shadow snuggled next to me again. Extending his neck, his head rested across my lap. He lay still, defiant, clearly with no intention of being locked in the barn, and though I may have been concealed from the outside, I knew I had no chance of staying hidden. Benedict opened the door. 'Shadow— Pandora! What are you doing here?'

Shadow did not move: he was clearly staying. Coming into the smokehouse, Benedict tried to hide his shock. 'I'm sorry. You obviously have a reason to be out here. Do I intrude?' There was hurt in his voice, a hint of embarrassment.

'No, you don't intrude. I am waiting for someone but it's not a prearranged tryst. I thought our prowler might return.' He was in his night clothes, his coat pulled round him, his ankles bare in his shoes.

'You're watching in case there's another burglary?' He closed the door, leaving a small gap. 'But you're watching the tower? The burglary took place because the kitchen door was left unlocked – an opportunist taking advantage of an unlocked door.' I said nothing and he drew closer. 'Only, he wasn't an opportunist, was he? The girls tell me the terror has returned. The feather... the mandrake? There's a nervousness about you, and Miss Mitchell looks increasingly anxious.'

I shook my head. 'I can't tell you.'

'You can. Pandora, what's going on?'

A sudden stab in my ribs. 'I can't tell you. You'll tell Grace and that would be very unfair. She's suffered enough already. I want her and the girls shielded until... well, until all this gets resolved.'

'I won't tell anyone. Nothing will pass my lips.' Sliding down the wall, he squeezed beside me. 'Pandora, the girls are intuitive, they know things without being told. What's going on?'

Sitting side by side, I pulled the blanket over his cold feet. I hardly knew where to start, or even if I should. He listened in silence, Shadow staring up at us, looking first to one and then the other. Benedict was clearly horrified. 'This is far too much for you to bear alone. You need legal representation and a nightwatchman. The grounds must be watched at all times. I understand Miss Mitchell believes she's made her school safe, but when my men leave you'll be completely unprotected.'

The thought of him leaving St Feoca seemed suddenly unbearable. 'Nightwatchmen cost money. And there'd be talk. We can't allow a hint of this to reach others. Our school is about to be closed. We have... maybe a week... to bring it back to life. Everything depends on us keeping free from rumour and wicked speculation.'

'You've taken legal advice?'

'Our attorney is to visit on Tuesday. Aunt Hetty will give him the mandrake and the manuscript. Our tormentor is someone who knows the churchyard. Someone who's planned this to the minutest detail.'

'Pandora... you're shaking.' His hand closed over mine, firm, warm, holding it tightly. 'I'll stay and watch now. And I'll ask my men to set a watch. They can take a night each. They know you were burgled because Susan keeps telling them she's glad to have six strong men under her roof. But you must ask your aunt to seek help.'

'Shadow will take care of any prowler. If that was him tonight, he won't be back. But if it was a badger, or a fox, he may still come.' Clouds obscured the moon, the smokehouse icy cold: a comforting heat as Shadow drew closer. Sitting side by side, Benedict's shoulder was touching mine, his thigh warm beneath the blanket, and I fought the terrible yearning of wanting it to be me he loved, not Grace.

His voice was a whisper. 'This is not what you expected when you boarded the *Jane O'Leary*.'

It was hard to speak. 'Not what I dreamed of at all. I always thought Mama would be with me. That St Feoca would be like in my memories. I thought that by reuniting Mama with Aunt Hetty, we'd all be so happy. I thought they would teach the girls and I would . . .'

He waited in silence. 'You'd paint miniature portraits? That's what you really want to do, isn't it? There's such joy in your paintings. You have a rare gift.'

The tenderness in his voice threw me. I must not let him see the sudden tears in my eyes. 'We can't always do what we want. You know that. You're a chemist – you love your work. The only time I've ever seen light in your eyes is when you talk of precipitation, or extraction . . . or distillation and reactivity. You're hiding what you really want to do. I'm to be a head-mistress, and you're to be a surveyor – fleecing people out of their land for a ten per cent cut!' I had not meant to sound so harsh. I was being cruel, punishing him for loving Grace. For wanting to give her a beautiful home, a secure future, a handful of children, all with her beauty and talents.

'I don't deny that. None of it.' He took his hand back, running it across his hair. 'And I don't deny I would like it otherwise. But I have obligations, Pandora. I've been the recipient of great generosity. My parents gave me everything – their time, their love, their savings. My brother was sensible, secure, solid as a rock and as generous as they were ... encouraging my studies, slipping me money when he knew I was struggling. I was given so much. Oxford is an expensive place — board, lodgings, food ... books. My studies were their priority. My parents gave the same to my brother, but whereas he was a safe recipient of their love and money — a good investment — I just kept needing more funds. Matthew wanted to follow Father into the Church, but I should have been more honest. I fought my reluctance. I was trying to please them.'

'You left without qualifying, and feel you wasted your parents' savings?'

'Yes.' Shadow followed our voices as he stared from one of us to the other. 'My interest in minerals started as a child. Reverend Gregor — the one I told you discovered titanium — was Father's friend and my teacher.' He sounded hesitant, yet his voice grew stronger. 'Like a sponge, I soaked up everything he could teach me. I thought, like him, I could find a quiet parish and continue my studies.' He coughed, his voice hoarse. 'But I won a scholarship to London. I wrote an essay for the Royal Society and won. I left Oxford without qualifying to take up more studies in London. That was rash and inconsiderate, yet my parents encouraged me, sending more money to support me.'

'Then you've nothing to feel guilty about.'

'I can't speak of it.' His voice was stony; in the darkness his mouth drew tight.

'Maybe you should, Benedict. There's a shadow over you. You made me tell you everything. You said I should break from under my hard shell, and maybe you need to? I poured my

318

heart out to you, so it's only fair you trust me.' He remained silent and I tried to keep the bitterness from my voice. 'Or at least tell someone. Maybe Grace?'

He shook his head. 'It's too hard to speak of it.'

Shadow seemed to sense his pain; his eyes deepened, his stare intensified. Benedict drew a deep breath. 'My father died on my mother's fifty-fifth birthday. We always celebrated Mother's birthday. Father always took the day away from his parish so we could have lunch on the beach. His parish was St Kew. I was raised by the sea. Every year, Father, my brother Matthew and I would walk the six miles, and Mother and my sisters would take the cart. Only as the years went by, my sisters would walk beside the cart because the cart became fully loaded – overflowing with produce, and buckets, and a tarpaulin to protect us from the wind. Every year, without fail. *Every* year.'

I could feel his shoulders tensing, the muscles in his arms harden. Clearing his throat, his voice rang with pain. 'But last year, I was to present a paper to the Royal Society on the same day. It was my dream and I . . . wrote apologising that I couldn't be there for her birthday . . . that I'd try to come soon afterwards.' He looked down, grasping his head between his hands. 'That day – the day I wasn't there – the sea was moderate but the wind was picking up. From what I'm told, two boys were playing with a dog on the beach. The dog ran into the sea to get a stick and started struggling in the waves. Both boys waded out to save him, and both boys got pulled out to sea.'

He cleared his throat. 'There's danger in those waves, a

hidden current can sweep a good swimmer out to sea. The boys were struggling and my brother was not a good swimmer. Even so, he went to their rescue. Only he misjudged the strength of the tide, the pull of the current. It looked calm in the centre, but he . . . he . . . floundered. My family were on the beach. His wife and children. All of them watching from the beach as he struggled against the tide . . . watching . . . until they couldn't see him struggle any more.'

He kept his hands against his face. 'The shock was too great for my father. He rushed to the water but suffered a heart attack and fell to the ground. My mother had just lost her son, and now she was in danger of losing her husband.' He swallowed, his hands shaking. 'My father died in the cart on the way home. My brother's body was washed up six miles down the shore. The two boys were never found.'

I wiped the tears from my eyes. 'It wasn't your fault, Benedict. It was *not* your fault.'

I could hardly hear him. 'But it was. And it feels like it still is. I should have been there – I'm the strong swimmer in the family. I should have been the one to swim out. Not my brother. Not a husband and father. I would have stopped Matthew going. Instead, I was glorifying in the applause of people I neither knew nor cared about.' He wiped a tear from his eye.

'I can't speak of the guilt I bear. The nightmares are lessening but in them I'm swimming out to him. I'm forcing my way through thick waves and getting nowhere. My brother is dipping beneath the water and I just can't get to him. I can't save him. And I wake each morning with such remorse. Such guilt. My brother was my idol. My big brother who helped me carry rocks because they were too heavy for me to lift. He never teased me about my collection, just cleared more space. He'd carry them upstairs and make room for them in our bedroom. He was my rock. He was clever, amusing, but serious. He was driven by compassion... by his humanity. He used to feed birds and squirrels from our bedroom while I poured vinegar on to the rocks. I had a hammer to break them open to find crystals, and he would watch me from the window, throwing bread to the doves. He was a gentle man, a loving son... a wonderful brother.' In the silence, he wiped his eyes. 'I'm sorry. It's just I never talk about the... the... incident.'

I wanted to reach for his hand, hold it between mine. Wrap my arm about his shoulder and hold him. In the half-light, his face looked drawn, his fist pressing against his lips. 'Tell me more about your brother. You told me I should speak of my anger at Father, yet I think you should speak about your love for your brother. Of this terrible loss that won't leave you.'

'Matthew was destined for high office... for great distinction. He was a humble man with such generosity of spirit. He had a greatness about him. He never criticised me for leaving Oxford nor for my wilder moments. In fact, he encouraged me. It was he who told me to play my fiddle. He said everyone fed the musician – that I'd get free suppers and free wine. And he was right. Money was always tight and I played for my supper. He knew I was not destined for the Church, but he was. He was destined for greatness – the family's bright future. And now I must attempt to fill his shoes. I, who have only ever followed my own interests.' His voice grew firmer. 'Now, I have only the interests of my family at heart. They are my only concern. My mother and my sisters must have the stability my brother would have given them.'

'And now you're well placed to bring that stability. I understand why you came to my rescue in Falmouth. You thought me a widow, like your sister-in-law. You came to my rescue, and when you thought I was shamefully pretending to be a widow, you were angry.'

'Yes.' The first tentative cry of a cockerel rang across the field and Shadow raised his head. His ears twitched as it called again, stronger, more resolute, getting closer. Above the tower, the first pink streaks of dawn were lighting the night sky. Benedict straightened. '*There is a time for many words, and there is also a time for sleep.*' He smiled. 'That's the only part of the *Odyssey* I remember. But it seems somehow relevant. Thank you, Pandora.' He bit his lip. 'Thank you for listening.'

I smiled, trying to hide my heartbreak. 'I don't suppose anyone will get any sleep now that cockerel has discovered my hens!'

'No!' His laugh was rueful. 'This is highly irregular, Pandora. We'd better not be found.' Yet he pulled the sacking tightly round us as if reluctant to leave. 'Will you save your school, do you think?'

'The school's my life. My *life*.' I was going to cry. Dear lord, I was going to cry. I should disentangle myself from the sacking, pat the dog, rise, and return to my room; forgo the pleasure of sitting so close to him. I had thought I would never love a man. Never allow myself to be manipulated and dictated to, yet it was my heart doing the dictating, my heart tearing up all my resolutions. I had never imagined love could be so painful.

His voice was soft. 'You know there are rumours about Sir Anthony and Miss Mitchell? They say their marriage is imminent.' He wiped his mouth. 'Is there any . . . good reason you have to stay *unmarried*? Your grandmother was a married headmistress. Surely you could allow yourself to love?'

Heat seared my chest. Mama would have sat like this, maybe exactly here, whispering words of love with Father. 'I do understand what it is to love,' I whispered. 'I understand wanting to be with someone, to ache for them. For their touch. To think only of them, to be desperate to be with them. I do *understand* that. The lure of love is very strong but knowing who to trust is where I stumble. Love fades. It's not constant. Trust is more important.'

'Love doesn't fade.' His words seemed torn from him. 'True love endures and strengthens. It builds that trust. It is constant. It allows each to feel fulfilled – two halves, making a whole. Each with their strengths and weaknesses, yet always enriched by the other. You have your grandparents as an example – I have my parents. Their love was constant; their trust in each other complete.' His chest was rising and falling, his arm against my arm; underneath the sacking the heat of his body scorched mine. 'Don't judge every man by your father, Pandora.'

I knew I must go. Of course I must go. He broke the silence, his voice a whisper. 'There's another rumour . . . and many would welcome it. Mr Cador Ferris has not the arrogance of his father. He's to inherit a baronetcy and a very fine park.'

'You think I should marry for money? Benedict, how little you know me!' Shadow pricked up his ears, and I lowered my voice. 'You expect me to marry a wealthy benefactor and *play* at running my school?' I was fighting the hurt. The terrible desire to cry.

'No! No, that's not what I meant at all. I meant that if you felt you could, or rather, if you *did* love him then . . . maybe you should. He's clearly very attentive – the orchids . . . your beautiful pearl earrings. Only the girls say—' He stopped, his hands clasped together.

'What do the girls say?'

He seemed to struggle to find the right words. 'That you've *lost your heart* and everyone knows it except you.' The tension in his tone made it hard to hear him. His breathing had quickened, his hands gripping the filthy sacking.

'I shall *never* marry a man for his money!'

Neither of us moved, Shadow relaxing back, still keeping a wary eye on the crack in the door. Yet I needed to ask about Grace. I needed to know. Words formed on my lips, but I could not say them: anything to prolong this pleasurable intimacy rather than ask the question I did not want to hear answered.

'What about you, Ben?' I tried to sound happy. 'The girls are similarly convinced that you're in love. Mollie says the men could have finished the road *weeks* ago, and Kate says they told her mother you've been dragging your feet.'

'There may be some truth in that.' He stared ahead.

'I need to thank you for their labour, and for your kind offer of gypsum. You must send us an invoice.' I was speaking without thinking, jealousy twisting my stomach. *He had all but told me he loved Grace.*

He shook his head. 'There'll be no invoice, Pandora. I'm just glad to be able to help — and the men need work. My brother used to call me Ben. It sounded very pleasant coming from your lips.' The stab was back. Fiercer, too painful to bear.

Suddenly, Shadow pricked up his ears. Standing up, he started wagging his tail. Falling on his forepaws he began barking, his whole body twisting. 'Hush, Shadow . . . Shadow, stop.' Yet still his tail would not stop wagging, his bark even louder. 'Hush. You'll wake Aunt Hetty.'

Benedict threw back the sacking. 'We can't risk this any longer.' Opening the door, he peered across the courtyard. 'Dawn's breaking.' A grey haze was rising in the east, the bands of pink merging into one. 'Pandora . . . it was fate we met in that downpour. I know you're angry with The Fates, but I'm not. Every day I'm grateful for bumping into you. Meeting you and Miss Mitchell . . . and the girls.' He frowned, looking over his shoulder at the dimly lit cobbles. 'Pandora . . . there's something I need you to know.'

Shadow was barking again, louder, twisting round, his tail knocking against me. 'Ben, we mustn't be seen like this. I must get back.'

'Yes . . . of course.'

Dew covered the cobbles, a slight mist. Perched on the wall a cockerel was crowing. My fingers fumbling with the key, I looked round. By the coach house, Shadow stood at Benedict's heels. Both were watching, waiting for me to slip silently through the door, and I looked back at Benedict Aubyn. Like Mama would have looked at Father.

The pain was excruciating, violent, tearing me apart. *Mama. It's so painful.* She seemed suddenly close, as if standing beside me, reaching out her arms. Understanding my pain.

Chapter Thirty-four

St Feoca Manor: School for Young Ladies
Monday 13th April 1801, 10:00 a.m.

The library window was open, a blast of cool air filling the room with the scent of flowers. Grace was not one to open windows, but I wanted to blow away the musty smell of the books. Or was it because I wanted to watch the man I loved in the courtyard outside?

Dressed in his Sunday clothes, Jacob Carter drew a deep breath. ''Twas simply a muddle. I was under pressure at the mill. The grain was spoiling an' Sir Anthony had been that good to me. I never, never, thought to cheat ye. I didn't load the carts. I thought the right grain had gone to the right place. I paid ye the difference, Samuel.'

Samuel Devoran was stockier than his brother-in-law, though with the same black hair and dark looks. Also dressed in his Sunday clothes, they stared across the table at each other. 'Well, that's the point, isn't it? Ye put Sir Anthony first. An' it weren't the first time. Ye milled his grain *first*. Ye left mine seven days in the damp. That's *not* our agreement an' it's disrespectful to Miss Mitchell. It's her mill, not Sir Anthony's.'

'I'd left his longer. Honest, Sam. His had been waitin' nine days. I'm workin' a quarter of the time I used to work. I've only the incoming tide. And if Sir Anthony has corn to grind then I've every right to grind his corn. Ye know that. It's our agreement.'

There was a slight lessening in their anger, at least that was something.

Outside, the girls were watching Benedict harness the cart. 'Ye want to weigh the carts?' Gwen sounded cross, shrugging in dismay. 'But that means ye'll charge some carts more for the same miles. That don't seem fair.'

Benedict straightened. 'It is fair because the suspension's better and they're doubling their loads.'

'But that's good. Double the loads and there'll be less wagons to block the road. Ye said there's too many as it is. Why not let them double their loads?'

He glanced at me through the window and I tried not to smile. 'Because the toll will be for the amount they carry. If I can get this weighing machine built, the tolls can be charged per weight of the carriage or wagon. There's got to be a way of measuring the loads, Gwen.'

Mollie was equally unimpressed. Standing by her cousin, she shook her head. 'What Gwen means is them carrying coal or stones will pay more than them carrying straw. Yet they cover the same distance!'

'Yes, because it's not the distance we have to calibrate – it's the damage to the road. Heavy loads cause more damage. Thus the toll will cover the cost of repairs.'

Kate joined them, standing firm. 'I think ye just don't want heavy wagons on yer new road. Mamm says yer new road should be good enough for heavier loads. The men say it won't rut, but ye're saying it's goin' to.'

Benedict shrugged. 'Well . . . yes . . . in theory, Mr McAdam's roads shouldn't rut, but the suspension on coaches has improved . . . the stagecoaches get piled high. These new wagons are twice, three times, as robust as previous ones. What do you think, Sophie?'

Sophie bent to pat Shadow. 'Gwen's right . . . and Mollie's right. And so's Kate. But that don't make ye wrong, Mr Aubyn. If having a weigh machine stops the arguments, then that's what's needed. Something to stop the arguments.'

Both men had stopped talking, both listening to their daughters in clear surprise. Jacob Carter coughed. 'They talk some sense, those lasses. Fancy them arguing with Mr Aubyn like that.'

I pulled my papers nearer. 'They're not arguing, Mr Carter. They're bright, intelligent girls who've been encouraged to question. That's why our school *has* to thrive. Gentlemen, I'm not leaving this room until you give me a clear plan on how you're going to cooperate. You think me cocooned from want and hunger. Well, that's not the case. I know what it's like to be evicted for rent arrears . . . to pack in a hurry and leave before dawn. But that doesn't soften my resolve. I'm not going to let this school fail for want of revenue from either your farm or your mill.'

Samuel Devoran stretched his hand across the table. 'It starts now. You heard my Sophie. *No more arguments.*'

Jacob Carter reached forward, taking his brother-law's

hand in a firm grip. 'Ye want bones grinding, I want to grind. There's evidence this gypsum works. Ye've read the reports?'

'Plenty evidence comin' through. Smith of Highstead says clover manured with gypsum is always preferred by horses and cattle.'

'Aye. An' Lord Leicester in Holkham Hall.'

'An' the bone-crushing mills in Sheffield? I read they sold six hundred ton. Lincolnshire's been using bones. I've read they pay sixpence a bushel.'

'And fish bones. I read one village in Cambridgeshire made *two thousand pounds* in one year from the Fens alone.'

Benedict was ordering Shadow off the cart for the third time. Picking him up, he placed him at Gwen's feet. Samuel Devoran smiled. 'He's a good man. Dogs know who they can trust.'

'You're not angry Mr Aubyn plans to build his turnpike right by your farm?'

His eyes flashed under their heavy black brows. 'No, Miss Woodville. That road will bring us prosperity. I may be prepared to fiddle-faddle around with horses too delicate to step in mud, but my sons won't tolerate it. Thoroughbred horses who cost more to keep *per day* than whole families per week?' He looked down, his chest rising and falling.

'Don't stop on my account. Tell me, what do your sons propose to do on my aunt's land?'

He cleared his throat. 'We've stabling for forty horses. There's little enough income from the farm, but stabling on a busy turnpike? Ye've heard of manna from heaven, Miss

Woodville? Well, this road's heaven sent. So, no, I'm not angry with Mr Aubyn. Not angry at all.'

Jacob Carter's voice was just as firm. 'Aye, the man knows the land. He's surveyed every inch of it. He's promised me gypsum an' I believe he'll deliver. My main concern is with no stream flushing it, it won't take long for the mill to block completely, but Mr Aubyn's addressed that. He lent me six strong men to dig and clear the ditches. So, I've no problem with him either.'

'Use the silt, Jacob. Dry it, an' add it to the mix. 'Tis good minerals in there.'

I think I offered them paper and ink but it was all I could do to stop myself glancing out of the window. I caught Benedict's farewell wave and heat seared my cheeks. The cart clattered over the cobbles, the girls waving goodbye, the dog barking. In the ensuing silence the cockerel jumped on to the wall and fluffed up his feathers.

Kate laughed. 'Look at him all proud and preening! What shall we call him?'

'Poppycock,' replied Mollie.

'Poppycock!' Holding their stomachs, the girls bent double.

Their giggles brought smiles to all our faces. The two brothers-in-law shrugged and shook hands and I breathed deeply. Together, we would make the mill prosperous again, fertilise our fields, run the best coaching inn in Cornwall. The school would rise like Venus from the waves. The girls would return and laughter would fill the courtyard.

That would have to be enough for me.

My new paints were of the highest quality. The undercoat had dried on five of the shells, and one was already painted – the huge black cat from the shop which I would send to the shop-keeper as a thank-you. I hardly dared look at the portrait I was painting. I ought to put it aside and stop my foolishness, yet the more I looked at it, the more I was drawn back to finish it. I had captured his eyes completely, captured his half-smile. Captured the strength in his jaw. His intelligence. His kind-ness. Captured his warmth. Captured his prominent Adam's apple. Captured the way his hair fell forward, the way he held his shoulders. Captured his air of respectability. Captured his sadness, his shyness when he spoke of love.

Chapter Thirty-five

St Feoca Manor: School for Young Ladies
Tuesday 14th April 1801, 9:30 a.m.

We watched Francis Polcarrow hurrying up the drive; his case looked heavy but his step was light. 'Bring him straight up, Pandora. We won't be overheard in here.'

Running down the stairs, I saw Grace leaning over the hall table, an open newspaper in front of her. 'Grace, what's the matter?' She did not move but stood staring down at the paper. 'Has someone you know died?'

She looked ashen. 'This is an *advertisement*. For a *teacher* in our school.' Clasping her hand over her mouth, I thought she might cry. 'A *teacher*. Look. Read here.' In the centre of the page, an advertisement had a thick black box around it.

Required with immediate effect: a teacher, or a lady
who has held a position as governess, is invited to apply
for a position in St Feoca School for Young Ladies.

The applicant must be educated to a high degree, be in her
thirties, and be steadfast in her support of female education.

Salary and conditions of service will be discussed at interview.

All applicants to write to Lady Clarissa Carew of Trenwyn House.

'Pandora . . . look. Miss Mitchell is leaving the school – the rumours about her and Sir Anthony must be true! Only I don't want her to leave. Is that very selfish of me?' Tears welled in her eyes.

I put my hand of her shoulder, desperate to keep my voice steady. 'We can't keep her here, Grace, not if she chooses to go. But you can always live here . . . this is your home. You can stay here for as long as you want.' I looked away. *Until your marriage to Benedict, that is.*

We turned at the knock on the door. Opening it, a ray of sunshine followed Francis Polcarrow through the door. 'Miss Woodville.' He bowed, his eyes immediately turning to Grace. In the sunshine, her hair was the colour of ripe corn, her blue eyes filled with tears. Clearly an angel in distress.

'May I introduce Miss Elliot? One of our teachers.'

He bowed, forgetting to take off his hat. Bending to rescue it from the floor, he brushed her shoulder as she, too, bent to retrieve it. Blushing, he stammered. 'Forgive me, Miss Elliot. You're very kind.' His blush deepened. 'A lovely bright day for a trip downriver. Very pleasant.' He fumbled with his bag. 'What a very long drive you have . . . very pleasant. What a bright day.'

I had to cough to catch his attention. 'Miss Mitchell is in her study upstairs. Do, please, follow me.'

At the top of the stairs he glanced down to take his leave of Grace. 'Miss Elliot is a teacher here? What a very . . . very . . .'

A bitter taste soured my reply. 'Bright day?'

There was something about his smile, something in the lightness of his step. 'I do mean that, Miss Woodville.'

Aunt Hetty remained sitting at her desk. 'Please sit, Mr Polcarrow.' She waited for him to draw up his chair. 'Thank you for your letter. You haven't found my father's will?'

Emptying a wodge of papers on to the desk, Francis Polcarrow separated them into three piles. 'Unfortunately not. You've not found it either?'

Aunt Hetty peered over the rim of her glasses. 'I've searched everywhere. If it was in Father's study, it's been taken. Our night visitor has had plenty of time to go through the files. I imagine there might even be other documents missing.'

Francis Polcarrow reached for the first pile of papers. 'I've been thinking about that. I believe your prowler must have read both the will and the constitution. Whoever he is, he not only knows Mr Richard Compton is heir to the estate but also what is needed to ensure the governors are forced to close the school.'

Sunlight drifted across the room. Dressed immaculately, Aunt Hetty looked pale, through striking, her hair more softly dressed, her sapphire earrings catching the light. Round her neck, she clasped her gold locket between her fingers. 'You spoke to his agent, Mr Banks?'

Francis Polcarrow's eyes seemed to darken. 'I did. *Eventually*. He likes to have his palms well oiled and I nearly didn't get an appointment. Until, that is, I made out I was interested in purchasing your land. I let him register my name . . . and he might have been led to believe I was enquiring on behalf of my brother!' Aunt Hetty's lips pursed and his smile deepened. 'As we suspected, the man employing Mr Banks is indeed your father's heir – Mr Richard Compton – and, if we're to believe

Mr Banks, Mr Compton was informed he is to inherit the estate by *you*, Miss Mitchell.'

'Me?'

'Yes, and the letter – in your name – stated you were voluntarily closing your school and he was not to contact you personally but to deal entirely through an attorney.'

'That's preposterous!'

'A detailed map of your land was enclosed. Apparently, Mr Compton has several manufacturing interests in Birmingham and though his businesses are doing well, extra investment would be beneficial and he would be keen to raise more money – hence he's sent Mr Banks to *ascertain* how much interest there would be in your land.' He looked up, his smile mischievous. 'As it is, time has been against the person insti-gating your downfall. A year ago, when the troubles started, he was no doubt expecting an easy and profitable purchase! But not now. The perpetrator of your school's *demise* must be furious the new turnpike has garnered such interest. It raises the price of your estate considerably.'

'Mr Banks has no authority – no legal right whatsoever – to gather such information. How dare he?'

'He states he's acting on behalf of your estate. The rumours you're to sell your land have become widespread and no one knows he's acting on behalf of Mr Compton.'

'But who would write to Mr Compton?'

'Anyone who wants your land; believe me, there are many interested parties.' He reached for a sheet of paper. 'Four *interests* have been recorded for the farm – two open bids and two closed. In which case, Miss Mitchell, we cannot rule out your tenant, Mr Devoran, as our perpetrator.'

'No. He'd never want the school to close.'

I leaned closer. 'Four have registered an interest in the farm? Do they all want to turn it into a coaching inn?'

'Two want to turn it into a coaching inn, one was undisclosed, and Mr Yoxall wants to turn it into a wagon park. One interest has been registered for the house – that's Major Trelawny on behalf of the militia. And *four* interests have been registered for the shoreline.'

'Four!'

'Yes, Miss Woodville. Mr Banks was reluctant to divulge who they were but I managed to wheedle out who the contenders are. Here are the names, beginning with the Carnon Streamworks. Mr Henry Lakes of the Blowing House in Calenick wants to build a new smelting house with good access to a port, and Lord Entworth has put in a considerable starting bid, so has a firm called Roseland Holdings.'

Aunt Hetty remained silent as Francis Polcarrow reached for another piece of paper. 'Here's how the land's to be divided up.' Sliding a map across the desk, we stared at the different shading. Some had vertical lines, some cross-hatched. The shoreline had been left blank. 'If you notice, three people are interested in the gatehouse.'

I peered closer. 'And two for Tallacks Wood?'

'The gatehouse is to be made into lodgings for visiting investors . . . or for those who miss the tide to Truro.' His eyes sharpened. 'So we can't rule out your tenant, Mr George Penrose. Nor can we rule out Mr Jacob Carter from the mill. Both would benefit from investment.'

'Neither would want the school to close.'

He caught the frostiness in Aunt Hetty's tone. 'Forgive me, but we must be rigorous. Now, as for the members of the Turnpike Trust, there are *five* declared interests where the proposed tollgate is to be sited. That's because the Turnpike Trust have reverted to the original plan – Lord Entworth had switched it to his side of the river, if you remember?'

'Rich pickings indeed.'

'Very much so. If the Falmouth Gate is anything to go by, the annual income could exceed four hundred and twenty pounds – after deducting rent and expenses.'

'Lord Entworth gave way?'

'Eventually – after a barrel load of complaints. Members of the Turnpike Trust must not seek to profit from any land deals. They do, of course – all of them grasping and grabbing everything they can – but, given the swell of public opinion, which remains very strong, Lord Entworth, being the chairman, mustn't be seen to profit. Hence, the tollgate and its income will be on your side of the river.'

Aunt Hetty sank back in her chair. 'Vultures, the lot of them.'

'But here's the interesting part, Miss Mitchell. Mr Banks let drop a consortium from Falmouth want to extend the ferry services and are interested in your land adjacent to Harcourt Quay.'

I turned the map round. Harcourt Quay lay squarely between St Feoca land and Tallack Creek. 'But you've not marked it as having anyone interested?'

'Precisely!' Rubbing his hands, he could barely conceal his excitement.

Aunt Hetty frowned. 'The harbinger of such horrific news and you consider it fit to smile?'

His smile broadened. 'The whole time I've been working on this I've been growing hugely despondent. Your trust in me weighs heavily. I'm all too aware it's a race against time. We must presume Richard Compton has a copy of your father's will and anticipates becoming a very rich man. Only if we keep within the terms of the constitution can we hope to stave him off.'

A pulse throbbed in Aunt Hetty's throat. '*Stave him off?*'

Nothing seemed to daunt his inexplicable spirits. 'Miss Mitchell, you remember I said a consortium sought to extend the ferry service? Well, I happened to see a letter.'

This time there was a returning smile. '*Happened*, Mr Polcarrow?'

'I told Mr Banks the person I represented was particularly keen to buy the land adjacent to the quay. And the aforesaid replied that the land was unavailable – that it was already under a *subcontract* and therefore unable to be sold.'

He reached for another piece of paper. 'And, like a dog looking for a bone, I went scurrying back through every account I could find. Miss Mitchell . . . aren't you intrigued?'

'Yes, I am. I had no idea dogs hid their bones among office accounts.'

'They most certainly do!' His cheeks were flushed, a sparkle in his eyes. 'Eighty years ago, the owner of St Feoca agreed a ninety-nine-year lease with the owner of Harcourt Quay for a strip of land which lies adjacent to the quay. This strip of land measures no more than *fifteen* yards. You can see it here

– adjoining the land owned by Harcourt Quay. Eighty years ago, the owners of Harcourt Quay needed to extend their quay in order to berth larger ships and this lease still runs. *And so does the rent.*'

Aunt Hetty studied the map. 'I don't recall any rent from this strip of land. I've no knowledge of this at all. You've seen this lease?'

His dark hair shook. 'It's not among the school accounts, nor is there any mention of it in your father's file. However, I found out who negotiated the recent sale of Harcourt Quay and buttered him up.'

'*Buttered* him up?'

Francis Polcarrow shrugged. 'An expensive dinner, Miss Mitchell, because I was forced to buy a bottle of Reserve Portuguese claret – which I tasted none of. I put the dinner on my stepfather's account.' He looked down, a slight blush.

'We'll cover the cost.' I stopped. 'At least...I hope you're going to tell us there's enough money to cover it?'

His cheeks glowed. 'Several times over! Since the original lease, Harcourt Quay has been sold *twice* – forty years ago and a year ago – and the rent's been paid *diligently*. Indeed, every five years the rent's been adjusted as specified in the lease. The present owner of Harcourt Quay is paying four pounds two shillings into a bank in Truro under the name Harcourt Quay Extension, which is registered to the St Feoca Estate.'

I tried to calculate the sum. Mama had been twelve when they arrived from Exeter. 'The account's in St Feoca's name?'

'Yes, and it's valid. There's one hundred and two pounds in the account.'

'*A hundred and two pounds?*' Aunt Hetty gripped the edge of her desk. 'For a strip of land measuring only *fifteen* yards? Are you certain?'

'Absolutely. The previous owner of St Feoca was an astute man. He priced the rent high because he recognised its future value. He withdrew his money when he sold the estate, but your father left the money to accrue in the bank. Maybe he didn't know about it?' Francis Polcarrow reached for his papers, shuffling them into a neat pile. 'In short, that's enough money to employ any number of teachers, maids, gardeners, grooms. Your school has funds again, Miss Mitchell. Enough to get it restarted.'

'Mr Polcarrow . . . I can't thank you enough.' Aunt Hetty seemed lost for words.

'But the knives are still out, Miss Mitchell. We need three teachers and ten pupils in place within the week. You've enrolled more pupils?'

Her mouth tightened. 'We have names of four endowment girls and our four charity girls. We'll need another teacher, but not by next week. The problem is any new pupil must be fee-paying or we'll have difficulty persuading the governors the school's viable – not some frantic cobbling-together to pretend the school is functioning.'

Francis's smile vanished, replaced by a frown of concern. 'The governors are right. Their concerns are valid, but once restarted you're bound to attract fee-paying pupils. A virtuous cycle, so to speak. Parents need to see the school is viable and attracting pupils before they themselves will be attracted.'

Aunt Hetty opened her drawer and unrolled a piece of cloth. '*If* we get started, Mr Polcarrow. This mandrake root was found in a basket of vegetables left at our door. It may look like a parsnip, but it's deadly if consumed. Could you keep it with the dolls as evidence we've been the target of vicious threats?'

The colour drained from his cheeks. 'This changes everything. An altogether different matter. Left accidentally, we can prove no malice was intended, but not left accidentally and we're talking of *intent to kill*. Who knows about this?'

'Everyone in the house, though we emphasised it must have been an accident. No one knows about the other threats. But this, we found recently in the library. I believe several of the pupils must have read it.'

Opening the drawer, she handed him the scorched manuscript. Reading with horror, he flicked through the pages. 'It's written in brown ink – to make it look aged! He's clearly soaked the pages in tea . . . and burned the edges. How despicable! How appalling to frighten the girls like this – they must have been petrified.' He stopped. 'I wonder if it's the work of the same person who wrote to Mr Compton? If the writing compares to the letter Mr Compton received, I believe we could link the two. It's a thought, isn't it?'

Tall, sombre, showing no signs of his previous exuberance, Francis Polcarrow bid us good day. I was about to show him out but swinging round, his voice hardened. 'We need to take a very close look at everyone who attended the Turnpike meeting. I didn't think much at the time – just another member of the Turnpike Trust lining his pocket – but we must consider everyone. And that includes Benedict Aubyn, the trust surveyor.'

Sudden dizziness made me catch my breath. 'Benedict Aubyn?'

A puzzled frown. 'Yes. As the owner of Harcourt Quay, he stands to gain more than most. Without his quay no one can import or export anything. He can rack up his rents and harbour dues as much as he likes. Everyone wants access to the sea.'

Aunt Hetty gripped the arms of her chair and I reached for mine. Fighting my giddiness, I tried to speak. '*Benedict Aubyn* owns Harcourt Quay? Are you certain?'

'Absolutely certain. Don't forget, he's surveyed your land. And not just for the Turnpike Trust, either. Carnon Stream-works commissioned him to survey the river mouth. His name's on their report.'

Aunt Hetty's voice was a whisper. 'Has he declared an interest in any of my land?'

Francis shook his head. 'I don't recall his name, but I'll go through the list again. I'll find out exactly who's put in an interest for what.'

This time, her voice was stronger. '*Butter up* as many people as you need, Francis. I want the names of everyone who seeks to profit from the sale of my land.'

I stared after him as he hurried down the drive. My chest felt tight, my throat constricted. I needed to stop the blood rushing from my head. In the library, Grace was laying out material for the girls to sew, her basket brimming with ribbons and coloured threads. She was humming, absorbed in her preparations, and I hurried past, desperate not to catch her eye.

Usually when Susan was in the kitchen, happy chatter would echo down the corridor, but I heard only low tones and whispers. Both had their backs to me, Annie handing Susan a handkerchief and patting her arm. 'I just said . . . if you don't mind, I'll have none of that filth talked here. Then George told him to leave. But the man just handed him his card and said he'd be waitin' his instructions.' Susan wiped her eyes. 'Only, that's the third one that's come. The first said he'd set it up as rooms for investors but this one clearly meant it to be a . . . You know. For the soldiers' pleasure. Honest. To have my home turned into some pleasure house for soldiers. *Gateway to Heaven*, he said he'd call it.'

I tiptoed back along the corridor, fearing I might be sick. Right from the start Benedict had lied to us. Hurried footsteps sounded and Aunt Hetty rushed across the hall. 'Lady Clarissa's coming. I've just seen her coach from my window.'

Four horses swept to a stop outside the front door. Two groomsmen dismounted, pulling down the steps and, if Lady Clarissa looked angry, Mrs Angelica Trevelyan looked furious. Shaking the creases from her gown, she helped Mrs Lilly dismount. Behind her, Reverend Penhaligan clutched a newspaper beneath his arm. 'Oh dear,' whispered Aunt Hetty. 'The full set. That's never a good sign.'

Stepping forward, she curtsied. 'It's always a pleasure to

welcome you to St Feoca but something tells me this visit is not for pleasure.'

'Unfortunately not.' The feathers in Lady Clarissa's hat caught the wind. 'I'm sorry not to give you notice, Harriet, but we came as soon as we could. 'You've seen today's *Mercury*? No, I can tell you haven't. Well, my dear, there's something you need to read.'

Chapter Thirty-six

Placing his newspaper on the hall table, Reverend Penhaligan had no need to turn the page. What they had come to show us was written in large letters across the front. IMPOSTER SEEKS FUNDING FOR *SO-CALLED* SCHOOL. No fire burned in the grate, the room growing colder as I read. A SEDITIOUS AND CYNICAL ATTEMPT TO ROB GOOD PEOPLE OF THEIR MONEY.

Reverend Penhaligan helped Aunt Hetty to sit, likewise offering me a strong arm as I sank into a chair. Lady Clarissa swept up her silk gown and sat at the end of the table, Mrs Lilly unbuttoning her coat to sit opposite. Angelica Trevelyan did not sit, but kept striding backwards and forwards, her stout boots and severely cut jacket giving her an air of authority. 'By a concerned . . . no, by an *enraged* member of the public. Anonymous, of course, who believes his lies must be brought to the attention of the *gentle and generous benefactors in our illustrious town.*'

Aunt Hetty held her hands to her face. 'Read it for me, please, Pandora.'

A wave of nausea churned my stomach. *'It has been brought to my attention that a woman, for she is no lady, masquerading under an assumed name, claims she is the niece of Miss M— whose school has been failing for over a year. More precisely, an establishment where parents have withdrawn their daughters due to unnatural occurrences. A place where devilment and witchery go hand in hand – to this very day.'* I looked up. 'An assumed name? How does he know that?'

Angelica Trevelyan turned on her stout heel. 'Names of passengers are clearly listed in the ship's log as well as the harbourmaster's debarkation lists. I intend to enquire into this. But this accusation of devilment? Who knows about the raven and the dolls?'

Aunt Hetty looked at me for confirmation. 'Only Pandora and myself – and Francis Polcarrow. And the man who wrote this. No one else knows. Read on, please, Pandora.'

The heat in my cheeks made my eyes water. *Benedict Aubyn knew.* I wanted to run from the room, loosen my neck scarf yet I managed to keep my eyes on the words blurring in front of me. *'The woman claiming to be the niece, a Miss W— is a fraudster, a runaway, intent on spreading disorder and disturbance. She is a violent agitator: a dangerous instigator of uprisings and riots. Indeed, she was the first to throw a stone into the window of Telward's bakery during the recent appalling breach of peace in Truro. A wild, pernicious woman intent on debauching our young girls with her radical and seditious views—'*

'Outrageous!' Angelica Trevelyan's cheeks were the colour of plums. 'Maybe there's *some* truth in the runaway bit but to smear your name like that! How dare he imply such a thing?

You were nowhere near the riot. Certainly not throwing any stones! Read on . . . it gets worse.'

I could barely speak, a searing pain making me light-headed. 'I didn't throw any stones but he's right. I was in the middle of it.'

Gasping in unison, Mrs Lilly looked wide-eyed; Lady Clarissa, speechless. Reverend Penhaligan sat down, even Angelica Trevelyan stopped striding. 'You were in the middle of the riot?'

The band round my throat grew tighter. 'I was in the road and in their way. I was swept up by them . . . caught in the swell. They held me by my elbows to keep me from getting crushed. It was impossible to break free. But I wasn't there to riot, though I believe they may have reason for their complaints.'

'Of course they have reason for their complaints!' Angelica's tone matched her frown. 'But to be seen amongst them can only do you harm. Someone saw you – the writer of this scur-rilous article knows you were there. He knows you can't deny this claim.'

She was terrifying: beautiful and furious. 'No, I can't deny it. I don't know who saw me. I can't think who knew me to recognise me. Maybe it was when I went to the Turnpike meeting? That was very crowded.'

Tell them. I fought to breathe. *Tell them he knows that, too.*

'Innocent or not, this does not bode well.' Lady Clarissa placed her hand on Aunt Hetty's elbow. 'But at least she wasn't arrested for instigating the riot like he claims. I'm sure a lot of people were caught up in the crowd that day. We can ride this out. Do continue, Miss Woodville. I'm afraid it gets worse.'

I tried to clear my throat. '. . . *radical and seditious views. Many of our gentle and generous benefactors in our illustrious town have been approached to bestow endowments to line the coffers of this failing school. But who do they propose to teach? Servants, is the unfortunate answer. The endowments are merely to pay for their servants.*'

I caught the compassion in Mary Lilly's eyes. She must have seen my eyes were full of tears. 'We know that's not true, but many may well believe it to be. You're not the first to suffer slurs like this, and you'll not be the last. We'll find out who wrote this and expose him for the liar he is. Take courage, my dear – though I must warn you it now turns very scurrilous.'

I could barely focus on the print. '*We must ask ourselves, who is this woman who is to have such sway over the innocent minds of our children? Well, let me inform you. A woman born out of wedlock, or rather, a woman born to parents who were forced to avoid the scandal of her conception. A marriage which not one single person favoured. She is the daughter of a disgraced gentlewoman and that, Ladies and Gentlemen of Truro, is who proposes to teach the delicate flowers of our bosoms. Are our innocent young girls to be debauched and tainted by such association?*'

A tear trickled down Aunt Hetty's cheek. Another, and another. Reaching for her handkerchief, she dabbed her eyes.

Lady Clarissa's grip tightened. 'That part we may not be able to refute. I'm so sorry, Harriet. The man who wrote this article intends to inflict a fatal blow. A mortal wound. And I must say, the damage is considerable.' Reaching into her bag, she drew out a pile of letters. 'We've lost half the funding for the endowments. The promised money is dwindling. Actually, it's more than halved. And this is just the first morning.'

Mary Lilly's white hair was coiled beneath her green bonnet, her cheeks flushed, her looks feminine and delicate, but her eyes held steel. 'Not the charity girls. The funding for your estate girls is perfectly safe and always will be. You have my word on that. And we'll raise the endowment funds again. It's just at times like this you realise how fickle people can be. All it takes is a scurrilous, defamatory article and opinions are immediately swayed. As the writer clearly knows.'

Reverend Penhaligan was watching me from above his half-rimmed glasses. 'Maybe it's better if you don't read any more, Miss Woodville. I think you've read enough. Maybe I should have the paper back?'

Lady Clarissa and Mrs Lilly nodded but I gripped the paper, not letting them slip it from my hands. Already I knew what it would contain. '*And as for the dishonourable man who debauched the gentlewoman of which I speak. A one-time tutor at our illustrious Grammar School, a Mr W— who was dismissed for incompetence and banished to the Windward Isles. The man was an imposter. A fraud. An un-schooled liar claiming to be a scholar. And I can only warn you, with dire and heartfelt misgiving, that this woman seeking to debauch the very angels amongst us has the same bad blood, the same depravity of spirit as her father. Liars and fraudsters must be held to account. We must hold fast against her wicked influence and save our daughters from ruin.*

I remain a concerned, no, an enraged, member of our hard-working and illustrious public. Mr J P S—'

They must have been waiting for my instant indignation,

a tearful tirade in favour of my father, yet as my silence continued, their expressions grew increasingly concerned. Perhaps they thought me to be in shock. I was in shock. I could hardly pull my thoughts together. Spinning round my head were just three words – *who else knew?* I could hear nothing, the room a blur. I hardly saw them, hardly heard them. Benedict Aubyn knew about Father, about the raven, the dolls, and about me being in the centre of the riot. Only Benedict Aubyn.

Like in a dream their voices came and went. 'We must refute that! His slurs are outrageous.' Lady Clarissa reached for the newspaper and folded it quickly. 'We'll draft a reply. We cannot let that go unchallenged.'

'I'm afraid we'll have to let it go unchallenged.' A searing pain ripped through me. I was leaning on a field gate; keeping warm under musty sacking; standing straight-backed in church; staring through the window at a man holding a dog. Yet I had to find my voice. They had to know. 'Father *is* a fraud. His qualifications were awarded to his cousin and he thought no one would ever think to doubt him. Grandfather sent him away the moment he found out. Reverend Cardew told me the day of the riot. He said Father was lucky he didn't have him publicly horsewhipped. Everything in that article is the truth.'

'Oh, dear Lord . . . Harriet, is that true?'

'I'm afraid it is, Lady Clarissa. Pandora told me the moment she knew.' Elegant, immaculate, not a hair ruffled, her tears still glistening on her cheeks, she smiled and the last shreds of my heart tore completely. 'I think we all can hear the death knell tolling. A fatal wound, indeed.'

I could hear wailing, someone howling: piteous crying, the hurt so deep, the pain unimaginable. A guttural, animal howl. Lost, plaintive, filled with agony. 'My dearest . . . dearest Pandora. Come here.' Aunt Hetty's arms closed round me.

'It's all my fault. *All my fault.* I bring ruin to everything. *Everything.* Father named me well – Kalon Kakon . . . Beautiful Evil . . . sent as calamity to man. Aunt Hetty, I've ruined you. I've brought all this about.'

'What utter nonsense!' Her voice was sharp, filled with fury. 'With or without these slurs, the knives have long been sharpened. I won't have you take any blame.'

Angelica Trevelyan was striding again, and with great purpose. 'Well, I don't hear the death knell. I won't have this school closed.' I caught the draught of air as she passed. 'So what he says is true. That's fine. You're the target of his vicious malevolence and, as such, you may have to leave the school – for a while, at least. You can stay with me. I shall take you to every function I attend and believe me, I shall attend *every function.* I'll make people acknowledge you. Very publicly. As will Mrs Lilly, won't you, Mary?'

'Indeed. Come and stay with me – be my guest. We shall host a charity ball. If not several. Lady Polcarrow will help. She's one of our main sponsors and will give us every support.'

Outside, Susan was collecting up empty tankards from the footmen, Annie bustling round with a plate of tarts. Grace and the girls were admiring the horses, asking the coachmen their names. Shadow was at Gwen's heels, not barking, but sitting to command. The sky looked to be darkening, a band of clouds thickening, threatening rain.

Another draught of cold air as Angelica swung round. 'You can no longer be headmistress, Pandora. That's the only sensible way forward. I will stand surety for the endowment girls – though I believe two names may well have been withdrawn. How long do we have, Lady Clarissa?'

Lady Clarissa clasped her hands. 'Days, Angelica...' She sorted through her pile of letters and held one up. 'Mr Richard Compton *requests* a meeting at my *earliest* convenience. He wishes to know the exact date of the closure of St Feoca School.' She let the letter drop to the table. 'Now, I may not get this letter for a week as I intend to be out of town for a while! But that's as long as I can stall him.'

No further draughts, but a wry smile. 'Then we have less than a week to find four girls whose parents don't mind their innocent young girls – *the delicate flowers of their bosoms* – being *debauched and tainted* by association with St Feoca School.'

Angelica Trevelyan was magnificent: strong, furious, beautiful; intelligent, articulate and fearsome. Everything I aspired to be. I had dressed my hair like hers, altered my gown to be like hers. I had worn my headband to be like her. A perfect product of St Feoca School for Girls. Aunt Hetty must have been thinking the same. 'You ran away from here five times, I believe, Angelica? There was a time you'd gladly have instigated the closure of my school.'

Angelica's smile flashed across the room. 'Not once you introduced me to your alternative syllabus. That changed everything. That's why I'll fight tooth and nail for this school. How else will our delicate flowers bloom under such harsh conditions?'

Reverend Penhaligan altered his glasses, his heavy brows lifting. 'What was that you said, Angelica? *Alternative* syllabus?'

One glance at the others and Mary Lilly leaned closer, her sweet Irish lilt lifting her words. 'No alternative syllabus, Opus, my dear. No, no, no, goodness no.'

His brow remained unconvinced. We were all looking at him, me with the same creased brow. The four of them were smiling, yet not smiling, looking at him yet not catching his eye. Each with a shrug as if they, too, had not heard of any such thing either. He cleared his throat. 'I didn't hear that, did I?'

Mary Lilly patted his arm. 'No, Opus. You didn't.'

Angelica Trevelyan reached for her bag and Aunt Hetty stood up. 'There's been no response from the advertisements? No applications from any teachers?'

'I think we can presume there won't be any now.' Lady Clarissa swept the letters into her bag, the blue feathers in her hat swinging. 'Your father did you no favour whatsoever, Harriet. I've long thought he reacted foolishly to Abby's marriage. He should never have entailed the estate.'

'I asked him to.' Aunt Hetty's voice was firmer than I expected.

Her eyes softened. 'My dear . . . I understand. Believe me, I understand. But though I've never been a realist and never hope to be one, I feel we need to face reality.' She looked at each of us in turn. 'We have one week to find six pupils and one teacher. If not, I will have to close the school.'

'That's seven whole days!' Angelica Trevelyan was already halfway through the door.

We stood on the drive, the girls waving goodbye. The coachman whipped the reins and Reverend Penhaligan leaned from the window waving his hat. The wind felt fresher, a few tentative drops of rain. Aunt Hetty pulled her shawl tighter. 'Those clouds look ominous. I'm afraid it's the end of our sunshine. Come, girls, back to your lessons.' Ushering Grace in front of her, she turned. 'Gwen, tell Annie we won't dine formally tonight. Just a tray in our rooms. And when Mr Aubyn gets back, tell him I want to speak to him the moment he returns.'

Chapter Thirty-seven

The weather was worsening, rows of heavy grey clouds stacking up over the sea. Unable to be in my garden, I took refuge in Grandfather's study. Accounts lay open on the desk, my idea of writing to former pupils growing less attractive by the minute. Falmouth was no longer visible, just the grey mist, grey rain, grey sky, grey sea. The tree tops in Tallacks Wood were swaying, a scattering of white crests building at the exposed entrance to the creek. Turning to the next window, I had to brace myself. The track leading to the farm was only just visible; the muddy fields were beginning to darken, water pooling in the ruts. Beyond that gate was another gate and a stream where kingfishers darted across the cool water.

The moment I saw him arrive, I would go to Aunt Hetty. She was not the only one who wanted to speak to Mr Benedict Aubyn. The clock struck four, the fire almost out, just two logs remaining in the basket. Adding them, I watched the flames leap, but the ice around my heart would not melt. He should have told us he had so much to gain.

I almost missed his return. He was taking the short cut, huddled against the downpour, his coat and hat dripping. He passed from sight, entering the courtyard, and I ran to Aunt Hetty. Pointing to a chair at her desk, her mouth tightened. 'Sit there, my dear. I'll do the talking.'

'His explanation will come too late. My trust in him has gone.'

She handed me a glass of water and squeezed my shoulder. 'I know. That's why it's important I do the talking and you do the listening.' Hurried footsteps sounded on her steps, a knock at the door. 'That's him now. Straight back. Deep breath.'

He had changed out of his muddy boots, his jacket dry, his smile fading at the severity of Aunt Hetty's frown. Bowing, he glanced in my direction but I kept my eyes down. We were seated yet there was no chair for him. 'You wish to see me, Miss Mitchell?' There was hesitancy in his voice, tension in his tone.

'Mr Aubyn, you are the owner of Harcourt Quay?'

His fists clenched. 'Yes, I am.'

'And you thought it not important enough to tell us?'

'I missed the opportunity to tell you. And once that opportunity had passed, I thought it would complicate matters.'

Aunt Hetty's laugh was brittle. 'Which it certainly has. How did you *miss* this opportunity, Mr Aubyn?'

He took a deep breath. 'I was on my way to introduce myself to you as the new owner — I had every intention of insisting you pay for half the road repairs.' His voice grew stronger. 'Which legally, you are obliged to maintain. But when I walked up your drive and noticed all the potholes, my immediate thought was that you'd not be able to afford the repairs.'

'So you thought to butter me up and offer your kind services to an impoverished spinster whose land you had every intention of buying.' Leaning back, she fixed him with her fiercest stare. 'And you just happened to be in the area when the Turnpike Trust required a surveyor? Your quay is vital to them. Without your quay they cannot transport their goods. You stand to be a very wealthy man, Mr Aubyn – once the vultures get their talons in to my land.'

'Miss Mitchell, I bought the quay when your school was *thriving*.' A note of defence entered his tone. 'On my father's death, my family were required to look for somewhere else to live. My friend, Mr John McAdam, was at my father's funeral. I had inherited a small sum on my father's death and it was he who advised me to buy the quay.' His hands clenched. 'I needed an investment with an income. My family needed somewhere to live. As it turned out, the cottage on the quay was too small for them, but the income from the businesses was sufficient to cover the rent of a larger house. I thought it a sensible solution.'

His voice remained firm. 'But recently, I became aware that the income from the quay was insufficient for my family's needs. They were hiding their want from me. I was advised, at the time of purchase, that road improvements would add value to the quay and when Mr McAdam kindly stepped in with an offer of employment, I was grateful for his timely intervention. His new road technique is in its infancy – he needed to convince the Turnpike Trust to adopt his new ideas, and I needed the income.'

I glanced up. His cheeks looked less gaunt, his eyes not too narrow at all. With his hair no longer covering his forehead, his face held new strength. No sign of his lost-boy vulnerability, he stood square-shouldered in the face of Aunt Hetty's hostility. I stared back at my hands, determined not to fidget, not to let him see my heart was torn in two.

A slight raise of her eyebrows. 'Are you aware Miss Woodville arrived here in Falmouth under an assumed name?'

Not a flicker, not a glance in my direction. 'Yes. She arrived under the name of Mrs Marshall. We bumped into each other under an overhang and I was asked where the coaches left from. I was told she needed to get to Penzance and I paid her fare as she had no money.'

A slow intake of breath, but Aunt Hetty's stare did not waver. 'So you surmised she had run away?'

His eyes held hers. 'I did. But then she told me so herself – the day she learned her father was a fraudster. The day she was caught up in the riot and nearly trampled underfoot.'

'You saw her in the riot?'

'I helped her avoid the militia who were closing in on the protestors. It turned very ugly. On the way back, I bathed her cheek and she told me about her father.'

I thought she might hear the pounding in my heart. Aunt Hetty remained silent, taking her time. 'You knew her father was dismissed from the Grammar School and sent away? Are you aware her mother is considered a *disgraced* gentlewoman?'

'Yes. Miss Woodville told me the first fact, and I believe the second is only supposition. Idle gossip.'

'You know how close we are to closing the school?'

'Everyone knows – it's the talk of Truro and Falmouth. But that wasn't the case when I bought the quay. I didn't introduce myself to you then because your mother had just died and I didn't want to intrude on your grief.' The tension in his voice returned. 'But I was aware of it when I suggested you sell some of your land. I saw it as a perfect opportunity for you to raise funds to restore your school. And I still see it as an opportunity. A lost opportunity. Selling land is not a sign of weakness. It's a commodity. You'd get a good price and you could pour funds back into your woefully neglected estate.'

'Well, that's telling me.' She interlocked her fingers, leaning forward on the desk. 'Were you aware a raven was found in the kitchen... and hideous dolls and a manuscript? As well as the mandrake root?'

'Gwen and Sophie told me about the mandrake and Miss Woodville told me about the raven and the dolls in the smokehouse the other night.'

The blood rushed from my head. I thought I might faint but if Aunt Hetty was shocked, she hid it well. 'The *smokehouse?*'

'Yes, Miss Mitchell, the smokehouse. Shadow was barking and I went to silence him.' Not even glancing in my direction, his eyes remained firmly on Aunt Hetty. 'He led me to Miss Woodville who was watching the tower. She told me why she was there and I urged her to consider employing nightwatchmen.'

'*In the smokehouse?*'

'Yes. We stayed keeping warm under the sacking until the cockerel warned us it was dawn and the household would soon wake.'

Not a glance in my direction, and I was glad of it. My cheeks were burning, my heart pounding. He had no need to tell Aunt Hetty that: some things were better left untold.

'Have you read the newspapers recently, Mr Aubyn?'

'No. My work has kept me busy in Redruth.'

Reverend Cardew might have been persuaded to break his silence, the writer of the article would know about the devilment because he perpetrated it, and anyone could have read the disembarkation list. I caught Benedict's eye: not a quiver, not a flutter, not a downward glance. Not like the men in Government House who would try to tease their way out of any accusations. Not like Father with his weasel eyes and false smile. Benedict was neither smiling nor frowning, merely waiting for Aunt Hetty's next rapier thrust. Gone was her playful cat-and-mouse teasing, her raised eyebrows and pursed half-smile. This was a duel, and Aunt Hetty's sword was sharp and swift.

'Have you declared an interest for some of my land, Mr Aubyn? I believe you surveyed my shore for the Carnon Streamworks?'

Just the ticking of the clock and Aunt Hetty's absolute stillness. He stood watching her, a pulse beating in his neck. 'I was in need of money and references. The Turnpike Trust would not have given me the position of surveyor without clear proof I knew what I was doing.'

More silence, just the pounding of my heart. 'You haven't answered my question, Mr Aubyn. Are you intending to bid for my land?' Aunt Hetty remained motionless, her stillness unnerving. I was used to Father's angry shouts, his temper flaring at the slightest provocation. Of heated fights, not icy coldness. *Say no. Say no.*

He cleared his throat. 'Yes. I have declared an interest.'

I felt a knife twist in my back. Anger burned my throat, my eyes, my cheeks. So underhand, such betrayal. Aunt Hetty felt it too. Her mouth hardened. 'Mr Penrose tells me there are plans to repair the Old Tudor Quay in Tallacks Creek. That tenders have been invited to strengthen the quay for barges to moor alongside. I presume you've declared an interest to bid for Tallacks Creek and the mill?'

His eyes held hers. He remained silent, head back, chin in the air and a new frostiness entered her tone. 'How very convenient for you to set your men to work before your purchase is complete. When did you order the gypsum – when you decided to bid?'

His jaw clenched. 'Mr Carter needs financial help. Someone needs to invest in his mill and if you had . . .'

'Don't stop on my account, Mr Aubyn. You think me neglectful?'

'The estate has been woefully neglected. Both families need investment. They cannot survive as they are.'

'And if I had sold some of my land like you suggested, I could have saved my school?'

'*Can* save your school.' His look held defiance, his voice rising. 'The truth is I can't understand why you don't. Landowners must move with the times. The neglect of your estate is causing great hardship. I'm sorry to offend you but you can't expect my sympathy. Sell your land, invest in your estate, and allow Miss Woodville the chance to rebuild the school. You owe it to Miss Woodville. Even if it takes her years, you owe her the chance to rebuild her school.'

'Well, I must say, you've made your point very clear.'

'I meant no offence. I'm sorry, I shall pack my bags directly.'

I sat upright, straight-backed, poised, my hands calm, no sign of the turmoil tearing me apart. At the door he turned. 'I don't seek to profit from your land, Miss Mitchell. Far from it. I wish you only well. Good day.' His eyes burned mine. 'Miss Woodville.' He shut the door and Aunt Hetty breathed deeply, her fingers tapping her lips. She raised her finger for me not to speak and I went to the window, watching the gathering dusk.

Missed the opportunity to tell the truth. So much better to find out the truth now, rather than later. Better to know than to be caught out like Mama and be lied to. Better to know who to trust, who was keeping things back. Aunt Hetty remained motionless, her calmness soothing me. Or so I thought. Benedict was striding down the drive, Shadow at his heels. He swung round, ordering the dog back and Shadow sat and waited. When Benedict turned, the dog ran after him, and a tear trickled down my cheek.

'He's had to bring the dog back. Shadow won't leave his side.'

Aunt Hetty's voice was gentle. 'A night spent together in the smokehouse is not easily forgotten.' My heart sank; it was clearly my turn to face her rapier questions. 'Did he kiss you?' I shook my head. 'Well, he missed a trick there. Most men try to seal your fate by sealing your lips.'

Dragging him by the scruff of his neck, Benedict returned

the dog to the front of the house. Walking away, the dog followed yet again. 'Aunt Hetty . . . do you think he wrote that article?'

She shook her head. 'No, I don't. He doesn't know about the constitution. If he knew, he'd know the land is held in trust and I couldn't sell it even if I wanted to. He thinks lack of money is our only problem.' She reached for my arm, pulling me closer. 'And he couldn't possibly have written that article.'

'Why not?'

'Because, my dearest, the poor man is desperately and completely in love with you. I'm not even cross with him. I believe everything he's told us. He's right about my neglect – I've been too absorbed with my own interests – and if he didn't show interest in my land, I'd think less of him.'

I caught my breath. 'Do you mean that?'

'About his bid, or about him being in love with you? My dear, he's been in love with you for a while now.'

'But I thought . . . I thought you thought he loved Grace.'

A shake of exasperation. 'What a lot you have to learn! The poor man can't take his eyes off you. And when a man can't take his eyes off someone he concentrates on other people in the room. He's pleasant and polite and carries on long conversations because the only person he really wants to speak to twists him in knots and makes him too tongue-tied to talk.' She gave my arm a squeeze. 'When do you think he's going to realise he needs to tie the dog to a post?'

I was smiling, trying to stop my tears, yet the more she squeezed my arm, the more my mouth quivered and the more my tears splashed.

'And when a man finds he can't tear his eyes off the woman he loves, he uses what he thinks are subtle ways to hide his adoring glances. Like staring at her reflection in the coach window. Or choosing to turn the pages of music so he can look up at her.' She shrugged. 'I even told him I would be expecting his proposal but I think his mind was on the map he was about to present to the Turnpike Trust.'

'But Aunt Hetty . . . you've just sent him away! He thinks you're furious with him – that he's unwelcome and must never come back.'

'Yes, absolutely furious. Of course, he must think he's banished.'

'But might that not be a bit . . . counterproductive?'

This time a laugh accompanied her shrug of exasperation. 'What a lot you have to learn, my dear. Give him a day or two, and he'll come striding back with even greater ardour, to stand with that defiant look in his eyes and claim you from me.'

'But you really did look very cross, Aunt Hetty. You may not know how severe you can look sometimes. What if he doesn't come back?'

Her hair was dressed more softly now, framing her fore-head, a curl down either side of her high cheekbones. Her lips looked redder, as if rubbed by beeswax, her complexion flawless, a slight glisten in her eyes. 'Then you'll have years of practising how to look equally severe. A mirror helps, but not too often, and not for too long. You don't want to get lines. It's very ageing.'

Below us, Benedict Aubyn was carrying the dog back to the

courtyard and her frown returned. 'Your father did *not* name you, Abby did. All that ridiculous nonsense about *Kalon Kakon, Beautiful Evil, sent as calamity to man*. I presume your father told you that?' I nodded and her eyes flashed. 'Yes, Pandora's jar was full of all the evils in the world – and yes, she unleashed them into the world – but the one blessing she kept back was Hope. One of Father's favourite saying was: *Of all good things that mortals lack; Hope in the soul alone stays back.*'

Crossing the room, she opened the bottom drawer of her desk. Returning with a small book, she held it to the dying light. 'This was Father's. It's an illustrated anthology of Greek gods and goddesses. Abby and I loved it as children.' Her voice dropped. 'I didn't know it was missing, or rather, I never looked for it, but two years ago it came to me through the post. All the way from *Philadelphia.*' She wiped a tear from her eye. 'I realised then that Father must have given it to Abby when she left in such a hurry.'

She opened the red leather cover and the pages fell open on a picture of a beautiful young lady holding a large Greek jar: an amphora, almost as big as she was. Slipped inside the book was a piece of paper and I recognised Grandfather's writing. *We live in Hope.*

My hand trembled as I held it to the light. Underneath, four more words were in Mama's familiar writing. *I live in Hope.* 'At first, I thought Father had given it to her when you left for America, but then I realised it must have been when they left for Bristol. That's why Abby named you Pandora. And why I knew Benedict Aubyn had fallen so deeply in love with you. I saw the hope in his eyes, the sudden igniting of new life. He played that piece about Orpheus and Euridice and talked of Greek myths. He mentioned hope. You bring hope, Pandora. You've always embodied hope to me.'

I tried to stop my mouth from quivering. Tears blurred my eyes, splashing my cheeks. Impossible to stem, she let me cry as if she knew it would do me good: washing away the past, the hurt, the lies; filling me with courage, with strength, with determination. In the growing dark Benedict was hurrying down the drive unencumbered by the dog. 'If he turns round to glare at my window, you can be sure he'll come back.'

I swallowed, my mouth dry. 'How do you know that, Aunt Hetty?'

'Because Anthony Ferris didn't.' She smiled. 'And Orpheus did.'

He was too far away, his black coat merging with the gathering dusk. Soon he would be out of sight. I held my breath; I even think my heart stopped beating. I could only just make out his dark coat, his hat pulled low, a bag in both hands, and I gasped. 'But he doesn't know I love him. He thinks I'm never going to marry because I mistrust men . . . because they curtail women and control our lives.'

I felt her squeeze my arm. 'He has a point.'

'But I do love him, I do. I've tried not to but it's overwhelming. It just seized me one day and turned me inside out. It's actually a horrible feeling – like wanting to be sick all the time, like being in pain. Like my heart is aching. Is this how Mama felt?'

She kissed my cheek. 'Yes. But your mother chose the wrong man. I knew that the moment I met your father. Dogs always growled at your father. Dogs know who they can trust.'

Through the gloaming, his clothes were too indistinct, his figure lost to the darkness. 'He didn't turn round. Aunt Hetty, he *didn't* turn round.' We should have lit a candle, the embers were casting a red glow across the room. She remained motionless, silent, deep in thought. 'What are we going to do?' I whispered. 'Lady Clarissa's right. We have to be realistic.'

I was not expecting such a vibrant smile. 'We're going to do what your grandfather and mother tell us to do – *live in hope*. I can't think why I've been so slow. The answer's staring us in the face, or was, until he walked out of the door. We're going to bid for the house. I'll take out an advance on the three hundred pounds a year I'm to get from the estate and use some of the one hundred and two pounds as a deposit.'

I felt almost breathless. 'We'll bid for the house – keep the school but not the land? Aunt Hetty – it's the obvious answer. Will we have enough money?'

She squeezed my arm tighter. 'Perhaps we might take a leaf from your despicable father's book. We'll sell some silver. It only needs polishing and we won't have time for that. We'll sell everything we don't need. We'll keep the house, even if we lose the land.'

Of course, I was smiling, laughing, hugging her. I lit the candles, stoked the fire, and held Mama's book to the fragments of my heart. Aunt Hetty's transformation was complete. She was skipping like a girl, giggling, pouring a glass of wine from a decanter in her cupboard. Raising our glasses, she looked radiant and I hoped I looked the same. Yet the room was too hot, the wine too strong. I wanted to run from it, throw myself on my bed. *He didn't turn round*. He had no idea of my feelings for him. He thought I wanted only to be a teacher, wanted only to have my own school.

Chapter Thirty-eight

St Feoca Manor: School for Young Ladies
Wednesday 15th April 1801, 11:30 a.m.

A slight break in the clouds saw me reach for my umbrella.
Drawn to the quayside, I watched the water lapping
against the iron ladder on the fifteen yards that made all
the difference to how many ships could moor alongside. I
knew not to look for him: the cart had been returned and
George Penrose was already filling it with the next load of
logs. Hammering echoed behind me, the brightly painted
sign *Roseland Holdings* newly positioned above the door. Three
men in tall hats were staring across the river, not watching
the seagulls, or the egrets, or the sandpipers, but a dredging
machine being pulled up the creek by a barge.

An icy wind was blowing down the River Truro and I
stood watching the bargemen adjust the sail. Falmouth was
a grey haze in the distance and I pulled my cloak tighter, yet
I needed the fresh air after such a sleepless night. A splash
of oars and I looked up: the ferry from the Passage Inn was
crossing the creek, the ferryman no doubt cursing the barge
for delaying him so long. A woman was sitting in the stern

and it seemed a lifetime since I had been rowed across like that.

The ferry drew closer. Hugging her cloak, the woman had her hood pulled low. 'It's a north wind, that's why it's so cold. It'll be even colder going up to Truro.' They drew alongside, and she spoke again. 'Is St Feoca School easy to find?'

The ferryman slipped his rope round the iron ring. 'Aye. Straight up the drive from the castle gate. Shall I see ye safely off?'

She was already holding the rails. 'No, I'll climb the ladder. I've only a small bag.' She was nimble, her movements lithe. Reaching the top, I could not help but look twice. She smiled, pulling back her hood, confirming what I thought.

'Miss Meredith Trelawney?'

'Yes . . . goodness. How do you know me?' Recognition flashed across her eyes. 'Of course. You're Ben's friend on the cart that day! We saw each other very briefly, but I don't know your name.' Aged about thirty, she was bright-eyed, alert, with a look of intelligence Father might consider *would cause her problems*. She looked amused, even happy. 'Are you by any chance Miss Pandora Woodville?' I nodded and her smile grew broader. 'I'm answering your advertisement for a teacher. The one in the *Gazette*? I hope I'm not too late to apply? Only I thought I would stop off and see the school before I go on to Lady Clarissa.'

'Not too late.' I bit my lip, following her to the gatehouse. She was walking with such energy, striding ahead, looking round, admiring the oaks. 'Did Mr Aubyn send you?' I managed to ask.

Her laugh was immediate, joyful, full of intimacy. 'No one *sends* me anywhere, Miss Woodville. I'm not a chattel to be *sent for* or sent *somewhere*. I choose where I go and what I do. Does that shock you?'

I tried to match her long strides. 'No, Miss Trelawney, it doesn't shock me. It thrills me.'

'And it's *Meredith*. I hear Miss Mitchell has a fearsome bark?'

I was almost breathless trying to keep up with her. 'Yes, she has. A fearsome bark.'

My answer seemed to please her. Eyes sparkling, she pointed to the mended potholes. 'Ben said he'd been working on your drive.'

Aunt Hetty was not barking, though she did look fearsome. Yet every question she darted at Meredith, the answer came back equally swiftly, with humour, not even a glimmer of being intimidated. I was in my usual seat: Aunt Hetty had told me she would do the talking, but Meredith seemed to be doing rather more talking than Aunt Hetty.

'Yes, I have two brothers – Henry is a major in the militia and James owns land not far from here. They've both offered me a home – as have my parents, who live in St Kew. I could share my time between them – and because I know this will be your next question – they've tried very hard to marry me off. They won't stop either and if anyone they produce can contemplate the idea of me continuing to do what I like, how I like, when I like, then I may consider his proposal. But that isn't going to happen, is it?'

'Isn't that a bit *rebellious*, Miss Trelawney? You surely don't think that sort of behaviour is encouraged here at St Feoca?'

'I like my independence, Miss Mitchell. I like the independence that teaching in a school brings. I enjoy using my brain. I enjoy the concept of learning, and I like to impart knowledge. Husbands consider their wives their property – and call their daughters *the flowers of their bosoms*. They control where their wives go and consider those who don't adhere to these principles as wayward, forward and inviting trouble. We must marry and give up our freedom, or we must become governesses under another man's control. Until men grasp the idea that women are capable and *highly intelligent*, they will not change. Society needs to embrace the idea of a woman having a certain degree of independence. I like teaching and I do it very well. Can you imagine a husband allowing me to apply for this position?'

Aunt Hetty drew a deep breath. 'You've read that article?'

'Yes. And it was like a red rag to a bull. Girls are not flowers to be watered. They are to be educated.'

'And the fact that our school is all but closed?'

Straight-backed, she exactly mirrored Aunt Hetty. Yet whereas Aunt Hetty was in black, Meredith was wearing apricot. Once free of her heavy cloak, she looked dainty and petite. Her jacket was close-fitting and trimmed with velvet ribbon, a ruff at her neck. Beneath her angled hat, her fair hair curled at shoulder level. Pearls swung from her ears, her gown slim fitting, ending just above her ankles. Her boots looked delicate, yet sturdy enough to take her long strides. 'My brother told me the militia have put in a bid for the house.

He told me the circumstances of the sale and I knew I had to come.'

'You know Benedict Aubyn. Did he tell you we're angry with him?'

'Yes, he made that very clear. We were almost brought up together. But no one can stay angry with Ben for long – except his family, who remain furious with him.'

I sat watching Meredith Trelawney with growing regard. She was poised, elegant, respectful, yet strangely youthful, as if convention and etiquette had not taken their toll. Aunt Hetty sat for a moment before leaning down and opening her bottom drawer. 'Your references are impeccable. Why did you leave Bath? I know the school has a formidable reputation.'

'To be near my parents, who, though very well, are not as young as they were. And I missed Cornwall. It draws you back. I shall not leave Cornwall again.'

Placing some plain paper and a quill in front of Meredith, Aunt Hetty drew out a page of what looked like printed questions. 'I wonder if you might write what you consider to be the answers? Not every pupil takes this examination . . . and it goes without saying that none of their fathers know about this. Most of their mothers know, but not all. Am I making sense, Miss Trelawney?'

'Perfect sense, Miss Mitchell.' Her pen scratched the paper, her writing fluid, racing along the page just as she raced up the drive. She reached for another page, filling it quickly with arithmetic, grammar, dates, kings and queens, lists of first ministers, political parties. Next came parts of flowers, an answer about the circulation of the blood.

Aunt Hetty held up her hand. 'You may stop. Just answer the last question if you wouldn't mind?'

Meredith turned the page. '*Who benefits from a woman being educated?* This question tests them on their knowledge on *The Vindication of the Rights of Women* but you ask for just two words?'

Sliding the paper across the desk, I caught her answer. *The World.* Aunt Hetty smiled. 'One of our governors wrote that. Most of the girls write, *our society*; some write, *our children* . . . some write, *our daughters.* There's no right answer, of course.'

Rising, I thought the interview had ended but Aunt Hetty straightened and stood quite still. 'The sad fact is we need four more pupils or within the week our school will be forced to close, my land will be sold, and your brother's men will trample their muddy boots all over my polished floors.'

'Which must not happen, Miss Mitchell.'

'No, it must not happen. Which is why I intend to bid for the house myself – in which case, I shall be in direct competition with your brother.'

A slight shake of her head, a swing of her pearl earrings and Meredith smiled. 'Then I'd better ask him how much he intends to bid – so you can override it, Miss Mitchell.'

Aunt Hetty's eyebrow rose, a returning smile. 'You don't have any nieces, by any chance, do you, Miss Trelawney?'

'Not of school age, unfortunately. My six nephews attend the Grammar School. Why do you ask?'

'My land is in jeopardy because of a constitution put in place by my father. If the school fails, and by that they term fewer than ten pupils and three teachers for more than six months, the house and land resorts to the heirs of the estate. That time is now. Did your brother not tell you that?'

'He told me you've been struggling with numbers. That, reluctantly, you must close the school. Which is so clearly not the case. The case is you're being forced to close?'

'Not yet. We will fight on.'

I thought I would be asked to escort Meredith round the school, but Aunt Hetty indicated to a door I had never entered. Her hand rested on the door knob. 'After that scurrilous article, the governors think it best Pandora keeps her head below the parapet, so we must take her off our list of teachers.' She paused. 'There's something you both need to know.'

The door opened to a large attic. Despite the greyness of the day, light was streaming through the roof windows. A long table took up most of the room with further tables lining both walls. A glass-fronted cabinet stood at one end, books and papers piled on shelves at the other. But if the room surprised me, the contents of the tables drew me completely. Each held a microscope, each with piles of paper by its side, each with a tray of sharply pointed pencils and quills the size of an eyelash.

Aunt Hetty ushered us in. 'At first, I was content with handheld magnifiers until Father bought me this Cuff microscope. I was overjoyed and thought it was all I'd ever need until Mother bought me this model, which had been adapted – very similar to the one used by Robert Hooke.' We followed her round the room, her elegant fingers caressing each microscope in turn. 'Which works extremely well, but not quite as well as this newer version, which has the same single lens but with far greater curvature.'

Each of the microscopes was different, some with gleaming brass handles, others with duller, tarnished rims. Varying in size, each had a polished wooden base, each with rows of dishes grouped at their side. In the centre of the large table stood a tank of murky water. Opening a large book, Aunt Hetty pointed to a page of exquisite drawings. 'This book was published six years ago. It includes the work of Antonie van Leeuwenhoek which is well known, but this edition includes drawings by others who study Natural Philosophy.' She turned the page. 'Each drawing is what we term an animalcule – a little animal – and each one can be seen only through the high magnification of a microscope.'

She drew a deep breath. 'I was disappointed in love, Miss Trelawney, and thought never to be happy again. But the pain of heartbreak lasted less than three weeks – if it was heartbreak at all! My father knew exactly what he was doing when he bought me my first microscope. It was liberating, like finding my real soulmate. Can you imagine any husband allowing me to spend so much time peering down the rims at these magnificent creatures?'

Meredith pointed to a pile of papers. 'May I?' Aunt Hetty nodded and she spread out several pages of exquisite drawings, identical to the ones in the book. 'You've replicated his findings?'

'I thought to replicate them as a way of learning, but it became my passion.'

'Aunt Hetty, these are beautiful. You draw so well.'

'Your grandmother was a very fine artist. She taught us both. Imagine my pleasure when I found two, then three, animalcules that no one else had ever drawn. It was exhilarating, to say the least. Since then, I've found two more.' The tips of her fingers trailed over the microscope. 'Two years ago, Mother read about a new microscope made by Georg Brander, the famous Augsburg instrument maker. This one here. It was extremely expensive and only a few were finding their way to England, but Mother insisted I must have one and wrote to the Royal Society. She paid the sum outright. My name was put on the list of buyers, and a year ago it arrived wrapped in silk, cocooned in cotton, triple-boxed, and nailed into a rather large crate.' She held my eye. 'All the way from Augsburg.'

I stared back at her. 'You wish to concentrate on your *studies* – not . . . to marry?'

'Yes, Pandora. I want to concentrate on my studies and a husband would only get in the way. When Mother died I found solace in my work and when the school's closure became a reality, I thought it a way to spend more time on researching these animalcules. This microscope has opened a new world for me. I have *several findings* I wish to publish.'

'Of course you must. You must write a paper and send it to the Royal Society.'

I thought Aunt Hetty was cross. Her mouth clamped, her chin held high. Then I saw she was trying to contain her tears. 'Miss Trelawney, will you take the position of headmistress of St Feoca School?'

Meredith Trelawney's smile lit the room. Her pearl earrings swung, her fair hair bouncing off her shoulders. 'I would consider it the greatest honour, Miss Mitchell. But I have to warn you, I have a fearsome bark.'

Aunt Hetty dabbed her eye. 'Perfect. Now all we need to do is find you some puppies to bark at.' She returned the piles of paper to their neat order and stood silently looking down at them. Intuitively, we both knew to keep silent. Finally she spoke. 'Why is Benedict Aubyn's family furious with him?'

Meredith's eyes were the shape of almonds: blue-grey and filled with purpose. 'Ben has nine sisters, one sister-in-law, and two nieces. His mother is one of the most intelligent, kind, loving women I've the pleasure of knowing. She *never* gets angry. Yet despite being very angry, Ben will not listen. He's told you of their reduced circumstances – that they were evicted from the rectory and are living in cramped lodgings until Ben can recoup their fortunes?'

'He's told us very little.'

'I'm not surprised. They say he's being particularly stubborn. But in his defence, I know he's been deeply affected by the tragedy. They all have. When Ben realised they were struggling, he came rushing back to Cornwall but the family want him to return – to finish his work – but Ben won't listen. He says he must provide for them.'

Aunt Hetty shut the door of her laboratory. 'He has a very good position with the Turnpike Trust. He will make money.'

'Yes, but he's a chemist, Miss Mitchell, not a surveyor. His work's far too important. The family believe in him – they always have. They don't mind how little they have, or how long it takes, so long as he finds a way to separate that gas.'

'Toxic gas . . . from mining?' I could remember his passion, his anger at men paying too high a price for their labour. 'He's trying to separate noxious gas from the fumes the workers have to breathe?'

'Yes. The tin they mine contains arsenic – which they burn off to get the pure tin. But Benedict wants to find a way of solidifying this arsenic gas once it's burned – so that it can be safely removed. Or used. Though deadly, he believes arsenic may have therapeutic properties, and only when arsenic is understood and calculated – and treated with due caution – will the mine owners agree to invest. To separate the toxic fumes, that is. Most believe he won't find a way and can't do it. Most want to deny arsenic even kills. But he knows he can do it, he just needs to perfect a technique.'

'To ensure the arsenic stays in solid form and is not breathed in by the miners?'

'Yes. And when he does, thousands of lives will be saved.'

Aunt Hetty walked swiftly across the room, reaching for Meredith's cloak and gloves. 'How old are his sisters?'

Meredith struck her forehead. 'Lord, how slow I've been! Rachel must be twenty-three – she's engaged but not yet married – Sarah's twenty-one, Leah's nineteen... Deborah is seventeen, Becky, sixteen... Letty is fourteen... Lizbeth, thirteen... Mary, eleven, and Little Lottie's ten. His two nieces are four and two.' She pulled on her gloves. 'Mrs Aubyn taught me everything. She and the rector ran the rectory like a school. Ben and I used to sit next to each other – he used to copy my work.'

'Will they come?'

'Of course they'll come.'

I stood staring at them, barely following their words. They sounded so in tune, their thoughts intuitive, as if speaking with one mind. 'You mean they'll come here . . . to live? They'll be . . . our . . . pupils?' I stammered.

Meredith Trelawny was halfway to the door. 'Yes, Miss Woodville. Your new pupils. Well, maybe not the older girls but certainly the younger – six fine, intelligent girls in need of both a home and an education.'

'Then . . . then?' I could barely form my words.

Aunt Hetty was smiling, blinking back her tears. 'It's perfect . . . the answer to our prayers. We have our school back – we have our new pupils, and we have our new teacher.'

Meredith Trelawny was racing down the stairs, pulling on her cloak. 'It'll take three days to get there and for them to gather up their things. I'll tell them Ben wants this. Which he does, only he doesn't know it yet! Which is probably the way to keep it. He says you've made it perfectly clear he must never return. Will that be a problem?'

'No, not at all.' Aunt Hetty opened the front door.

Meredith glanced round, shrugging at the gathering clouds. 'You have a beautiful school, Miss Mitchell. This is such a happy day, don't you think?'

We stood watching her hasten down the drive. Halfway down, she turned and waved. 'I thought . . . we all thought . . . you were going to marry Sir Anthony,' I whispered.

Head high, Aunt Hetty lifted her chin. 'Anthony's father marched Anthony down that drive the day after Abby's wedding. Neither gave a single backward glance. A month later Anthony was sent to London. Three months after that he was married into a wealthy family. Mother asked Lady Ferris to be a governor to show there were no hard feelings but Lady Ferris remained aloof and was often absent. Which suited us all very well. Anthony kept his distance, which was the right and honourable thing to do. So no. I have no intention of marrying Sir Anthony.'

She shrugged, her high cheekbones slightly flushed. 'After Mother died, Anthony showed me great kindness and generosity. I accompanied him to the theatre and his baskets of produce have been very welcome. Tonight, I shall write to him and thank him for his attention and apologise if I've given him any undue *expectations*. That my gratitude for his generosity may have been misinterpreted.'

She stooped to uproot a weed growing between the stones. 'Benedict is quite right: we're in urgent need of groundsmen.' Brushing the mud from her fingers, she stared at the empty drive. Daffodils were spreading beneath the trunks of the oaks, a dove preening its feathers on the ledge of the dovecot, and I stood willing him to come striding up the drive.

As if reading my mind, her hand slipped through my arm. 'He did turn round, Pandora. Only it was too dark for you to see.'

Stage Four

THE HERO'S RETURN

Chapter Thirty-nine

St Feoca Manor: School for Young Ladies
Thursday 16th April 1801, 12:00 p.m.

Gathered in the library, we waited for Aunt Hetty to help Annie to her seat. Acknowledging the girls' curtsies, she smiled. 'How very prettily you stand, girls. How tidy you look. Straight back, Mollie dear. Head a bit higher. That's better.'

I pulled out her chair and she motioned us to sit. 'I've written to the *Gazette* and it will be in tomorrow's paper. In two days' time, Mrs Aubyn and her family will take up residence in the parlour boarders' rooms and the rooms on the first floor. If you could get them aired and ready, please, Susan?'

I hardly recognised Susan. Wearing a dark blue housekeeper's uniform, her blonde hair was neatly tucked under a white bonnet. A lace collar frothed at her throat, further lace at her cuffs. Round her slim waist a bunch of keys jangled on a chain. 'I've aired the bedding and the mattress covers are off. Four girls have applied for the position of maid. Those I take on will make up the beds and stack the fires. I've opened the large kitchen and we'll scrub the larders and cupboards. George has four men to see this afternoon – three groundsmen and one groomsman. There's desperate need out there and plenty of applicants.'

'Excellent. Annie, do you understand why I want you to move to the room next to Grace? You'll be introduced as my mother's former companion and you'll be treated with due respect. You can advise on the menus, but Susan will employ a new cook and kitchen maids. The new cook will take your old rooms.'

Grace reached for Annie's hand. 'I'll help you move your possessions, Annie. It'll be lovely having you next to me.' She had pins in her apron, the girls' pieces of fabric beginning to take the shape of aprons on the table in front of us. Her heightened colour reflected her sudden clumsiness. Spilling a tin of ribbons, her hands could not keep still. 'Will the elder sisters teach? Only they may not think I'm good enough.' She bit her lip.

Aunt Hetty's eye filled with compassion. 'That's something we'll need to discuss, but your position as our established and *much loved* teacher will not change.' She waited for Grace to nod and smile, then reached for her paper. 'Our new pupils are . . . Deborah, Rebecca, Letitia, Elizabeth, Mary and Lottie – that must be Charlotte. I want you to show them the warm welcome we expect for our pupils at St Feoca.'

She left to write to the governors. Grace and the girls were to resume their lessons, and Susan and Annie were to prepare to interview the maids. I tried to match their busyness, yet my thoughts were all over the place. One moment, I believed Aunt Hetty that Benedict might love me, the next I was convinced she was mistaken.

The thought of meeting Benedict's family was tying me in knots. They would love Aunt Hetty and adore Grace, but they would find me lacking in so many ways. Crossing the courtyard, I sought solace in my garden. The night's fierce rain had filled the water trough to overflowing; drops still clung to the cherry blossom, the tips of the asparagus glistening in the mud. Strutting round the puddles, Poppycock eyed me with disdain. 'You're very fine, Mr Poppycock. Very fine indeed. I think I might paint you with those glossy feathers of yours.'

Trailing my fingers over Grandfather's sundial, I reread the inscription, *Pereunt et imputantur*. Grandfather's riddle would have led Mama to the well. *You have found the silver and found the gold*, but what if time was the answer to the next clue, not water? Time *well* spent. A soft whimper made me turn: Shadow had positioned himself by the gate and, head on his paws, lay watching me through his solemn black eyes.

Suddenly, his ears pricked up and he bolted from the garden. Men's voices were growing louder in the yard. 'She might be in her garden.' Turning, I had no time to compose myself, no time to slow the beating of my heart. Benedict stood at the gate, Shadow at his heels. He looked drawn, hardly able to hold my eye. 'Miss Woodville, forgive me, but may we trespass on your time?' Beside him Jacob Carter held a roll of paper in his hands.

I could hardly hear him for the pounding in my ears. 'Of course. How can I help?'

'Mr Carter has something he wishes to ask Miss Mitchell, only we thought it best to channel it through you.' He looked up, his eyes defiant. 'It's about the land north of his mill.' His eyes held mine. 'Mr Carter is the one who's instigated this, not me. He asked for my help and I'm willing to give it – for the good of the mill. If he could show you his findings?'

I took a deep breath. 'Shall we go inside? They're busy in the kitchen and the library. Maybe we could go into the coach house?'

Jacob Carter pointed across the garden. 'It won't take long. Is there room in that potting shed to spread out a map, Miss Woodville?'

Opening the door, the smell of musty earth mingled with iron and old leather. Gwen had sharpened the shears and oiled the spades, her newly emerging seedlings standing in neat rows. Pots cluttered the window sill but the small table was clear. 'Stay outside, Shadow.' Benedict stood back to let me go first.

Squeezing into the confined space, Jacob unrolled a map. 'Yesterday, I followed the path of the old leats as far as I could. They've dried so gradually, I nearly lost my way. In Father's day we had a steady stream. I've tried to clear them over the years but there's no flow – just a series of stagnant pools. But – with all this rain – I thought the natural springs might show up. Father used to say small trickles lead to small streams an' small streams lead to small rivers.' He pointed to his map. 'I never trespass, Miss Woodville. I'd never think to. Besides, the woods are set with traps – George nearly lost his foot – but I was that intrigued. Mr Aubyn gave me the idea. He said 'twere a shame the stream weren't on my land. So I went further than I should.' Removing his hat, he wiped his forehead.

He pointed to his map. 'There's no springs. Nothin' on our land. It's that dry, despite the rain. Puddles, yes, and sodden, but everythin' overgrown an' no sign of the old leats. And I started thinkin' how good Sir Anthony's been to me. He's given me work an' kept me goin'. And my thought was this: if Miss Mitchell could ask Sir Anthony if Mr Aubyn could survey his land, then maybe he could find a way of filling the leats? Maybe, Sir Anthony . . . knowin' his friendship with Miss Mitchell . . . might be willin' to help?'

The more I stared at the map, the more my heart thumped. 'Was this drawn at high tide, or low tide? Our wood ends here?'

'High tide. That's the periphery fence. It's well fenced, Miss Woodville.'

Fury swept through me. Not for a long while had I felt this angry. 'You've surveyed our land, Mr Aubyn. Does Mr Carter's map match yours?'

'Completely. He's a good draughtsman.' He must have seen my cheeks burning. 'Pandora, I did *not* instigate this. You cannot think this is my idea.'

It was all I could do to keep my voice steady. 'Please leave this map with me. Thank you, Mr Carter. You may leave. Thank you.'

'You think me presumptuous, Miss Woodville? But you'll ask Miss Mitchell?'

My anger was mounting. 'Yes, I'll ask. Thank you. Good day, Mr Carter.'

I caught Benedict's deep intake of breath, his clamped mouth. 'Good day, Miss Woodville.'

'No, not you, Mr Aubyn. I'd like you to stay.'

We waited while Jacob stroked the dog and left the garden. Benedict shook his head. 'Pandora, you *cannot* think I instigated this. I was wrong not to tell you about my ownership of the quay, and I understand you're cross about my interest in Tallacks Wood, but I didn't—'

'Ben, that stream we stopped at was on the right of Sir Anthony's drive, wasn't it?' My heart was pounding.

He looked puzzled. 'Yes. Then it dries to a trickle or finds its way underground to the creek.'

I was right, I was surely right. 'The land Grandfather sold Sir Anthony's father was *above* the stream. And our wood ends right at the tip of the creek. Not halfway up.'

'Your grandfather sold some land?'

'Yes, a strip of land to construct a drovers' lane. Only it wasn't used for the drovers, it was used to build the drive up to his house. Ben, there's something I need to show you. Can you come?'

We walked sedately across the courtyard, taking the short cut to the front door of the tower. Rushing up the spiral steps, he was hardly breathless as I pulled back the heavy bolts. 'This is Grandfather's study. Shut the door. I don't want us overheard.'

Searching the shelves, I remembered which file it was in. I knew to turn to the very last letters. The embossed letterhead was there, the map with the land outlined in red. 'Look. I'm right, aren't I? Does this map match your map?'

Studying it carefully, his frown deepened. 'No. The stream on this map distinctly remains on your land . . . here's where it enters the tip of Tallacks Wood.' He looked up. 'But Jacob's quite right. The stream does dry up.'

The answer to the riddle *was* water. Not time. Sir William Ferris and his family had plenty of time, he just needed the water. I could barely speak for my fury.

'Grandfather knew the value of water. The land was sold to extend a drovers' lane – to give the cattle access to water – but Sir Anthony's father was being devious. He knew Grandfather would assist a drovers' lane because Grandfather loved cows and would want to support the drovers – but the lane was never opened. There was *never to be* a lane. Just a vast sweeping drive up to Tregenna Hall. And lakes. Two huge lakes. And fountains, and rills.'

Benedict leaned closer. 'You think they've redirected the stream?'

'Yes, I do. That's why the Abbot's Pond is dry and the mill pond has silted up. They've *stolen* our water.' I handed him the letters. 'These letters imply there was to be a union between the families.'

He read them, his frown of concentration deepening. 'But they never married. Why?'

'My mother's disgrace; her rushed marriage tainted any further connection. Sir Anthony never proposed but I think it's worse than that. I think Grandfather believed they'd purposefully cheated him out of his land. And I think Aunt Hetty thinks the same. It was just an excuse to wheedle good land out of Grandfather. Both of them were furious. Aunt Hetty said she would never marry and she's not going to marry Sir Anthony now – I'm not sure she even likes him. She's grateful for his benevolence, but I think she's still angry with him.'

He remained studying the map. 'They've fenced off the head of the creek...effectively taken the top strip of the wood where the stream should filter down to the millpond. Why would your grandfather allow that?'

'He didn't. Grandfather died before the drive was built. They waited until Aunt Hetty was too busy, Grandmother hardly left the house, and Jacob Carter wouldn't think to question the perimeter fence.'

'They must have redirected the stream sluice by sluice. I imagine they laid pipes under the drive when they constructed it; a system of tunnels channelling the water away from the stream and into their lakes. That's why Sir Anthony has put in an offer for the mill and the woods. So no one finds out what he's done.'

'He's to bid for the creek? How do you know that?'

Walking to the window, he stared across at Tallacks Wood. 'When I declared my interest, Mr Banks merely snorted. He couldn't resist laughing. *I don't think Sir Anthony will find you a threat* were his actual words. I presumed Sir Anthony wanted to buy the wood for your aunt.' He turned. 'For the woman he loves. So she can retain the creek she loves...keep the memories of her family safe...her childhood – everything that's dear to her.' He turned away, his chin held high.

'But...what if he doesn't love her? What if he never has? What if he says he wants to buy the woods to save her school, but what if he just wants her land? Like the last time?' A chill made me shiver. 'To hide his deception about the stream?'

'Or to own the land for its value.'

'Value? But he's made the mill worthless, or is there a fortune to be made in fertiliser?'

He kept his back to me, staring across the water. 'There's a good living, but not a fortune. It must be to cover his tracks. Your aunt has every right to close the sluices he's put in place. The stream is on your land and once full, it will gravitate to the river. Once his channels are closed, the river will find its old course and the millpond will refill. So will the Abbot's Pond.'

'Of all my aunt's land, the wood is the most worthless. What if we're wrong and doing him a disservice? That he's genuinely in love with Aunt Hetty and thinks only to give it to her as a present.'

'I'd like to think that.' He gripped his hands together, tapping his chin. 'Pandora, you must believe me. Your aunt is right. I have decided to restore the Old Tudor Quay – simply to enable Jacob Carter to run his business.' He turned, and my heart seemed to burst. The hurt had returned to his eyes. 'He can take the lease and receive the harbour dues. I'll *not* profit. I promise you, I will not profit.'

'So, that day, when I came across you, you weren't surveying the old mine to see if it could be made profitable?' I tried to sound light-hearted.

'I was searching for where they might be hiding our stolen stones but as the old shaft was right there—' He stopped, the shadow of his half-smile. 'Yes, I was surveying the old mine.' He looked away, holding himself upright.

'In the hope of making it profitable again?'

'No. Absolutely not. I promise, I have no intention to profit from your aunt's land. It's just . . . Well, the truth is there's a specimen in your grandfather's cabinet – it's bright and shiny and labelled silver – but it's fool's silver, which surprises me as every other specimen is labelled correctly.' He pressed his hand to his forehead. 'This bright specimen of so-called silver is labelled *found in Tallacks Mine*, which I knew couldn't be the case but I thought to have a look – out of curiosity.'

Silver from Tallacks mine. Mama's treasure she always spoke about.

'I think it might have been left over from one of Grandfather's treasure hunts which he never changed back. I found a riddle in *Candide*. The clue for gold was Eldorado and the specimen in the cabinet might have been the clue for silver. But Grandfather knew it wasn't real silver as the riddle said *minerals may trick you and falsely shine*. Ben, what is it?'

He shook his head. 'No, it's too much of a coincidence.'

'What is? What coincidence?'

'A year ago there was nothing but talk of rich silver seams. Two mines were estimated to earn thousands of pounds in revenue.'

'I remember you telling us.' My heart began thumping. 'A year ago – that's when the terror started.'

'Maybe there are rumours there's silver to be found in Tallacks Wood? Your grandfather was a serious mineral collector. Why would anyone who saw that specimen doubt his word?'

'Anyone could have seen it – certainly all the pupils and their visiting parents. Aunt Hetty has open days – she says she often shows off Grandfather's collection.'

'Anyone could have seen it, but the question is: who's put in an offer for the woods? Only Sir Anthony Ferris.'

A shudder ran down my back. 'What if it's *him*? What if he's been playing us along like his father did before him? What if he left the dolls and that horrible manuscript? He could have written to the paper and left that mandrake, only it wasn't in *his* basket, which of course would clear him.'

Coming to my side, he took my arm. 'Pandora, sit down. You've gone very pale.'

'Ben, do you know anything about the school's constitution?' He shook his head. 'No, we thought not. It governs the closure of the school – and no one knows about it. *No one*. Except the school governors.' I thought I might be sick. 'But now I think about it, we missed someone off our list. Sir Anthony's late wife was a school governor and she could easily have told him about the constitution. Only the school governors know the land is held in trust and Aunt Hetty can't sell it. Anthony Ferris must know the school has to close before he can buy her land.'

'The land is held in trust?'

'Ben, it's him. That sense of dislike when I met him – which I put down as jealousy – was mistrust. All that charm . . . all that consideration. What if he wants Aunt Hetty's land and is prepared to poison us for it?'

His arm tightened round me. 'Put your head on your lap. Take a deep breath.'

'Ben, there were *two* sets of footprints – what if Cador is his accomplice? No, that's not possible. He wouldn't. He's too kind. He's too self-effacing – he's a sweet man.'

'Is he?' His voice was strangely fierce. 'He's younger and quicker and would scale the ladder with no difficulty. I know you have every reason to think well of him, and I wish it otherwise. I once thought him honourable but I now believe him to have a roving eye. I saw him wink at Grace in church. Not once, but twice. I was going to tell you that night in the smokehouse – had you shown an interest in marrying him, that is.'

Nausea made me grip my stomach. 'The tracks I followed led to the jetty – just across from their land. What if they had their skiff waiting? Ben, it's them, I know it is. They want the mine. The *silver*. Sir Anthony has fenced off the wood and set traps to prevent anyone from prying.'

'And as Miss Mitchell couldn't sell the wood even if she wanted to—'

'He set about the closure of her school. Because he knew the land was in trust to the heirs of the estate.' I ran my hand across my mouth. 'Someone must have told him about the silver in the cabinet.'

His breath was warm against my cheek. 'You said the collection is open to view. Anyone could have seen it – the girls, Susan, all the maids – certainly Lady Ferris would have seen it on her visits.' He glanced at the clock. 'We need to tell your aunt.'

It was all I could do to stand up. 'I'll go to her now. But he's too late. We've saved the school.' He swung round, a sudden, searching look, and I hardly knew how to tell him. 'The constitution stipulates we have to have ten pupils . . . so we've had to seek more. We have our four girls, and hopefully four charity girls, though there may just be two, but we needed four more pupils.'

He must have sensed something. A flicker of doubt entered his voice. 'Needed?'

'Meredith said your family would come . . . to help us save the school.'

He turned but not before I caught a flash of hurt. 'My family does not need charity. Meredith had no right to suggest they do. I will provide for my family. No one else.'

'Ben, please understand. Your family will save our school.' Tense, his shoulders stiff, he stared out of the window and I took a deep breath. 'It was both Aunt Hetty's and Meredith's suggestion – and Meredith has already left. We need your family. We're relying on them to come.'

He clasped his head in his hands. 'Ben, it's the perfect solution. Meredith told us your mother ran the rectory like a school. Aunt Hetty wants to ask her to teach. Maybe your eldest sisters could as well? They might relish the chance to contribute to your family's income?'

'My sisters will *not* take endowment places. I will provide for my family. I will not accept charity.' He stood stony-faced, biting his lip.

'You're angry? You're not happy for them to come?'

He seemed to be struggling to find his words, his voice a whisper. 'How can I be angry when I know how much they will love it here – just as I do? The moment I walked down the drive I thought, *Imagine if this was Mother's school and she had no money to pay for the drive.*'

I wanted him to draw me to him, hold me tightly, to whisper

the words I was so longing to hear. But he drew himself stiffly upright, holding back his shoulders, standing tall and proud. 'I will pay for my sisters' education. In full.'

'Ben, you are already. You may not know it, but your money has saved the school. Our attorney found an account from the sub-lease Harcourt Quay pays us to extend the quay. It may only be four pounds a year but it's been left untouched, and it gathered interest. It's more than enough to enable us to start again.'

A note of formality entered his voice. 'Then I'm happy to have helped. You can fulfil your dream now. Your school will rise from the ashes, like the phoenix.'

Returning the papers to the shelves, I looked back across the room. The fire was stacked, Grandfather's chair beside it. I could imagine him reading *Candide* and nodding off to sleep with his pipe in his hand. *Rise from the ashes*. Suddenly, the floor spun beneath me. 'Pandora, what's the matter? Pandora, what is it?'

I could hardly speak. 'Sir Anthony is going to use fire.'

'Pandora, I hardly think—'

'He's going to burn us down – tonight, while there's only just the four of us. Before the groundsmen come . . . before the maids come . . . before your family arrive. Before too many can see him do it. He's already warned us – it's in *The Coming of the Devil* – only he's the devil and he's going to watch us burn.' The room began to reel. 'He knows Aunt Hetty has saved the school because she's written to tell him. She's stopped him from proposing. He'll be laughing like the devil laughed . . . watching the house burn because he knows *there's no water*.'

I felt a welcome stream of air as Benedict fanned my face with a book. 'He knows there's *no* water in the Abbot's Pond. *No* water to put out the flames.'

'The manuscript threatens fire?'

I could feel the heat, smell the smoke. 'The house burns down and she's consumed by flames. He's that evil, that perverse. He's planned this all along. And it will be tonight.'

Chapter Forty

The clock struck two. The chimes faded. 'They'll come along the shore road like they did last time and follow the track along the hedge. They'll cross the lower field to the back of the washhouse. I know that because I followed their footprints. They'll leave their boat on the shore — and row back to their jetty on Tallacks Creek.'

'We need to catch them in the act of setting fire to the house; otherwise it's just wild speculation.'

'It isn't wild speculation. They'll come tonight, I know they will. And he's not going to make any mistakes. He'll want the whole building to go up in flames.'

Benedict reached for my hand. 'That won't happen. We can't risk this. Even if we're wrong it's better to be safe than sorry. I'll tell Susan the men and I are leaving today. Once we're gone, Sir Anthony will think the school is unprotected. I'll get my men to surround the school and lie in wait. Nothing must seem out of the ordinary — go about your day with the excitement you would normally be feeling. The fewer people we tell the better.'

'Just Aunt Hetty and the others. Sir Anthony and Cador don't know we've strengthened the windows and added the new bolts. They'll think it'll be the same as the previous times. You can catch them going up the ladder. Maybe they'll both go up?'

'We'll surround the ladder and if by any chance they get through the window, the bolts will hold them off long enough for us to arrest them.'

I nodded. 'Then do the others need to know? Might it just frighten them? What if I stay awake and watch the corridor. I can alert them if there's any smell of smoke.'

He crossed to the west window. 'Maybe that's for the best. I hope we're wrong, but if we're not I'll bring someone with the necessary authority to arrest them. They must be caught entering the premises. Preferably setting fire to it.'

'Don't tell anyone who we suspect it is. Tell them an unknown madman's been threatening us. I'll watch from my aunt's stairs – if I smell smoke I'll wake the others and leave from the front door.'

'I hope it doesn't come to that.'

I felt dizzy with fear. 'There are fire buckets in the barn. We've had a lot of rain. Might there be enough in the Abbot's Pond to form a chain?'

'A trickle, no more.' Returning to the north window, he stared across the sodden fields. 'I wonder how long it would take to reverse the stream? There must be a good flow if it fills his lakes and all his fountains and rills. I'll take my men and see if we can find where he's built the sluices and shut as many as we can. That might help. But we mustn't be seen. We'll have to wait for the cover of darkness. How many wells are there round the house itself?'

'Just the water pump and the well in the courtyard. The one in the garden is covered by a grille.'

'No pumping cart?' Shaking his head, his eyes grew stern. 'Your aunt's been very remiss. She should have a pumping cart and no well should ever be covered.'

I remembered an earlier conversation. 'Aunt Hetty told me Lord Carew's got a fire cart. Why not go to him? He's got plenty of groundsmen to call upon.'

His eyes held mine: filled with purpose. 'I'll go now and put everything in place.'

'You'd better storm down the drive. If they're watching, they must think we're angry with you. I'll keep Shadow in the barn tonight or else he'll bark and warn them off.' My heart jolted. 'You don't think it was them the other night, do you?'

Reaching for his coat, he opened the door. 'Quite possibly.' Bolting the study door, we started down the spiral steps. 'Lord Carew is a magistrate; he'll know who to bring. After I talk to him, I'll go to the wood and release as many drains as I can. When it's dark, I'll wade downstream with my men and close all the sluice gates.' Bending under the ancient lintel, he drew me back, strong, dependable, standing by my side. 'They will be caught, Pandora. Caught and brought to justice. I'll blow a whistle the moment we've got them.'

My mind flashed: a memory of Grandfather marching me into the wood. 'My grandfather used to give us his whistle to signal – one whistle to say we've found his clue. Two whistles to say we're coming back. Three whistles meant we needed help and he'd come and find us.'

Pulling his hat low, he turned to go. '*One* whistle. And one whistle only. Then this will all be over.'

No need for pretence, his fierce strides crunched the gravel. Even the girls looked horrified. Coming to my side, they stared after him in dismay. Mollie slipped her hand into mine. 'He'll come back, Miss Woodville. Honest he will. He'll have to, anyway, now that his family's coming.'

Sophie gripped my other hand. 'Then you can stop yer quarrelling and just... well, ye know. Let him love you.'

Kate was practising hopscotch. 'He does nothin' but say how clever ye are... how we should all be like you. The kind of things *sweethearts* say.'

Halfway down the drive, Ben stopped and turned round. 'You think it's *me* he loves, not Grace?'

Doubling up, they each gripped their stomachs. 'Honest, Miss Woodville!' Gwen could hardly stop giggling. 'An' ye think we should come to school?' Their laughter grew. ''Tis plain as the blush on yer cheeks. As certain as night follows day.'

Mollie began pulling up weeds, Kate still playing imaginary hopscotch. 'Will they like us, Miss Woodville?' whispered Sophie.

My heart was ready to burst. I crouched down. 'Yes. They'll love you. All of you... As do I.'

I never imagined what being kissed by four girls all at once would feel like: it felt overwhelming, humbling, making my tears run and my heart soar. Not one kiss, but two, now three.

Four kisses from each of them, the girls reaching out their arms, holding me in their tightest embrace. We almost fell over and I had to steady myself with my hands.

'We're going to sleep here from tomorrow onwards,' Sophie whispered. 'In our *own* beds. With sheets and a *diderdown*.'

Across the drive, one of the windows in the new wing slid open. Grace saw us and waved, and we waved back, smiling, laughing, without a care in the world. Or so everyone must believe.

I kept glancing at the clouds. Though threatening rain, they were moving fast, the wind picking up. Annie walked around her new room in almost hushed awe, remembering how my grandmother used to sleep in the bed: telling us how she used to lay out her clothes, how she would dress my grandmother's hair and they would talk. She had known my grandmother before she was married: Grandmother, she kept repeating, was her entire life.

Accompanying Aunt Hetty round the school, I watched her lock every window and slide across every bolt. The windows were shuttered, everything secure. Trying to match her excitement, I praised the cleanliness of the rooms, the softness of the eiderdowns, the piles of crisply ironed linen pillow cases. Tomorrow, the new maids would make the beds, but for the moment the rooms were well aired, the remains of the fires glowing in the grate. 'They'll not find anything amiss,' she had said, surveying the newly rolled-out carpets and polished floors.

I could not eat but pushed the food around my plate. Grace was clearly nervous, going through her lists, making sure everything would be perfect. 'Will they really like me?' she had whispered and Aunt Hetty had nodded. 'They'll love you. You can teach the piano and sewing. Annie will help. I wonder if you could keep a special eye on her? I think all this disruption might unsettle her. She may feel a little lost.'

Retiring to bed, Aunt Hetty bade us goodnight but Grace drew me aside. 'Annie's very troubled. She thinks she's putting Mrs Mitchell to bed. She says she'll just brush Mrs Mitchell's hair and will go down directly.'

Through the open door, Annie was clearly confused. 'Grace, when you helped bring up her possessions, did you find some cherry brandy?'

She blushed, nodding, biting her lip. 'It's something she started a while ago. A nightcap to help her sleep. It's in her bottom drawer. Shall I give her some? Perhaps she'll settle better to sleep.' I nodded and she added, 'If I leave my door open, I'll be able to hear her, but maybe I should stay in her chair until she's asleep? I'll help her undress.'

It was nine o'clock. With the cherry brandy, Annie should sleep soundly but my thoughts were hardly with them: I was planning where to sit, where to keep watch. Benedict would be opening the sluices, Lord Carew bringing his men. I would not change from my day clothes. Nor must I light a candle.

Leaving my door open, I heard Grace singing a soothing lullaby to Annie, as if she was singing to a child. The clock chimed ten and I reached for Grandfather's silver whistle. Aunt Hetty had been amused I had remembered it, smiling as she handed it to me. 'Of course you must have it — he would have wanted that.'

Listening to the stillness, the house seemed quiet. Tiptoeing from my room, I glanced through Grace's open door. She was not in her bed but waved at me from the chair by Annie's fire-place, her white nightgown and lace night cap glowing in the firelight. 'She's asleep,' she whispered, reaching for her candle and leaving the room. 'I'll be able to hear if she gets restless. Goodnight, Pandora.' She bit her lip. 'Are you sure they'll like me?'

She looked vulnerable, her face pale. She had been clearly nervous during supper, deciding she would re-polish the glasses, maybe even some of the silver. Reassuring her, I bade her goodnight and waited by my door until she was out of sight. Grabbing my blanket, I shut my door firmly and tiptoed to Aunt Hetty's stairs.

Benedict would be opening the sluice gates, Lord Carew gathering up his men.

The chimes faded. Twelve o'clock, and I settled back on the middle step wrapping my blanket around me. From my vantage point, I could see both their rooms. Though dark, a faint red glow lit the corridor. Shadows flickered from Annie's room, a comforting light as I continued my vigil. Two hours: they would come in two hours. The stone walls were icy to touch, a draught coming from under Aunt Hetty's door. Three hundred years had left their mark: the steps were worn in the middle, the oak handrail rubbed as smooth as glass.

I heard a soft tread, the faintest sound of footsteps. Peering into the darkness, my heart began to race. It was only Grace, checking on Annie, and I settled back, trying to calm my fear. I heard her bank up the fire, the glow grew brighter, her white nightgown silhouetted against the flickering light as she returned to her room.

I felt numb from sitting but did not move. Like a hunter, my instincts told me to keep still and she passed silently in front of me. She was worried enough about Annie to add further fear and I was there to protect them. The first sound of the whistle and I would go down. *If* it was Sir Anthony and Cador, would they come together? The walls felt as cold as a tomb. Gripping my blanket round me, I pulled it over my head. I should have brought two blankets, not one.

One o'clock. Half past one. More footsteps. Grace was checking on Annie again. She was clearly not sleeping, most likely thinking about Benedict's family, or her list of what still needed to be done. I saw the firelight glow, the comforting flicker of light behind her as she returned to her room. At her door, she paused. Turning back, she shut Annie's door, and we were plunged into darkness. Impossible to see, she must have felt her way back to her room as I heard her door shut.

A sensation of movement. The hairs on my arms began to prickle. I could see nothing, hear nothing, just a change in the air, an impression of someone passing. No sound at all, but an eerie sensation that someone had walked straight in front of me; someone making their way silently along the corridor, going down the stairs.

Gripping my whistle, I followed through the darkness.

Trailing my hand on the banister, I tried to calm my fear. *No one can get through the tower window.* No doubt it was Grace getting more candles or emptying Annie's pot. I could not see her, nor could I hear her, I could only sense her movement.

I made no sound. Halfway down the stairs, I breathed deep for courage. This was where the dolls had been left, the grotesque image still vivid in my mind. Suddenly, the blood rushed from my head and I gripped the rail, my heart hammering so fast I thought I might faint. Not the thought of the dolls, but another terrifying thought. Grace knew about the silver. Grace had made a study of the minerals and had even discussed them with Ben. I had to clutch the banister, control my giddiness.

Grace knew every mineral in Grandfather's collection. She knew about the silver, about the riot, she had seen the box arrive on the cart. She could have put the manuscript in the library, the mandrake in the basket. But why? Why Grace?

Did she know Cador Ferris? Ben had said Cador had winked at her in church, the man I had seen running from the house was strong, agile, with his exact physique. What if Cador was used to entering through the tower? The kitchen door had often been found open, Annie's nightcap a useful ruse to keep her from hearing. What if Sir Anthony and Cador knew about the heavy bolts across the study door?

I could hardly keep my hands from shaking.

Grace has warned them. She's going to let them in.

Chapter Forty-one

The gabled windows of the great hall were shuttered, no light filtering through the top. The last of the embers glowed in the fireplace, and I strained to hear the slightest sound. It was too dark to see anything, no sense of movement, no passing shadow: no sound of the front door bolts being slid across. Grace must be planning to let them in through the kitchen or the back alley – or maybe the scullery, or the drying room? I gripped my whistle. I had to keep my nerve: they must be caught entering the house. If I blew my whistle too soon, they would be alerted and get away.

The corridor to the kitchen was pitch black and I reached out, trailing my fingers against the wall. The library door was shut and I crept forward. The kitchen door was open and I stood straining to hear the slightest sound. Silence, just the ticking of the clock, the flicker of embers in the grate. I nearly jumped as the clock chimed two. The chimes faded, surely I must hear her soon. The glow from the fire was too faint to see by, but I would sense her movement, hear her reach for the key.

The stillness was eerie. Someone must have visited each time the kitchen door had been found open. Both of them, or was it just Cador? The clock struck the quarter hour and I tiptoed slowly forward, peering round the door. The kitchen looked empty: Grace must be waiting in the scullery. The back alley would offer perfect concealment, no one would see them go there and no one would think to look. My hand round the whistle was tight with fear. They must be caught entering the house.

Inching forward, I made no sound. I would unlock the kitchen door for Ben and wait. The door to the scullery was shut: the moment I saw anyone enter the kitchen, I would blow my whistle and call for help. Reaching for the handle on the housekeeping cupboard, I opened it without a sound. Annie's keys were kept in the top drawer. Fumbling in the dim light, I could feel nothing. No cold iron, no chain.

My stomach jolted. Grace must already have them and by now she could be anywhere. The keys would give her access to the conservatory, the music rooms, the new wing. I had wasted precious time. I was angry now, furious with her: Sir Anthony and Cador could already be in the house. Making no sound, I hurried back towards the library, trailing my hand along the wall. I had wasted half an hour, maybe longer.

Edging round the long table, I suddenly smelled smoke. It was coming from the music-room corridor and I tore to the door, grabbing the handle, shaking it, pushing against it, desperate to force it open. It remained firmly locked.

Racing back up the stairs, I flung myself through Aunt Hetty's door. 'Aunt Hetty... Aunt Hetty... Quick.' She was in her bedroom and I called from her desk. 'Where are your keys? Grace is setting fire to the new wing – she's locked the door behind her.' Finding them, I raced back, almost stumbling as I ran. My fingers shaking, I turned the lock to the music-room corridor.

The first music room was untouched, the second likewise, yet the smell of smoke was growing stronger. It seemed to be coming from the third room and I fumbled with the keys. I hardly ever handled the keys and panic made my fingers tremble. I tried two, three, finally turning the lock and flinging open the door. Chairs were stacked against the fireplace, the fabric on the seats already on fire. Black smoke billowed into the room, catching my throat, making my eyes sting. Pulling a chair from the fire, I grabbed a cushion and started beating the arms where the flames had caught.

The fire in the fireplace was blazing, a chair falling on its cracked leg. Grabbing the chair next to it, I threw it to one side. It was blackened, the seat smouldering, and I smothered it with as much force as I could muster. Smoke curled from the horsehair seat and I smothered it again. Looking round, I saw the curtains draped over a chair and about to catch fire. Pulling them free, I thought they had caught but they were merely singed and, as yet, unburned. More chairs rested against the wooden panelling, another set of curtains positioned for the flames to follow.

The log basket with its contents had been thrown on the fire, the flames blazing, but it seemed contained to the fireplace and I rushed to the door. I had to follow her – find her next fire – but I turned back. The flames could spark and

411

catch the rug. Pulling it free, I tried to think where she would go next — not the conservatory as it was sparsely furnished, the glass roof too tall, but the bedding in the bedrooms would easily catch fire. Racing along the corridor, the door to the new wing was locked. Again my fingers fumbled. Again, I could smell smoke.

'Take this.' Aunt Hetty thrust a dripping blanket in my hand. 'And these.' She handed me a pair of thick leather gloves. 'Try to smother the flames.' She ripped a strip off her night-dress. 'Cover your nose and leave the moment you feel it's too much. Your life's more important than the building.' Finding the right key, she turned the lock.

'Ben's outside... he's got men. We think Anthony and Cador are behind the terror — and Grace. I could whistle for help only I don't know if Ben's caught them yet. It might alert them.'

'Anthony's behind this? And you *expected* they'd come tonight?' Her mouth tightened. 'You should have told me.'

We began running up the sweeping staircase. 'We thought they'd try to enter through the tower. I thought we'd be safe. I had no idea about Grace — she must have warned them about the bolts.'

'*Grace?* Are you certain?'

'Yes, Grace. It's definitely her.'

We reached the first floor, Aunt Hetty just ahead of me. 'Don't open any windows. The wind will fan the flames. Hold still...' She ripped my gown to expose my knees. 'This will catch.' Tearing her own nightgown, she exposed her legs. 'If you get a spark, wrap yourself in your blanket. But don't let it come to that. How many men does Ben have?'

'He said he'd bring as many as he could. He's warned Lord Carew. He knows where the fire buckets are . . . he's hoping there might be enough water in the Abbot's Pond.'

'Possibly – though I doubt it.' She tied a thick band of nightdress round her nose and mouth. 'Let's see what we can do. I'll check the floor above. No heroics, Pandora . . .'

The four doors on the corridor were shut but could not be locked. Opening the first, I reeled back in horror. The horsehair mattresses had been pushed against the fireplace, beneath them, a pile of blankets and eiderdowns. Again, the end of the curtains were draped across the mattresses. Pungent smoke was rising, curling from the sides, flames breaking free, and I grabbed the top mattress, then the second, then the third. Most of the top bedding had not yet caught but the more I took off, the more the fire seemed to blaze. Two, three, four blankets saved. An eiderdown had caught, the flames beginning to take hold, and I pulled it free, smothering it with all my strength. Turning round, I saw another eiderdown flare and threw my wet blanket over it. Dragging it to the floor, I smothered it quickly. The fire seemed contained, just the fiercely burning logs inside the grate.

Aunt Hetty stood by the door. 'No fires upstairs. I'll take the next room.'

The fire in the third bedroom had started to take hold. Ripping away the mattresses I pulled off the blankets. The heat was fiercer, a crackle to the fire. I could feel my face burn. The smoke was thicker, the flames shooting sideways. Pulling away what I could, I thumped everything with my blanket. Again and again. Thumping, thrashing, until only black rims remained. The fire in the fireplace still roared, the heat making me stand back, yet it seemed confined. Pulling everything further away, I judged I could leave it. Glancing back, it looked safe: the drapes and wooden panelling were untouched.

Racing to the last room, I pulled away the mattresses, once again smothering the flames on the eiderdowns. Grace had planned this to the last detail. The fires had been lit earlier to air the rooms, the log baskets stacked in welcome. The bedding was folded on the beds so all she had to do was stoke the fire and pile everything up. The heat of the third fire seemed slightly less, but as I moved the eiderdowns the flames leapt. Clutching the wet blanket against my face, the stench of burning feathers filled the room. 'How dare you? How *dare* you?' Never had I been so angry. Thrashing the flames, I could have been thrashing Grace. The hem of one curtain had caught and I rolled it into a tight scroll. I could feel the heat through my leather gloves and had to let go. The hem was charred but no longer burning. My heart racing, I swung round.

Aunt Hetty wiped her forehead, leaving a smear of black from her leather glove. 'Where did you see her?'

'I didn't. I just know it's her. She didn't see me – nor hear me. I don't think she knows we're on to her.'

'If it is her, she's moving quickly. She has a clear plan. She must have gone down the back stairs.'

'What if she goes to the library? Aunt Hetty – your books!'

'She can't be that far ahead.' At the top of the servants' stairs, she pulled me back. Smoke was rising, the sound of crackling. 'She's used lantern oil – I can smell it.' On the

414

landing, flames were leaping from two huge wicker baskets, black smoke billowing, swirling up the walls. 'She's blocked the stairs – she's heading for the laundry – setting everything on fire behind her.' Aunt Hetty wrapped her blanket round her and held it across her face. 'Those baskets are on wheels. We need to get them off this wooden floor and on to a stone floor. There's one in the privy. There's water there. Keep your blanket tightly round you. Can you do it?'

Nodding, I pulled my blanket over my head and hurried behind her. Flames were building, the wicker baskets in danger of collapse. Pushed against the wooden panelling next to the banisters they were perfectly placed to set fire to the stairs. The heat was building, the smoke almost blinding, but the wheels ran free. Holding the wet blanket round my head, I grabbed the handle, pulling it at arm's length. The heat burned my glove but I would not let go. My only thought was to get them to the safety of the privy.

The privy was instantly cooling. A large room, the cubicles contained jugs, basins and china soap dishes. The walls were lined with marble and stone, the floor tiled in black and white. Two large copper tanks stood at each end and Aunt Hetty reached for a tap. Water splashed to the floor and she pulled down her face covering. 'Wet these towels. No . . . wait. push the baskets over – let the water flood them.' Turned upside down, the flames slowed but the baskets remained burning.

Opening another tap, more water splashed to the floor. 'Wet your blanket again. Soak your gloves.' Her hair fell across her eyes, her face flushed. 'We collect rain on the roof. There are two full tanks up there.' She opened a tap above a copper bath. 'We'll fill this bath — and come back for the water.' Placing her gloved hands under the stream of water, she looked at the baskets. 'These will burn themselves out. Nothing can catch. Drying room next — take a pitcher of water with you.'

Scooping up a pitcher of water, we raced down the back stairs. Grace had left nothing to chance. She had chosen the rooms with the most fabric, with wooden floors and panelling. Ahead of us the laundry door was locked. 'More smoke!' Ripping off her heavy gloves, Aunt Hetty reached for her keys. 'She's set fire to the sheets — that's why she insisted on hanging them up to air!'

Chapter Forty-two

The smell of pilchard oil mingled with the smoke. In the darkness the sheets formed an armada of ghostly sails and I pushed them aside, passing round them, diving under them. They had been splashed with oil and Aunt Hetty shouted, 'Don't get oil on your clothes.' My foot knocked against something hard and I stood back. A barrel lay on its side seeping oil on to the floor. It was yet to catch but the sheet to one side of it was burning. Two others were beginning to flare. Aunt Hetty was behind another. 'Stand back . . . better wet our gloves.'

Plunging my gloves in the water, the flames were easy to see in the darkness. The sheet above the oil was flaring. Ripping it down, I smothered it with my blanket. More sheets looked to be catching. 'There's no water in here – but there's water in the wash room.' Aunt Hetty's fingers trembled as she turned the lock.

Wooden cupboards lined the walls but at least the floor was stone. Pulling down the burning sheets, I had to be careful not to soak them in the oil. Heaped in a pile, I gathered them in a tight roll. The flames looked contained but the smoke still lingered, the smell of pilchard oil growing stronger. Turning, my heart seemed to stop. Another barrel was on its side. 'She's set a trail of oil. It leads down the corridor – towards the kitchen.'

Once again, the door was locked and Aunt Hetty reached for her key. 'She can't be that far ahead.' Turning, she glanced at the windows. 'What was that?' The alley was in darkness but there was just enough light to see the outline of the window frames. 'I heard something. A piercing sound.'

'A whistle? It's Ben. That's Ben's signal.' I ran to the door. It was unlocked and I reached for my own whistle, blowing it with all my breath. One . . . two . . . three piercing blows. My hand was shaking. I could smell smoke drifting on the wind, the sound of shouting. 'There's a fire outside – across the courtyard.'

Aunt Hetty was halfway down the corridor and called back. 'We have to stop her before she sets light to the library. There's sand in the sand buckets. We'll pile that up.' She stopped. Two of the buckets lay upturned, the other two empty. 'She's tipped them up. Check the kitchen, I'll check the library.'

Turning round, I saw two more sheets smouldering and about to flare. Rushing back, I rolled them in a ball and hauled them through the back door into the brick alley. Even if they burned, the mullion windows were made of stone and the sills would not catch. The smoke had long made my eyes water, my protective band making it hard to breathe. Loosening it, I chased after Aunt Hetty. The kitchen looked empty. No sign of fire. The clock struck three and her voice echoed from the library. 'She's not in here. I'll check upstairs.'

Fear filled me. 'Annie's fire's still hot. Grace kept banking it up.'

I heard Aunt Hetty tear down the corridor, but something made me turn. A log had been added to the fire, shadows dancing across the ceiling, and in the dim light I searched the room. Grace was not hiding under the table, nor in the pantry. The back door was still locked, yet something looked different. Earlier, the scullery door had been closed, but now it lay slightly ajar. Like a hunter, I froze. Yet I felt the prey. I could feel her eyes burning me from behind the door. If she overcame me, she could lock me in the scullery. 'I'm coming,' I shouted. 'I'll check the music rooms.'

Making my footsteps as loud as I could, I hurried towards the library, but doubled back to the kitchen, staying out of view. The scullery door creaked open and I held my breath. It opened wider, hurried footsteps crossing the kitchen. Grace bent over the fire, her back to me. In her hand was a poker, the tip bound in rags and soaked in oil. She was waiting for it to catch light and had not seen me, but she must have sensed me. Swinging round, she ran from the room.

I tore behind her. 'Grace . . . stop this. STOP THIS NOW.'

Racing back to the laundry room, I lost her to the darkness. The flames were out, just dim moonlight filtering through the window. No sound of footsteps, no sound of her breathing. She could be hiding behind any of the sheets or weaving between them to keep from sight. 'How could you do this, Grace?' I caught the faintest movement, the outline of her edging towards the wash room. She would lock the door and escape through the window.

'How?' Her voice was brittle. 'How? Well I can, and I have.' Her laugh sent shards of ice down my spine.

She was edging closer to the door. She seemed to reach for something. 'Grace, listen. There's no silver in that mine. You've been fooled. Tricked into helping them. Sir Anthony and Cador are using you. Did you tell them about the silver — or did they suggest it to you? What reward could possibly be sufficient? What reward to burn the house — to terrorise the pupils — to let Sophie believe the devil took her tongue?'

'You think Cador *likes* you? Well, that's the biggest joke of all. He doesn't. *Not one tiny bit.* He detests you as much as I do. How jealousy clouds your thoughts!' Her laughter was callous, a sneer in her voice. 'You think I haven't seen the envy burning your eyes? Eating away at you every time I play my music. I've watched you, and I've glorified in every scowl, every flash of jealousy — sending me out to teach *servants* while you primp and pose.'

'Grace, stop this. Please. Just stop and think of the consequences.'

'You *sicken* me. You and your jealousy — your ugly scowls and sullen looks. Your sense of entitlement. Your arrogance. You're nothing. *Nothing.* You're a whore's daughter. A fraudster's daughter. You think you're better than me. Do this. Do that. Take the lessons, sit in a freezing barn. Your false airs and graces! Your grandmother would have laughed at your attempts to be like her.'

'Grace, you've been *used.*'

'Ha! You're just like the others – all of them sneering at me, thinking me no competition. That I've no rank – that I haven't the breeding to catch the eye of the gentry. Well, you're wrong. All of them wrong.' Her laughter grew waspish. 'We laugh at you. Your talk of grand receptions; *Oh yes, the Governor's daughters were like sisters to me.* You're a laughing stock. Barging back here pretending to be a lady.'

I could hear her reaching for her keys. She seemed to be counting them, knowing exactly which one was which. Soon she would reach the key she needed. Her laughter grew cruel, even more vindictive. 'Well, here's something for you to chew on. It's me Cador loves. *Me* he wants to marry. Let that sink in. I'm to be the next Lady Ferris. How d'you like the sound of that?' The vitriol in her voice sliced like a knife. 'The school will burn, the land will be sold, and Cador and his father will have the silver. *Our* silver, Pandora. Not yours.'

'There's *no* silver. Grace, you're a fool. How do you possibly think you can get away with this?' I started edging closer.

'Oh, but I woke and heard a commotion... just like you did. I came running down and found this door wide open. Someone must have entered – and I've been fighting to put out the flames. See... I've even got burns to show for it! I shall be recognised for my bravery. For my selfless attempt to save the house – a heroine, trying to save the school she loves.' Her hatred rang across the room. 'What a shame I couldn't manage to put out the flames.'

'The bedrooms are saved. You've failed, Grace. Failed completely.'

'Not yet. There's still time. Only *you've* seen me. No one else.'

She sounded sharper, crueller, her voice chilling. 'Aunt Hetty won't believe I could possibly be involved. Oh, do you have a problem with me calling her Aunt Hetty?' Fleeting moonlight flooded the room and I saw she had a rope coiled in her hand. The darkness returned and I thought to hide behind the sheets. Or should I run to the back door and shout?

Suddenly, my legs were pulled from beneath me. My back crashed to the ground and pain seared through my body. The force of the fall left me winded. I tried to get up but she leapt astride me. I could not roll away, nor slip from beneath her. She was stronger than she looked, kneeling on my chest, making it hard to breathe. I felt my wrists gripped, forced painfully behind my back, and I kicked with all my strength.

'That's enough.' It was a man's voice. A scuffle followed, and I heard Grace scream. Benedict's voice rang with fury. 'Stay still. Biting won't help. These gloves are too thick.'

Moonlight returned and I saw the ghostly sheets part. Two men came striding across the room. Gripping Grace by the wrists, I heard the rattle of handcuffs. 'Stay still, you can't run. We all heard you.' Someone was lighting a lamp: a tinder glowed, a flame caught, and Ben helped me up. I could barely stand and he drew me to him, my whole body shaking. 'You're safe . . . safe now.' His arms closed around me, pulling me against him. 'Are you hurt? Did you knock your head?'

'No – it's just the shock. Have you got them?'

'Yes.' He kept his arms around me, holding me as if he would never let me go. 'So it was Grace! All this time it was Grace spreading the rumours and terrorising the pupils. She must have warned Sir Anthony and Cador not to use the ladder.

The barn nearly caught; Lord Carew turned up just in time.'
His hair was ruffled, his jacket smelling of smoke, and I leaned
into him, my legs almost crumpling beneath me. Now it was
over, I seemed to feel more fear. 'Sir Anthony and Cador are
handcuffed to the cart. They didn't go near the tower and that
threw us. Fortunately, we'd set someone to watch the barn.
They came down the farm track – a direction we hadn't fore-
seen. They knew exactly what they were doing and we only
just got to their fires in time. Sir Anthony set fire to the end of
the barn, and Cador was caught in the coach house. He almost
got away. There was quite a tussle. The barn's out of danger
but Lord Carew's men are dousing the thatch just to be sure.'
I nodded, resting my head against his shoulder and his voice
dropped. 'I heard your whistle and ran straight here. Thank
goodness you thought to blow one.'

The two men held Grace between them. Both looked official, both with florid faces beneath their tall hats. The first
pushed her forward. 'You've a long journey ahead, young lady.
All three of you. Lord Carew wants you taken to Bodmin.'

She turned round, glaring back at me, and I could barely
keep my voice civil. 'You had so much. Aunt Harriet gave you
everything and you've thrown it all away.'

The door closed, the first man holding up the lamp as he
strode down the alley. Darkness engulfed us, and Benedict's
arms tightened. Bending his head, he rested his forehead
against my hair. 'I'd better do something about this oil. We're
still in danger until it's cleared up. Are you all right?'

I nodded. 'The fires in the bedrooms might not be out –
not properly, at least. My hands are fine, but I have a burn on

my leg. I'll soak it upstairs. There's water in the privy – Aunt Hetty has two tanks of water on the roof.' Again, his arms tightened. I had never been held like this before, never felt so secure. I wanted him to hold me for ever, never let me go.

He drew away but reached for my hand, pressing my palm against his heart. I could feel it beating, pounding, his chest rising and falling. 'Leave everything to us. You've done enough. Bathe your burns and see to Annie and Miss Mitchell.'

'Did you open the leats? Did it work?'

It was as if he could not let go of my hand. Pressing my palm harder against his heart, he seemed to struggle to find the right words. 'The water will soon trickle back . . . not enough for tonight, though. We're lucky the thatch was damp – lucky with the recent rain.' His voice caught. 'You saved your school, Pandora. You, and you alone. Without your foresight . . . your quick thinking . . . your instincts . . . your aunt could have lost everything.' Again he seemed to struggle, yet kept my hand pressed against his chest. Darkness engulfed us and I wanted him to raise my chin, feel his lips seek mine.

His body tensed, and he let go of my hand. 'I'm glad I was able to help – and glad my family can help.' He sounded matter-of-fact, a stranger's politeness entering his tone, yet he seemed to struggle again. 'I . . . I . . . hope my family do you proud. I'm certain your school will prosper. It will rise like the phoenix and . . . and I wish you all the happiness in the world.' He turned, coughing to clear his throat. 'I'll see to this oil now.'

A lamp shone in the kitchen. There was the sound of bustling, Aunt Hetty issuing instructions. 'Thank you, Susan. Yes, pour all the men a drink. There's brandy in this cupboard

– and there's some ale. The men will need something to eat; do we have anything we can offer them?'

Ben stepped away. In the dim light I wanted to fling my arms around him. I wanted to tell him how much he meant to me. That I loved him. That I adored him. That Aunt Hetty was not cross with him, nor ever could be, but the door was thrown open and a tall man with a ruddy complexion entered. Dressed in a leather coat with several layers of dripping capes, he stood beaming at us from the back door. 'I must say, this all works up quite a thirst. That was a good night's work, Benedict. My goodness, what a toad. Never liked either of them, but this is well wide of the mark. They'll repent at leisure.'

Stepping forward, he removed his hat to a bald head and bushy white eyebrows. His white side whiskers almost met under his chin, his face flushed: for a man in his early seventies, his physique was strong and, but for his accent, I would have judged him a farmer. 'Ah, my dear. Let me guess – you must be Pandora? Splendid. Well, my dear – you've saved your school. Your *Barn School*, as Clarissa likes to call it.' I curtsied, blushing furiously at my exposed legs, yet in the half-light, he seemed not to see them. 'Time to go through and see what Harriet has for us – something to quench the thirst? Benedict, you'll join us in the kitchen?'

Bowing, Benedict took a step back. 'Thank you, Lord Carew, but no. I'll check the bedrooms and get some sand on this oil.'

I felt a large cloak wrapped round me, heard a voice I loved so well. 'Ah, I see you've met each other. Lord Carew, may I present my niece, Miss Pandora Woodville?'

He held out his arm and Aunt Hetty slipped hers on to his. Turning, he offered me his other arm and we stepped forward as if going into a formal dinner. 'Clarissa is quite right – how like your dear grandmother you are. Such rare beauty. And such courage. She says you have your aunt's qualities – a certain independence of mind!' His laughter was warm, throaty, filling the air with affection. 'Harriet was quite a rebel, you know – your poor grandmother used to despair.'

Aunt Hetty raised her eyebrows and Lord Carew pretended to be admonished. 'Yes, well, another time and I shall tell you more.' Pausing at the door his voice boomed across the kitchen. 'Is that brandy I see you pouring, Mrs Penrose? Splendid! And cake. My goodness, that does look good.'

Lanterns lit the courtyard. Through the open door, shouts rang across the yard. I could hear wagon wheels, the clatter of hooves. Her apron pristine, hardly a hair out of place, Susan swept in and out, carrying trays of cake and cups of wine. Finishing his brandy, Lord Carew replaced his hat and we followed him into the crisp dawn air. Two fine horses were being led across the cobbles. 'Splendid.' Lord Carew pointed to the horses. 'You found them? Excellent. Harness them to the back of the fire cart and we'll take them with us.'

By the barn, two carthorses stood harnessed to a wagon carrying a huge water tank and an iron pump. Men were reaching up, pulling down, pumping the water through a long pipe. They stopped. 'That's the last of the water, Lord Carew. The thatch won't catch now.'

'Splendid.' Lord Carew turned to us. 'A good night's work. You've done well. A terrible business – I'll see justice done.'

He bowed, striding towards the coach house, and I wrapped my cloak tighter. Shivering against the early chill, I caught a glimpse of Sir Anthony and Cador Ferris on George's cart. Dressed head to foot in black, they merged into the darkness, yet I saw their hands tightly secured behind their backs and the ropes binding them to the cart. Hunched next to them, Grace was glaring at us with no sign of remorse. Shuddering, I would have turned away but Aunt Hetty stood firmly by my side. 'Your grandmother used to say beauty on the outside turned ugly without beauty on the inside. She never thought that highly of Grace. She often said she'd like to see more grit in her.'

'I believe she was envious of the other girls – angry they saw her beauty and accomplishments as no threat. It riled her that they assumed she would not marry well. She was quite happy to terrorise them and close their school.'

'So she set her cap at Cador Ferris, not realising that it was he who was using her. She was sixteen. Naive, foolish, vulnerable. Clay in their hands.'

Susan joined us, standing on my other side. 'She's a wicked, wicked girl, burning our school like that, without a second thought. Well, there's nothing we can't get straight. Nothing we can't put right.' She stood glaring at Grace. 'Nothing we can't rectify. The maids arrive tomorrow and we'll get to work. Annie's still sleeping, bless her heart. This will hit her hard.'

I, too, stared at Grace's impassive face. 'She gives Annie strong brandy at night. That's why she sleeps so well.'

Lord Carew stepped on to the cart and George flicked the reins. The fire wagon was to lead, the cart to follow. Waving to the men on the wagon, we stood in silence as the cart passed. Aunt Hetty's eyes were piercing, yet not one of them looked round. Staring straight ahead, Sir Anthony remained sullen, Cador snarling rough words at Grace. He looked furious, his sudden vitriol making Grace sob.

Aunt Hetty's mouth tightened. 'Strong brandy would make anyone talk. Grace must have wheedled all Mother's secrets out of Annie. Mother told Annie everything and Grace told Anthony and Cador. They used her as their spy. That's how they found out Mr Compton was Father's heir – and about your father's fraud . . . and your mother's *indiscretion*.' The cart became lost from sight and Aunt Hetty took a deep breath. 'Anthony wanted my land. He might even have got his way, but for your timely arrival.' She slipped her hand through my arm, squeezing it tightly. 'I'll make a list of the damage for the insurance company tomorrow.'

'We're insured?' Tears sprang to my eyes. I could barely hope. 'I thought . . . maybe . . . ?'

Aunt Hetty's squeeze grew tighter. 'I doubled our premiums after I read that horrific manuscript. Mother always insisted on insurance.' She kissed my cheek. 'It's your school now, Pandora. Always keep it insured. Keep tanks on the roof and keep the Abbot's Pond full. I've been very neglectful. I've been too caught up with my studies.'

Susan handed me a clean white handkerchief. 'You just keep on with your studies, Miss Mitchell. We'll see to the school. We'll raise money for a fire cart. We'll arrange a fete. We'll stage plays and theatricals. We'll make St Feoca the best school in Cornwall.'

Shadow came silently to our side, sitting obediently without being asked. On the garden wall, Poppycock stretched out his long neck and gave his first tentative cry of the morning. Red streaks lit the dawn sky, the smell of smoke giving way to the scent of jasmine. Aunt Hetty straightened, her chin in the air. 'We have two whole days before Richard Compton comes marching down our drive.'

Chapter Forty-three

St Feoca Manor: School for Young Ladies
Friday 17th April 1801, 10:00 a.m.

Opening the shutters, bright sunlight streamed into the room: not the past grey rain, but a glorious spring day with only a handful of white clouds drifting across the sky. I had no idea I had slept so late. Susan must have been in as a tray of fruit and fresh bread lay on my dressing table. A glimpse of yellow caught my eye: a silk gown was hanging against the wardrobe door. Slightly too long, and more than slightly out of fashion, the lemon fabric shimmered in the sun and I ran to it, feeling the quality, holding the silk against my cheek. Pinned to it was a letter.

My dearest Pandora,

It is time for a new beginning. Mother and Abigail would want this, as do I. We shall end our outward mourning and keep our inward mourning to ourselves. Mother and Abby will always remain lodged deep within our hearts. They will never leave our thoughts. They will never be absent from our lives — they are as much a part of us as we are a part of them. But we must look to the future. Your new school must be a place of happiness — they would want that. Their laughter is everywhere, echoing across the hall, ringing around the courtyard. Abby's footsteps still race down the stairs, Mother giggling as Father chases her and tries to kiss her. They are in the fabric of every room, every page in every book, always with us, and will never leave us. We will honour their memory, not by mourning, but by joining them with our laughter, our joy, our unswerving dedication in the pursuit of the education of women.

I don't mind how you alter this gown. Do whatever you like as I'm sure you will make very fine adjustments. Make one of your headbands to match, and then, perhaps, you might make one for me?

My love for you knows no bounds.

I remain, your fondest aunt,
Hetty

Fighting my tears, I pulled my stocking over the lint bandage on my calf. My burn had barely blistered. Nor were my hands sore, but my shoulders and back ached. Hardly taking my eyes off the beautiful lemon gown, I dressed in my black one, tidying my hair as best I could. The water I had splashed on it the night before had done its damage: a mass of frizzy curls framed my face. Reaching for my band, I placed it over my forehead, deciding I would paint Aunt Hetty the most beautiful headband anyone had ever seen.

Halfway down the stairs, Susan looked up from the polished floor. Clutched in her arms was a basket of cloths and a jar of beeswax. 'Good day, Miss Woodville. Miss Mitchell is in the tower – she'd like to see you.' Behind her, six maids dipped a curtsy. Holding mops and buckets, they wore crisp white mobcaps and starched white aprons. Susan looked equally immaculate. 'We've done the music rooms and the drying room. Just the bedrooms to do.'

'Can we use them, do you think?'

Her blonde hair shook under her housekeeper's bonnet. 'Not those bedrooms – but we've plenty others we can use. Word is, they'll be here tomorrow afternoon.' She turned to her troop behind her. 'I'll introduce everyone later, if I may? We'll carry on now. Oh good, here are the girls.'

Gwen and Sophie ran from the kitchen, closely followed by Mollie and Kate. Beaming up at me, they stopped to curtsy. 'Good day, Miss Woodville.' They followed the others to the music rooms and the hall fell silent. I could smell onions frying. Someone was singing.

Opening the front door, two men in brown tweed were weeding the drive. Raising their hats, they bowed in greeting. 'A fine mornin', Miss Woodville.'

Wondering if I should curtsy back, I smiled instead. 'A very fine morning. Oh, forgive me, I didn't recognise you – you're the road builders – you helped last night. I'm sorry, I don't know your names.'

'Frederick Shire and John Barny. Two of your new grounds-men.' The older of the two men held his hat against his chest. 'Fact is, we thought we'd stay. Fact is, four of us are staying. We've plenty to do here and . . .' He had a wrinkled, weather-beaten face, his eyes kind, smiling a shy, respectful smile. 'A place like this is hard to leave.'

432

A lump caught in my throat. After so much evil, such fortune made it hard not to cry. I had to look away. Everything I dreamed of was coming true. We were a school again – a proper school. Every dream coming true, well, not quite every dream. I cleared my throat. 'Is Mr Aubyn still here?'

They shook their heads. 'No, Miss Woodville. He left an hour ago.' Frederick Shire gripped his hat. 'If I may say, what ye did in those bedrooms was nothing short of heroic. Fact is, we saw what ye'd done. Fact is, ye put out those flames like, well, like we'd never have thought possible.' He shuffled his foot. 'Mr Aubyn's right. Ye saved this school. No doubt about it.'

'Thank you, Mr Shire. And thank you, both . . . for wanting to make St Feoca your home.'

Running up the spiral stairs, the study door was open, Aunt Hetty sitting at the desk. She was not dressed in black but in a beautiful amber gown with a matching jacket. Her jacket was trimmed in cream, no lace, but with a row of cream buttons and a soft ruff at her throat. Round her neck, her gold locket glinted in the sun and I drew back, immediately fearful. She was clutching a handkerchief against her face.

Grandfather's Bible lay open in front of her, a mass of papers spread to one side. Rereading a piece of paper, a fresh bout of tears made her dab her eyes and I stood frozen to the spot, almost too scared to go in. 'They aren't coming, are they? They won't come. We've lost the school.'

'No, my dear, it's the best possible news.' She reached for a letter. 'I've just received this from the vicar who baptised you. Come and read it.' She held it out and I realised her tears

433

were tears of happiness. 'Your mother didn't lie about your birth. She told us the truth. Look...' Her hand trembled as she passed me the letter.

Dear Miss Mitchell,

I can confirm that your niece, Miss Pandora Elizabeth Woodville, was born in my parish on January 23rd 1780 and christened in my church, St John's, on January 30th. Indeed, I remember your sister, Abigail Woodville, very well. She was a charming addition to our parish and frequently helped my wife with her parish duties. I particularly remember her because I tried to persuade her not to call her daughter Pandora. But she insisted, and so I relented. I am very sorry to hear of her death and I would like to extend my sincere condolences to you and your niece.

I remain your servant,

Edward Ramsbury,
Rector of St John's Church, Bristol

She blew her nose. 'Goodness, this won't do at all.' Opening the Bible, she turned to the page of dates and dipped her quill into the ink. 'I should have known there had been no *indiscretion* – no urgency, except her desire to marry. She simply forced Father's hand.' Her writing was swift, firm, undoing the wrong. There was hardly any space, only just enough room for the date. Turning the Bible for me to see, she straightened. 'Of course, this changes everything. We can now be very vocal and refute that scurrilous article.' Looking down, she rested the tips of her fingers against her lips and I knew not to speak. Her

434

silences were what I loved most about her: her deep concentration, her clear lines of thought something I must emulate. Father had never thought before he spoke, never considered things deeply.

The sun beat in at the windows, the sky a brilliant blue. The tops of the trees in Mama's wood were bursting into life, the sea sparkling, the clear outline of Pendennis Castle standing sentry over Falmouth. I knew what Aunt Hetty was thinking, and I knew she was right. 'This mustn't change anything, Aunt Hetty – Meredith Trelawney must be our new headmistress. She's perfect for our school and I want her to be in charge.' She seemed relieved, a slight shrug of her shoulders. 'And I love my new gown. Thank you . . .'

Her amber hat with its matching cream trim brought out the hazel in her eyes: without any frills or lace, she looked elegant yet demanding of respect. Something else I would have to emulate. 'There are other gowns but I thought the lemon would suit you.' A sudden frown, and her voice grew stern. 'I should have been sharper – Anthony may have known about the constitution but not who was heir to the estate. Richard Compton isn't named in the constitution. No one's named. Apart from me, Annie is the only other person who could possibly know. Unless they have Father's will.'

'Anthony and Cador knew the school had to close, and when they thought it was certain they wrote to Richard Compton.'

'They must have investigated Richard Compton's businesses and believed he'd sell the estate.' She reached for my hand. 'But you turned up and gave us all hope.' Gathering up the loose pages, she slipped them carefully back into Grandfather's

Bible. 'Anthony or Cador must have searched this study, but how did you suspect them? That's what I want to know.'

'Because... Aunt Hetty — there's something I must show you.' Pulling the file from the shelf, I went through every detail: the stolen water, the falsely labelled silver, the treasure hunt clue I had found in *Candide*. She sat resting her fingers against her lips, silent, calm, a smile where I thought there would be a frown.

Leaning forward, her eyes glistened. '*Omnia vincit amor.* Father only ever wanted us to marry for love. Reaching for her handkerchief, she dabbed her eyes. 'I need to be alone. Spend the rest of the day sewing your dress. Susan will sort everything out.' She blew her nose. 'Abby won that treasure hunt. I thought the answer was water — Father knew the value of water — but Abby was right. The answer was time — *time well spent.*' She dabbed her eyes. 'Go now. Enjoy your sewing.'

With bright sunlight pouring into my bedroom, I settled myself by the window and began cutting the seams. It was as if Mama was leaning over my shoulder. *Take the fullness out first — discard the worn parts — see if any fabric can be turned.* Running footsteps sounded down the corridor and stopped outside my open door. All four girls ran to my side. Smiling, they fingered the yellow silk. 'We've put flowers in all their rooms.'

'What a kind thought, Gwen.'

Racing out, Sophie stopped at the door. 'You're going to look so lovely, Miss Woodville.' She was gone, and I settled back to my scissors. I would shorten the bodice and raise the waist.

The buttons would remain as they were, so, too, the sleeves. The scoop neck was very pretty and could be left untouched, so, too, the hem. All very similar to the other three gowns I had altered. Footsteps again, but this time they did not stop – the maids must be going to their attic rooms above. The clock chimed two and the new seams were pinned.

Susan's voice echoed down the corridor. 'Yes, that piece of chalk. Thank you. Now, where's my list?' Silence followed, just the ticking of the clock, then running footsteps again, the girls tumbling back into the room.

'Miss Woodville, you have to come.' I was grabbed by both hands, Sophie and Kate pulling me down the corridor, their newly washed hair bouncing as they swung round. Flushed with excitement, Gwen pointed to the recently written slate. 'Look – *Gwendoline* Devoran, Sophie Devoran, Mollie Carter, Katherine Penrose. Come and see.'

Sun streamed on to the iron bedsteads, lighting up a brightly coloured rug. They had already chosen their beds and ran to claim them, their legs swinging freely. Sophie could not stop beaming. 'We've got a whole bed to ourselves.' Different shades of damask covered the beds, a satin eiderdown folded at the base. By each bed, a chair stood next to a small chest of drawers.

Mollie pointed to a painted door. 'We've got a *hanging* wardrobe as well. And there's a mirror behind you.'

Unable to sit still, they slid off the beds and gripped my hands again. 'They have their own room, too. Come and see.' Gwen led us down the corridor and stood by another beautifully written slate. 'Leticia Aubyn, Elizabeth Aubyn,

Mary Aubyn and Charlotte Aubyn.' The room was identical: the same damask counterpanes, the same satin eiderdowns. Gwen's eyes were sparkling. 'The daffodils and forsythia came from the garden – the catkins from the hedge.'

Kate smoothed an eiderdown and straightened a chair. 'The Mrs Aubyns and the older Miss Aubyns are to sleep in the top rooms of the new wing until the parlour rooms are ready. Miss Trelawney's going to sleep where Miss Annie was.'

Twisting her fingers, Sophie beamed up at me. 'Miss Annie's going back downstairs. She said she's the cook here and the cook sleeps by the kitchen. She won't change her mind. She says she's addenment.'

'Adamant.' I smiled. 'Well, it looks like you've got everything organised.'

Returning to my room, I reached for my needle and re-checked the new seams. My stomach fluttered, a rush of expectation. My nerves were getting the better of me; not the sewing, that was the easy part, but the thought of meeting Benedict's family. Since he held me like that, my body could not stop tingling, imagining him reaching down to kiss me. A fresh flush of heat seared through me.

The sound of running footsteps, the girls tumbling in again. 'Mrs Lilly's sent our dresses! We've got *two* each. And *underclothes*.' Gwen had tears in her eyes. 'And stockings, and handkerchiefs . . . and new shoes.'

'And nightdresses. Honest, you've never seen anything so beautiful.'

This time, I secured my needle. My hands were grabbed and they raced me down the corridor. Their new clothes lay on their beds: two blue woollen frocks, three pairs of white woollen stockings, a selection of undergarments and a flannel nightdress. Mollie held her nightdress against her cheek. 'They're from Mrs Lilly. We're her charity girls.'

'Come, girls.' I drew them to me, my arms stretching round them, squeezing us together. I had never felt more certain in my life. 'You're *not* Mrs Lilly's girls. And you're *not* charity girls. You're St Feoca girls, and I'm very proud of you. Very, *very* proud of you. Promise me, you'll always be who you seem to be.'

Gwen's cheeks dimpled. 'You mean like *Esse Quam Videri*, only in English!'

'Yes, I suppose I do.' I joined in their laughter, the five of us squeezing together, almost toppling on to the floor. Their hair smelled of lavender, their faces flushed. We straightened and the girls ran from the room. At the door Sophie swung round.

'No wonder Mr Aubyn loves you so much.'

Chapter Forty-four

Another glorious spring day; everyone scurrying around, with last-minute preparations in full swing. A knock on the front door made Aunt Hetty swing round. She walked sedately to open it. 'Ah, good day, Mr Polcarrow. You received my letter?'

Francis Polcarrow bowed. 'Indeed I did.' He was smartly dressed in a blue jacket, his silk cravat pinned with an enamel pin. 'Good day, Miss Woodville. How . . . well you . . . look.' He seemed suddenly embarrassed, as if he might have said something wrong. 'Considering your ordeal, I mean . . . but that is a very fetching gown.'

'Thank you.' I had to resist the temptation to swirl round. It was the most beautiful dress I had ever worn. 'Is there any sign of the Aubyns? We're expecting them any minute.'

'George is waiting for them by the ferry with his cart.'

Ushering him to the library, Aunt Hetty sat at the head of the table. 'Did you see Miss Elliot? I hear they're to be taken

440

to Bodmin.' She showed no sign of anger, just a matter-of-fact tone.

His mouth tightened. 'I did. And they left this morning. I told Miss Elliot what you asked me to tell her – that you'll send her clothes and pay for her representation. She said very little – but nodded when I told her your instructions were for my stepfather to take her case.' He cleared his throat. 'I did add that her only hope for leniency rested on her turning King's evidence against Sir Anthony and Cador Ferris. I said she must tell the truth about the dolls and the manuscript.' He looked up. 'I also told her Tregenna Hall is to be searched. The letter to the *Gazette* was written in the same brown ink as was used in the manuscript which, if I'm not wholly mistaken, they'll find hidden in Sir Anthony's study.'

Aunt Hetty took a deep breath. 'And the mandrake?'

'*If* we can believe Miss Elliot the mandrake came as a shock. She admits she left *all three* baskets on their instruction but claims she had no idea there was mandrake in it. Which may well be the case. I pointed out that everyone in the house, including her, would be the target of their murderous intent and that seemed to strike home.' Opening his leather case he drew out a list. 'She was smitten with Cador Ferris and believed he was in love with her. Though I believe he has since been very cruel to her. She believed they were to be shortly married.'

Laughter rang from the kitchen, someone was singing; a flurry of footsteps followed by the sound of barking. Francis Polcarrow frowned. 'Sir Anthony may have told her he was only after the silver in the wood but that's clearly not the case.

I doubt he even thinks there's silver there. I have received confirmation that Sir Anthony Ferris owns Roseland Holdings and, as such, he's declared an interest in buying not only your land along the shore, but your mill and all your land east of the river. What's more, it was Roseland Holdings who enquired about the quayside for a new ferry service.'

'They dangled the prospect of a title and great wealth over Grace and her naivety proved fertile ground. How is Miss Olwyn Ferris?' Aunt Hetty might have been able to remain calm but I could hardly hide my fury.

'Taking it badly, Miss Mitchell, as you would expect. Her aunt has been sent for and I believe will be staying with her.'

Voices drifted from the courtyard. Mrs Devoran and Mrs Carter were saying goodbye to their daughters. Glancing up, Aunt Hetty smiled. 'Forgive me, Mr Polcarrow — Pandora, do you think you should have a quick word with them?'

The kitchen rang with activity: Annie was stirring a large pot of stew, one of the maids slicing a cabbage. One was piling up plates, another laying out crisp white napkins. Outside, the girls were showing off their beautiful new dresses and ran to greet me. Holding my hands, they swirled me round. 'Miss Woodville! How beautiful you look.'

'And how beautiful you all look.' By the garden gate, Mrs Devoran and Mrs Carter stood fighting their tears.

Mrs Carter wiped her eye. 'Be a good girl now, Mollie.'

I had not met Mrs Devoran before. Dark-haired like her sister, the family resemblance was striking. She stood biting her lip. 'Mind your manners. Do us proud. We'll see you after church on Sunday.'

They turned to go and I called after them. 'Mrs Devoran, would it be possible for you to bring fresh milk every day – maybe at seven each morning? Gwen and Sophie can help you put it in the dairy. And Mrs Carter, if you can, could you bring us fresh flour every morning? Also at seven, so that Mollie can help you carry it to the larder?'

Smiles flooded their faces. I would have liked to have stayed and talked but hurried back. The library door was open, Aunt Hetty wiping her eyes. Yet Francis Polcarrow was smiling. Standing as I entered, he pulled out my chair.

Aunt Hetty's voice was stern. 'Nothing has changed, Mr Polcarrow. The constitution still holds.'

'But surely?' He stopped, and I caught a glint of warning in Aunt Hetty's eyes. Poor man, he hardly deserved it.

'Before Benedict Aubyn left he insisted he would pay the full fees for all six of his school-age sisters. He's adamant they are not to take an endowment place from another girl.'

Francis shrugged his broad shoulders. '*Six* school fees? That's quite some sum!'

Aunt Hetty returned his shrug. 'His mother and eldest sisters are to be teachers. The third eldest is to help reorganise our library and his sister-in-law and her two daughters are to live in the parlour boarding rooms. Benedict Aubyn also insists on paying for their board and lodging. He won't hear otherwise.'

'He's clearly a very proud man.'

'Indeed, I expected no less and, as such, I've written to Mrs Angelica Trevelyan to send us all four of her endowment girls. We shall soon have fourteen girls in our school, and three teachers, so the constitution's requirements are fulfilled. And it can continue *as it is*.'

Francis Polcarrow reached for his papers. 'On the closure of the school, your father's heirs will inherit the estate.' I hardly heard them. Heat seared my cheeks, the thought of Benedict's family increasingly petrifying. Francis Polcarrow was not looking at me but mirroring Aunt Hetty's stern expression. 'I believe . . . on careful consideration . . . that there may well be some legal means by way of selling some of your land, Miss Mitchell. A distinct possibility to release certain capital.' He leaned closer. 'Any lease should be for twenty-five years, no longer, and I suggest the rent should be increased every five years. Your land's going to double in value. The mineral rights alone make it worth a fortune.'

A shout of instructions, sudden footsteps hurrying down the corridor. A maid knocked on the door and Aunt Hetty turned. 'Yes, Ruth?'

She was middle-aged, grey-haired, and I recognised her as the lady in the ferry who had sold my shells to the other passengers. 'If you please, Miss Mitchell, they're coming up the drive. Mrs Penrose's gettin' everyone together.' She glanced at me and smiled. Everyone was coming back: everyone coming home. Giddy with nerves, I tried to appear calm.

Aunt Hetty reached across the table and squeezed my hand. 'Are you ready to meet the new members of your school?' I nodded, though it was all I could do to breathe. 'Good. Let's go and greet them.' As we stood, she reached for the gold locket hanging round my neck. Opening it, she smiled at my burning cheeks. 'It's a good likeness — a very good likeness. You've captured him perfectly.'

Susan positioned everyone in a long line by the front door. Halfway up the drive, two little girls were sitting next to George on the cart. Trunks were piled high behind them, Meredith Trelawny striding ahead with two ladies, and I recognised the tallest as the woman in the inn who had pleaded with Ben. No one was speaking, each gripping their bags and staring ahead: walking up the drive with the same mixture of excitement and hope as I had done.

Ben was by his mother's side, his sisters spilling around them. Ranging in height, they had the same purposeful stride, each with ribbons in their bonnets, each wearing a warm cape and sturdy footwear. Mrs Aubyn looked as refined as I expected. The closer she drew, the more my heart thumped. Grey hair framed her oval face. She looked strong, competent, her head held high. She smiled, and instant warmth surged through me. She had Benedict's blue eyes, the same straight nose.

They reached the drive and stood in a circle. Benedict looked at me, our eyes met, and I tried to smile. He bowed in greeting, bending to tell the two little girls to curtsy, and I thought my heart would break. The girls were clutching his hands, looking up at him with such love. Picking up the youngest, he held her in his arms. Aunt Hetty stepped forward. 'Welcome . . . welcome to St Feoca School. I hope you will all be very happy here.'

Gwen and Mollie held bunches of flowers tied in yellow ribbons. Curtsying, they presented them to Mrs Aubyn and Miss Meredith Trelawny. 'Welcome to St Feoca.'

Meredith took the flowers and smiled. 'Thank you, they're lovely. What are your names?'

They glanced at me, filled with pride. Gwen stood tall, her voice respectful. 'I'm Gwen from the farm.'

Mollie stood equally straight-backed. 'And I'm Mollie from the mill.'

Next, Sophie and Kate stepped forward, presenting Mrs Martha Aubyn and the eldest Miss Aubyn with more beautiful flowers. 'I'm Kate from the gatehouse.'

'And I'm Sophie from the farm.' They looked round with equal pride and my heart swelled. Stepping forward like that, telling everyone who they were and where they were from. Now it was my turn to speak, my turn to welcome everyone, yet my tongue felt tied. Grandmother's school had been saved – Aunt Hetty's school – and now *my* school. The sudden enormity of it all seemed to strike me: Mama's dream was coming true; I was going to be a teacher.

I must have managed a curtsy, probably even a smile. 'Thank you so much for coming.' It was as if Mama was by my side, Mama welcoming everyone to their new home. 'Thank you for believing in our school. Together, we will make this the best school in Cornwall. I'm so happy you're here.'

What was wrong with me? If I had been alone, I would have crossed my fingers behind my back. Benedict's solemnity tore my heart. Carrying the youngest, he stood back, holding the eldest's hand while Meredith introduced his mother and sisters to me. I must have been smiling as they were certainly smiling back; each was elegant and refined, their deportment exemplary. Each had Benedict's intelligent eyes, each greeting me with growing excitement.

Aunt Hetty introduced Susan, who curtsied deeply. Without an apron, her blue dress with its double row of brass buttons gave her instant authority. Turning, she led Meredith and the two Mrs Aubyns down the line of maids and groundsmen. Smiling, they repeated everyone's name. *Always use people's names — servants as well as fine lords. Remember that, my love.* A shiver ran down my spine. It was as if Mama approved. As if Mama was smiling back at them.

The introductions complete, Susan issued instructions where each trunk was to be taken. Aunt Hetty stood back, ushering Meredith and the Mrs Aubyns through the door, and any fear we had that they would not like the school was instantly dispelled. They could not have looked happier. 'What a magnificent hall. What a lovely fireplace. Look at those stairs – are those angels peeping between the banisters?'

'Yes. I think that's why my parents bought the school.' Aunt Hetty cleared her throat. 'You must want to freshen up – Susan will show you to your rooms and I'll leave you to settle in. We can gather here in – shall we say – an hour?'

I looked round. Benedict was walking towards me, his eyes burning mine. 'Miss Woodville.' He bowed. 'Your dress suits the day perfectly – a glorious bright colour. Perfect for your school's fresh start.' He caught the swing of my earrings and looked down.

'These pearls were my grandmother's,' I whispered. 'She's wearing them in her portrait.'

He glanced up at the painting. 'So they are. And how very lovely they look on you both.'

Chapter Forty-five

The fire was roaring, the long table laid with china teacups and plates. 'There's more cake and more tarts.' Standing by the silver urn, Susan surveyed the table. 'That'll do nicely.' She winked at the girls who were beginning to look nervous and I went to stand by them. Aunt Hetty was sitting at one end of the table, Francis Polcarrow next to her. Spread in front of them were several papers. They were deep in conversation but rose when the others entered.

The sea of new faces swam before me. Two of the elder sisters had Benedict's dark curls, two had auburn tints. All had blue eyes, the youngest six wearing brightly coloured dresses. The oldest three were in grey, the two Mrs Aubyns in black. Voices were rising, excited chatter beginning to fill the room. Holding Sophie and Kate's hands, I ushered Gwen and Mollie over to the youngest Aubyn girls. 'Let me guess, you must be Leticia . . . Elizabeth . . . Mary and Charlotte.' Addressing them in order of height, I hoped I was right. They seemed delighted and I left them all smiling.

Benedict's middle sisters were standing next to the mineral cabinet, clearly absorbed with what they saw. The eldest curtsied. 'I'm Leah, and this is Deborah and Rebecca.' They looked bright and lively, returning to their examination of the minerals. 'Benedict told us about Reverend Mitchell's collection. He has a fine collection of his own – that's what's in the heaviest trunk! Do you like minerals, Miss Woodville?'

'I'm interested in them, but I know very little about them.'

They had a warmth about them, a sense of energy; all with broad foreheads and highly intelligent eyes. All of them seemed educated. All, no doubt, highly accomplished. They would sing and play the piano. They would recite poems I had never heard of and sing operas I did not know existed. Leah smiled. 'Benedict's told us how well travelled you are – how well you know the world. How good you are at Greek and Latin. There's nothing I like better than a page of Latin.'

The other two seemed unable to contain themselves. Smiling broadly, they exploded into giggles. 'No you don't. Take no notice of her, Miss Woodville. She hates Latin and Greek. She likes mathematics and astronomy. She spends all night gazing up at the stars. Do you like astronomy, Miss Woodville?'

Laughing, I smiled back. 'I've never studied it, but I'll join you if you'll teach me.' I swung round. Benedict had entered the room, his little nieces clutching his hands and looking round.

'They love him so much,' the younger of the three whispered. They, too, looked at their brother in adoration. 'We don't like his hair short like that. He doesn't look like Benedict at all. He hates his new position with the Turnpike Trust. It

450

may be making him money, but it's quite horrible to see him so torn. Mother's very cross.'

Panic struck me. 'Your mother's cross you've come?'

'Oh no. She's over the moon about coming here. We all are. We can't think of anywhere we'd rather be. It's just she thinks Benedict should be in Bristol, that his work's far too important to just abandon it like he has. But he says he won't go back. He says he needs to stay in his new post.'

I had not heard the carriage, nor the knock, but saw Ruth rush to open the door. Lady Clarissa swept in carrying a large basket of fruit: Angelica Trevelyan followed, behind her Lord Carew and Henry Trevelyan, who I remembered from the Turnpike meeting. Aunt Hetty rushed to greet them, immediately introducing them to Meredith and Mrs Aubyn.

Lady Clarissa's voice rang across the hall. 'A welcome basket of fruit for you all. How was your journey? Such a glorious day to travel.'

The noise level was rising, laughter echoing round the rafters, and I knew I must step forward, not show the trepidation I was feeling. Among such happiness, I had to stop my panic. Mama's dream was coming true, everything she had longed for, just as she would want it. *Mama's* dream, not *my* dream.

Benedict clearly knew Henry Trevelyan well. Smiling, he bent to introduce his little nieces, everyone braving their grief and embracing their new beginning. Everyone except me. Grandfather was surveying the scene from his heavy frame, so, too, Grandmother with her intelligent eyes and gentle smile. I stared back at her, my panic rising. She did not seem to be watching the others but seemed to be looking at me. Just me. Her eyes purposeful, piercing my heart as if in understanding.

Another knock on the door and Reverend Penhaligan entered with his wife, a kind-looking lady, not unlike Mrs Aubyn. 'My goodness me.' Reverend Penhaligan adjusted his glasses. 'I must say, this is all very welcome.'

Angelica spun round, her cream gown shimmering in the light. 'Fourteen pupils once the other four arrive.' I would paint her just like that: her eyes shining, the pearls on her headband glittering. She looked thrilled to meet the Mrs Aubyns. Another knock on the door and Ruth rushed to open it. This time it was Mrs Lilly and a rather stern-looking man dressed in black. Angelica Trevelyan turned and smiled. 'Father! How lovely.' Slipping her arm through her father's, she smiled at Mrs Lilly. 'Now we're complete – just the four new girls to bring tomorrow.'

The youngest girls were getting on splendidly, or were, until I heard Gwen's raised voice. 'No, that's just not possible!' She looked furious and I knew I must join them.

'It *is*, I promise you.' Benedict's sister Mary was standing her ground. 'Mother wants him to go back to Bristol. She's adamant he must. She says his heart is there, but he won't hear of it. He says his heart is *here*. In Cornwall.'

'He can't go!' Mollie and Kate were both frowning, Sophie on the point of tears.

All four sisters had embroidered bags hanging from their waists: each reached inside and drew out one of the painted shells Benedict had told me he had sold in Truro. 'Don't worry. He won't go – he says he's going to stay in his horrible post.

We think it's because he's fallen *in love* – and we think it must be the lady who painted these.' They held up my shells. 'He said they were painted by a lady with great courage. Someone we should aim to be like. And that sounds like *lovers'* talk.'

I stared back into my grandmother's eyes. All these years planning to come home, all the heartache, all the longing. All the sleepless nights, the loneliness, my very own Odyssey stretching for what seemed an eternity. Everything I loved was in this room, everything just as I knew it would be. I held my grandmother's gaze, feeling her strength. It was not the buildings I craved, not the bricks, not the stone staircases, the carved mullion windows. Not the angels peeping through the banisters, not the beams, the rafters, not even my beautiful garden. It was family I craved. My sense of who I was, and where I came from. It was love I sought.

Love, staring straight at me, his smile broadening.

Aunt Hetty stood at the head of the table and beckoned everyone to join her. Meredith sat on one side, Lady Clarissa on the other. Mrs Aubyn sat down next, the eldest Miss Aubyn leaving a space for me. Francis Polcarrow pulled out young Mrs Aubyn's chair and took his place opposite Angelica Trevelyan. Reverend Penhaligan flicked out his coat-tails, smiling as he sat. Opening his leather case, he drew out his minute book, his bottle of ink and his quill. 'Excellent. I believe we're ready.'

They turned, one by one, smiling at me from across the room. An empty space awaited me, a look of happy expectation in all their faces, and I slipped my hands on to Sophie and Kate's shoulders. 'Please allocate who's to teach what without me.'

'Without you?' Benedict, Henry Trevelyan, Lord Carew and Mr Lilly were deep in conversation. Stopping mid-sentence, each turned quickly round. Mrs Penhaligan and Benedict's older sisters also swung round. 'But surely you'll want to teach Latin and Greek? There's no obstacle to you teaching now – Miss Mitchell has made that very clear.'

Lady Clarissa was not the only one to sound shocked. Everyone was clearly stunned. Only Aunt Hetty seemed unperturbed, a slight smile as she tapped her fingers against her lips.

'I don't think I'll be any good at teaching . . . so I've decided it's best not to. I'm going to go to Bristol instead. To perfect how to paint miniature portraits. *In Bristol.*'

'Paint miniature portraits? My dear, I think that very foolhardy!'

'I'll never know if I don't try, Lady Clarissa. My home is here – my beloved home – and I shall always come home. I love every inch of every room, every beam, every crooked door, every archway. I love the shadows that cross the lawns, every petal on every flower in my garden. I love Aunt Hetty with a passion, and Annie and Susan. And the girls. I love my grandparents being in every turn of every stair. I love the way the house creaks, every loose floorboard. There's nowhere I love more. But I'm going to do what I've always wanted to do. What I've always dreamed of doing. And that is to paint miniature portraits.' I looked deep into the eyes of the man I loved. 'In *Bristol.*'

Benedict's voice faltered. 'But Miss Woodville, there's no money to be had painting miniature portraits *in Bristol*. No money, no security, and little prospect of success.'

He was staring so intently, his eyes brimming with hope.

With love. With incredulity. I was speaking freely for the first time in my life. It was me speaking. Me. Not hiding behind Mama's dreams, not shielding behind my aegis. Not crossing my fingers. 'I believe you're wrong, Mr Aubyn. I believe there's every prospect of not only happiness but enormous success, *painting miniature portraits in Bristol.*'

'But *painting miniatures* does not provide for when . . . *smaller* miniatures . . . come along. It barely provides wood for the grate, or food for the table. It can only be considered reckless and rash. There is no security to be had. None whatsoever.' His words seemed forced from him.

'I will not be put off, Mr Aubyn. My heart is set on painting miniatures *in Bristol.*'

He cleared his throat. 'Painting miniature portraits is all-consuming. When you paint miniature portraits you forget to eat – you forget to sleep. Painting miniatures requires endless nights of . . . *painting*. And more often than not the painting doesn't come to anything. The . . . painting . . . dries too early, or dissolves. Or evaporates.'

'Then, I'll paint them again with or without logs on the fire. If my paintings dry too quickly, I'll try again the next day. And the next day. Until what I've set out to do is done. I'll not be put off, Mr Aubyn. I intend to become very proficient in painting miniatures. In *Bristol*. With or without food on the table.'

Beside me, Elizabeth whispered, 'But he's never painted a miniature portrait in his life! He's no idea about painting!'

Gwen, Mollie, Kate and Sophie shook their heads. 'He's not talking about *actual* painting. He's telling Miss Woodville he can't afford a wife. *In Bristol.*'

'Why would he do that?'

'Because it's *her* he loves,' they whispered in unison.

Benedict ran his hand through his hair. 'I'm sorry – if you could just excuse us for a moment?' Striding across the hall, he reached for my hand, pulling me behind him as he rushed me to the music room. Safe inside, he held my hands against his heart. 'Pandora, what are you saying?'

'I'm saying I love you, Ben. That I've loved you for a very long time, only I thought you loved Grace. And as that isn't the case, I think we should go to Bristol.'

'But . . . but I thought you didn't agree with love? That you mistrusted men.'

I must have been smiling, certainly I was the happiest I had ever felt. 'That was before I fell so deeply in love with you. I believe you're right: true love does endure and strengthen. It builds trust. It is constant. It allows each to feel fulfilled – two halves, making a whole. Each with their strengths and weaknesses, yet always enriched by the other.' Love shone from his eyes and a wave of heat scorched my chest. 'Aunt Hetty knows and she approves.'

'She approves?'

'Yes. And Aunt Hetty's *never* wrong. It's because you turned round on the drive . . . and because dogs trust you. She never liked Father, but she's very fond of you. She doesn't know about us going to Bristol yet but Ben, you *have* to finish your work. You have to find a way to separate and solidify the arsenic. Everyone's agreed on that.'

'But . . . but . . .' He ran his hand through his hair. 'Are you *proposing* marriage? It's just this is too . . . too . . . impossible.

I meant what I said. I have so little means. There will be no money.'

I could not stop smiling. 'I can't leave it to you, Ben. If I left it to you, you'd take too long. It might take you years before you considered yourself in a position to propose – and I can't see the point of waiting. I don't mind one bit if your family need all your money, because we'll have each other.'

'Pandora . . . you're most perplexing. Hadn't you set your heart on teaching in your own school?'

'I thought I had, only I realise now it was what Mama wanted – but I've always wanted to paint. Only, I didn't realise quite how important it was to me . . . or how much I wanted it until now.' I stopped, suddenly nervous. 'You will say yes, won't you?'

'Oh, yes, yes, yes. My sweet darling, yes.' His smile ripped through me. Leaning slowly towards me, I threw my aegis to the floor and his lips burned mine. 'But Pandora, we must be sensible. We must wait. Without the turnpike job we'll have no money. The rent from the quayside will only just cover my family's expenses. What's left will be a pittance. I've so little to offer. Only my love. My deep and passionate love. And my respect. And my complete adoration.' He reached for my lips again. Never had I thought my body could burn so fiercely.

'You forget, I'm used to getting by on very little. One day, you'll be a famous chemist, renowned for saving lives, and I shall be a famous portrait painter. In the meantime, I can sell my shells and I'll teach painting – I'll do anything except teach Latin. Ben, I'm being true to myself for the very first time. My true self. I've brought Mama home and that's really important to me. I can feel her here, but I realise it's not the bricks and mortar that brought me home – though I love them with a passion – it's finding who I really am. Finding love. Finding you. It was as if I knew I would find love here. And I have. So much more love than I could ever imagine.' I stopped while his kiss took hold. Never did I imagine love could consume you so completely.

'Dearest Pandora. You have such talent. Everyone will want to have their portrait painted by you – my beautiful, brave, bringer of hope.' He straightened his cravat. 'We'd better go back. Do I look remotely respectable?'

I hardly knew who said what, or whether I replied. All I knew was that everyone had tears in their eyes, especially his mother, who kissed me so warmly. As did Aunt Hetty, and all nine of his sisters. As did his sister-in-law and his two adoring nieces. And Gwen and Mollie and Kate and Sophie, all of them skipping round and clapping their hands. Susan stood by her urn with her handkerchief in her hand.

Henry Trevelyan clasped Benedict round the shoulders. Mr Lilly patted his back, everyone congratulating us; Lord Carew was beaming, telling everyone how splendid it all was. Henry Trevelyan's voice rang across the hall. 'This must call for a tune. Benedict, have you a fiddle with you?'

On Henry's command Benedict returned from the music room with a violin held high in his hand. 'Take your places, everyone.' He smiled. Not a half-smile, but a smile filled with radiance. Standing on the foot of the staircase he swung his arm and all nine sisters rushed to form two lines. Joining hands, they tapped their feet, counting down.

'Three, two, one.' Suddenly they were rising and dipping, holding up their arms for the others to pass under. The Aubyns could certainly dance: the youngest girls took our girls by the hand, showing them how to wait for the counts before joining in. Francis Polcarrow was just as nimble, a perfect partner for Benedict's second eldest sister. Lord Carew was particularly sprightly, Lady Clarissa laughing as he spun her round.

Now Mr Lilly pulled Mrs Lilly in to the dance. Giggling like the girls, they ducked and swirled. Henry Trevelyan lifted Angelica high in the air and all the while Grandfather and Grandmother looked down from their frames as if wanting to join in; their smiles seemed broader, their eyes brighter. Laughter had returned to their school, the sound of running feet, an explosion of giggles: everything Mama had remembered, and I held my locket to my lips, kissing it softly.

Ben stopped playing and I slipped my hand through his arm. Aunt Hetty came to join us. 'Benedict, a word of business. I'd like to take the lease on that empty building on your quay – the one Roseland Holdings no longer requires.'

He smiled. 'That's very kind of you, Miss Mitchell, but I'm sure it won't be left empty for long.'

'No, you misunderstand me. I intend to start my own ferry business.' She took a deep breath. 'May I?' She opened my locket and pursed her lips. 'I don't like Bristol, Pandora, and I never will. But talent like this needs to be nurtured. I believe your grandmother would want you to go. As do I.'

Benedict stared at his portrait. 'Have you ever been to Bristol, Miss Mitchell?'

'No. Of course not! Why would I ever leave here?' She raised her immaculate eyebrow. 'What does this laboratory in Bristol have that we can't build here in Cornwall?'

His hair was ruffled, his cheeks flushed. Best of all, he had that burning look in his eyes. 'Nothing we can't build here.'

'Very well then. That's decided.' She raised her chin. 'It's long been my dream to have my own laboratory. I shall name it in honour of my mother. When we have the funds, Francis will oversee the building of it. You may like to give him a list of your requirements – how and where to store these corrosive gases of yours.' Her earrings swung, her chin firmly in the air. 'So, I'm to ask Reverend Carew to read the banns, am I? You're quite determined to live in poverty in Bristol? Nothing can change your minds?'

We stood smiling back at her. 'Nothing at all.'

'Well, I suppose that settles it, then. You're to marry for love, not money. That's how it should be and how Father would want it. He made that very clear.' Turning, she raised her fan, beckoning for Francis Polcarrow to join us.

Flushed from dancing, his cravat slightly askew, Francis stood beaming at her side. 'Am I to tell them now, Miss Mitchell?' Aunt Hetty smiled and he cleared his throat. 'I have found Reverend Mitchell's will.'

'Well, you must tell Mr Richard Compton he will have to wait a little longer.'

His smile broadened. 'I'm afraid I can't, Miss Woodville. Because it's not what we thought. In his will, Reverend Mitchell states that his entire estate is to be divided equally between you and Miss Mitchell. *You* are the heirs to his estate.

Both of you, equally. Mr Compton is not mentioned in the will. At all.'

The room seemed to spin. '*We* are his heirs?'

Aunt Hetty wiped her eye. 'You're to marry an heiress, Benedict. Father left the estate to Pandora and myself and as Pandora is my sole beneficiary your children will inherit the estate in its entirety. Father's love of riddles was designed to keep fortune seekers at bay. He may have let drop everything was to go to Richard Compton but it was never the case.'

'Aunt Hetty, I can't quite take this in.'

'It's my fault, really. I should have been sharper. Mother stopped me from attending the reading of Father's will by sending me on some wild goose chase. At the time, I thought it just bad timing, but now I can see she arranged for me not to be there.'

Francis Polcarrow nodded. 'I knew the will had been officially read, and legally discharged, but it wasn't filed in any of the correct places and it got me wondering. Why, when everything else was so well documented, could we not find a perfectly legal will? It didn't make sense. I searched everywhere – the files of *lands in trust* and *estates in arrears*, *lands under dispute*, even *lands registered to the deceased*, but to no avail. It had simply disappeared. Until one of the clerks remembered my stepfather's locked drawer holding *papers held in confidence*. We tried every key we could find and finally we opened it. And there it was – a file containing your grandfather's will and his very specific instructions.'

Benedict handed me his clean white handkerchief and I wiped my eyes. 'Why go to such lengths to keep his will secret?'

'Because a letter accompanied the will, Miss Woodville.' Francis glanced at Aunt Hetty, who nodded. 'In which Reverend Mitchell made it abundantly clear he was not prepared to let a single penny go to your father – through your mother – but he wanted half his estate to go to you. He also stipulated in *no uncertain terms* that his will was not to be shown to either of his daughters. Both were to be told that all his possessions had been left to his wife, and the estate held in trust for his heirs, which he *hinted* would be his cousin's son. Only when Miss Mitchell decided to close the school would the truth be known.'

'Why didn't Grandmother say anything? Why go along with it?'

Aunt Hetty drew a deep breath. 'I believe Father made Mother swear on the Bible she would never tell me.'

'But why? Aunt Hetty, it hardly makes sense.'

'Because Father wanted someone to marry me for love, and only love. He'd been tricked into giving up land to Sir Anthony and could see how vulnerable I might be when he was no longer able to protect me. He was determined to deter any more fortune hunters.'

'And you never suspected?'

'No, never. Once the constitution was drawn up, I never thought to question it. Father drew it up after Abigail married your father. He was furious with them both – furious Abby had been the target of a malevolent man – and wanted to shield me from the same. If I was ever to tell a prospective husband I would not inherit the land, Father believed the fraudulent ones would back away. The more I thought about it, the more

462

I liked the idea of being so free. I had stability, independence, a fulfilling occupation, and I thought it a perfect solution. I thought the school would thrive and that one day I'd hand it over to you.'

I dabbed my eyes again. 'He cut Mama out of his will but gave her share to me.'

'He never stopped loving your mother. Nor you. Never stopped hoping you'd return. And you have. And that's the only thing that matters. Except you're going to Bristol!'

Benedict's arms closed round me. 'We'll come home, Miss Mitchell — every Christmas and every summer until we've built your laboratory.'

'*Our* laboratory, Benedict. I intend it to become the pride of Cornwall. But first, we must restore the estate.' She kissed my cheek. 'I'll need your agreement and signature on the leases Francis is to draw up — any land we sell shall be a joint deci-sion. But I thought we might consider an auction of leases on the strip of land *north* of the new road? I suggest six leases — one for a cooper, one for a wheelwright, one for a blacksmith and one for a saddlery. One plot could be used for a printing press, and one to be run as a charity kitchen. Do you agree?'

I smiled. 'And Mr Devoran's sons will run a coaching inn?'

'If they so wish.' She glanced round the room. 'Now go . . . go while no one's watching.'

I felt my hand gripped and we ran down the corridor, past the library and into the kitchen, laughing and smiling as Annie stopped to kiss me; across the courtyard, the moon shining on the cobbles; not into my garden, nor into the coach house, Benedict's hand warm and strong. Shadow leapt to join us, running quietly by our side. Lanterns were burning on the front of the house, the coaches waiting, the horses stamping their feet. Above us, the moon shone with such intensity. Not down the drive, but down the track leading across the fields, Shadow at our heels.

Slower now because the ruts were wet. A puddle loomed and Benedict swung me over it, continuing across the field, his hand in mine. At the gate he stopped, his arms tightening round me. 'I told you to marry an heiress,' I whispered.

His laugh was rueful. 'Your aunt knew I'd never propose if I knew.'

'And Aunt Hetty's never wrong,' we said in unison.

'And I knew you wouldn't propose because you thought yourself too poor.'

He bent his head, resting his forehead on mine. 'Darling Pandora. Darling, darling Pandora. I was drawn to you the moment I saw you. Or rather, the moment I bumped into you. That day when you told me about your father I felt such admiration for you. You were so strong, so correct in your condemnation. But it was here, right here, at this gate, where I fell so deeply in love with you. It was like the sun blinding me, a warmth flooding through me. I knew, with absolute certainty, you were the only woman I could ever love. Light had entered my world again – a reason to hope. We were standing side by side,' his lips brushed my cheek, 'and I felt such an ache, such intense longing. I knew I had to spend the rest of my life with you by my side. My beautiful, brave bringer of hope.' His lips sought mine, kissing me softly.

'I've always argued with The Fates! I've always been angry

464

with them for taking me away. But they brought me back.' His lips brushed my hair, my ear, my throat. 'And if they hadn't taken me away, I'd never have been on that ship, and we'd never have bumped into each other. I don't want to wait. Not one week longer than we must.' The pressure of his lips mounted, and I felt myself melting with intense pleasure. Moonlight sparkled on the gate, lighting the fields and the trees in Mama's wood. The scent of salt carried on the breeze and he held me like he would never let me go. 'Side by side,' I whispered, 'for the rest of our lives.'

'Side by side,' he whispered back.

I thought my heart was going to burst. Side by side with the man I adored. And side by side with the dog, who was making it abundantly clear he was coming with us.

Acknowledgements

The Cornish Rebel is my seventh novel and I'd like to extend a warm thank-you to my agent, Teresa Chris; to my editors, Hanna Keene and Sarah Hodgson; to my copy editor, Alison Tulett, and to the talented team at Atlantic Books. Without you, my books would not be the books they are. A huge thank-you to my husband, who often wonders which century I am in, and to my family and grandsons who are never-ending in their enthusiasm and support. So, too, the team at Kresen Kernow, Redruth, who make researching my books so much fun. Thank you, all of you.

This book is different from my others in that it contains a map. I met the very talented artist Sally Atkins at a book event in Lostwithiel and immediately loved her work. I knew she was the right person to draw Benedict's map and, sure enough, she managed to find the original map of the proposed Turnpike and copied the style exactly. A huge thank-you, Sally. If you would like to contact her or see more of her artwork, her website is www.thesunnycupboard.co.uk.

St Feoca School is entirely fictional, though Benedict Aubyn and Miss Mitchell are based on real people. John Loudon McAdam was in Falmouth at the time and the Turnpike Trust were indeed planning the new Truro to Falmouth Turnpike as early as 1801. I haven't included historical notes here but you can find them on my website www.nicolapryce.co.uk.

Thank you for choosing to read *The Cornish Rebel*. If you would like to get in touch do join me on my Facebook page – Nicola Pryce-Author – or contact me through my website. I would be delighted to hear from you.